LORDS
of
CIRCUMSTANCE

Chance favors the prepared mind. - Louis Pasteur

MIKE LEACH

This is a work of fiction. Any similarity to persons living or dead (unless explicitly noted) is merely coincidental.

ISBN: 1453635645
ISBN-13: 9781453635643
Library of Congress Control Number: 2010908996

Dedication

∾

In memory of Barbara L. Clark,
my high school English teacher,
who knew me before I did.

mjl

PART I

Born of pain and bitter plight,
Tinctured red by cruel sight.

Chapter 1

༄

In the small, Veterans-of-Foreign-Wars town where I grew up, there was little for young people to do. After dark, there was even less. The sidewalks were rolled up at eight, and a tentative silence fell across the asphalt streets and freshly-mown lawns. Mosquitoes and crickets ruled. The few teens that lived there were particularly frustrated by this, so they cruised up and down the state-named streets in Buicks, Plymouths or other tired wrecks salvaged from local junkyards, burning barrels of twenty-nine-cent-a-gallon gasoline.

Most of these journeys stretched well into the night, with no real destination in mind. But they satisfied the restless demands of youth and passed the time until morning. The greatest challenge for participants was simply to return home unscathed by local law enforcement.

During those forays, who you ran around with defined your social rank, and I was always at or near the top. It was easy to excel in such matters, since the entire pool was made up of only a handful of competitors.

For some reason, I gravitated toward the more adventurous of the breed, fueled by the fear that we extracted from daring physical feats. This is how we tested and eventually broke through limitations, which, of course, is what the teen years are all about. When we were lucky, no one got seriously hurt.

I hung out with Bill, who left an indelible impression on both my mind and body. First of all, he was brilliant. He possessed a very high I.Q. and was strikingly handsome, with steel-blue eyes and a razor-sharp jaw line that spoke of power. He was an exceptional athlete, serving as quarterback of the high school football team. This made him popular among the other students, who considered him to be a reasonable risk. His teachers liked him – his coaches loved him.

But he shrugged off most of this attention, viewing it as secondary to his forte. And we were all privy to what that was.

Bill was a *fighter*, born to the challenge and fostered by a physically abusive father who had retired from the railroad years before. His mom had fled under extreme duress when he was four years old. His father had assured her that he would kill both her, and her son, if she tried to take "his boy" away, if she said anything to the police, or if she ever returned.

He could be very convincing, so Bill was left to fend for himself under the iron tutelage of his father's hands.

It was an unfortunate circumstance. On Monday mornings, you could never be quite sure who had tattooed Bill's face – whether it was another teen aggressor, or just his dad getting drunk again. Either way, I admired Bill's resilience and, over time, came to respect him for the quintessential warrior that he was.

We were both physically fit, but even back then I understood that my friend, Bill Hunter, belonged to an entirely different breed – a throwback of a sort, to whom violence came as naturally as eating or sleeping, and as instinctively as any animal executing its territorial imperatives.

I always seemed to be in the wrong place at the wrong time with Bill. When he erupted into violence, it was usually sudden and without forewarning. More than once, I was sprayed with his victim's blood before I even realized that a problem had commenced. Perhaps I was just slow, but I prefer to attribute it to his lightning speed, developed through numerous clashes with unfortunate opponents.

Bill was not predisposed to warning his adversaries, for he knew that it was best to start well, regardless of how you finished. Always in close proximity, I learned to protect and cover rapidly. I also learned the vicious nature of such engagements, but will admit to being more fascinated by Bill's techniques than afraid of their outcomes.

Standing beside him at a high school dance, I was embroiled in a battle that erupted between Bill and the older brother of his latest victim, backed by four of his cronies. The older brother – a two hundred and fifty pound, twenty-two-year-old adult – barged in through police security at the perimeter of the building and charged up to Bill. Before a single word was spoken, Bill busted him in the face so hard that it sounded like a small, twenty-five caliber pistol discharging, instead of bone meeting skin.

Police converged upon the brief riot that followed, spraying mace into a crowded room that boiled with flying fists and grappling bodies.

I eventually escaped the melee and stumbled outside, where my girlfriend's sister found me. She thought I'd been seriously injured, since my eyes were streaming crocodile tears, and my face was swollen and blood red. But, this time, it was the chemicals – not the battle – that had taken its toll. She had to drive me home in my '66 Mustang, because I couldn't see two feet in front of my face.

Bill was hauled off to jail (until his angry father could retrieve him and double the pain), while I retired to the relative luxury of cold compresses and a bad headache.

Nevertheless, I was completely captured by his mystique, similar to the way humans are fascinated by the rare strength and beauty of a leopard or tiger that has just pounced upon its prey. Once you got over the initial shock, exhilaration followed – new highs of incredible intensity – an allure with all the addictive qualities of cocaine, and with similar costs.

I followed Bill through other such experiences, too numerous and embarrassing to recount, serving as both observer and participant. I won't hesitate to admit that I learned a tremendous amount from him, though he was probably unaware of it.

Our inevitable parting of ways followed high school, but I never forgot the pure power of his presence or the strange mixture of pain and joy that he could inflict. It served as a guideline in my own life to define the outer limits of human behavior, to understand when one must stand his ground as opposed to turning away, and as a reminder of the narrow separation between men and animals.

The thin veil of civilization is all that separates us from the beasts, and, through association with Bill, that veil was temporarily lifted. Even a brief glimpse of that world was sobering and educational – a potent reminder of what we all stand to lose.

After high school, the U.S. Marines found in Bill what I had already discovered – a beautiful savage, intelligent and efficient at warfare. They promoted him quickly, and he became a leader among his own kind, using his innate talents to serve his country. In short, he found his calling.

Years later, as an adult, I ran into him again, shortly after his military service had ended. Standing in line at a local movie theatre, he slipped behind me and secured the back of my neck in a vice-like grip. Even before turning to identify my assailant, I knew, at a subconscious level, that it was Bill. No one else would risk such a thing. He moved slowly around in front of me, never relinquishing his iron-handed control, and I was treated, once again, to his broad smile and piercing blue eyes.

Instantly, a phantom taste of blood crossed my mouth – the random product of memory. The unexpected sight of him catapulted me back in time to the ever-present possibility of danger that had intensified the warm, restless nights of our youth.

We spoke briefly of our shared past, then discussed his discharge from the military. But no mention of my own fate entered the conversation. For the time being, he relied on assumption, which was fine with me.

He knew nothing of the path I'd traveled. He was far too busy following his own – primarily the Ho Chi Minh Trail – where a lot of dead Viet Cong bore his mark. Bill had taken pride in placing his "seal of good faith" on the foreheads of fallen enemy soldiers, forged by an imprint of his high school ring. He heated the face of it with a cigarette lighter and stamped his approval on their silent expressions.

During this ritual, he recited the mantra, "Like moths to a flame." This confused his comrades, until the outraged enemy placed a bounty on Bill's own head, which drew a steady stream of angry combatants – like moths to a flame.

Bill knew that an adrenaline-charged, revenge-seeking enemy was far easier to defeat than calm, calculating soldiers. So, he motivated them accordingly. It was difficult to argue the effectiveness of his technique, since the HCM Trail was littered with the initials of our small-town high school's name.

It seemed like an entire lifetime had passed since we were fast friends. Yet, even in that brief conversation outside the movie theatre, I realized that nothing – not even a wisp of change was upon him.

Under the right circumstance, the thin veil could lift again, and the perfect man-beast – the leopard of my youth – would instinctively pounce.

Little did I know that this chance meeting would change the nature of every minute of every day of the rest of my life.

Chapter 2

༄

"Rise and shine, ladies!" The brutish prison guard raked his baton across a row of bars that fronted ten cells. It produced a sharp, staccato sound that hammered my pounding brain. Only nine of the cells were occupied now. The tenth cell's inmate had "retired" last week, courtesy of an irate Mexican who didn't take kindly to anyone touching his filthy yellow ball cap. A deep shiv sent his tormenter to the afterlife. These things happened.

"Survival time," the guard announced, with a tight grin on his ruddy face. "New day – you pay!"

The cell doors opened simultaneously, and we were routed downstairs to the prison cafeteria to suffer through yet another lousy breakfast of powdered eggs and cold, canned biscuits. I didn't eat much.

Most of the other inmates didn't seem to mind the food, wolfing it down like gourmet fare. I donated mine to the guy sitting across from me. He smiled, revealing a ragged lack of dental care.

After breakfast, we were prodded outside into the stark light of day. A few guys from cell block D already tossed basketballs haphazardly at rusting metal backboards.

I headed to the far corner of the pen, where two black men pumped iron and bragged about conquered women. They tolerated my presence, figuring that I was no threat to them. They were right. I was no threat to anyone anymore – a broken man with a broken soul.

The last four years were lost to me. During the briefest trial proceedings in the history of our county, I had remained a creature of stone. I had heard the words – the virulent, scathing accusations, the flurries of wild lies, mixed with occasional parcels of truth – but I was immune to it, floating above it all in a hazy firmament.

My publicly-appointed lawyer couldn't offer much in the way of a defense. He had little to go on. Knowing where all this was heading, he enlisted the aid of my mom, who pleaded with me through thick glass panels to stand up for myself, to explain my actions and tell the court what had really happened. She was sure that there was more to it, but I had separated from it all, drifting slowly away from the pain, retreating into a cool, silent vacuum.

After a while, I had difficulty determining exactly who my mom was and what she was doing there. Alone in a crowd of strangers, I released myself, and a great, black curtain descended. Clocks stopped their tedious rhythms, and I was clear of all the pain.

Following an unmeasured period of time, I found myself in state prison, wandering about in a stupor, caring nothing about anything. My only hope lay in the high likelihood that someone would soon put an end to my nightmarish existence.

They had already come close once. That time, I had supplied minimal resistance and was pummeled by fists and feet until I was unconscious for days. A blessed coma of still, cold darkness had enveloped me, while blood streamed steadily from my mouth and ears.

Following a week of off-campus hospitalization, I was returned to the prison infirmary when I made the mistake of opening my eyes again.

No one was more surprised than I was to be looking at anything other than the fires of the eternal pit. But that time, the professional kindness of strangers, who refused to take my ethics into consideration, was responsible for returning me to the temporary confines of hell on earth.

I knew it would be a brief reprieve – nothing good was left in this life. Each day was an empty vessel, and I was unable to rehydrate my withered spirit. Nothing I could imagine would ever renew it.

"It's just a matter of time," I told myself, unable to fathom sixteen more years of a mandatory sentence.

In nature, the weak and sickly are certain targets. In prison, it's no different. An easy kill advances an inmate's status as merciless – a low-risk, high-yield feather in his cap.

Sure enough, within a month, I caught the hungry eyes of death examining me again from across the quad.

I knew exactly what was going down. I'd already noticed them clustered tightly in a small group, eyes darting quickly to and from my position. They were planning the approach, the close and the cover.

Others were timing the guards, searching for the briefest window of opportunity when their attention would be focused elsewhere.

There was no mistaking their intent.

An icy chill stirred at the base of my spine, and I steeled myself for what was to come.

As I waited, I glanced down at the small tattoo on the back of my right hand. Bill, who oddly possessed artistic talent, had put it there. It depicted two strong right hands clasping, affirming their mutual bond.

In the distance, a dove cooed, ridiculously out of context to the situation.

In the dizzying blur of a moment, I recalled something that Bill had said to me once in high school, when we were picking ourselves up off the ground, following a brutal beating by two Cubans. We had foolishly picked a fight with them, but they were older and stronger – fresh from the hard labors of sugar cane fields and barroom brawls. They had dispatched us quickly and without remorse.

"Damn, that was fun!" Bill had said, wincing through the pain of cracked ribs and a broken nose.

He fed off that pain, and used it as motivation to track them down a few weeks later, two towns away. He surprised them at a family gathering and settled the score with sober efficiency. When his first opponent hit the ground hard, the second one pulled out a knife. Bill put both of them in the hospital, one of them no longer able to father children.

I called to mind the terrible pain of my first prison beating, hoping that it might spark a defense. But nothing happened.

Then, slowly, something stirred in the crowd. Someone was quickly approaching. In a matter of seconds, a wide-arcing spike flashed through the brilliant sky, and the words, "Die, Jefe!" rang out.

I reacted only with a slight twist to one side and a quick bob of my head. In slow motion, I followed the crudely-fashioned wooden handle at the base of the spike, tightly seated in the fist of my attacker. It passed just above the left side of my head and continued its descent.

The business end of the homemade weapon embedded itself in the arm of a large skinhead standing just to my right. He threw his head back and roared in pain.

Off balance, the attacker stumbled, and I launched my fist upward, under the base of his ribcage. He went down flat on his stomach. The skinhead took one step forward and crushed his heel into the back of his neck, snapping it like dry wood. He spat on his victim, creating the bizarre impression of water hitting a hot frying pan, as a raspy, well-timed death rattle wafted up through the crowd.

I folded myself quickly into the mass of gathering inmates and disappeared.

Apparently, the will to survive remained inside me, though I had no idea why. My reaction had been more a property of instinct than of conscious choice.

I didn't sleep well that night, convinced that my sentence would soon be upgraded to life. Shadowy figures climbed the walls of my mind. I turned over and over, soaking the cheap mattress with feverish sweat. At three A.M., I bolted upright and peered into the abyss.

"So be it," I said aloud in the middle darkness of my five-by-nine cell.

I stood up and walked to the front bars, gripping them tightly. A small lightning bug, sucked in through a ceiling ventilation fan, floated down the hallway. Its tiny chemical factory periodically illuminated the gray concrete walls with a faint, green glow of redemption.

Chapter 3

❧

"**M**r. Garrett, please come in."

Once a week, a state-funded clinical psychologist dropped by to amuse the rapists, killers and sadists that shared our cozy little bed and breakfast. He examined the dark under-belly of society through wire-rimmed glasses. Inmates revealed their sordid histories while he extracted patterns and tendencies from their words.

Afterwards, he spent hours writing detailed psych reports that dissuaded parole boards from releasing them. Even I knew that society owed this man a huge debt of gratitude. And the inmates couldn't really blame him – he was just doing his job.

I figured my summons was meant to soften the impact of a sudden change in sentencing. I was right.

"Mr. Garrett – or, uh, Matt? May I call you Matt?"

"Sure," I replied. "Call me anything you want."

"How are you doing today?" he asked. He gestured toward the wooden chair opposite his desk.

"Fine," I lied, and sat down, wary of the outcome.

"Matt," he continued, reaching for a thick pad of paper on his desk. "I was hoping we could talk a little this afternoon."

"About what?" I replied, feigning ignorance.

"I'd like you to tell me a bit about what brought you here – about what happened out there that changed things for you. I'd like to know how you feel about all that now – about what impact it's had on your life and how you view your future."

I made no reply. Was he referring to yesterday's attack, or the events that surrounded my original incarceration?

Why had I been summoned? The state certainly wasn't concerned about my *feelings* – not now, not for the next sixteen years, not for the rest of my life.

What was he trying to do? Was he writing a dissertation on inmates' *feelings* at the precise moment their sentences were extended? Was he hoping to document my emotional response when informed that, from this day forward, I could only leave this place in a box? It didn't make any sense to me.

I studied my shoes.

"You don't want to talk about this, Matt?" he inquired, tilting his head slightly to one side. He paused briefly, and then took a deep breath.

"All your test scores indicate that you're an intelligent young man, Matt. Is there some reason that you don't want to talk to me? Do you think that I am your enemy?"

Again, I said nothing.

"I understand where you're coming from, Matt. It's not easy to trust someone you don't really know. But, believe me, I'm here to help you. What you did in the past – right or wrong – isn't really as important to me as who you are right now – where your head is.

How did the events that brought you to this prison change your view of the world outside these walls?"

It was simultaneously clarifying and confusing. It didn't sound like this meeting was related to yesterday's incident in the prison yard, but I couldn't be certain. Maybe he was just taking the long way around, toying with me.

I looked up and studied him, trying to read between the lines. More questions surfaced.

Why would he care what I thought about the world outside these walls? That world had nothing to do with me. Unless I sprouted wings and had my face rearranged by a plastic surgeon, there was absolutely no relationship between *that world* and Matt Garrett.

Life outside these walls went on without me, and, as far as I knew, that was perfectly fine with pretty much everyone out there.

What's more, there was no happy reunion in the works – not for a very long time – perhaps forever. So, why was he asking me these questions? Why didn't he just cut to the chase?

He studied my reaction and waited patiently for a reply. The silence grew uncomfortable, and I repositioned myself in the chair, placing my right foot on top of my left knee and pulling it closer to my center.

I spotted a fly on the wall and focused on it. It kept turning sharply in different directions, unable to decide which way to go.

"It's O.K., Matt," the psychologist said reassuringly. "I can wait."

Chapter 4

❧

I picked up Keri at noon on Saturday and headed for Twin Lakes. We'd grown up swimming there since childhood. We both loved the sun and the water, and were virtually inseparable when it came to boy-girl activities.

As early as the fifth grade, I was convinced that this was the person that I both wanted, and needed in my life, and carefully-laid plans began to take shape. It would require a windfall of good luck, and the odds didn't favor me. But Keri did.

She bounced into the passenger seat of my burgundy Mustang and, in the same movement, leaned over and kissed me on the cheek.

"Hey, there!" she said excitedly, revealing a smile that kept me awake at night. "Where ya been?"

Long brown hair stretched to the base of her spine, and soft brown eyes swallowed any hope of resistance. She was eighteen and beautiful.

"If I told you that, I'd have to kill you," I replied. "And then, who would I have to swim with? Sharon Zellar?"

A sharp blow struck my right arm.

"You'd better *forget* about Sharon Zellar!" she warned. "Besides, I doubt she'd be too impressed with your soprano solos in the choir on Sundays." She laughed, knowing full well that she had no competitor on the planet.

"Oh, I don't know," I teased, struggling to reach a higher octave. "There's something kind of special about a fine tenor voice coming out of a guy like me, don't you think?" She ignored the comment and reached into the backseat, opening the lid of the cooler.

"What'd you bring me?" she asked excitedly.

"Pig's feet and peanut butter," I replied. "You can make a meal out of that, can't you?"

"Come on," she pouted. "What's for lunch? I'm *really* hungry." Her expression changed to petulance.

"Mom made chicken salad on croissants," I yielded. "There are a few deviled eggs in there, too."

"Yummy!" she said, truly delighted. "Your mom makes the best chicken salad sandwiches ever. Can I have one now?"

"No!" I insisted. "You'll have to wait until we get there. If you get into that stuff now, there won't be anything left for me."

"Well, then," she explained, "you'll just have to live off my love."

She snatched a sandwich from the cooler, tore the wrapper open and took a giant bite out of the moist croissant. I could almost taste it.

"A guy could starve to death," I whined.

She chewed the bite and swallowed it, exaggerating her pleasure. Happy with the result, she leaned over and planted a long, slow kiss on my lips. For a moment, I lost sight of the road.

"*That* should tide you over," she said, proud of the slight blush she'd put on my cheeks.

As she withdrew, her long, straight hair flowed like gossamer across the top of my right forearm, a sensation that would linger for years – a silken legacy, frozen in time.

"Thanks," I said, "But let's try to get there in one piece, O.K.?"

We turned down the access road to Twin Lakes and parked under tall pines that sheltered picnic tables near the beach. Children ran to and from the water, chattering excitedly about their discoveries. Occasionally, moms corralled them to apply suntan lotion. Dads stoked charcoal grills, pressed hamburgers and joked about being over-worked. A few of them wore comical aprons.

We selected a table of our own, covering it with a red gingham cloth. I placed the cooler at one end and removed paper plates and napkins from a plastic bag, setting two places adjacent to each other. Keri peeled back the aluminum foil from a plate of deviled eggs and popped one into her mouth. I came in a close second.

She poured two Cokes into plastic glasses that were filled to the brim with chipped ice. Potato chips and onion dip rounded out the menu. We sat down beside each other and tore into it.

"Not bad, huh?" I commented.

"I'll gain five pounds," she replied, her mouth half full of chips.

"You *need* some meat on your bones anyway," I said. "You're a little too skinny for me."

"Give me a couple of weeks," she countered.

"How are your mom and dad doing?"

"Great," she answered. "They're really excited about the fact that we're both headed to the same college this fall. I showed them your dorm when we were up there last weekend. I could tell that my dad was pleased to see that it was located all the way across campus from mine."

"Smart man," I said, knowing that he was a good father, who took a serious interest in his daughter's welfare. I respected him for that.

"He likes you a lot," she added, "but he likes me even more! You know how it is with fathers and daughters – right?"

"Sure," I said.

I paused a moment, thinking carefully about my next words.

"The only thing that worries me a little is that there's going to be a lot of competition for your attention up there. I don't want you to feel like you have a collar around your neck, but, at the same time, I'd like to be included in your long list of suitors."

She laughed. "I'll save you a place at the end of the line."

"No," I said, struggling to explain myself. "I'm not kidding. I just want you to be happy."

She set her drink on the table and turned toward me, lifting my chin slightly with the tip of her fingers. Her brown eyes examined mine. For a moment, she looked puzzled, but gradually her expression resolved into a warm smile.

"I *am* happy," she replied in a soft, serious tone. "And nothing's ever going to change that."

She stood up suddenly, planted a playful kiss on the top of my head and shouted out as loudly as she could.

"I love this guy!"

Everyone in the picnic area immediately stopped what they were doing and turned toward the source of the disruption.

Trapped, I shifted to one side and slid slowly beneath the surface of our table, escaping the embarrassing outbreak of friendly smiles and knowing chuckles that followed. Spontaneous applause erupted and spread quickly across the pavilions. Keri just stood there and beamed, enjoying every inch of my descent.

When the applause finally diminished, I stood up, threw a towel over my head and walked down to the beach in defeat. A tiny little girl in a bright pink bathing suit bounded up to me and placed a handful of warm, wet sand on top of my right foot, patting it firmly into place.

"There, now. That's better, isn't it?" she said, looking up at me with an impish grin.

Chapter 5

❦

Twin Lakes was formed by two lakes, joined by a slightly narrower middle section. From above, it took on the whimsical shape of a large peanut. It was refreshingly spring-fed, considered to be one of the cleanest lakes in the state.

Swimmers, water skiers, pleasure boaters and fishermen enjoyed its abundant space, which included picturesque vistas and a healthy large-mouth bass population. Majestic oaks, slender pines and occasional cypress trees graced its shorelines. The beaches were packed with fine white sand, extending out as far as an adult could walk and still keep their head above water.

Keri removed her T-shirt, revealing the trim body of a model, restrained by a sleek, coral bathing suit. She was already tanned to light brown perfection from the long days of summer. She passed by me at the edge of the water, en route to greater depths. More than one set of male eyes monitored her progress.

There was something completely congruent about the way her body integrated with the elements of earth and sky that surrounded her. The water also welcomed her presence, yielding softly to her graceful movements. She dipped the back of her long brown hair beneath the surface and called for me to join her.

"Come on in!" she cried. "The water's great!"

I removed my shirt and left it on the beach. I strolled slowly out to meet her, allowing my sun-warmed body to adjust to the cooler water temperatures. When I came within range, she executed her plan.

"You sissy!" she taunted. "Here – let me help you." She scooped two handfuls of cold water from the surface of the lake, spraying it across my face and chest. It landed like a quick jolt of electricity.

"Thank you – thank you very much," I said, delivering my best Elvis impression. Then, I dove headlong under the water and disappeared.

"Matt," she said worriedly, knowing that payback was likely. "Matt, don't you do it. You'd better behave yourself!" she warned, half pleading.

Using only my hands, I pulled quickly across the bottom of the lake, deep enough to avoid detection. The surface of the water remained completely undisturbed. I passed beyond her a good twenty yards and then surfaced quietly, careful to control the sound of my breathing as I replenished my lungs.

Undetected, I slipped beneath the surface again and moved into deeper water, searching for anything that might serve my purpose. A long, thick piece of Spanish moss, blown into the lake during afternoon thunderstorms, rested on the bottom. It had turned from gray to green, ideally aged and ready for action.

Keri was growing uncomfortable with my prolonged absence. There weren't any structures nearby to hide a person, and I had been submerged for quite a while now. She turned from side to side, searching for any indication of my whereabouts.

Keri knew that I was a strong swimmer, but this was getting a little ridiculous. She stopped worrying about herself and started worrying about me. She reminded herself that we had entered the water very soon after eating, and her heart rate quickened. Her heightened anxiety set the stage perfectly.

Shaped into a letter "C", I curved the moss around the front of her legs, careful not to touch them. I released it just above her knees, allowing it to sink at its own leisurely pace. The tentacles of the long, slimy piece of Spanish moss brushed down the face of her legs, catching her completely off-guard.

She screamed and jumped halfway out of the water. In the process, she drew her legs up underneath her body, leaving ample room for my escape. When her feet met the bottom again, they landed right on top of the pile of moss, which generated a second leap of Olympic proportion.

By now, she'd caught the attention of the picnickers on shore, who watched intently as the drama unfolded. She clamored toward the beach, squealing. When she reached the sand, she turned back toward the water anxiously.

I surfaced well away from the site of her distress and called out to her.

"What happened? What's the matter?"

Though I tried desperately to restrain it, a tight grin crept slowly across my face. It was all just too delicious.

Gradually realizing the source of her distress, she stood there with her hands on her hips, glaring at me.

"Matt Garrett!" she shouted. "You'd better just *stay* out there until tomorrow!"

She picked up my shirt and flung it into the lake. Then, she turned around and stormed all the way up to the picnic tables.

I laughed so hard that my sides hurt.

Chapter 6

෨

Keri wasn't one to hold a grudge for long. After some gentle coaxing and a few dozen apologies, she forgave my transgression. We went back down to the beach and stretched out on two large beach towels, positioned to take full advantage of the afternoon sun.

She smiled at me occasionally, but suggested that I remain vigilant, since the possibility of sudden retaliation existed. She explained that she was still refining the details of her plan.

Chances were it'd be a good one.

She spread cocoa butter on her arms, legs and stomach. I was granted the privilege of putting some on her back – somewhat surprising, considering the sheer terror that I had induced just thirty minutes earlier.

The smell of tanning lotion, mixed with her natural scent, was intoxicating. God's gifts were many and diverse, but this topped any olfactory experience that I had ever encountered. I took my time.

Too soon, she indicated that enough had been applied, so I rolled onto my back and tried to inhale every luxurious particle that floated through my space. I struggled to understand what I had done to deserve her friendship. Eventually, I accepted the unexplainable and drifted off to sleep.

A half hour later, I awoke to the cold touch of ice melting on the surface of my lips. Keri moved a small cube of chipped ice across them, enjoying my slow return to consciousness.

"Wake up, you old lake monster! You need to turn over now or you'll look like a lobster tomorrow."

I turned over on my stomach and placed the left side of my face on my folded hands. She lay on her side, propped up on one elbow, and lightly combed her fingers through the back of my hair.

"I love you," she whispered.

"Yeah, I kind of got that a little while ago," I quipped, unsure of my right to the correct response.

Later in the afternoon, we played volleyball with a couple of families that needed extra team members. Keri had natural athletic ability, and I was always proud to see her talents on display. She always made light of our victories and happily blamed me for any defeats. She knew that I would get even with her for such comments, which is exactly why she enjoyed them.

We finished our match in the mid-afternoon sun, winning by a narrow margin. Hot and sweaty, we headed back down to the lake to cool off. On the way, she suggested that my serve could have been a whole lot better and then bolted ahead of me to avoid the consequences.

"You wait until I get my hands on you," I called after her.

"Promise?" she replied, diving headlong into the lake.

The water had achieved perfect daytime temperature. We swam for an hour or more, occasionally stopping to talk about friends, family, college plans and movies we'd like to see before the summer ended. For a while, I supported her by placing one hand under her back as she floated across the surface of the lake and chattered.

Later, when our conversation waned, we stood facing each other, toe-to-toe in neck-deep water, exploring the boundaries of touch. Occasionally, we kissed briefly, careful to observe standards related to the public display of affection.

Keri wrapped her hands around my neck, while I traced the gentle curves of her body beneath the surface of the lake. She invited me into areas that were welcome and instructed me in those that were not. I understood and complied. For now, that was enough.

The sun tracked lower in the sky, and the long afternoon reclined.

At six o'clock, we packed all our stuff and loaded it into the car. I cranked the Mustang's engine, and we headed down the access road.

By the time we joined the main highway, Keri was already asleep, her head resting comfortably on a towel pressed against the passenger-side window. It had been a wonderful day – a rare pleasure in a bright landscape that had folded time.

The steady purr of the Mustang's engine anticipated the road as we approached the outskirts of town.

Chapter 7

A screaming blast of twisting metal and shattered glass slammed into the right side of my car, with all the explosive impact of a bomb. A splash of red blurred my vision, and everything went silent.

Between earth and sky lies a middle space, void of sound and feature. Time is not measured in that frail habitat, and movement dissolves into perfect stillness. I lingered there for seconds, then minutes, uncertain of my ability to return. Something deep inside told me not to – not to open my eyes ever again.

Until I remembered Keri.

A huge gasp of air entered my lungs, and I awoke to find her misshapen head peculiarly angled alongside my right knee. Her skull was clearly fractured, and her long brown hair sprawled into a puddle of blood on the floorboard. She was completely unrecognizable.

"Oh, my God!" I screamed over and over, in a voice that belonged to someone else. "Keri! Keri! Wake up! Wake up, Baby!"

I shook her violently, but got no response.

Great shuddering sobs welled up inside me and escaped into the terrifying atmosphere. I screamed at the top of my lungs.

"Help us! Help us, please!"

But no one responded.

I already knew that she was gone, but refused to accept it.

I crawled out the driver-side window, dragging her lifeless body behind me. Her ribcage was crushed, and her lungs had collapsed. She had taken her last breath. I kneeled over her, closing my eyes and wailing savagely.

When I opened them again, the driver of the other car was stumbling out into the street. He approached slowly, listing slightly to the left. There was a small abrasion just below his hairline, and one of his two front teeth was broken in half, though he was unaware of it.

The massive weight of his Caddy had absorbed most of the impact within the first three feet of its engine, leaving the driver relatively unharmed.

The radiator of his car spewed steam, while rock and roll music issued from its plush, leather interior. There were no other cars in the area.

As the at-fault driver drew nearer, the sweet smell of liquor preceded him. I could see that he was doing something with his mouth, but it didn't make sense to me. Was he choking? Retching? Was he hysterical?

I was too distraught to decipher it.

A few steps closer, it hit me, stunning my senses. He was giggling – actually giggling like a little girl.

"Whoa, Man! *That* was *incredible*," he declared loudly, giddy with alcoholic euphoria.

I recognized him immediately. He was the useless son of a local car dealership owner who operated the only place that you could buy a new Cadillac within three counties.

His father had sheltered him from the law on numerous occasions, bringing to bear his wealth and political connections in the community to gloss over his son's penchant for expensive booze and non-stop partying. So far, it had cost his father only a fraction of his considerable net worth.

Now, he could add vehicular homicide to his son's list of accomplishments.

But not for long.

I stood up and wiped the blood from my eyes and forehead. My vision cleared, and my heart went cold.

I moved quickly to meet him, bringing my fist sharply upward, under the base of his nose. Bone and cartilage tracked northward, driving directly into the front of his brain. He fell backward – stiff and straight, like a severed tree – and the giggling stopped, permanently.

Far in the distance, sirens approached, alerting people to an emergency that no longer existed.

Apparently, I managed to walk about fifty feet in the direction of town, and then collapsed, curling into a fetal position by the side of the road.

A man in a gray Ford pickup stopped and placed a blanket over my trembling body. Through a thick mind-fog, I uttered "Thanks" and then passed out.

Chapter 8

❧

Iawoke somewhere in the night, startled by the clanging sound of metal doors. The smell of stale urine and alcohol-tinged vomit hung in the air. The incessant chattering of two prostitutes, fresh from late-night labors, drifted down the hallway. A faint hint of early light brushed the jail room floor, and I struggled to right myself.

My body was racked with horrific pain, and my eyes had swollen to narrow slits. Several cuts and abrasions remained untreated on my face and arms, and my mouth was dry as cloth. I was stiff and bruised beyond anything that I could remember.

"He's awake," I heard a deputy say.

Moments later, the hallway door opened, and a large, chesty man with beady eyes walked up to my holding cell. I recognized him from pictures plastered on large billboards in the area. It was Bob Winfield – the father whose son now took up space in the city morgue – the same morgue that housed my beautiful Keri.

"You scrawny little bastard!" he cursed. "I'll watch you gasp for your last breath of cyanide inside of a month. You'll pray for death, and you'll cough your worthless guts up all over the chamber floor! I'm going to see to it that it gets televised all over this state, so your worthless parents get to watch it, too! Would you like that? Huh? I'll bet you would, you bastard, you *sick* little worm!"

He was unaware of the fact that my dad had died of meningitis when I was ten, leaving only my mom for him to persecute. I turned slowly to meet his dark eyes and addressed him in a controlled manner.

"Why don't you go home and screw that useless, fat-assed wife of yours?" I said coldly. "Come to think of it, maybe you'd better call first and make a reservation. I understand that she's pretty popular with the guys down at City Hall."

He lunged forward, shoving his right arm through the narrow opening between the bars. It wedged tightly at the shoulder, and his right hand flailed wildly in the air, inches from my face.

Two deputies moved forward and restrained him. They half-dragged him down the hallway toward the exit. He continued yelling hysterically.

"I'll see you dead, you son-of-a-bitch! I'll see you dead!"

"You're repeating yourself," I said calmly.

I lay back down and closed my eyes, immersed in a stream of hazy nightmares.

Early the next morning, Bob Winfield beat his wife so badly that she required several hours of surgery. She told authorities that she had fallen down the stairs. They'd heard it before.

Chapter 9

❧

"**I** was involved in a car accident," I said, abruptly breaking the long silence that had lasted almost twenty minutes. "Afterwards, I killed a man."

"How did you kill him?" the prison psychologist inquired.

"With my right hand," I answered.

"And did he deserve to die?"

That question took me completely off-guard.

"Doesn't matter, does it?" I responded defensively. "The state didn't seem to think so. They were more interested in the testimony of a witness who was sitting on his front porch, almost ninety yards away from the scene of the accident."

I still couldn't understand why this psych guy was asking me all these questions.

"But, what do *you* think?" he asked, seeming genuinely interested in my answer. This question also struck me as odd, since what I thought was logically irrelevant.

"I never really thought about it," I replied. "I guess I didn't give him much say in the matter. It all happened pretty fast."

While he digested my response, I stirred up the courage to confront him.

"Why are you asking me all these questions?" I said boldly.

He took a deep breath and looked up from his notepad. I thought I knew what was coming, but I was wrong.

"Bob Winfield was found dead in his own bed last weekend, Matt. Seems his wife buried a kitchen knife in his chest while he was sleeping. Then, she went downstairs and had coffee and a bagel. When she finished her breakfast, she called the police and politely requested that they remove his body from the house."

He paused briefly, checking my reaction. I remained blank, so he continued.

"When they got there, she was washing dishes. A bloody towel was hanging on her refrigerator door. She told them that she 'needed to wash that thing, too.' They transported her up to the state mental health facility about ten o'clock Monday morning."

"Tough break," I said.

"There's more," he replied.

"As she was escorted to her room on the hospital ward, she told the orderlies to be sure that the police read her will immediately. At first, they didn't think much of it, but she was insistent. She wouldn't settle down until they promised to comply with her request.

"In the end, her persistence paid off. They conveyed the information to her doctor, who passed it on to the authorities. The state police, her lawyer and an officer of the court went down to the bank and had her safe deposit box opened.

"When they removed her will, they found an extra hand-written letter folded up inside it. She had signed and dated it three days prior to her husband's murder. It revealed that he had bribed that witness you mentioned earlier to swear under oath that you had provoked a fight with his son. He was paid well to deliver his statement with absolute certainty, indicating that Winfield's son had been completely innocent of all wrong-doing. Evidently, Mr. Winfield had coached the witness to include vivid details of a lengthy argument that had preceded your attack, with his son begging pitifully for mercy while you struck him repeatedly.

"Shortly after reading her letter, the state police arrested that same witness in an upstate county. He was driving a nice Cadillac, even though he'd been unemployed for years."

It was stunning news. I wasn't sure what to make of it. The psych guy leaned forward and provided more details.

"The letter also revealed evidence of jury tampering, as well as a sizable amount of cash paid to the county medical examiner to alter his son's blood alcohol report. They took the M.E. into custody shortly before noon on Wednesday. Under considerable pressure, he admitted that the Winfield boy's blood alcohol level had actually been three times over the legal limit at the time of the accident."

I stared at him in disbelief. When I started to speak, he raised his hand.

"Wait, Matt. There's one more thing. Some overly-ambitious news reporter, named Booger Hayes, lied his way through two telephone operators and an administrative assistant up at the state capitol building, claiming to be our new governor's aide. He managed to speak directly to him, providing the governor with all the messy details of what had happened down here.

"According to Booger Hayes, Governor Rice was 'mad as a wet hornet' when he heard the story. He told the reporter that your father, James Garrett, was one of the finest men that he'd ever known. Apparently, they had served together in Korea. Did you know that, Matt?"

"No," I replied, "I had no idea." My voice was a little shaky. "My father was a quiet man, who rarely spoke of his military experience. I knew that he had served in Korea, but that's about the extent of it."

"I'm not surprised," the psych guy said. "I see a lot of that."

He settled back into his chair and displayed a subtle change in demeanor. When he spoke again, his voice was even more serious.

"Anyway, Matt, I think it's only fair to warn you that you may want to prepare yourself for what I'm about to say."

"What? What is it?" I said anxiously. "Is my mom O.K.? Tell me."

He dropped the bomb.

"Your sentence has been commuted, Matt. You're being released. Your mom and your lawyer are waiting downstairs for you right now. I think she's pretty excited about all of this. I hope you are, too."

He waited for my response. When none came, he provided gentle instructions.

"Right now, Matt, I want you to go back to your cell and gather up your things. I'll have the guard escort you down to the visitor center. You'll have a few papers to sign, and then I want you and your mom to walk out of this place together. And, Matt, don't take this the wrong way, but I don't ever want to see you again."

A broad smile spread across his face.

I stared at him for a few seconds, disconnected from the meaning of his words. Then, slowly, it all began to sink in. When comprehension arrived, it staggered my weakened foundation. I buried my face in my hands and sobbed for the first time in four years. The psych guy stood up, walked around the desk and placed his hand on my shoulder.

"You've had a rough start in this life, Matt. But there's absolutely no reason why you can't turn this thing around. You're a survivor, son. Put those skills to good use."

An image surfaced in the back of my mind of a little girl in a bright pink bathing suit, playing with sand at the water's edge.

"There, now. That's better, isn't it?"

Chapter 10

The next morning, I woke up in a double bed with fresh, white linens. The wonderful smell of bacon and coffee stole beneath the bedroom door, beckoning me toward the kitchen. I stood up, pulled on a pair of jeans and a T-shirt and traced the intoxicating aromas to the kitchen table. Mom had placed a warm pan of homemade biscuits in the center of it, covering them with a white cloth. A bowl of scrambled eggs and a plate of crisp bacon and freshly sliced fruit waited on either side.

She was standing with her back to me at the kitchen counter. She hadn't noticed when I entered the room, so I turned around and just stood there quietly for a minute, taking it all in. The furniture, the lamps, the pictures on the wall, even the rugs on the floor – every little detail was exactly as I remembered it.

Turning back toward her, I moved quietly into the kitchen. In a moment, I was standing behind her. She whirled around and faced me, smiling from ear to ear.

"Uh-huh," she said, "I had a feeling that the smell of hot biscuits might get you out of that bed!"

She wrapped herself tightly around my diminished frame and hugged me longer than usual. It was immediately apparent that I wasn't the only one who had suffered. She'd done far more than her fair share.

When she finally disengaged, she turned quickly back to the kitchen counter, wiping her tears with a dish towel that left streaks of flour on her face. I placed both my hands on the back of her shoulders and waited.

"Go sit down and eat now, before it gets cold," she said.

Wanting to diffuse the situation, I turned back to the kitchen table, pulled out a chair and sat down cheerfully.

"Wow! This looks great, Mom. You really shouldn't have done all of this. But, since you did, let's not let any of it go to waste!"

She regained her composure quickly and placed a pot of coffee and some cream on the table. She sat down across from me and ate, sharing the details of recent events.

The story of the phone call that she'd received from the governor was both remarkable and compelling. Word had spread quickly through the small community, and the excitement that it had generated was still fresh. Words poured out of her so fast that I had to ask her to slow down.

It was clear to me that I was in the presence of a remarkable woman. The last few years had taken a toll on her, but she had weathered the storm with the tenacity of a badger. Her strength was returning now, and she was sharing it with me.

I consumed every detail of her stories and ate real food for the first time in years. It was beyond heavenly.

Chapter 11

❧

Two weeks later, David T. Hayes, locally known as "Booger" Hayes, returned home from a weekend trip with his wife and two daughters to discover that the aging front steps of his house had been replaced by sturdy, new two-by-eight construction. The solid wood steps joined the front porch precisely and had been sanded and painted to match.

For some time now, that project had languished on a long list of honey-do's that had suffered from the demands of Booger's job and the time that he devoted to his wife and children.

They had no idea who had built it until an elderly lady next door mentioned that she had 'served a quart of iced tea to a nice young man over there on Saturday' who had a small tattoo on the back of his right hand.

Chapter 12

〰

I had gone to the movies to get my mind on something else – anything else. Digging through my sock drawer the night before, I had come across things that shouldn't have been there. I hadn't seen my high school ring in four years – same for the photograph. They belonged to Keri.

Her parents had returned them shortly after the funeral. Six months later, they had moved out of state to escape the painful reminders that lurked around every corner.

I removed the items from the drawer slowly and sat down on the edge of my bed. Memories flooded into the long night. I was still staring at them the next morning.

Mom entered the room early and looked down at my hollow eyes, dark and drawn from lack of sleep. She removed the ring and couples photograph from my hand, gently returning them to the dresser drawer.

"Get some sleep now," she said, moving to the window and closing the blinds. "I'll have lunch ready when you get up."

She walked to the bedroom door, turning to add a final thought.

"Why don't you get out some this afternoon," she advised. "Go downtown and see a movie or something. Get your mind off things."

"Sure," I said. She closed the door, and I lay down and drifted off to sleep. Darkness swallowed me, and my mind surrendered to badly needed rest.

Five hours later, I got up and dressed. I went into the kitchen and made myself a sandwich. Mom chastised me for passing up a hot meal, but eventually let me have my own way. After lunch, I told her that I was going to walk downtown and see what was showing at the local theater.

She was pleased.

Chapter 13

❧

The night of the high school dance hall riot, Bill's dad had picked him up at the city jail and driven him home, cursing all the way.

When Mr. Hunter pulled into their driveway, he came around to the passenger side and dragged Bill out of the car, forcing him to the ground by the back of his neck. When he tried to get up, his father, angry at the inconvenience of having to leave his bottle for an hour, landed heavy blows on his son's face and chest. Bill absorbed all of this without a word. He just kept staggering to his feet, trying pitifully to escape his own front yard.

Finally, he crawled beyond the length of his father's interest and was free to lie on the sidewalk bleeding.

He showed up at our house just before midnight, with a badly split lip and a deep cut on the right side of his cheek. He was covered with bruises from the shoulders up. Mom and I took him down to the emergency room, where they stitched the cuts and covered them with gauze bandages.

When they finished patching him up, Bill hopped off the examining table and said, "Thanks, Doc. I'd better get back home now."

Mom took him by the arm and said, "No, I don't think so, Bill. You're staying with us for a few days. You need some rest." He knew there was no sense arguing with her.

Early the next morning, Marie Garrett left the house alone.

We found a note on the kitchen counter indicating that she had gone to the grocery store and would return shortly. It read, "Help yourself to what's in the fridge, and there's fruit and cereal on the table."

At the time, we thought nothing of it, and proceeded with the breakfast at hand. I should have known that we'd be feasting on a hot meal, if she hadn't been intent on more important things.

Five minutes after we sat down to breakfast, she was standing on the front steps of Bill's house, banging on the front door until his old man grudgingly got up from his recliner and opened it.

"What the hell?" he started to say, but she cut him off. His burly, unkept frame towered over her, but she wasn't intimidated.

"Mr. Hunter," she said calmly. "Your son will be staying over at my house for the next couple of days. I hope that will be O.K. with you."

"Hey, Lady" he replied sarcastically. "It's your dime."

"Fine," she said, relieved that he wasn't the least bit concerned about where his son stayed.

He stepped back to close the door, but she stuck her foot in it.

"Oh, and Mr. Hunter, there's one more thing." She stepped farther into the doorway, holding it open with her left hand. Her eyes fixed steadily on his, and her small physical stature seemed to disappear. She spoke to him in a low, threatening tone.

"If you *ever* injure that boy again, I'm going to bring my shotgun over here and spray your privates all over your living room wall. Do you get what I'm saying here, Mr. Hunter? Do you understand me clearly?"

His jaw dropped, and he muttered something indiscernible. It sounded a bit like "Yeah."

"Good day, Mr. Hunter," Mom said. She turned around and walked down the front steps at a normal pace.

An hour later, she arrived home with groceries and a smile.

Mr. Hunter returned to his booze and verbal abuse, but that was the extent of it. He died a few years later. His liver was a mess. At the time, Bill was fighting in Vietnam, and I was in prison. Not many folks attended his funeral.

Mom went out of respect for the family, but didn't carry a handkerchief.

Chapter 14

❧

"Come on. I'll buy you a beer," Bill said as we exited the movie theater. "We can catch up a little on the ghosts of our sordid past."

He knew about Keri dying in a car wreck, but I doubted that he knew much more than that. He had only been back in town a few days, and seemed completely wrapped up in the irony of our chance encounter.

"O.K.," I said.

"Is the Blue Grill still open?"

"I think so," I replied. "Let's walk down there and see."

A block or two out of the city limits, we found the Blue Grill still churning out thick, grilled hamburgers and cold bottles of beer. I knew I wasn't supposed to be in a place where alcohol was served, but I ordered a Coke with my burger and fries and Bill followed suit. We sat down at a table next to a jukebox playing James Taylor music.

"Listen, Man," Bill said right off the bat. "I was really sorry to hear about Keri. I know that you two had big plans together. It was a tough break, losing her like that. Sometimes life really sucks, doesn't it?"

"I still can't shake loose of it," I replied. "I'm not really sure that I want to."

"Well," Bill said, "I lost a lot of good friends in Nam, but none of them were as beautiful as she was. I can only imagine what you've been through."

"I try to remind myself every day that I'm not the only one who has lost loved ones," I said, looking down at the surface of the table. "But, somehow, that doesn't seem to make a whole lot of difference. I'm just going to have to deal with it."

"Take your time, Matt," Bill advised. "And hold onto some of those memories, too. That's how we honor those who meant something to us."

His comment was strange. It was obvious that Vietnam had changed him. Most guys had returned home bitter and damaged. Others were ill, their spirits broken and directionless. But Bill had grown stronger from the experience. He had matured and was more at peace with himself, more grounded.

I wasn't really all that surprised. Bill was at home in warfare. He thrived on challenges that determined whether or not a person continued to breathe. And he appreciated those who fought alongside him. It made sense to him to remember them – all of them.

I smiled back at him, but knew that the worst was yet to come. I would have to tell him where I'd been the last four years and why.

"I killed a man," I said abruptly. "I've spent the last four years in prison." I looked directly into his eyes, searching for a reaction.

"I killed fifty-three men," he replied. "And I've spent the last four years in hell." His gaze did not waver.

"That's different," I said. "There was a war on."

"To my knowledge, Congress never declared a war." His reply took me by surprise.

"So, why did you go?" I asked.

"Seemed like the right thing to do at the time," he answered. "I suppose it was the same for you, right?"

"I guess so," I replied, thinking about it.

"You *guess* so?" he questioned. "Let me ask you something, Matt. If you were faced with the same situation today, would you do anything differently?"

"No," I admitted. "I wouldn't."

"There you go," he said. "You did what you thought was right at the time, and you still do. Enough said, my friend – you don't need to explain anything else to me."

It was the reprieve that I had sought, and it settled over me like cool water.

"Thanks," I said.

I stood up, excused myself and went to the john. Bill kept working on his hamburger, washing it down with a second Coke.

A few minutes later, a light brown man entered the front door and walked over to Bill's table.

"Hey, hombre, remember me?" said a voice in broken English.

Bill looked up at him. It was the Cuban that he had neutered back in high school. The man reached behind his back and pulled a thirty-eight caliber handgun from his belt. He brought it up slowly and pointed it directly at Bill's face from across the table. Bill locked eyes with him and displayed a sardonic smile.

"How they hanging, Amigo?" Bill inquired, mindful of the fact that they weren't.

The Cuban cocked the gun's hammer and managed a wide grin of his own. He hesitated just long enough to relish the moment.

I lunged through the air, slamming into the Cuban's left side, wrapping both of my arms tightly around his shoulders. The gun went off. The bullet passed effortlessly through the jukebox and embedded itself in the wall behind it. We crashed to the floor, and I struggled desperately to gain control of his right hand. The gun discharged again, boring a hole through the baseboard, through which daylight now streamed.

Bill stood up and slammed his boot down on the Cuban's right wrist. Then, he bent down and removed the firearm from the man's painfully-opened hand. He bent down, placed the barrel of the gun against the Cuban's temple and moved his deadly face uncomfortably close to his terrified opponent. He paused for effect, and then whispered something to him in Spanish. His steel-blue eyes penetrated the Cuban's soul.

I knew that Bill was going to kill him, and that I would be returned to prison immediately. The psych guy would be disappointed.

I closed my eyes tightly to avoid the spray, preparing for the deafening blast of the thirty-eight.

Seconds passed. Then, Bill stood up. He called me off, releasing the Cuban. The guy scrambled out the front door and raced up the street like a man possessed. I turned to Bill, who seemed completely unaffected by the incident.

"What did you say to him?" I asked incredulously.

"I told him that he was a lucky man."

"Let's hope he understood," I muttered.

Bill walked over to the bar and handed the gun to the proprietor. He apologized for the damage and offered to pay for it. The owner was so thrilled that no one had been injured that he refused payment and insisted that we sit back down and finish our meal.

"It's on the house," he declared. "I won't tell anyone if you won't!"

Things calmed down quickly as we returned to our meal. The jukebox played on, demonstrating amazing mechanical fortitude.

"You're just full of little surprises, aren't you?" Bill said, watching me carefully as I ate.

"What do you mean?" I asked, puzzled.

"You just saved my bacon, didn't you?" Bill insisted.

"You would have figured it out on your own," I replied.

I could tell that his mind was racing, but the finish line was completely obscured.

Chapter 15

❦

Bill had come home to clean out his dad's house and list it with a realtor. He had no desire to live there – too many bad memories. He was building a place of his own somewhere down in the lower islands, but I wasn't sure where. He hadn't said.

It seemed to me that he'd had enough of governments and killing, and just wanted a little peace in his life. He'd certainly paid his dues, so I was happy for him. Maybe one day I'd get to visit his tropical hideaway, and we could go fishing together. But first, I'd have to get a job and put away some money.

I went over to his house the next day and helped him box up more stuff. He wasn't interested in trying to sell it. Either he didn't need the money, or handling it was too painful for him. We distributed most of the furniture to a couple of local charities and took several boxes of trash to the dump. There wasn't much left when we sat down on his front porch later that evening.

"You're coming over for dinner tonight, right?" I asked him. "Mom said she talked to you about it yesterday."

"Yep," Bill replied. "I'll be there."

"I'm really glad to hear that. I need the company. She's invited someone else to join us. When I asked her who it was, she refused to tell me – said I'd have to wait and see. She's been acting a little strange lately. I'm starting to wonder if she's got a boyfriend or something that she's afraid to tell me about. It could make for an interesting evening."

"No doubt," Bill agreed. "But, whatever it is, take it easy on her. She's been through a lot, you know."

"Yeah, I know. I've got to find some way to make it up to her."

"You will," Bill said.

"When will you be leaving us?" I asked.

"Next week," he replied. "I'm going up to see a buddy at the V.A. hospital in D.C. on Monday. I'll be leaving my Jeep at his place. On Tuesday, I'll fly down to Miami to order a few more building materials for the island house. If I'm lucky, they'll arrive by boat in a couple of weeks, so I can finish my roof. It's really nice to have something over your head when it rains down there.

"Hey, why don't you ride up to D.C. with me on Monday? You can keep me company, so I don't fall asleep at the wheel. You can take a bus back on Tuesday. It's only thirty bucks. And, being the generous sort of guy that I am, I'll even pick up the tab!"

"Thanks," I said, "But I really need to get busy and find a job around here. It's not going to be easy with a criminal record hanging over my head. Besides, you don't need me tagging along to visit your injured war buddies. I'd feel a little out of place."

"He's not a patient," Bill said. "He's an administrator. And he'll be happy to meet you. I've told him quite a bit about you already."

I was surprised that Bill would have mentioned anything about me to anyone. I was always the student – he was the teacher. I had learned from him – not the other way around. What could he possibly have found in me that was worth sharing with someone else?

"Come on," he insisted. "You've been out of a job for four years. What difference will a couple more days make?"

I was wildly curious about what he'd told his friend about me. But I wasn't going to ask him. There was an easier way to find out.

"You'll come with me, won't you?" Bill said. "It'll give us a little more time together before I leave the mainland."

"Maybe," I said. "Let me think about it."

I had already made up my mind that I was going with him.

Chapter 16

As a civilian contractor to the military, my father's job took him up and down the eastern seaboard and into the great iron and steel mills of the Midwest and northern states. He sold machine parts to the military, earning a sufficient salary to keep us afloat, in exchange for having to spend weeks at a time on the road.

Periodically, he mailed us brightly-colored postcards, with short, printed messages that reported his whereabouts. They were postmarked in cities like Pittsburgh, Flint, Chicago, Detroit, Ironton and Bethlehem. I marveled at the pictures of faraway places and hung on every word printed on the back of them.

When he came home for three or four days at a time, he brought me small airplanes and toy soldiers made of metal. They fit easily into his leather suitcase. I lined them up along a shelf on my bedroom wall and did everything I could to bring them to life. I imagined them in action against tyrannical enemies and slept with naive visions of warfare in my head.

In the afternoons, we played baseball together in the backyard, concentrating on the fundamentals of fielding and proper batting stance. He taught me how to oil a glove and place-hit to left or right field. There was never enough time to learn everything I wanted to know from him. Dinner always interrupted our progress at the very moment that I wanted most to continue. He was amused by my impatience and would always get another few swings in with me after dinner, before the sun finally set. It was as much as I could have of him, but I always wanted more.

As with every childhood, certain memories are more vivid than others. Some left indelible stamps on my identity and forced critical lessons into my hapless brain. I struggled to retain as much as I could of the time that I spent with my father, but school, sports, teachers and friends demanded their own space. At certain times, though, external influences took a back seat.

A neighbor of ours had served in World War II. He was one of the lucky ones who made it through the landings on Omaha Beach. He spoke of it only when prodded and attributed his survival to powers that remained beyond his comprehension. He had earned the Silver Star and two Purple Hearts during that operation, but downplayed their significance, saying only that "a lot of good men died there." When I was in the fourth grade, he passed away of natural causes.

My father attended his graveside ceremony and took me with him. I didn't like wearing a tie, but, as it turned out, I was underdressed. The local VFW Honor Guard posted seven men in crisp military uniforms alongside his gravesite and waited. A local protestant minister delivered the eulogy, dressed in a black three-piece suit. It lasted fifteen minutes. During this time, my mind wandered from his flag-draped coffin to the battlefields of Europe and beyond. For a moment, I was among them.

The explosive, simultaneous report of seven M1 Garands caught me completely off guard, snapping me back to reality and boring through my small frame like a jackhammer. Twice more the same shockwave jolted my foundation, and I looked up at my father with terror in my eyes. He put his arm around me and spoke reassuringly.

"It's O.K., son," he said. "They're just getting God's attention."

I calmed down, but maintained physical contact with my father to settle my nerves. I had heard of a twenty-one gun salute before, but had never actually experienced one. It was a clarifying moment in my life, after which I seemed to understand more about almost everything. I can't explain it – it's just what happened.

The ceremony ended as the flag was removed from his coffin, folded into a tight triangle and placed in his wife's waiting hands. She sat quite still, surrounded by friends and family. My father went over and spoke to her. I didn't hear what was said, but she seemed to appreciate it. Gradually, more people moved toward her, offering their condolences and then departing.

We walked back to our car, careful to avoid stepping on other graves. Many of the headstones had military markings on them, some dating as far back as the Civil War. I thought of the small metal soldiers back home on my bedroom shelf. Some of them carried tiny rifles that I now realized were M1 Garands.

A question formed in my head.

"Why do they do that, Dad?" I asked, looking up at him with a puzzled expression.

"What do you mean?" he replied.

"Why do they fire those rifles like that?"

He could tell that I was serious about an answer.

"It breaks the grip of death," he replied, "so the living can begin to release their pain."

I thought about it, remembering the tears of the family. The shock of the blast had certainly jerked all of us back to reality – back to the present, where life continued, despite the loss of a husband or father, neighbor or friend.

My father knew things that mattered.

Chapter 17

When Bill and I arrived at my place for dinner, there was a black automobile parked in the driveway. It had a subtle air of importance about it, but no real markings of any kind. Three small antennas rose just back of the rear windshield. I assumed this was my mom's mystery guest, who either worked for a funeral home or had no interest in frivolous matters like color, style or taste. Most likely, he would be older, balding and desperate to impress. I shared my prediction with Bill as we pulled into the driveway.

"Not even close," he replied, taking me by surprise.

"What do you mean?" I said. "Do you know this guy?"

"I've never met him, but we've talked before," Bill replied.

"So who is he?" I demanded. "And why is he here?"

"Let's go in and find out," Bill said, enjoying his advantage. He opened the Jeep's door and hopped out, striding quickly up the front walkway ahead of me.

"Probably a visit from my new probation officer," I muttered, annoyed at Bill for not telling me what he knew about this guy earlier.

When we got to the front door, I could see through the living room window. A man in a crisp, black suit stood with his back to us, talking to my mom. He had a thick head of black hair, broad shoulders and a solid, imposing, six-foot frame. He exuded self-confidence in a way that seemed out of place in our little neighborhood. But he was gentle as he stepped forward and gave her a quick hug. Bill said something about my lousy intuition as we opened the front door and stepped inside.

"Hello," I called out. "Sorry, we're a little late."

"Matt! Bill!" Mom said, stepping around her mystery guest. The man turned toward us at the same time and began to walk toward me, extending his hand. He froze halfway, staring at me in disbelief, as if I were a ghost. The momentary lapse in his forward progress left me in an awkward situation and, for an instant, I wasn't sure what to say or do.

"Incredible," the man said, brow furrowed, as if trying to solve a riddle.

Mom stepped between us and broke the growing silence.

"Matt, I'd like you to meet someone."

"Sorry," the man spoke up. "You kind of took me by surprise. It's incredible how much you look like him – really unbelievable." His eyes moistened, presenting yet another uncomfortable element.

"Look like who?" I asked.

"Matt," Mom said, "I'd like you to meet Governor Owen B. Rice – the man responsible for your release from prison."

I stood staring at him like an idiot. The governor of our state? In *our* home? What was he doing in *our* little house? He had come alone – no press accompanying him to capture his descent into the abode of commoners – no assistants to take notes for a later press release on the extravagant thanks that I was about to heap upon him. *"Stop thinking," I told myself, "and get busy!"*

I reached forward and grabbed his hand, shaking it profusely until it was in danger of dislocation.

"Man, am I ever glad to meet you," I said. "You really saved my life. I can't begin to tell you how much I appreciate it."

"My privilege," he responded. "Turn about is fair play."

I had no idea what the man was talking about, but nodded my head in agreement.

"Sometimes life comes around to meet itself perfectly," he added, a distant look in his eyes. Almost immediately, he broke it off and suggested that we all sit down and chat.

Before sitting, Bill stepped forward and shook his hand, too. "Glad to finally meet you, sir."

The governor smiled at him.

"Once again, the privilege is mine, Lieutenant. We all appreciate your service to our country."

"Semper fi," Bill replied and sat down beside me on the couch.

Governor Rice settled into the single chair opposite us and studied me once again, shaking his head slowly from side to side. "It's remarkable," he commented. "I wish your father could see you now."

"He died of meningitis in a Maryland hospital when I was ten years old," I replied mechanically. "They brought him home for burial in our local cemetery. I can still remember how cold it was that day."

"I can only imagine," he replied, looking over at my mom who sat alone on the beige sofa to our right. I noticed that she was studying her shoes and fidgeting with a small piece of paper that she passed nervously back and forth between her hands.

Suddenly, she looked up at us and said, "Could I get you boys something to drink?"

Before we could answer, she got up and walked briskly into the kitchen. Something strange was going on, but I had no idea what it was. Had I missed something? I turned to Bill with a puzzled look on my face, but he turned both hands up and shrugged, indicating that he, too, had no idea what was happening. I turned back to Governor Rice to ask him if he knew, but he stood up quickly and followed her into the kitchen. We could hear them talking in subdued tones – the governor obviously comforting her, and Mom clearly worried about something. At times, she almost seemed to be pleading with him. I didn't like the sound of it, but out of respect for both of them, I waited patiently in the living room with Bill.

In a few minutes, the governor returned to his chair and sat down quietly. Mom came in right after him with Cokes and coffee on a tray.

"Here we go," she said. "Help yourself, boys. Governor Rice, could I pour you some coffee?"

"Yes, thank you," he answered.

She filled a cup to the brim and placed it on a saucer, adding a tiny pitcher of cream on the side. She handed it to him and returned to her place on the sofa. He took a sip of it and set it down on the coffee table. He sat upright in his chair and took a deep breath, as if preparing for something important. From my perspective, things were getting stranger by the minute, but I remained quiet, figuring that whatever it was would soon be made clear to us all. I hoped it wasn't bad news.

"Matt," he began.

"Wait," Mom said, sliding up on the front edge of her cushion. "Let me."

I could tell that she was tormented by something, which clearly meant this wasn't going to be good news. *"Brace yourself, ole boy," I told myself. "The honeymoon's over."*

"Matt, I need to tell you something – something that you're not likely going to understand very well. It's something that's been bothering me for a long, long time, especially since you went to prison. But, the truth is, I wouldn't be telling you any of this right now, if it hadn't been for that, and Governor Rice getting involved in your release."

She was worried, and I couldn't help but feel sorry for her.

"What is it, Mom? Whatever it is, it's not your fault. I can take it. Just tell me."

She looked at me with a stony expression and replied.

"Oh, but you're wrong, Matt. It is precisely my fault. You have no one to blame but me for what I'm about to tell you. I am the one who has kept this information from you for so long, and you are the one who's going to hate me when I tell you."

I laughed.

"Don't be silly, Mom. What is it? What could possibly make me do anything other than love you? You're my mom – right?"

I smiled at her in a failed attempt to calm her fears.

"Indeed, I am," she replied, "which is exactly why I should have told you this a long time ago. It just wasn't possible. I felt I had to protect you. I felt you were better off not knowing – that you would somehow have a better life if I kept it to myself. But, you know, things like this have a way of catching up with us. The truth always manages to find its way home."

"Okay," I said, growing impatient. "So, what is it?"

"I know how much you loved your dad, Matt. And it was cruel of me to keep the truth from you. I only hope that you will forgive me."

She stopped, put her face in her hands and began to cry softly. Governor Rice stood up and moved next to her. He leaned down and placed his hand gently on her shoulder.

"Let me finish this, Marie," he said. He straightened himself somewhat, and looked at me, a grave expression on his face.

Chapter 18

❦

October 23, 1950, 0647. Chosin Reservoir, Northeast Korea. Temperature: Forty degrees below zero.

Sergeant Owen B. Rice had struggled for hours to stay warm before finally drifting into a fitful sleep. Two hours later, he awoke to a blaring cacophony of human outcries pouring down the mountainsides just above his unit. White ghosts descended in dizzying numbers that boggled the senses. The nightmare had begun.

During the night, Chinese forces had slipped quietly over the mountainous borders, clad completely in white, blending perfectly into the snow-covered terrain. Completely unexpected, the foreign invaders rained down on X-Corps like white locusts, descending in savage waves of human flesh. Their sheer numbers were overwhelming. Many Marines lost their lives where they lay. X-Corps would be annihilated unless they could quickly extract themselves from the sparse warmth of their blankets and initiate a rapid response.

Owen barked his squad to life and they swung into action. M1 Garands, M1 Carbines and .45 caliber

Thompsons ripped through the early morning light, cutting large swaths through the first contingent of Chinese attackers. They fell hard, their rifles bouncing like toy sticks across the frozen ground. Owen's squad took up defensive positions just in time for a second wave to swarm down the mountainside, picking up the weapons of their fallen comrades and bringing them to life again.

Two of Owen's men fell, 7.62x39mm shells opening mortal wounds in their chests. A third member of his squad was shot in the head.

Owen ordered his remaining men to fall back, fighting every step of the way as they withdrew. Whenever possible, they launched grenades into the mongrel hoard, with devastating effects. Arms and legs separated from their attackers, brilliant splashes of red spraying across their cold, white uniforms. Still, the Chinese advanced, folding their growing losses into the landscape, content to exchange one Marine's life for ten of their own.

Owen could feel the stiffness of his half-frozen extremities coming to life again as blood and adrenaline coursed through his veins. His head was spinning, in search of tactics that might free them from this onslaught. But there was nothing that could possibly apply to this situation. There was no time to think – no time to plan – no time to do anything other than fight or be killed. Their back was to the wall, which, of course, was when Marines were at their very best. He had already lost three of his men – he wasn't going to lose any more.

He found a vantage point between two boulders that offered a forty-five degree angle of fire directly across the path of the oncoming Chinese. From this position, he could temporarily delay their advance all by himself. His men could fall back to join other Marines, with a chance of survival if they could fight together in larger numbers. There was a brief lull in the attack, and he took advantage of it. He turned quickly to PFC Dave Warren.

"Give me your Thompson and three grenades. Take my rifle and withdraw the men to the next Marine unit you can find. Take the dead with you. Do you understand me, Private?"

"Yes, sir. But what are you going to do, sir? I mean, you can't just stay here by yourself, sir."

"Do as you're told, Private. That's a direct order. I'll catch up with you later on."

Dave Warren paused briefly, then detached three grenades from his belt and turned over his Thompson Auto. He returned to the other men and relayed Sergeant Rice's orders. Grudgingly, they obeyed, moving quickly to gather their fallen brothers and withdraw to the east, where other Marine units were engaged in similar fighting.

Owen Rice was alone now, but there was no time to think about it. He pulled the pin on his first grenade and lofted it over the rocks into the next wave of Chinese as they advanced down the narrow path that formed a natural gauntlet in his favor. They bunched together as they approached, funneled into the changing landscape.

Owen knew this provided maximum effect for grenade fragmentation and automatic rifle fire. The powerful blast took out six of them, and he followed it up immediately with scathing automatic fire. Bodies fell over bodies, piling up as they came closer to his position. The second grenade sprayed shrapnel through even more of their teeming numbers. They took shelter behind the bodies of their fallen comrades, frantically firing in his direction with wild attempts at accuracy. He could feel tiny bits of chipped rock embedding themselves in his face and arms, but he was well trained to ignore any pain, which left his fighting capabilities intact.

He sprayed the advancing troops again, the heavy forty-five caliber bullets occasionally lifting their slight bodies into the air. Heavy smoke rose from the barrel of his Thompson Auto in the bitter cold air that surrounded him. He gave it a brief rest and reached for his third grenade.

A hot round from a Chinese SKS rifle tore through his left shoulder and spun him around. He came to rest on his knees, with the grenade still tightly gripped in his right hand. He immediately pulled the pin with his teeth and hurled it backwards over the top of the boulders. Judging from the sound of the blast, it had only managed to travel a few feet in the direction of his relentless attackers. But when he turned to peer through a crack in the rocks, he realized that the placement had been perfect, since they were almost upon him now. He had bought himself a few more seconds to live.

He picked up the Thompson Auto with his right hand, determined to finish well.

"This is it, " he said to himself.

He moved to the edge of the boulders to face the inevitable, committed to taking as many Chinese with him as possible.

Chapter 19

⁓

MacArthur's forces had driven the North Koreans all the way back to the Yalu River on the southern border of China. A successful conclusion to the war seemed close at hand. But the Chinese government had warned that, if U.N. forces crossed the 38th parallel, Chinese forces would enter the war in support of the North Koreans. Unfortunately, no one believed them. With no seat at the United Nations and no diplomatic relations with the U.S., their warnings went unheeded. As a result, 20,000 UN troops, including the U.S. Eighth Army and X-Corps, were quickly surrounded by 200,000 Chinese soldiers. The U.S. First Marine Division, parts of the U.S. Seventh Infantry Division and the Independent Commando Royal Marines were trapped in a vast net of Asian fighters. They were fish in a barrel.

Blood froze quickly and bodies turned to brick in the sub-zero temperatures. "Frozen Chosin," as they called it, was bitter cold – fast becoming a giant freezer, filled with frostbite and death.

As he moved to the edge of the boulders that had protected him, Sergeant Owen Rice raised his

Thompson Auto to address the enemy one last time. He sprayed his remaining rounds directly into the newest wave of Chinese who had grouped tightly together to charge his position.

"Fools," he thought. Seven or eight more soldiers fell as he exhausted the rest of his ammo. He settled back behind the rock and looked up at the icy, gray walls of the hillside opposite his position. He drew his combat knife, knowing he would likely have no chance to use it.

Suddenly, another figure flashed into focus – a fellow Marine, moving quickly to establish a superior angle of fire to the right of his position. He carried a long, heavy Browning BAR, discharging full-auto rounds of 30.06 into the gauntlet of Chinese attackers.

While Owen's .45 caliber Thompson had knocked down one soldier at a time, each one of the Browning BAR's 150-grain 30.06 rounds, traveling at supersonic speeds of 2800-feet-per-second, tore through three or four soldiers at a time. As the newcomer emptied each twenty-round clip, he raced parallel to their numbers, using any and all available cover, swapping out clips at an astonishing rate as he ran.

The awesome display of automatic firepower and sheer determination panicked the Chinese, and they turned back to seek cover. But, the Browning BAR was inescapable, mowing down their ranks indiscriminately. Forty or more Chinese were killed by the stranger as they stumbled over their own comrades in full retreat.

Owen Rice turned to look at the hole in his left shoulder. The blood had already coagulated, and a frozen cap was quickly forming over the wound. The pain was beginning to dull, but he knew it would return with a vengeance when it thawed. Still, he was grateful that his legs worked, and his right arm was fine. He got to his feet and listened intently.

In the distance, the Browning BAR finally went silent. A .45 caliber handgun could be heard discharging periodically along the attacker's path, silencing the last cries of wounded Chinese soldiers. Captain James R. Garrett appeared a few minutes later, the Browning BAR slung over his shoulder, smoke still rising from its barrel. He was an imposing figure, well built for the task at hand.

"What say we get out of here, Sergeant," he said, offering his hand and a quick smile. "Those bastards can go find their own entertainment. I'm running low on ammo anyway."

Owen extended his right hand, too, and thanked him sincerely. "You saved my life, Captain. I won't forget that."

"No problem," James Garrett replied. "If we can fight our way out of this shooting gallery, you can buy me a beer."

Owen Rice understood the Captain's make-light response, but catalogued every detail of what had just happened, permanently committing it to memory. One day – one day he would find a way to repay this man.

In late November, X-Corps executed a "fighting withdrawal" to the south, headed to the seaside city of Hungnam, where naval ships awaited them for evacuation. When asked if he were retreating, the commanding officer of the First Marines, Major General O. P. Smith, responded, "Retreat, hell! We're not retreating. We're just advancing in a different direction."

Along the way, they completely destroyed seven divisions of Chinese soldiers, inflicting ten times their own number of casualties.

After obliterating the city of Hungnam, the First Marines caught a ride south and immediately re-entered the fray, fighting alongside UN forces in southern Korea. An armistice was declared in July of 1953, establishing the 38th parallel as the line of demarcation between democratic South Korea and communist North Korea.

Chapter 20

❧

An uneasy feeling hung in the room. I felt certain
that I wasn't going to like whatever came next.

"I met your father in Korea, Matt." Governor
Rice began. He spoke slowly and deliberately, as if
explaining something to a child.

"So I've been told," I interrupted. "What was he
like back then? How old were you guys when you
met?"

"We were young, Matt – far too young to die,
but plenty old enough to dance. And dance we did,
my friend, all the way to the top of Korea and back
down again. He was a brilliant soldier, your father –
an exceptional Marine. He saved my life at Chosin
Reservoir in 1950, and I guess you could say that's
what got the whole thing started."

"Got what started?" I inquired. "What do you
mean?"

He took his hand off my mom's shoulder and
returned to his chair. He sat down slowly, picked up
his coffee and took a sip. He studied me above the
rim of his cup. Then, he set it down and continued.

"By the time the war was over, Matt, your father and I had become best friends, with just enough hardware between us to get ourselves noticed."

"What kind of hardware?" I asked.

"Service metals," he replied. "Combat metals."

"Interesting," I said, completely confused. "He never showed any of them to me."

"He wasn't allowed to," Governor Rice replied. He went on, ignoring the puzzled look on my face. "You see, after the war, we returned to the states together and accepted government jobs that turned out to be – well, let's just say *unique.*"

"I don't know what you mean," I said. "After the war, my father was a civilian contractor who spent the rest of his life selling machine parts to the military. I still have a shoebox full of postcards that he sent us from all the places that he worked up north."

The governor looked at my mom, who still had her face in her hands. He cleared his throat.

"Those postcards were written by government staffers, Matt. Your father was overseas at the time, doing what he did best – serving his country."

"Wait, wait, wait a minute," I stuttered. "What are you talking about? Are you saying that my father was still in the military, even *after* the war?"

"In a manner of speaking," Governor Rice replied.

"But that's not true," I argued. "He was a civilian contractor. He came home every few weeks. I saw him. For God's sake, we played ball together in the backyard."

"Like I said, Matt, your father was an exceptional man."

I looked over at Mom. "Is this true? What's he talking about? Why didn't you tell me about all of this?"

She gave no reply.

As it sunk in further, another thought hit me. I winced.

"Wait a minute. Are you saying that Dad *chose* to be away from us?" I asked incredulously. "Why? Why did he do that, Mom? What was more important to him than we were?"

She raised her head, tears running slowly down her cheeks.

"Nothing, Matt," she replied softly. "Absolutely nothing."

I felt anger rising in me, but kept it under control. I stood up and began pacing back and forth across the living room floor, rapid-firing questions at both of them.

"What was he doing overseas? What branch of the military was he working for? What was he trying to accomplish that was so all-fired important? Didn't he know that we needed him here at home? Didn't he know how much we missed him? What was he thinking? And why the hell didn't he tell us what was going on? How could he be so selfish? We needed him here. *I* needed him! And he was out gallivanting around the globe? It's the most ridiculous thing I've ever heard."

I stopped and glared out the front window of our house. I could feel the pressure building up inside me – the kind that usually releases itself in the form of a big mistake.

Feeling completely betrayed and painfully embarrassed, I shouted suddenly, "If I'd have known what he was doing, I wouldn't even have gone to his funeral!"

The governor stood up. I turned to face him, fully expecting an unpleasant exchange. Instead, he replied calmly to my outburst.

"As a matter of fact, Matt, you didn't."

Chapter 21

∽

Things were getting crazier by the minute. My world was spinning out of control, coming apart at the seams in the living room of my own home. Reality was dissolving into whatever design these people came up with. Worst of all, I still wasn't gaining any ground on it. The truth felt consistently beyond my reach. I was moving from an understanding of almost everything into a morass of deception and betrayal, where I understood absolutely nothing.

I projected my fear on the governor.

"Are you frigging crazy, Man? I *went* to my father's graveside service and almost froze my ass off. There was an Honor Guard from the local VFW. My father had an American flag draped over his coffin. Mom still has it. He's buried right down there in Mount Peace cemetery! You can go see for yourself, if you'd like. Mom knows. She was there with me. Right, Mom? Tell him!"

It was her turn now. She sat up straight and looked at me.

"I can't, Matt," she said.

"What do you mean, you can't?" I said angrily. "You were there, weren't you? Or did I just dream that you were there?"

"Yes, I was there, Matt," she replied. "But your father wasn't."

"What's that supposed to mean?" I complained. "If Dad's not buried there, then who is?"

"No one," Governor Rice said. "It's an empty coffin."

"What?" Matt cried. "What are you talking about? Why would you bury a coffin with no one in it? That's insane!"

"We did it to protect you, Matt. It was best for you and your mom that way."

"I don't understand," I replied. "If no one was buried there, then where's my Dad?"

"He's dead, Matt. He died almost fourteen years ago in western Russia."

"Russia?" I asked, dumbfounded. "What was he doing in Russia?"

"Serving his country," the governor replied.

"So, he died of meningitis in Russia?" I asked, emphasizing each word for clarity.

"Not exactly," he answered.

"O.K.," I said, stretching out each word carefully. "So, exactly what *did* he die of, and where did they bury him?" I was tired of the cat and mouse game. "And what was the charade of burying an empty casket supposed to protect us from?"

"It's complicated, Matt," his mom replied. "Sit down a minute."

I sat down on the couch again and looked over at Bill.

"Did you know about all of this?" I asked him.

"Not until a few weeks ago," Bill replied.

The governor intervened.

"First of all, Matt, we're not absolutely sure what your father died of. All we know is that he died in Russia of an illness that lasted less than a day. The exact nature of that illness remains a mystery. His body was not available to us, so there was no way to verify the exact cause of his death."

"So, how do you know that he died that quickly?"

"We know, Matt. For now, you'll just have to accept that. We felt that it would be best to provide him with a normal burial here at home. This eliminated the possibility that the Russians would further pursue any knowledge of him that they might have obtained. The intent was to provide an extra level of security for you and your mom. But, now that you're older, you need to know the truth about what happened to him, particularly in light of what I'm about to discuss with you."

He continued to monitor my reactions carefully. I felt that I was being examined.

"Great," I said, sarcastically. "So, what's next? Are you going to get around to telling me exactly what my father was doing when he died?"

"I already have," the governor replied. "As much as I can, until we finish this conversation."

I sat back, crossed my arms and took a deep breath, frustrated by the slow speed and incomplete nature of the information that he was providing.

"Relax, Matt," he said. "We've got a long way to go."

"You're telling me," I replied.

I reached into my pocket and fumbled with the small, metal soldier that I carried with me all the time. It was the one connection to my father that remained unchanged.

Chapter 22

❧

"**H**ave you thought about what you're going to do with your life now that you're out of prison, Matt?" the governor inquired.

"Get a job, I guess, like most folks," I said. "I've already put in a few applications around town."

"Sounds good," he remarked. "Had any response yet?"

"Not yet," I said.

"What type of work are you looking for?" he asked.

"The kind that pays," I quipped.

"Uh huh," he muttered. He moved to the front window and looked out across the lawn. He seemed to be waiting for me to say something.

"I know it's not going to be easy, with my prison record and all. But I'll find something. I'll dig ditches, if I have to."

"Uh huh," he repeated again.

"Uh huh, what?" I said, sounding a little irritated.

"Well, I was just wondering, Matt..." His voice trailed off. He glanced back across the room, preparing his next words. He paused for a second, with a distant look on his face, as if he were visiting foreign lands. He wrapped his right hand around the back of his neck and rubbed it.

"What now?" I thought, waiting for the hammer to drop.

"Before we can continue this conversation, Matt, I'm going to need you to sign some paperwork. The information that we're about to discuss is highly classified by the U.S. government, and I need to guarantee, beyond all doubt, that it will remain in the strictest of confidence. I am personally responsible for the protection of this information – failure to do so could put other lives at risk."

He moved back to his chair and took an important looking document out of the briefcase that rested alongside it. It was immediately clear that there had been advanced planning and forethought associated with his actions. He had come well prepared to discuss whatever it was – a matter of utmost importance, judging by the official seal on the document. I was both captivated and frightened by the gravity of it. Suddenly, things were becoming much sharper – more focused and real.

"Before we start, Matt, I need you to know the general nature of what we may, or may not discuss here today, so that you can make a reasonable decision about whether or not you wish to proceed. Some of this information concerns your father. Some of it concerns you. Ultimately, it will make a choice available to you that could shape your future in ways that you can't even imagine right now.

"I won't kid you, Matt – there's a downside, too, which is that there will most certainly be serious risks involved. Either way, since this information directly affects the lives of others, you will be legally obligated to protect it, even at the risk of personal harm, up to and including the possibility of your own death. Do you understand what I am saying, Matt?"

"Jesus Christ!" I said, stunned. "What are you talking about? Have you all gone mad?" I looked around at the others. Mom and Bill remained calm, immune to my kneejerk reaction. They were taking this thing just as seriously as Governor Rice, leaving me no room to divert the conversation.

Bill folded his arms and looked directly at me, communicating without words. Somehow, I understood him. I knew that he wouldn't be here if he wasn't already privy to this information – a fact that was oddly reassuring to me. But an uneasy presence permeated the room, and a sense of entanglement surfaced. My past, present and future all seemed to be merging into this single, decisive moment.

"What if I say no?" I blurted out.

"Then this conversation ends here, Matt, and your life goes on exactly as before. No harm done."

"But what about my father?" I demanded.

"I will have told you everything that I can," the governor replied. "I'm sorry, Matt, but that's the way it has to be."

"And if I say yes?" I inquired.

"Then everything changes," he replied coolly. "But, unfortunately, I can't describe those changes to you unless you sign these papers. It's up to you, son. Take your time - read it carefully."

I picked up the document and read it quietly to myself. It described information regarded as critical to "the safety and security of those involved," as well as to "the national interests of the United States of America, both at home and abroad."

Further along, references to "public safety" and "our survival as a nation, as well as a species" came into view. The reference to "species" was definitely confusing, but I continued to read. Failure to follow strict guidelines concerning this information would result in legal action, including, but not limited to, "federal prison terms," or, in such cases where others were lethally impacted, "the possibility of execution by a military firing squad."

It was far and away the most intimidating document that I had ever read. Further along, the language became more esoteric, and, for a while, I felt that it was beyond comprehension. But, any way you looked at it, there was no mistaking the fact that it was a serious document, bearing weighty commitments. My fingerprints, signature, social security number and witness signatures were required on the affidavit, giving it an air of official finality.

Governor Owen Rice and Lieutenant Bill Hunter's names already appeared on the professionally prepared document. If I signed it, they would have to follow suit, assuming direct responsibility for my involvement. I didn't want to do anything that would harm them or damage their reputations, so I knew that, if I went forward, there would be no turning back – no mistakes on my part, regardless of the circumstances.

It was one of those defining moments in life that had arrived virtually out of nowhere.

"Is any of this going to impact my mom?" I asked. "Is she going to be safe if you share this information with me?"

"Absolutely, Matt," the governor replied. "We'll see to that."

"Who's *we?*" I asked.

"The U.S. government," he replied, "as well as a handful of others who operate independently."

I had no idea what he was talking about, but it sounded good to me.

"O.K., then," I said, drawing a deep breath. "I'll sign it. I don't have any problem keeping a secret, as long as you can tell me what happened to my father and can assure my mom's safety afterwards. If he was a spy or something, I want to know that. And I want to know how he died. But, most of all, I want to know *why* he died."

"Sign the document, Matt, and I promise that you'll know all of that and more," the governor said. "Just be sure that you understand the commitment to absolute secrecy that is required of you. Once you know why, I have a feeling you won't have any problem fulfilling that obligation."

I placed the document on the coffee table. The governor took a black-ink fingerprint pad from his briefcase and handed me a pen. He rolled all ten of my fingerprints onto a series of small square boxes at the bottom of the document. Then, I wiped my hands with a dry towel and signed and dated the paperwork on the appropriate line. The governor and Bill added their signatures beneath mine to complete the authorization.

"O.K.," I said. "What's next?"

"Dinner," Mom said. "We can talk about all of this afterwards." She rose and headed toward the kitchen. The three of us looked at each other and smiled. She had a way of keeping things in perspective.

Soon enough, a slow-roasted pork loin – one of Bill's favorites – graced the table, along with mashed potatoes and gravy, fresh-cut green beans and pickled beets. The intoxicating aroma of home-made yeast rolls also filled the house as she brought them into the dining room on a large silver tray. Iced tea and coffee were served, but not before Governor Rice unexpectedly offered to say grace.

This surprised me a bit, coming from a man who had obviously led such a physical life, who had killed other men without remorse and had risen to such a powerful position in state government. To me, it all seemed a bit surreal, but we bowed our heads and listened to his prayer, delivered with the sincerity of a church minister, and with equal eloquence. This was a man to be reckoned with, I decided. Apparently, there was a good deal more to him than met the eye.

The tensions of the last twenty minutes faded quickly as we realized how hungry we were. The conversation soon turned to the wonderful quality of the food that Mom had prepared. She smiled for the first time that evening and even managed to blush a little when, halfway through the meal, Bill inadvertently commented that she was "the best mom he had ever had."

I knew how much that meant to her and winked at him in approval. Governor Owen Rice took it all in and requested another yeast roll.

Chapter 23

❧

After a warm cherry crumb cake dessert, we returned to our places in the living room and settled in for the remainder of the evening. Governor Rice complimented Mom again on the wonderful meal she had served and then stood up and took the lead in the discussion. He paced about the room with a sense of purpose, while we remained seated, listening intently to every word. He began with a high-level overview.

"As you know, Matt, the world is changing rapidly. When your father and I fought together in Korea, we knew exactly who the enemy was, and we understood his motivations. We were intimately familiar with his weapons and tactics and were well equipped to deal with them. Back then, the enemy wore uniforms, so we knew exactly where to aim. The lines of disagreement were clearly drawn, and they ultimately settled on the 38th parallel, where they remain to this day."

"I know," I said. "It's still one of the hottest flashpoints on the globe." The governor nodded his agreement and continued.

"Then came Vietnam, and the lines began to blur somewhat." He looked over at Bill, in deference to his first-hand experience. He seemed to be looking for permission to proceed. Bill nodded his head in agreement and the governor continued.

"Bill can tell you that we faced a very different kind of enemy there, who fought with different weapons and tactics. Vietnamese soldiers turned into civilians. And those same civilians fought as soldiers. Women and children became part of the enemy's arsenal, as dangerous as any well-armed man. Guerilla tactics replaced head-on combat, and our forces had to adapt to new ways of fighting. At the same time, widespread dissent at home made it an unpopular war in the public's eye. Sadly, politicians effectively bound the hands of our forces, ultimately contributing to the loss of 58,000 American lives."

I looked over at Bill, whose expression had darkened considerably. I could tell this was a sore topic with him.

"But now, Matt, we face a new enemy – one that's even more insidious. It has no easily identifiable shape or form. Few people are even aware of the threat that it poses, because its identity and potential impacts are difficult for the average person to grasp. And, frankly, even if they could fathom it, they'd probably choose to ignore it for the sake of sanity.

"The new enemy rests in the hands of laboratory scientists and military researchers, and its current forms are varied and somewhat mysterious. The nuclear arms race has completely diverted our attention away from Pandora's Box, whose lethal contents have grown from a fledgling science into a dark, underground race for power and control.

"The problem is that everyone involved in this pursuit is, to some extent, flying blind."

He turned and looked back across the room at me.

"You're familiar with the myth of Pandora's Box, Matt?"

"Yes," I replied.

"Then you know that the wrong kind of curiosity can sometimes lead to unexpected dangers. Right?"

"I guess so," I answered, not entirely sure where he was headed.

"What we've come to understand, Matt, is that, once certain lines are crossed, there may not *be* any turning back. Things can get out of control quickly, with potentially unimaginable consequences. So, it's important for us to keep track of what lines are being crossed – when, where and by whom."

"O.K.," I said. "I understand. But what does all this have to do with my father, or, for that matter, with me?"

"It has everything to do with both of you," Governor Rice replied. "Let's start with your dad."

He continued to move about the room, speaking with a palpable sense of urgency.

"After the Korean War, Matt, your father and I were called to Washington D.C. to be briefed on an area of growing concern to the U.S. government. We spent weeks in exhaustive presentations, meetings and discussions.

"At the conclusion of all that, we were asked to form a small, elite group of military specialists who would receive several months of high-level, classified training in biological warfare. We were new to this game, but were aware of the fact that this type of warfare had been around since medieval times. Back then, the dead bodies of diseased soldiers were catapulted over the walls of besieged cities in hopes of spreading cholera, yellow fever or bubonic plague within the enemy's encampment. It worked to some extent, but wasn't a particularly reliable strategy. Refinements were needed in both products and delivery systems.

"World War I introduced the horrors of mustard gas and other chemical nightmares, and World War II brought us experimentation by the Nazis with various chemical and biological agents, using helpless human beings as guinea pigs. What we did not know, but had to quickly come to terms with, was that the U.S. government was actively engaged in similar bio-warfare research, using non-human subjects – mostly primates – with the idea in mind of actually deploying weaponized versions of those agents in Vietnam.

"In the 1960's, a series of secret government tests, conducted on and around a group of remote Pacific islands, produced results that were particularly disturbing and highly problematic – not because they had failed, but because they had proven far more successful than anticipated. Unbeknownst to us at the time, Soviet agents observed those tests, collected samples of our biological agents in Petri dishes and returned them to the Soviet Union, instantly advancing their own bio-warfare research programs by decades.

"President Nixon ultimately dropped plans for the use of those biological agents in Vietnam because they had no way to avoid massive civilian casualties alongside those of enemy combatants. Instead, in 1972, the U.S. rushed to sign the 'Convention on the Prohibition of the Development, Production, and Stock-piling of Bacteriological and Toxin Weapons and on Their Destruction,' more commonly referred to as the 'Biological Weapons Convention.'

"The United States, Great Britain and the Soviet Union offered themselves up as exemplary followers of this new doctrine, though little is known or verifiable regarding their actual observation of that agreement. U.S. experts suspected that bio-warfare sciences were continuing to advance throughout the world, and that the threat of accidental releases of weaponized biological agents remained not only plausible, but highly probable at some point in the not-too-distant future.

"With this in mind, your father and I were asked to form one of the earliest task groups to look into this growing threat, particularly as related to the Soviet Union, which the U.S. government viewed as their greatest threat. Over the next six months, our hand-selected team of men were schooled in the tenets of biological warfare, weaponized agents, dispersion techniques and some of the key scientific elements to look for once we had tapped into a credible source of information inside the Soviet Union.

"Six other members of our group were assigned in pairs to St. Petersburg, Sverdlovsk and Minsk to search for similar information on Russia's developing bio-warfare programs.

"Posing as grain dealers, your father and I were sent to Moscow to negotiate the on-going sale of U.S. wheat to the Soviets.

"Having grown up on a Kansas farm, I had some first-hand knowledge of grain sales and their related market influences, which I shared with your father. I was amazed at how quickly he picked it up. He was speaking the language within a few weeks, as competently as any grain salesman I knew. We used that knowledge to establish our reason for being in Moscow. We were tasked with immersing ourselves in local Russian culture, learning what we could about advances in Soviet biological sciences and monitoring and reporting any attempts to develop biological warfare agents that had the capacity to threaten the safety and security of the United States of America or any of its vital interests. The plan was to collect information, while avoiding any overt actions that might reveal our true mission.

"Since our actions were covert and highly classified, they were executed independent of all other government agencies at the time. If we were caught, the U.S. government would deny any knowledge of our activities, leaving us completely at the mercy of the Russians, who weren't known for their patience or tolerance of foreign intervention. Frankly, the thought of being sent to a Russian prison, or, worse still, summarily executed, didn't interest us much, so we were extremely careful about how we proceeded. Fortunately, we were given carte blanche to achieve our goals, answering only to the Joint Chiefs of Staff and the President of the United States through secure, diplomatic channels.

"In the spring, we moved to Moscow, settling into a neighborhood where a Soviet scientist by the name of Dr. Uri Kavalov lived. He worked at the Institute of Applied Microbiology at Obalensk, just south of the city. He was a middle-aged, spectacled man, with dark brown hair and a neatly-manicured beard. He was thought to be a significant player in the Soviet biological weapons program, though no one was really certain of this.

"The U.S. government had a special interest in him because one of our eastern European agents, who had disappeared the previous winter, had communicated a brief, cryptic message to them suggesting that Uri might be 'turned.' It was unclear why this was the case, but the agent had implied that something had frightened him. Exactly what that was remained a mystery, but, back in Washington, any possible information regarding the direction of Soviet bio-warfare programs was enough to pull out all the stops. This particular lead was tantalizing – an opportunity that they couldn't afford to miss.

"We were able to determine that Uri had a wife and two daughters who lived comfortably in a second-floor flat in a clean, modern apartment building, located in a well-cared-for neighborhood near Soviet Plaza.

The residence had been provided to them at no cost by the Russian government, while Dr. Kavalov graced them with his considerable scientific knowledge and laboratory skills. His wife and daughters appeared to be happy and well-adjusted, seemingly oblivious to the nature of his work.

"While in Moscow, your father and I tracked Uri's movements for months, waiting for the perfect opportunity to make contact with him in a low-risk environment. We knew there were no guarantees – the Soviet government had eyes everywhere, and odds were they kept them on their most prized possessions. To say the least, we had to be discreet.

"Our opportunity presented itself on a Saturday afternoon in mid-July at an outdoor produce market on the banks of the Moscow River. A sizable crowd had gathered there on the weekend, eager to select fruits and vegetables transported downriver on small boats and trucked into the city from nearby farming cooperatives. Vendors lined the stone walkway where Uri shopped, busily negotiating prices with potential customers. Baskets of bright red tomatoes, leafy green vegetables and variegated melons leaned out at passing customers, hoping to be selected over the next booth's offerings.

"Your father and I positioned ourselves next to a booth where Uri had stopped to buy radishes, placing them in a woven basket on his left arm. As he turned to exit, James brushed by him, deftly placing a small loaf of bread wrapped in brown paper on top of his vegetables. In the crowded conditions, Uri took no notice of it until several minutes later when he added some vine-ripe tomatoes to his basket. Spotting the loaf of bread, he hesitated briefly and then carried on as if nothing had happened. We weren't sure whether he thought the vendor had added it as a gift, or if he just hadn't registered its sudden appearance. His reaction gave no real clue.

"We left the marketplace immediately, hoping that he might contact us later that evening. The interior of the brown paper contained the address of a small restaurant, a proposed meeting time of nine P.M. and the first name of the agent who had vanished the winter before. It was a huge risk – perhaps life-threatening – but the note itself contained nothing of real substance and was our best chance at opening a line of communication with Uri. If he turned out to be a patriot, we might have to eliminate him and flee the country. But, if he showed up alone and was willing to cooperate, we might gain valuable information on the progress of the Soviet bio-weapons program. Either way, the die was cast."

Matt was spellbound, as Governor Rice continued to reveal the story of his father's parallel existence – a life that had been kept from him, for reasons that remained unclear. He spiraled down into the tale, becoming a silent spectator, completely absorbed in the liquid flow of it.

Chapter 24

❧

*Z*oya's was a small side-street café, named after the female Soviet partisan, Zoya Kosmodemyanskaya, a member of the Russian resistance during World War II who had fought so bravely against the invading Nazis. Following her capture at the age of seventeen, she was subjected to a night of barbaric torture by the Germans, who ultimately marched her into the village square and hung her. Her fellow citizens were forced to watch as they bayoneted her lifeless body repeatedly for refusing to reveal information about her partisan comrades. The Germans left her hanging in the village square for days as a warning to those who would aid the resistance. Her memory was still fresh in the minds of the Soviet people, and the white plaster walls of the small café, decorated with heroic paintings that symbolized the triumph of the Russian people, served as a memorial to her courage and sacrifice.

James Garrett and Owen Rice entered Zoya's just before nine P.M. that evening. Uri Kavalov already stood at the bar, nursing a glass of Stolichnaya vodka. The Americans moved to the back of the room and sat at a small table, looking around for any company that might have followed him. There was none. Government agents had become fairly conspicuous to them over the last several weeks. They'd even managed to identify a few of them through information collected by other U.S. agencies. Only two other couples shared the café, both in their sixties, and both were chattering loudly in Russian, completely oblivious to their presence.

James ordered vodka and pirozhki – small pastries filled with meat, potatoes and cabbage – for both of them. The waiter, a tall, thin man with a look of perpetual exhaustion, scribbled the request on a small pad of paper and disappeared into the kitchen.

The bartender was a rotund woman with rosy cheeks, inspired only by red wine and the stool that she sat on. She offered a stark contrast to the proud patriots who graced the café walls.

James took a small loaf of bread wrapped in brown paper out of his shoulder bag and laid it on the table. Within a minute, it caught Uri's eye and unnerved him a bit. He turned back to the bar and ordered another vodka, downing it in two swallows. They used this brief delay to review the environment, searching for anything that seemed out of place or unusual. Nothing was amiss.

Soon, Uri pushed back from the bar, took a deep breath and turned around. He had an unremarkable expression on his face, but they could still sense conflict in his movements. Both fear and urgency were present in his advance, but anyone watching would have failed to detect it. He had mastered his emotions in a way that suggested extraordinary self-discipline and control. An overwhelming sense of importance drove his feet forward, but at a leisurely pace that disguised his intentions.

"Dobrenecha," he said, as he approached their table. They replied in kind.

"Ah – you are American?" he asked politely, speaking good English, with a slight Russian accent. He had studied both languages in school from the time he was a boy.

"Yes," James replied. "Won't you join us for a drink?"

"A drink?" he inquired. "Yes, yes – a drink," he said, smiling as he stood opposite the two men, pondering his next move.

Owen asked him if he would like vodka.

"Sure," he replied. "Vodka is good."

Owen motioned to the bartender to bring them another round. The woman slid off her stool and filled three glasses.

Uri pointed at the loaf of bread on the table.

"Did you buy that bread at the Moscow market this afternoon?" he inquired.

"Indeed, I did," James replied. "Would you like to share some with us?"

"I've already eaten, thank you," Uri replied.

They knew immediately that he had made the connection – he already understood who they were and why they were there. He was a gifted and intelligent man, which made it easier for them to communicate without having to go through a lot of cautious, tedious dialogue.

As he spoke, the strange mixture of fear and urgency in his manner continued to evidence itself. It was dangerous business for a Soviet scientist to be seen talking with two Americans in a Moscow restaurant, regardless of the topic of conversation. They assumed that this was the source of his apprehension.

"Did you know my good friend, Peter?" Uri asked suddenly, as he pulled out a chair and sat down across from them.

They were shocked that he had come to the point so quickly and that he was actually willing to sit down with them.

"Somewhat," Owen replied. "But we haven't seen him for a while."

"It's not likely that you will," Uri said quietly, as if there were no real mystery to Peter's disappearance.

"Do you know where he is?" James asked.

"No, I do not," Uri lied. The grave expression on his face suggested to Owen that poor Peter might never be found.

"We need to talk," Uri said abruptly. "But not here."

"O.K.," James replied. "When and where?"

The bartender delivered three Vodkas, overhearing their conversation on the soaring demands for wheat and other grains as winter approached.

"I'll let you know," Uri replied as the bartender walked away. He tilted his glass of vodka up and drained it. With that, he stood up and smiled, pushing his chair back under the table.

"Dusvedonia," he said, turning around and exiting the restaurant with another dose of carefully measured restraint.

Chapter 25

❦

Captain James R. Garrett moved carefully through the narrow streets, lowering his face as he passed Soviet citizens returning from their day labors. Uri had requested that only one of them meet him at the Zverev Bridge, the oldest pedestrian crossing in downtown Moscow. He felt that a smaller group would attract less attention. When James arrived at the footbridge, a steady flow of businessmen and craftsmen strolled across its narrow span, discussing the events of the day. He took up a position on the west side of the Vodootvodny Canal and waited.

Uri wasn't the kind of man to be late – he was far too focused to delay matters of importance. At precisely six P.M., James saw him approaching from the opposite side, wearing non-descript clothing and a plain, brown hat. His stride carried him just beyond where James was standing, and then he turned back to ask for a light. James removed a small, silver lighter from his shirt pocket and lit Uri's dark brown cigarette. Uri thanked him and inquired of his work day.

"At the Kremlin's request, we added several more metric tons of wheat to their order. All in all, it was a very pleasant exchange," James replied. "And you? How did your day go?"

"Why don't you come with me?" Uri said. "I'd like to show you some of the work that I am doing."

James was a little surprised at his sudden offer, but more than willing to cooperate.

Uri led him back across the bridge and continued eastward through the business district. Soon, they turned down a winding, cobble-stoned street, lined by small shops and minor restaurants. Just as James started to ask him where they were headed, Uri turned suddenly down another side-street that was just wide enough for two men walking in opposite directions to squeeze by each other. Halfway down its length, he stopped beside an iron-framed wooden door, produced a key and opened it.

He had James enter first, then immediately followed him, locking the door again from the inside. A number of empty cardboard boxes were randomly stacked around the room, and an old wooden counter rested along the back wall. To their right, a cast iron staircase spiraled gracefully around a four-inch diameter metal pole, disappearing below them. Uri pointed toward the stairs, and they descended together about ten feet below street level. There, he took out a second key, which opened a windowless, solid metal door. Strangely, it revealed only six feet of hallway before encountering a third door, also metal, which had a small, Russian sign on it that read, "No Admittance." That door had an electronic keypad on it.

"These rooms were constructed by a group of wealthy private citizens during World War II to serve as bomb shelters," Dr. Kavalov explained. "They didn't want their families having to huddle below ground with commoners, so they kept this facility secret until the war ended. Afterwards, they sold the property. A failed export business used them for a while and then abandoned them. They fell into disrepair, and an elderly gentleman bought the property at auction, sight unseen. I leased the facility from him to use as storage units three years ago. I send him a small monthly check, and he leaves me alone. His health is declining, so he never comes around."

Uri entered a six-digit entry code that allowed them to pass through the third door into what looked like a small locker room. It contained two shower stalls, a wooden bench and a couple of large, floor-to-ceiling metal lockers. Hovering above the cold, white tile floor was a faint smell of exotic chemicals that James did not recognize, though he thought it resembled a disinfectant. Overhead, fire system sprinkler heads were mounted every five feet – possibly overkill, considering the concrete structure that they protected. Uri stopped suddenly in front of the lockers and turned to James.

"You'll need to put on a suit to come with me. It's very important that you follow my instructions and are extremely careful about what you touch beyond this point. I'll explain everything to you as we go. But, first, let's get you into this equipment."

He opened one of the locker doors and took out what James immediately recognized as a one-piece positive pressure bio-safety suit, ventilated by a battery-operated life-support system. James had worn a similar suit just six months earlier when he had entered a high-level containment lab at the U.S. Army's laboratories in Fort Detrick, Maryland. His eyes narrowed as he realized what was happening.

"Wait a minute," James said. "I thought your biological research labs were in Obalensk."

"They are, indeed," Uri replied. "But this is my own private lab. The government has no knowledge of this place or the work that I do here. That's precisely why I brought you to this location. I couldn't get you within a mile of our government facilities. If I tried, I would certainly be caught and executed immediately, along with my wife and children. The same goes for you and your family. The Russian government takes their military research facilities seriously, and any breach of security is guaranteed a rapid and, shall we say *thorough* response.

"I have access to small amounts of laboratory equipment through the University of Moscow, where I taught microbiology for many years prior to going to work for the government. I have several close friends who still teach at the university. They have supplied me with most of my needs. They don't ask a lot of questions, since many of them already have small labs of their own set up in their attics or basements. As a university professor, there's constant pressure to do research and publish the results. Many of my former colleagues work eighteen-to-twenty hours per day to meet those expectations. They put in twelve-hours-a-day at the university, and then go home and work six-to-eight more at night. Needless to say, they surrender their youth quickly.

"For the last three years, I have been carefully replicating my government experiments at Obalensk here in this lab, though on a much smaller scale. Carefully proportionate scale reduction does not affect the accuracy of my test results, so I have the freedom to exceed the progress of my Obalensk work here without government interference. I'm sure that you can see the benefits of this. I can avoid placing potentially disastrous products in the hands of unscrupulous government officials who would not hesitate to use them to advance their own status and power within the Soviet Union. Trust me. On two occasions already, this approach has delayed the Soviet goal of world dominance. If you will forgive me for saying so, I'm very good at what I do."

"So I've heard," James replied. "But why have you decided to share this information with me?"

"The answer to that question will become obvious to you in a few minutes," Uri said. "For right now, just put your suit on and remember what I've said about not touching anything without my permission once we enter the lab."

"What lab?" James asked. "Where is it?"

"Close," Uri replied.

Chapter 26

∾

James removed his clothing and put on the positive pressure suit, which was a little bulky, but not uncomfortable. Uri checked its air-flow and turned James around slowly, carefully examining the suit for any tears, punctures or leaks. James knew this was standard operating procedure before entering labs that contained dangerous materials, but he gave no indication of his knowledge.

When Uri was satisfied that James' suit was properly sealed and that he was breathing normally, he stripped down and donned his own equipment, motioning for James to examine it. He complied, noting that both suits had eight-hour batteries, which powered small motors that supplied HEPA-filtered air to their suits. An additional fifteen-minute battery backup was attached at waist level for emergencies, along with a small, waterproof flashlight.

With both equipment inspections completed, Uri went to the second shower door and opened it. He removed a bar of soap-on-a-rope from the interior wall, which was attached to a hook on a small suction cup. Then, he removed the hook, bent down and inserted it into a tiny hole in a corner tile and lifted it. Beneath the tile, a flat metal handle appeared. He raised and turned it ninety degrees to the left. The entire shower floor pulled up, revealing a hatch-like metal door just beneath it with a recessed combination lock. Uri spun the dial left and right, selecting various numbers. Then, he pulled the hatch up, resisted by an unseen negative air pressure that opposed any outbound air. Metal steps descended into a subterranean lab, twenty feet below ground level.

"You first," Uri instructed.

James descended the stairs, holding onto smooth, gray handrails as he entered a world of cold white tile, stainless steel containers, glass beakers, test tubes, syringes and bottles of sodium hypochlorite. Muted floor lighting provided sufficient guidance to enter the lab. At the far end of the room, two small monkeys sat in cages, hyper-alert to their presence. Uri closed the metal door behind them, which automatically relocked itself. He turned a small, corkscrew pressure valve that tightened the seal a bit more, and then descended to the lab floor.

A ten-digit electronic keypad was also located on the underside of the hatch above them, strangely providing outbound security. James realized that they were locked inside the lab now, all alone except for the chattering monkeys, the whirr of a small centrifuge in the middle of the room and the constant hum of positive airflow inside their suits. The place had a stark, sterile feel that reminded him of a hospital morgue.

"This way," Uri said, pointing toward a stainless-steel table next to the centrifuge.

A large, dual-view binocular microscope sat alone on the table, designed to allow two researchers to view the same specimen simultaneously. Its unusual shape and construction were unlike anything that James had seen back home. A large power-pack hummed on its side, and multi-staged lenses were stacked atop each other in the microscope's mid-section. Its design was uniquely complex, and its size suggested considerable power. Uri flipped a couple of switches on the scope that turned on its focal lighting. Then, he went to a side wall and switched off the overhead fluorescent lighting, plunging the room into near-total darkness.

He returned to the viewing table, bent down and opened the door of a small freezer unit underneath it. Using his flashlight, he removed three slides, labeled Alpha-9, Alpha-23 and Alpha-C, placing them carefully on top of the viewing table.

Uri selected the slide marked "Alpha-9" and inserted it into the microscope's carriage. He adjusted it carefully, focusing the lens before indicating to James that he should view the sample from the opposite side. James moved around the table and leaned over the microscope, pressing his face closer to the clear plastic facemask of his pressure suit. Immersed in the surrounding darkness, he approached the binocular lenses, entering the strange world of inner space. Tiny cellular structures came into view that housed tangled, spaghetti-like limbs. They lay cold and still, curled and twisted in random directions – motionless and seemingly dead.

"What exactly are we looking at?" James said above the din of his suit's airflow.

"A flivovirus," Uri replied. "Of no particular threat to humans – no more than, say, the common cold – but deadly to smaller primates. It kills them quickly – in a matter of days – a very unpleasant process to observe. After a few weeks, it burns through a percentage of their population and then stops as suddenly as it started."

James turned around and looked at the monkeys staring at him from across the room. They looked strong and healthy, though understandably agitated. They associated the presence of human beings with pain and were constantly in search of a means of escape. Each time he looked at them, they rattled their cages wildly, hoping that the doors would fly open so they could return to the safety of their beloved trees.

"Don't worry," Uri said. "They can't get out. The cages are made of heavy-gauge steel and there are tamper-proof locks on each of the doors." He removed the Alpha-9 slide from the microscope, replacing it with the one marked "Alpha-23." Once again, he positioned and focused the sample. James waited until he was finished and then leaned over to have a look at it.

There were clear similarities between the two samples. Uri explained that Alpha-23 was also a flivovirus, though it exhibited none of the random, aimless characteristics of Alpha-9's spaghetti-like appendages. Instead, Alpha-23 seemed to have a distinct goal in mind, having already penetrated the walls of the cells, protruding in clustered spikes that favored jacks or pinwheels. It was completely illogical, but James felt that this sample had purpose – a veiled type of organization that suggested intent. He wasn't sure why, but, to him, it appeared sinister – dangerous by design.

"Here, we see the same virus, but with a few changes," Uri began. "Some of the cell's proteins have been modified, creating what amounts to a nightmare virus for human beings. On the other hand, it poses no threat whatsoever to lesser primates. For reasons that we do not fully understand, exposure to this virus causes a human's internal organs to rapidly deteriorate, virtually liquefying them within a few days. To a medical examiner that autopsied such a patient, they would appear to have the internal organs of a cadaver that had gone unattended for a week or more. Most of the blood and bodily fluids would have long since evacuated the body, exiting quickly through every orifice. The skin would appear blotched and waxy, like a dehydrated banana.

"I personally engineered this virus a little over a year ago, using techniques that remain unknown to my contemporaries. Since its kill-rate is high – fifty-to-ninety percent of the target population – it would make a highly effective short-term instrument of war. It burns intensely, but has a finite lifespan, restricted to about twenty-one days. This is the only example of it in existence. I intentionally destroyed all remaining production of Alpha-23 to make certain that it never found its way back into the labs at Obalensk."

"That's very kind of you," James noted. "But why did you design it in the first place? And why didn't you destroy this sample as well?"

"Why design it?" Uri repeated. "It was simply a by-product of scientific inquiry – research for the sake of expanding my own fledgling knowledge of the cellular universe. The more I learn about viruses, the better I get at managing them. And, remember – not all such scientific research produces undesirable results. Many of the world's greatest medical discoveries have come from such inquiry. The dangers involved are justified by the vaccines and medicines that have resulted, saving countless thousands of lives. I'm sure you would agree with this."

"Of course," James responded. "As long as the researcher's objectives remain positive." He watched Uri's eyes, which remained calm and steady, revealing nothing in particular. For James, it was disconcerting.

"As for your second question," Uri added, "the reason that I kept a sample of Alpha-23 was to provide you with a means of comparison to Alpha-C, which rests on the last slide that I will show you. I completed this work two weeks ago – an accidental discovery of the utmost importance. I have secured this knowledge elsewhere, in case my lab is ever destroyed. It is absolutely essential that you understand this virus and what it could mean to the future of mankind."

"Sounds ominous," James replied. "Is it?"

"Depends," Uri answered. "Let's just say that it opens new doors."

"That's a little vague, isn't it?" James said. "Could you be a bit more specific?"

"Sure," Uri replied. "Let's start with the basics. As you know, most organisms on our planet are either dead or alive – there's no in between. Evidence of life-sustaining processes exists even in hibernating animals or in the deepest meditative states that humans can achieve. But, the complete absence of such processes results in cellular degeneration and is ultimately defined as death – a state readily verifiable with modern medical instruments."

"O.K., James said. "I'm with you so far."

Uri pointed at the slides on the table and continued.

"Some viruses, on the other hand, are quite unique in the sense that they never really die. They live in selected hosts, usually for a measured period of time. When the host dies, the virus simply goes dormant until another suitable host presents itself. If the virus's preferred method of transport is available, through physical contact, liquid transmission, airborne particles, etc., then the virus reawakens, jumps ship and begins to replicate itself in the new host. Eventually, it burns itself out, responding to internal mechanisms and schedules that we do not fully understand. Sometimes, viruses disappear at the peak of their activities, for no apparent reason. They behave in ways that defy explanation. As scientists, we should be able to understand them, but the truth is that we don't. Their logic continues to elude us."

James smiled.

"We'll catch up to them sooner or later. It's just a matter of time."

"Maybe," Uri replied. "But, meanwhile, we live in a dangerous world, with lots of unscrupulous people. Not all of them are looking to improve on man's condition. Don't you agree, James?"

James nodded his head, supporting Uri's statement, but feeling unsure of where he was headed with the conversation. After a short pause, Uri looked up at him. For the first time, James thought that he detected signs of weariness in him, mixed with a mild sense of defeat. But Uri's fatigue disappeared quickly, like a cloud blown across the sky.

"I guess that's a matter we'll have to leave to the philosophers," Uri said. "Right now, we must focus our attention on stabilizing the situation. To that end, let me continue with my explanation."

"Fine," James said eagerly. "I'm all ears."

"Usually, viruses are restricted to specific host species. They rarely exhibit cross-species adaptability. The first two slides that I have shown you are excellent examples of this fundamental singularity of purpose. Of course, that makes them extremely good at what they do. Familiarity with their respective hosts translates into a more effective, focused viral attack. With their uniquely-targeted knowledge, they ravage the host species, utilizing a single-minded approach – divide and conquer, replicate and destroy. But, as you know, fires that burn intensely consume themselves quickly. In the same way, such viruses do serious damage, but tend to go dormant faster than other viral agents."

Uri removed Alpha-23 and replaced it with the third and final slide, slightly larger than the previous two. The "Alpha-C" agent occupied a broader section of the mid-slide area. Uri moved its microscopic landscape around in search of a particular section of interest. When he found it, he stood up and spoke to James again.

"Have a look," Uri said, "And pay particular attention to the branching variations underway at the time that I terminated their progress. When I immersed them in bleach, it captured a stunning snapshot of the future of viral adaptation. One key protein was removed from the nucleus of this cell. I installed an engineered substitute, the structure of which is too complex to explain within the time constraints of our visit. Suffice it to say, it's never been seen before."

James felt a slight tingling sensation on the back of his neck as he leaned down to view the final sample. This one revealed a landscape that was completely different from the previous two slides. For James, it was a daunting task just to take it all in.

Alpha-C was a master flivovirus that had seized upon every available opportunity to transform itself. Cell lesions revealed a dizzying array of multi-shaped limbs, ranging from long, splayed, finger-like organisms to already-detached stars, anvils and long, crescent-shaped cords that lie frozen in the space between cells. Each viral entity was bordered by slightly different hues – colors most commonly found in the pale light spectrum of frozen hinterlands.

Of special interest to James were its spectacular transformations into a vast kaleidoscope of shapes and sizes. Small dot-sized versions flowed from one cell to the next, as if trailing a lifeline until they could penetrate the wall of the next cell. Larger weed-shaped versions forked and branched in every direction, taking on the abstract appearance of crackled ice. Spiraling away from the edge of his view, web-like viruses stretched across the face of some cells, glowing with a dark blue iridescence. Inside Alpha-C, one virus had become many, changing and adapting as it grew – a shape-shifting, moving target, halted only by the direct intervention of its creator.

"I'm not sure that I understand what I'm looking at, Uri," James said. "It appears to be a whole zoo of viruses."

"That's correct," Uri replied. "But Alpha-C began as a single virus. I watched it for several hours. It squirmed and morphed into a variety of viral agents, searching desperately for a new host. It's unlike anything that I've ever seen – perhaps more dangerous than smallpox. There's no telling what it's capable of. Further primate study is required to understand its behavior, and the results of that work must be kept secret. Meanwhile, I destroyed this slide sample."

"Good call," James remarked. "It looks like a virus that's completely out of control."

Uri did not reply. He stood up and removed the last slide from the microscope. "Now that you've seen it, we need to talk."

"I thought that's what we were doing," James quipped.

"About something else," Uri said. He placed all three slides back in the freezer and moved to the side wall, switching on the overhead fluorescent lighting. After taking a moment for their eyes to adjust, Uri motioned James upward, pointing at the hatch-like exit overhead.

"Let's finish this conversation upstairs," he said.

He flipped the overhead lights off again, returning the lab to its original, dimly-lit floor lighting.

Chapter 27

❧

Uri climbed the metal stairs and addressed the keypad on the underside of the hatch. His body blocked James' view of the numbers input – of little consequence to James, since he had no plans to return. Then, Uri pushed the hatch open, leading the way up into the shower room. James followed him out, closing the hatch behind them, assisted by the inbound airflow. It latched itself automatically, and he stood up and faced Uri again.

"We'll observe decontamination procedures before we proceed," Uri said. "First, please step into the other shower and I'll spray off your suit. Once that's done, you can do the same for me."

James entered the adjacent shower and Uri sprayed him down with a canister that contained pure bleach. He returned the favor, drenching every inch of the exterior of Uri's protective gear. Then, both of them removed their pressure suits, placing them on hangers on either side of the shower wall to dry. Uri stepped over to the adjacent shower and replaced the tile flooring that had concealed the hatch. He returned the clip to the suction cup on its wall and hung the soap-on-a-rope on it. Then, they crossed the room to their lockers and put on their street clothes. While they dressed, James wondered what Uri was thinking. His brow was furrowed and his muscles were tense.

"I fear that the Soviet authorities are growing suspicious of my dedication to their cause," Uri said abruptly. "They're not particularly happy with the results that I've provided them recently. They suspect that I might be holding out on them, and they want more. There have been subtle indications that, if my efforts at Obalensk don't improve, things could become dangerous for everyone involved. I am concerned for the safety of my wife and daughters. I don't want them caught up in this."

"Maybe you should have thought of that before offering them your services," James said. The words were no more out of his mouth than he regretted them.

"Were you under the mistaken impression that I had some choice in the matter?" Uri asked.

"Sorry," James replied. "I guess I was."

"In the Soviet Union, when you possess certain skills, choice is not always available," Uri explained.

"I see your point," James replied. "So, what are you going to do?"

"It's a serious paradox," Uri replied. "I love my country, but if I give them what they want, I could endanger not only my own family, but potentially the entire world. On the other hand, if I continue to provide them with only low-yield biological weapons that burn out quickly, I'm afraid that my services will no longer be required. What you have to understand is that, with my knowledge of their biological weapons program, they can't just ship me off to a Siberian labor camp. They couldn't risk it. The only way that they can secure that knowledge is to terminate it. And they will seal off any possible sources of leakage as well."

"Not a good position to be in," James replied. Finally, he knew where this conversation was headed. It was more than he could have hoped for.

"I want you and your friend to get us out of the country," Uri said decisively. "I want to defect."

"I'm sure that the United States of America would welcome you and your family," James said. "And I would consider it an honor to make that happen. We'll need a few days to set things up, but I can assure you that we'll do everything within our power to get you and your family out safely."

Uri offered him his hand. "I would be most grateful, James. It's important that we leave this country while we still can."

He turned away, hesitated a moment and then added, "You understand that you will be putting yourself at risk as well. Right?"

"Hey," James replied cheerfully. "Don't worry about me."

Chapter 28

❧

Earlier that evening, Dmitri Vasilii had arrived on the east side of the Zverev Bridge, about thirty seconds after Dr. Uri Kavalov had crossed it. Two subordinate agents stopped just behind Dmitri, awaiting his instructions. For the moment, he ignored them, focusing on the stranger on the opposite side of the bridge who had lit Dr. Kavalov's cigarette and struck up a conversation with him. Things looked innocent enough, until the two of them turned and began to cross the bridge together, walking toward them.

"Wait here," Dmitri said quickly to his colleagues. "And don't look at them." He started across the bridge in their direction, walking briskly, as if he were anxious to get home. Fifty feet away from them, he noted that they seemed to converse easily, free of the normal awkwardness present in first-time meetings. He sensed a certain familiarity between them, but couldn't be certain of it. Perhaps it was just his imagination.

Twenty feet away from them, Dmitri looked to his right and spoke to an elderly man walking alongside him.

"Good day, sir. It looks like we might get a little rain later this evening. Don't you agree?"

Somewhat surprised, the old man looked up at him and said, "What's that? Oh, yes, yes. We could certainly use some rain. It's been a little dry recently."

As the old man replied, Uri and the stranger were passing on their left, headed in the opposite direction. Dmitri caught a brief snippet of what the stranger was saying. "...several more metric tons of wheat..." was all that he could make out. It was an American accent.

Dmitri did not break his stride, continuing to the other side of the bridge, maintaining his casual conversation with the old man. Then, quite suddenly, he turned and bade him farewell, explaining that he had forgotten something back at the office. He hurried back across the bridge to his colleagues, who were still discussing the architecture of a high-rise building on the far side of the canal. Their conversation ceased the moment he rejoined them.

"Poloff," Dmitri said. "That stranger is an American. First, I want you to contact headquarters and update them. Then, I want you to go immediately to Dr. Kavalov's home and place his wife and two daughters under surveillance. Watch for any unusual activity and make sure they don't leave the city. If you have to take any of them into custody, tell them nothing until I give you further instructions. Victor, you come with me, and hurry – we must not lose sight of our primary objective."

Chapter 29

Uri felt like a terrific weight had been lifted from his shoulders. It had been a difficult decision, but he knew that what he was doing would provide the best protection for himself and his family. His research was important, and, hopefully, he would be able to resume it under more favorable circumstances abroad. James seemed capable and trustworthy, and he had not hesitated to offer his assistance. As a scientist, Uri knew that this was not his area of expertise. He needed someone with experience in this sort of thing – someone who had the right kind of contacts inside the U.S. government. And there was little doubt in Uri's mind – this man was not just a grain salesman.

He glanced at his watch. It was getting late, and he needed to get home. Tanya would have dinner ready, and she would be worried about him. If they left the lab now, he could make it home by eight.

He turned to James and said, "I think we should go now."

"Sure," James replied. "There's plenty of work to be done. I'll go directly to the embassy this evening. I need to access a secure line."

"O.K.," Uri said. "Could we meet again at Zoya's on Friday night to see what progress you've made?"

"Absolutely," James replied. "I should know something by then."

Uri punched in a series of numbers on the keypad of the metal door that exited the locker room. He opened it and moved into the short hallway. At the opposite end was the second metal door, beyond which was access to the spiral staircase. James followed Uri, closing the locker room door behind them. It snapped shut, and its internal mechanism automatically relocked. Then, they moved to the second metal door, where Uri removed a set of keys from his pocket. He unlocked the door, pushed it open and immediately froze in his tracks. Two men stood at the base of the spiral staircase. They stared briefly at Uri, but as soon as they saw James, they drew weapons with silencers on them and shouted in Russian.

"Get down on your knees! Both of you! Put your hands behind your head. And don't get up or I'll gladly shoot you both."

Uri knew that the silencers on their guns meant that they were government agents. He obeyed their commands, and James followed him to the ground, mirroring his movements. Uri began to plead with them in Russian, begging them to put away their weapons. He assured them that everything was all right, and that there was nothing to be concerned about. They ignored him completely.

Dmitri said something to Victor, who handed over his gun and approached the two kneeling suspects.

He searched them carefully for weapons, covering every inch of their bodies. Finding none, he pulled them to their feet, reclaimed his weapon and stood behind them, blocking any attempt at retreat. Uri began to shake, thinking that they were going to be executed on the spot, but he held it together. It was the first time that he'd ever had a gun pointed at him. James felt certain that they would not kill Uri, as he was too valuable an asset to the Soviet government. And that value would likely skyrocket as soon as they discovered his most recent accomplishment. On the other hand, James had little hope of a positive outcome for himself. Once they had a look around, things could get ugly.

"Who are you?" Dmitri said to James in English.

"I am an American businessman, here on a visa," James replied.

"Doing what?" Dmitri demanded.

"Selling wheat to your government so your people don't starve this winter," James replied.

"I'm sure that the Soviet people can feed themselves," Dmitri said. "What else are you here for?"

"To enjoy your fine Russian cuisine," James replied calmly.

"Perhaps you should try Zoya's. They serve wonderful pirozhki," Dmitri said, toying with him.

James made the connection immediately. The man who had glanced at them through the window at Zoya's the night before had been Dmitri. At the time, James thought nothing of it – a casual glance from a passerby that had lasted less than a second.

No one had entered the restaurant to question them and, to his knowledge, no one had overheard their conversation.

For the moment, they ignored Dmitri's comment. To acknowledge it would only incriminate them further.

"Let's have a look at what goes on here," Dmitri said. He pointed to the door behind them and said, "Open it."

"Please," Uri said. "This is my private study."

"Go!" Dmitri shouted.

The sound of his voice momentarily unnerved Uri. He turned around and walked back down the hallway. James followed him, as directed by Victor, who glared intently at him, enjoying his position of complete control. When Uri reached the locker room door, he stopped in front of the keypad.

"Open it!" Dmitri repeated.

Uri punched in six digits, with James standing beside him. He swung the door open and started to enter.

"Wait!" Dmitri shouted. "Before we go in, what numbers did you use?"

"06-95-37," Uri replied. James glanced at him, aware of the fact that those numbers indeed matched what he had just witnessed. Uri had calmed himself and was moving forward as if everything were normal. Anxious to see what waited inside, Dmitri did not question him further.

All four men entered the locker room in close proximity. Victor moved to each of the sidewall lockers and opened them. A few street clothes, some towels and a first-aid kit were all that he found. He trained his weapon on Uri and James while Dmitri went to the showers stalls. Two bio-safety suits hung on either side, the strong smell of bleach emanating from their smooth exteriors.

"Very interesting," Dmitri said. "What have you two been up to that would require this type of equipment?"

"Nothing important," Uri replied. "I was just showing James some infected animals that I'm treating."

"And what is the nature of their infection, Dr. Kavalov?" Dmitri asked. "And be careful of your answer."

"A respiratory illness," Uri lied. "I'm testing a new medicine on them. If it works, it may be worth researching as a treatment for pneumonia in human patients."

"And why do you need such protective gear to view these monkeys?" Dmitri inquired.

"We don't," Uri replied. "I was just being extra careful with my American friend here. We wouldn't want his trip spoiled by a lack of precaution on my part."

"Of course, Doctor," Dmitri said sarcastically. "We wouldn't want him to develop a cough in Russia." He smiled and looked at Victor, who raised his gun somewhat. James heard the safety release.

"Let's have a look at your little pets," Dmitri said to Uri. "I'm kind of fond of animals anyway. Where do you keep them hidden?"

"Please," Uri replied. "It's getting late. I must get home to my wife. She'll have supper waiting, and she'll be worried about me."

"This won't take long, Doctor," Dmitri assured him. "We'll be in and out as quickly as possible. I'm sure that you can understand our curiosity."

Uri looked over at Victor's gun, now pointed directly at his head, and capitulated. "If you insist," he said and moved to the second shower stall. He reached in, removed the pressure suit and laid it on the wooden bench behind them. Then, using the hook from the suction cup on the shower wall, he removed the corner tile, gripped the handle beneath it and lifted the shower floor, revealing the hatch and combination lock below.

"What have we here?" Dmitri taunted. "Is the State aware of these unusual accommodations?"

Uri did not reply, choosing instead to spin the combination lock on top of the hatch. Once it was unlocked, he pulled the hatch up against a light rush of inbound air, revealing the stairway leading down into the lab.

"Step back," Dmitri demanded.

Uri moved away from the hatch and Dmitri stuck his head down through the opening, while Victor kept his gun on Uri and James. Soon, Dmitri stood back up, a serious look on his face.

"O.K.," Dmitri said. "Let's have a closer look."

He sent Victor down first to secure the dimly-lit room. Uri and James went down the stairs next, stopping as soon as their feet met the floor. Dmitri started down last.

"Close the hatch behind you," Uri said. The room must be properly sealed before the lights will come on." Dmitri reached over his head and swung the hatch downward, noticing the electronic keypad on its underside just as the negative air pressure above them sucked it closed.

"No problem," he thought to himself. "I'm the one with the gun."

He turned and descended the gray metal stairs, listening to the nervous chatter of caged monkeys.

"At least that part of your story was true," Dmitri said to Uri, pointing at the cages on the far side of the room.

"Of course," Uri replied. "Why should I lie?"

Even to James, Uri didn't sound very convincing. Dmitri smelled blood, and he wasn't going to let loose of the scent.

Chapter 30

❧

When he reached the bottom of the stairs, Dmitri instructed Uri to turn on the overhead lighting. He would complete a thorough inspection of the lab, looking for anything suspicious to report to his superiors. Nine months earlier, he had received a significant promotion, and the thought of another one following so closely on its heels was exhilarating. He had already captured one prize – the American would be of great interest to the Soviet intelligence agency. But any incriminating evidence that he uncovered related to Dr. Kavalov could increase his status within the KGB exponentially. He felt like a kid in a candy shop.

Uri glanced over at James. James could see that he had already accepted his fate. The expression on his face suggested defeat, and his actions became mechanical. As Dmitri had instructed, Uri walked across the lab to the table situated along the side wall. He gripped the front edge of the table with his left hand and leaned across it, flipping on the light switches with his right hand. Simultaneously, he curled the fingers of his left hand underneath the table's edge, flipped open a plastic cover and depressed a small metal button beneath it. A video camera, mounted in a clear, fish-eye glass dome, whirred silently to life overhead. It recorded every inch of the lab, transmitting the output to a monitor-recorder concealed in the locker room above them. Then, he turned and walked back to a small desk, positioned between the microscope table and the monkey cages. He picked up a phone on top of the desk and began to dial a number.

"What are you doing?" Dmitri shouted, panicked by the possibility that Uri might be calling his superiors to report their intrusion. "Put that phone down!"

Uri continued to dial, completing the number as Dmitri shouted again.

"Put that phone down *now*, or you and your family will be arrested immediately!"

Uri spoke one word into the receiver. "Cerberus!" he said emphatically.

Victor's Walther nine-millimeter snapped twice in rapid succession, the first round tearing through Uri's right arm.

"No!" shouted Dmitri.

The second round had already ripped through the side of Uri's neck and continued on its path. It penetrated deep into the chest of one of the monkeys located directly behind him. In a single motion, Uri returned the handset to its cradle as he collapsed to the floor. The wounded monkey went ballistic, screaming and flailing about in its cage, blood spewing from its mouth and the gaping hole in its chest. In a matter of seconds, the animal fell silent on the floor of its cage, its blood spattered in every direction across the cold tile surfaces of the floor and walls.

"Fool!" Dmitri shouted. "You've killed him! You've killed Dr. Kavalov!"

Ignoring him, Victor crossed the room quickly and ripped the telephone cord out of the floor.

James rushed to Uri's side, went to his knees and applied pressure to the wound in the side of his neck. Uri was losing blood quickly, and his eyes were full of fear. His mouth opened and closed as he gasped for air.

"Which monkey?" Uri pleaded softly, a gurgling sound in his voice.

"What? What do you mean?" James asked, confused.

"Which monkey?" Uri cried, his eyes wide and insistent.

"The second one." James replied. "The one on the right."

Uri coughed up blood, and James raised his head, trying to open his airway. His eyes grew large and panicky. He was dying.

"In... infected..." Uri moaned. "Alpha-C..."

A raspy, clicking sound escaped his lungs, and his head slumped to one side. His eyes, glassy and jaded, rolled to the top of his head, his frozen gaze coming to rest upon the monkey cages behind him.

Chapter 31

❦

"Idiot!" Dmitri raged at Victor. "You've ruined everything! You've destroyed our only chance to extract critical information from one of our best scientists! We will both be punished for your stupidity. All we've got to show for our efforts is this useless American."

"Dr. Kavalov ignored our commands," Victor replied calmly. "He got what he deserved. I wasn't going to let him call in reinforcements. *You* might be willing to take that risk, but I'm not."

"So, you just shot him?" Dmitri exclaimed, incredulous at Victor's reply. "You're an idiot! I'll have you stripped of all rank by tomorrow. You'll be cleaning latrines for the rest of your life!"

Dmitri was livid with anger, his face crimson and strained. He would make certain that Victor paid for his mistake.

"I did what was necessary!" Victor shouted angrily. He'd had enough of Dmitri's criticism and wasn't going to listen to any more of it. He raised his gun and pointed it at his superior.

"What the hell are you doing?" Dmitri shouted at him.

The words barely exited his mouth when two more sharp reports issued from Victor's Walther. Dmitri's head snapped backwards, with neat, round holes in his forehead and right cheek. His mouth fell open and his expression went blank. His body arced backwards, beginning a slow descent that ended forcefully against the white tile floor. The sudden disturbance frightened the only remaining monkey, who barred his teeth and screamed like a banshee.

"Asshole," Victor commented, looking down at Dmitri's lifeless body. A tight grin spread slowly across his face. He had never liked Dmitri, who had been a source of constant criticism. At last, he had rid himself of the problem. Now, he turned his attention to the American.

James rose to his feet and faced Victor. Things had deteriorated so rapidly that he hadn't had time to think about his own fate.

"O.K.," James said. "What's next?"

"We get out of here," Victor replied, turning his gun on James and waving it towards the hatch above them. "I can salvage my career by telling my superiors that Dmitri shot Dr. Kavalov, and that you attacked Dmitri, shooting him with his own gun before I overcame you. I will be promoted for bringing you in alive for interrogation by our experts."

"That all sounds very nice, Victor, but I'm afraid it's a bit more complicated than that," James replied, a serious tone in his voice.

"On the contrary," Victor sneered. "It's all very simple. You Americans always think that you have everything figured out, don't you? Well, you're about to discover just how little you know about Soviet methods of interrogation."

"That's not what I mean," James replied.

"What are you talking about?" Victor insisted.

"Look around you," James replied. "Do you see any exits? The only one that I'm aware of is that hatch overhead – the one with the electronic lock on it. Forgive me for pointing this out, but, unless you're psychic, neither one of us knows what numbers to use on that keypad."

Victor looked up at the hatch, then back at James. His expression went blank.

"You're bluffing," Victor said finally, amused by the American's feeble attempt at humor.

"I wish I were," James replied seriously, staring up at the keypad himself.

"Get up there and open it," Victor demanded. "Now!"

"I'll be glad to," James replied. "Give me the numbers."

"You're lying!" Victor shouted. "Open it now or I'll put a bullet in your head!"

"Listen," James said calmly. "There's no reason for me to lie to you. We're both in this together. I want out of this place even worse than you do. Believe me, there's more going on here than what meets the eye. Probably more than you *want* to know."

"What do you mean?" Victor demanded, wary of the possibility of an impending attack by recently alerted co-conspirators. "Who did Dr. Kavalov call?"

"I have no idea," James replied coolly, trying not to further agitate him. "But that's not the issue."

Victor paused, his mind racing through the details of recent events. He tried to remember what Uri's last words had been, but he hadn't heard them clearly from where he stood. Was it something about an infected monkey? A disease of some sort? A code, perhaps?

"What did Uri say to you?" Victor shouted suddenly at James.

"He said that we're both going to die," James replied, looking over at the cages against the wall.

"That's insane," Victor declared. "Just because one of those monkeys has a respiratory illness doesn't mean that we'll be infected. Humans don't get animal diseases."

James stared at him and briefly considered mentioning such trans-species diseases as anthrax that infected both cattle and people or the bubonic plague that moved from fleas to rats to men. But it wouldn't make much difference anyway. He might as well just lay out the details of what they were up against.

"Listen," James began. "That monkey you just shot was infected with an engineered virus – a biological weapon of extraordinary design. And we're down here with no protective gear. Based on what I've seen of this virus, we're already hot."

"Liar!" Victor shouted. "You're just trying to scare me."

"It's the truth," James said firmly. "At this point, even if we *could* get out of here, it wouldn't make any difference. There's likely nothing that any doctor could do for us anyway, since, according to Uri, no one's ever seen anything like this before."

"I don't believe you!" Victor cried out, a higher-pitched tone of panic in his voice.

"You will," James said flatly.

Victor whirled around and fired his last two shots at the screaming monkey across the room, narrowly missing him as they ricocheted off the bars. This piqued the animal's fear and increased the volume of his hysteria. Victor moved quickly across the room and pounded his hand on top of the monkey's cage.

"Shut up! Shut up!" Victor yelled.

In a millisecond, the monkey swiped at the top of his cage, landing only a tiny scratch on his assailant's right hand. It went undetected.

Chapter 32

❧

Victor climbed the metal stairs and spent thirty minutes frantically punching in various numerical combinations, none of which worked. Then, he raced around the lab in search of something to use as a pry bar, but could only come up with a metal leg that he managed to break off a chair. It was poorly suited for the task, and his attempts to open the hatch were unsuccessful. He scoured the tile walls of the room, testing for weaknesses in their structure, but the World War II shelter had been designed to withstand bomb blasts far stronger than its inhabitants. Behind the tiles that he damaged, solid concrete walls stared back at him. He dug at them with the metal chair leg until his hands bled.

By nine P.M, Victor collapsed in a corner of the lab, exhausted from his efforts. Sweat poured from his face and hair, soaking his clothing to the bone. He balled up in a fetal position, wrapping his arms around his knees and placing his head on top of them. From across the room, James could see that he was finished for the night.

James laid down as well and drifted into a fitful sleep, visited by strange, ghost-like creatures that journeyed softly across his arms and legs. Not wanting to disturb them, he brushed them gently aside in his sleep, but they returned in greater numbers, determined to maintain their proximity. They seemed perpetually in search of a means of entry that eluded them. In time, they were sure to solve the puzzle, and James grew increasingly uncomfortable with their presence.

He awoke suddenly around ten o'clock that night, staring at the ceiling above him. It glowed with a pearl opalescence in the dim laboratory lighting, and, for a moment, the world seemed oddly at peace. Only an occasional moan from across the room disturbed the silence. Apparently, Victor, too, dreamed of foreign bodies.

For a while, James studied the keypad on the ceiling hatch above them. He had seen Uri punch in six different numbers on the second all-metal door's keypad when they had entered the locker room above the lab with Dmitri and Victor. He tried desperately to recall the digits, but could only come up with the first three; 069. The full sequence teased his brain, floating just beyond his reach. If only he could "see" those last three numbers, he would have it. Perhaps Uri had used the same set of numbers on the lab's hatch overhead. He struggled to retrieve the sequence from his memory, but nothing surfaced.

It wouldn't matter one way or the other, but thinking about the numbers brought him a certain level of comfort – a means of holding onto sanity in an insane situation. It was a skill that he had honed in Korea, and now he called upon it again.

"069... 069... 069..." he repeated over and over to himself.

The numbers cycled through his head – a mantra of lead that would not melt.

Before realizing it, he settled back and started to drift inward, toward another restless sleep.

"537" popped into his head, and he leapt from the floor. Victor continued to sleep, so he raced up the stairs and punched in the numbers... 06-95-37. He held his breath and pulled down on the handle. Nothing happened. He depressed the same six numbers again to verify his accuracy. The hatch remained locked.

"Uri was smarter than that," James thought to himself, descending the ladder in despair and returning to his own little corner of hell.

Chapter 33

৩

Tanya awoke at midnight to find that Uri was not beside her. Either he hadn't come home yet, or stomach distress had once again drawn him into the kitchen, where a glass of milk and some dry crackers sometimes offered him relief. Recently, his rest had been frequently interrupted, and she had chided him on several occasions to see a doctor. But he kept reassuring her that all was well. She was so busy with the girls that she didn't have time to pursue the topic as much as she wanted. Hopefully, he would eventually return to normal on his own.

She briefly considered rising to check on him, but remembered that she had an early start to the day herself, with both girls scheduled for school, gymnastics and piano lessons. She rolled over, pulled the warm duvet across her shoulders and drifted back into semi-sleep.

At half past midnight, a loud thud at the front door jolted her upright in bed. It sounded as if someone had tossed a large sack of potatoes against it, reverberating through the thin walls of the flat. She virtually leapt out of bed, pulling on a heavy cotton robe as she ran out into the hallway. Both girls were standing there in pajamas, clinging to each other with fear in their eyes. She instructed them to return to their room, to close and lock their door and not to come out until she gave them permission. They obeyed her immediately.

When she opened the front door, a small European man with matted hair and hollow brown eyes stared up at her from a half-seated position. He was bleeding from a wound in his right shoulder, but was nevertheless alert and functioning. His look was determined and serious as he spoke to her in Russian.

"Please, Mrs. Kavalov, please. You must come with me. Dr. Kavalov has sent me to get you and your daughters out of the city. There's trouble. We must go, quickly! I have a van waiting outside. Please, do as I say. Gather your children and leave everything else. I will lead you to safety."

She turned briefly and looked back into the kitchen. It was empty.

"Uri!" she called. There was no response. "Uri!"

The only sound was the soft whimpering of her two daughters behind their bedroom door.

"He's not here," the man replied, wincing as he shifted his position in the doorway.

"Who are you?" she demanded, turning back to the stranger. "And what are you talking about? Where is my husband? I don't know you, and I'm not going anywhere with you. Now please, go away and do not come back, or I'll call the police. Leave us in peace!"

She slammed the door, knocking the European onto his side. She could hear a muffled groan as he hit the floor. He struggled to right himself and spoke intensely through the door.

"Mrs. Kavalov. Please! I beg of you. Please open the door and hear what I have to say."

She refused.

"Mrs. Kavalov, my name is Peter," he said, breathing heavily. "Your husband is my friend. He asked me to relay this message to you: *'A winter storm pursues our fate that fails the heart of Cerberus.'*"

For a long moment, there was only silence. Then, slowly, the door opened, and Tanya peered out with a look of horror on her face. The European looked up into her terrified eyes and knew that she knew. There would be no need for further negotiation.

Chapter 34

With nothing to differentiate night from day, it was difficult to know what time it was when James awoke in the lab to the sound of Victor's coughing. He moved his watch closer to his face and saw that it was one A.M.

Victor was lying on the floor across the room, still balled up and moaning. The palm of his right hand was pressed against his forehead, and his breathing was erratic and labored. James stood up and started to walk in his direction.

Halfway across the room, he noticed that the back of Victor's right hand was swollen, mottled with tiny black scratches that gave the skin a web-like coverlet. A clear fluid drained from his nose, as if he had a cold, and his face was flushed and red. He was neither asleep, nor awake, but wavered feverishly in between the two states.

James immediately stopped in his tracks, deciding to withdraw to the safety of his original position. As he turned around, he caught a glimpse of the remaining monkey, huddled quietly at the back of its cage, out of character for its breed. It was hunched over, and its skin was splotchy with reddish-yellow pustules. The viral rash had ravaged its neck, face, arms and legs.

By two A.M., the monkey was dead.

Victor's moans grew louder and more frequent. By two-thirty, swelling tissue in his mouth and throat interfered with his ability to vocalize pain. He grew quieter, as the web-like rash spread across his arms and legs, climbing up his neck and eventually closing his swollen eyes permanently. He whimpered pitifully for a while, until his lungs filled with fluids and he finally stopped breathing. James noted Victor's time of death at 0245.

Captain James Garrett was alone now – the only sentient being left in the room. The last monkey had been infected by the blood, tissue or saliva of its fellow primate, or the virus had gone airborne, calmly floating from one cage to the other. Victor had received a direct, lethal scratch from the second monkey just six hours prior, which meant that, in its current form, this virus was the hottest agent known to man.

James sat down in his corner to await his own fate. He covered his mouth and nose with a piece of Uri's lab coat, all the while knowing that any material that he could breathe through would also admit tiny virus particles. It was a futile effort, but it was all that he could do.

By three o'clock in the morning, he began to feel feverish. His mouth went dry, and he searched for water. He went to the only sink in the lab and drank from its faucet, but the water was tepid and did not appeal to him. He scraped ice from the interior walls of the freezer and sucked on it, drawing cold moisture from the crystals. The skin on his extremities was reddening, and a dull headache began to interfere with his concentration.

The virus was clearly airborne. He had experienced no direct contact with Victor or the monkeys after entering the lab, yet his body was succumbing to the same biological agent. He scanned his mind for solutions, but none of his survival training applied to this situation. He knew what was coming, and he needed to prepare himself.

He thought of his wife and son, remembering the white spring dress that Marie had worn at Matt's baptism. It was simple, with small, yellow flowers on it and a lace collar that turned down gracefully at the neckline. Standing proudly beside her in a neatly-pressed suit, he was completely oblivious to the preacher's words, distracted by her natural beauty and amazing poise as a young mother. He had been fortunate, indeed, for most of his adult life, blessed with a beautiful wife, an amazing son and a country that he loved. He had survived the firestorms of Korea and had returned to serve his country yet again.

He fell asleep thinking of Matt's young fingers wrapping around a baseball for the first time.

The video camera overhead documented his fevered struggle, as the virus progressed at an alarming rate. The high-capacity tape, located in the base of the locker room monitor, ran out at 3:15 A.M., leaving no doubt as to the nature of James' fate.

Chapter 35

Tanya gathered her two daughters, instructing them to dress quickly and not to ask questions. The fear in her eyes was more than enough to convince them, and they pulled warm wool coats over their pajamas and added shoes and socks at a furious pace. Tanya stepped out of their room and opened a hallway closet door, removing her warmest coat and scarf, along with a small packet of travel documents, cash and a small jewelry box that rested on the upper shelf. She returned to her frightened girls and implored them to hurry.

In minutes, they were rushing out the front door and down the stairwell, where they passed the body of a man they did not recognize. Blood oozed from the corner of his mouth, and his eyes were sullen and glazed. It was Poloff, though only Peter recognized him. The sudden encounter frightened the children even more, and they clung to each other as they followed close on their mother's heels. Peter covered their exit, pausing only to remove a black Walther – the instrument of Peter's wound – from

Poloff's lifeless hand. Peter had two guns now – one more than he needed.

A dark gray panel van waited at the bottom of the stairs, vapor still rising from its exhaust. Peter opened its back door and hurried them inside, where they huddled on the floor on a mattress. He pushed the Walther into Tanya's hands and told her to put it in her pocket. Then, he slid into the driver's seat and started the engine. Satisfied that no one had witnessed their exit, he pulled away quietly into the night. The dark streets of Moscow were deserted, and they passed through the city unnoticed.

"Mother," said Alya. "Who was that man on the stairs?" Alya was the younger child, overwhelmed by the frantic whirlwind of events in the middle of the night. "And why didn't we help him?"

"We didn't know him, darling" Tanya replied. "And there wasn't time to stop. I'm sure that his family will take care of him."

"But where's Papa?" Alya whimpered. "Isn't he coming with us?"

"Not now," Tanya answered. "But I'm sure that he will join us later." She was completely unaware of her husband's whereabouts, but was absolutely certain of one thing; there was trouble – real trouble. She needed to get her children as far away from Moscow as possible.

Peter drove westward, exiting the city and continuing along deserted back roads. The countryside rose up beneath them, wrapping them in streaming bands of fog, the frail promise of morning still several hours away.

In just over an hour, Peter swung the van onto a dirt road that led down a narrow path into the woods. At the end of it, a small cottage appeared, silent and secluded, its outer walls laced with ancient ivy. An older, rusting vehicle sat alongside it, looking like an abandoned derelict. Peter stopped in front of the cottage, but left the van's engine running. He got out and disappeared around the back of the structure, returning quickly with a large can of petrol. He emptied it into the van's tank, then opened the passenger door and spoke to Tanya with urgency.

"I must go back for Uri," he said, breathing heavily. The wound in his shoulder was bleeding again, but he ignored it.

"Take the children in the van and continue westward until you reach the border. Show them your papers and tell them that you are going on holiday in the Ukraine. They won't know anything has happened yet, so they will let you pass. Good luck, girls, and may God protect you."

He turned around to leave.

"Wait!" Tanya shouted.

She exited the van quickly and removed her scarf, wrapping it around his shoulder and tying it across his chest. Then, she pulled a handkerchief from her pocket, folded it up and packed it tightly underneath the scarf, directly over his wound. Her eyes were moist as she pulled his face down to hers and kissed him gently on both cheeks.

"Thank you," she said, her voice trembling with emotion. "We will never forget what you have done for us."

"Go quickly," Peter said.

He stepped around her and closed the passenger door of the van. Tanya climbed in behind the steering wheel and shifted gears into reverse, turning the vehicle around and heading down the narrow path, away from the cottage. In a few minutes, they had exited the woods, turning west onto the two-lane country road that eventually led to the border.

Peter climbed into his old, rusty van and cranked its feeble engine. Black fumes rose from the tailpipe, and strong vibrations rattled its frame. In a couple of minutes, the engine smoothed out, and the vibrations decreased. He put it in gear, circled the cottage and exited the same way they had entered. Reaching the main road, he turned east, back towards Moscow.

With any luck, he would arrive at Uri's lab by three-thirty in the morning. If there were any signs of police or government authorities, he would not approach the building. If there were none, he would enter it, descend to the locker room and check the monitor to see if there had been an accident in the lab.

Either way, he dreaded what he might find.

Chapter 36

∽

Peter parked his tired van beside a small shop on the west side of the Zverev Bridge and walked across the Vodootvodny Canal, scanning up ahead for men who seemed out of place in the working-class business district. Finding none, he turned down the narrow, cobble-stoned street, maintaining his vigilance and slowing his pace somewhat. Eventually, he arrived at the small pathway that led to Uri's lab. Only two men walked up ahead, their backs moving rapidly away from him, until they disappeared entirely down another side-street.

Satisfied that he was alone, Peter withdrew a small key from his pocket and inserted it into the iron and wood door of the storage facility that Uri had leased. He swung it open slowly, stuck his head in and, seeing no one, cautiously entered the room. Then, he stopped and listened for a moment, searching for unfamiliar sounds.

Nothing unusual met his ears, so he proceeded to the spiral staircase and descended to the metal door below. He put his ear to the door and listened. There were no unusual sounds. He opened it with a second key and entered the brief hallway. At the far end, he punched in the numbers 06-95-37 on the keypad and entered the locker room. It was empty. No one was around.

Two positive pressure suits were draped over the shower walls. They smelled strongly of bleach, indicating that Uri had recently decontaminated them upon exiting the lab. This made no sense to Peter at all. If there were a problem in the lab, at least one of the suits would still be down there. Uri would not have entered the lab without it.

He turned to the lockers and opened them. Nothing was amiss. He moved to the back side of the left locker and pulled it away from the wall, using his good arm. An old Marlene Dietrich poster hung head-high on the wall in a thin wooden frame. Peter lifted it off the wall and set it on the floor, exposing a small door, behind which was a recessed monitor, with a video tape recorder in its base. A black and white picture of the laboratory below rested on its screen, with complete, real-time coverage of its contents. Peter moved closer to the screen, grimacing as he surveyed the terrifying landscape of Alpha-C.

Uri lay on the floor, face up. A pool of dark blood spread away from his neck and head, and his eyes were rolled up and fixed. His body was completely still. A second man that Peter did not recognize lay in a similar position, a few feet in front of, and perpendicular to Uri. Peter could just make out two neat holes in his face, with blood and brain matter ejected from the back of his head. He, too, was motionless.

On the back wall, both monkeys were still, with blood spattered on the white tile walls behind them and fluids draining from their cages. It appeared that one of them had died savagely and the other quietly, huddled in the back of its cage.

A second stranger lie in the far corner of the room, his back and neck arced strangely into an impossible position, completely opposite of the direction in which spinal columns normally flex. No contortionist – at least none that Peter had ever seen – could possibly achieve such a position. It was so bizarre that, for a moment, he considered the possibility of an anomaly in the camera's lens.

Moreover, the man's skin appeared blistered and swollen, tattooed with a strange, web-like lattice of black runners that covered his extremities. Dark fluids drained from his ears, nose and gaping mouth, and his swollen eyes protruded through eyelids that had disappeared behind them. Peter's stomach churned, and he turned away from the monitor, placing the back of his hand over his mouth and struggling for control. He had never seen anything like this before. What monster was responsible?

In a couple of minutes, Peter turned back to the monitor and studied a fourth person, lying opposite the contortionist, positioned on the near side of the lab. He, too, laid completely still, his skin covered with similar markings, though less pronounced and somewhat lighter in color. His face was turned to the wall, but Peter could tell from his clothing that he was not Russian. Uri had mentioned his plan to meet with an American – a matter of some concern to Peter. He had done his best to dissuade him, but Uri had insisted, saying that science overshadowed politics, and that no harm would come of it.

Peter rewound the video tape and hit the play button on the recorder. He fast forwarded through horrific details that streamed across the monitor, revealing a clear picture of what had happened in the lab. The American had been the last to succumb to the virus, possibly due to the fact that he had no visible open wounds. Opposite him, the most severely-impacted stranger displayed a gaping cut that ran the full length of his right hand, torn all the way to the base of his wrist by terrible swelling. Also, the American's posture did not include the severe, C-shaped backward curvature of the spine observed in his adversary across the room. He seemed to have been affected by a somewhat different strain of the virus, though the end result was the same.

Peter felt sorry for the American. Perhaps he had a family. His wife and children would never know what had happened to him. And, if the Soviet government found out, they might pursue a broader policy of containment that could place his innocent family at serious risk, even half a world away. He studied the problem and arrived at a solution.

He rewound the tape and removed it from the base of the monitor. Placing it in his coat pocket, he exited the locker room and ascended to the street-level storage room above. There, he located a thick, brown envelope in a box behind the counter. He pulled a pen from his pocket and addressed it to the American Embassy in Moscow. Then, he inserted the video tape and sealed the envelope tightly with packing tape that he scavenged from an old metal filing cabinet.

He exited the outer door cautiously, checking for any strangers that might have arrived in the neighborhood. Finding none, he walked back to the business district, where he entered a small bakery shop and paid a young man a hundred rubles to deliver the envelope immediately. Then, he retrieved his van and pulled it around the back of Uri's lab.

At this point, he had done all that he could do. Only one task remained; he must enter the lab and initiate emergency procedures to assure that the biological agent that Uri had designed did not escape. The decontaminate container at the back of the locker room would be switched out, replaced by an accelerant that would issue from all of the overhead sprinklers in the facility. A fifteen-minute delay timer, activated by a switchbox behind the locker room's monitor, would give him enough time to escape the area in his van before a phosphorus igniter in the lab initiated an intense inferno.

The accelerant would quickly push temperatures to several thousand degrees, reducing the entire facility to ash and cremating all of the unfortunate souls and organisms within it.

Chapter 37

❧

At nine A.M. on the worst day of his life, the phone rang in Owen Rice's flat. He jumped up from the table and grabbed it with the ferocity of a wrestler. James had been out of contact for over fifteen hours now, and Owen hadn't slept or eaten during that period. Something was wrong – seriously wrong. He felt certain of it.

"Owen?" said a heavy voice on the other end of the line. "This is Brad Weller over at the American Embassy. I think we have your answer. You'd better pack your bags and get over here. There's something that you need to see."

There was no further conversation. Owen hung up the phone and gathered his things. Something in his gut told him that he was headed home alone.

Chapter 38

❦

Matt Garrett stood up and walked silently over to the living room window, trying to sort it all out. Governor Rice had finished his tale, and the details were difficult to digest. Bill, still seated on the couch, stared at Matt with fathomless blue eyes.

After a while, Marie stood up, walked over to her son and placed her hand on his shoulder.

"He was so proud of you," she said, her voice trembling.

He took a deep breath.

"No more tears, Mom. Everything's O.K. now. At least I know what happened to him. I understand that he was doing important work. I just wish that we could have had more time with him."

"Me too, darling," she said softly. "Me, too. He was a wonderful man."

The governor rose and went into the kitchen to get another cup of coffee. By the time he returned, most of the tension in the room had dissipated.

"So, Matt, if you don't mind, I'd like to discuss one more thing with you. You can take some time and think about this – discuss it with your mom and

Bill. But I'll need your answer before I leave tonight. I'm going to take a little walk around town – stop by Mount Peace and visit your father's gravesite. But, I'll be back by nine o'clock to hear your decision. In a nutshell, I have a couple of friends in Washington who are interested in meeting and talking with you. Bill can introduce you to them, if you're willing to ride up there with him."

Matt looked over at Bill and shook his head. He had a feeling that he'd already been setup for just such a meeting, and he felt certain now that Bill's friend in D.C. didn't work for the V.A. He turned back to the governor.

"Talk to me about what?" Matt asked.

"About some pretty intensive training – in a very dangerous profession," the governor replied.

Matt turned to his mom. A mixture of fear and pride surfaced in her eyes, and a sense of destiny stirred inside him.

PART II

Forged in metal brought to bear
Against the gate of Satan's lair.

Chapter 39

⁓

At five A.M. the next morning, Matt shoved a small duffel bag into the back of Bill's Jeep and climbed into the passenger-side seat. Bill cranked the engine and let it warm up just long enough for Marie to rush out the front door of the house and cram a brown paper bag full of sandwiches into Matt's lap.

"You boys take care of each other," she said. She smiled and turned quickly away. Matt noticed a couple of tears on her cheeks, despite her attempt to conceal them.

"Thanks, Mom," he said. "And don't worry – we'll be fine."

Marie went inside the house and watched through the living room window as the Jeep backed out of the drive and headed up the street toward the main highway. Her eyes followed their vehicle until it disappeared from view. Realizing that the house was empty again, she wiped her face with the back of her sleeve and went to the mantel. She took down a small, framed picture of Matt and his father, studying it for the thousandth time. James leaned on an old baseball bat, with his opposite arm draped across his young son's shoulder. Matt wore a faded green baseball cap, and a tired leather baseball rested in his right hand. He looked up at his father with bright-eyed enthusiasm. It was her most valuable possession – a simple photograph that had sustained her through the darkest times.

"They were so good together," she thought to herself.

Smiling, she returned the picture to the shelf and headed into the kitchen. Her heart was heavy, yet it surged with inexplicable warmth.

At the highway intersection, the Jeep turned east toward I-95. An hour later, it merged into north-flowing traffic that hugged the Atlantic coastline as they began their long journey to the nation's capitol.

"You O.K.?" Bill asked.

"Yeah," Matt replied, a somewhat distant look on his face. He was a million miles away, but Bill knew exactly what he was thinking. It was etched on Matt's face, forming a permanent description of their shared experience.

Few people get to observe the untimely death of their own father. But Matt was one of the unlucky ones who had done just that. Before he and Bill left for Alexandria, Governor Rice had taken the two of them into Matt's bedroom, closed the door and played a copy of the secret Russian laboratory tape of James Garrett's demise on a small video machine. He wanted both of them to know the whole story, and showing them was far more effective than telling them.

Both young men had sat quietly on the edge of Matt's bed, taking it all in. It was a punishing affair, but Matt had insisted on knowing the truth about his father. As for Bill, the video tape had implanted a certainty in his heart that he kept to himself – it was not in his nature to discuss such things. For Matt, it had been devastating. For Bill, it was instructional – he decided immediately that there would be a reckoning, immune to any defense. That was just no way for a good Marine to die.

Matt would need time. Bill would need resources and funding. An extraordinary opportunity had been placed before them, and there was no doubt about their mutual commitment.

"Governor Rice asked me to give you this once we got underway this morning," Bill said, reaching into the inside pocket of his jacket and removing a plain white envelope.

Matt took the envelope, turned it over and slid his finger underneath the flap. Inside, he found a crisp one hundred dollar bill and a hand-written note. He stared at the money for a few seconds. It was the first hundred dollar bill that he had ever seen. Then, he removed the note and began to read it to himself.

Matt,

Having no doubt that you would accept my offer, this note was written yesterday evening at Mount Peace cemetery, just before returning to your home to collect your final decision.

Please thank your mom again for the wonderful meal and gracious hospitality that she provided. And tell Bill that it was a pleasure to finally meet him.

There's one last thing that you should know as you begin your trip to the D.C. area. Beyond having your prison sentence commuted, your slate has been officially wiped clean. As of midnight last night, no records exist of your trial or the four years that you spent in prison. I personally collected all related local court documents en route to Mount Peace cemetery, where a small pile of ashes now rests at the foot of your father's grave. My associates at the state capital, and in Washington, took care of the rest.

I wish you all the best. You are truly your father's son.

Owen B. Rice

Matt folded the note carefully and put it back in the envelope. He looked over at Bill.

"Looks like dinner's on me," Matt said, holding up the hundred dollar bill.

"Put it in your wallet," Bill replied. "It's already taken care of."

Matt frowned, but Bill ignored him, reaching across to the glove compartment and opening it.

"I've got a little something for you, too," Bill said.

He removed a dark, matte-finished Colt .45, Model 1911, with scored, black ivory grips. He removed the clip, cleared the chamber and placed the firearm squarely in Matt's lap.

"That's yours, my friend," he said. "Don't lose it. There's a box of shells underneath your seat."

Matt stared down at the weapon, struggling with the idea that it might actually belong to him. It was absolutely beautiful, customized by someone who knew what they were doing. He had always appreciated the craftsmanship and technical details of well-made firearms, and the quality of this one was beyond any that he could ever hope to own. A cursive quote, attributed to Louis Pasteur, was skillfully engraved on its slide. It read, *"Chance favors the prepared mind."*

"My God, Bill! It's beautiful!" Matt cried. "But... I mean... I can't take this. There's no way that I could repay you."

"You already have," Bill replied matter-of-factly as he accelerated into the passing lane.

Traffic thinned as they crossed the state line and continued northward through vast pine forests that emitted the sweet, sulfurous smell of pulpwood mills, swollen with harvested timber.

Chapter 40

❧

By noon, they had traveled six hours. The time had gone by quickly, as they spoke of the previous night's events and of what might lie ahead. Matt still held the Colt .45 in his lap, turning it over and over, admiring its details. He memorized the weight and feel of the weapon, balancing it in each of his hands to familiarize himself with its mechanical features and grip.

"Are you going to marry that thing?" Bill said, chuckling a little.

"It's your fault," Matt replied. "You can be the best man."

Finally, he put the handgun back in the glove compartment and reached into the back of the Jeep, retrieving the brown paper bag of sandwiches that his mom had prepared. He opened it and removed the one on top, wrapped in aluminum foil. Handing it to Bill, he pulled out a second one for himself. When he unwrapped it, he found a chicken salad sandwich on a fresh croissant. Instantly, his mind traveled back in time.

"Listen," Keri had said. "You can be anything you want to be... as long as you take me with you."

"You mean you want to ride on the back of a garbage truck?" he had teased.

"If that's what makes you happy!" she had replied without skipping a beat.

Returning to the present, he shook his head slightly.

"I'll always take you with me," he thought to himself.

Bill reduced his speed and exited the interstate, pulling into a small, two-pump gas station. While he filled the tank, Matt went to a vending machine and bought two canned drinks. They leaned against the Jeep and finished their sandwiches, washing them down with cold root beer. Then, each of them took a turn at the restroom, while the other stayed with the vehicle. In fifteen minutes, they were back on the interstate, feeling refreshed and heading north again. The afternoon sky was brilliant blue, with white, puffy clouds suspended above them in the warm southern breeze.

"So, where will we be staying?" Matt asked.

"In Alexandria," Bill replied. "Just outside D.C."

"In a motel?"

"No, we'll be staying at a place that belongs to my friend," Bill explained.

"And does this friend have a name?" Matt asked.

"John Sauter," Bill replied.

"And he works for the V.A.?"

"He works for the government," Bill said.

"Did you serve together in Vietnam?"

"For a while," Bill replied. "But he was called back to Washington shortly after the Tet Offensive in '68."

"You were there?" Matt inquired.

"Yes, I was," Bill replied. "It was a particularly nasty affair. Six thousand Marines held off twenty thousand Vietnamese."

"I heard about it," Matt replied. "It was a turning point in the war – right?"

"Both wars," Bill said.

"What do you mean?" Matt asked.

"Well, everything changed after Tet, for both soldiers in the field and civilians back at home. Civilian support went down the toilet, and many of the soldiers in Vietnam lost their sense of purpose. From that point forward, two wars existed; one fought with bullets, the other with the mind."

"It must've been tough," Matt commented.

"For some," Bill replied.

Matt knew exactly what he meant. Bill would not have concerned himself with such distractions. He would have taken note of their existence, but would not have been affected by them. Violence had been an integral part of his life since childhood, controlled only by his intelligence and military training. No one was better suited for Vietnam… or, for that matter, any other conflict.

"I should've been there with you," Matt said.

"I'm glad you weren't," Bill replied. "We've got more important things to do."

"Like what?" Matt inquired, fishing for information.

"Like getting you laid *before* you apply for Social Security," Bill replied, a wicked smile spreading across his face.

Matt frowned at him and took his fiancé out of the glove compartment to study her a while longer.

Chapter 41

෨

They stopped for dinner five hours later, three hours shy of their destination. They had steak, salad and baked potatoes at a very nice restaurant. Their hunger magnified the quality of the food, which was already superb. Once again, Matt offered to pay for the meal with his hundred dollar bill, but Bill pulled out a nondescript credit card and covered it, including a twenty dollar tip for the pretty, college-age waitress who had served them. They picked up a couple of mints on the way out of the restaurant, climbed back into the Jeep and hit the road for the last stretch of their journey.

In three hours, it was finished. Matt calculated that the entire trip had taken a little over fifteen hours, as they arrived in Alexandria at eight P.M. that evening. Turning down a few streets, they entered a quiet neighborhood of upper-middle-class homes, with neatly-manicured lawns and meandering sidewalks. Flowers adorned window boxes, and precision-cut shrubbery provided a sense of orderly boundaries.

At the end of a cul-de-sac, Bill pulled into the driveway of a white, Georgian-style home with black shutters. It blended nicely into the neighborhood and was equally well cared for. He pulled around to the back of the house, where an attached, two-car garage appeared. He left the engine running until, a few seconds later, the door opened automatically, and he pulled his Jeep inside, coming to rest beside a black Lincoln Towncar.

Bill shut the engine off and began to gather his things as the garage door closed behind them. Matt followed suit, pulling his duffle bag out of the back and opening the passenger-side door to exit the vehicle.

"Don't forget your fiancé," Bill said, pointing at the glove compartment. "Put it in your duffle for now."

Matt took the handgun and two loaded clips out of the glove box and crammed them down into his bag. It didn't look like the kind of neighborhood that suffered from break-ins, but he didn't like the idea of risking his trophy to common thieves.

A door swung open that accessed the house from inside the garage, and a tall, thin man with dark hair and smiling eyes stepped out to greet them.

"Welcome, strangers!" he said. "Glad to see you made it in one piece."

He moved toward Matt and extended his hand.

"And this must be our victim," he said with bravado, looking him over carefully while shaking his hand. He had a crisp, no-nonsense voice that conflicted with his relaxed attire. A Hawaiian shirt, faded dungarees and tan boat shoes gave him the look of a tropical bartender.

"Nice to meet you, Mr. Sauter," Matt replied.

"That remains to be seen, young man," he said, with a curious hint of sadistic pleasure. "But, please – call me John!"

"Sure," Matt agreed, still coming to grips with his unexpected appearance. He had pictured him as one would imagine a hospital administrator; with slacks and a tie, or perhaps a suit.

John released his hand and moved quickly past him, wrapping his arms tightly around Bill and lifting him off the floor in a joyful bear hug.

"Hunter! You old devil dog!" he cried. "How the hell are you, Man?"

"I'll be fine as soon as you put me down," Bill croaked, smiling all the same.

"It's been a long time," John said, releasing him.

"Not long enough," Bill replied sarcastically. "I hope you've got plenty of beer in the refrigerator."

"Indeed I do, my friend. Indeed I do. Come on in and we'll drain a few. Have you had anything to eat?"

"Yes," Bill replied. "We had dinner in Emporia. I hope you didn't wait for us."

"Who, me?" John responded. "I had Chinese at six."

"Was she any good?" Bill asked in a serious tone.

"No, but her mother made up for it," John replied, an equally serious look on his face.

He motioned the two of them into the house. They picked up their bags and followed him into the spacious living room. An Asian woman in her mid-thirties sat on the couch, reading through a stack of typed reports. She was neatly dressed, with the mannerisms of a legal secretary or businesswoman. Matt wondered if John's attempt at humor had contained any basis in reality, but he seriously doubted it. This woman carried herself in a professional manner and didn't look the part at all. She stood up as John introduced them.

"Ming," John said. "This is Bill Hunter and Matt Garrett. They're from the Deep South, so you may have to speak slowly if you want them to understand you."

"Gentlemen," Ming replied, nodding her head and smiling.

"You from VICORE?" Bill asked, glancing at the documents in her hands.

"I am," she replied. "Please sit down and we'll get started."

"You guys give me your bags, and I'll stow them in your bedrooms," John instructed. "I'll be right back, Ming."

He took their bags and disappeared down a hallway, returning to the living room within a couple of minutes. Ming sat down on the sofa again, poised and alert as Bill and Matt settled into adjacent chairs. She glanced at Matt again, then down at her papers.

"How's the investigation?" Bill asked. "Any progress?"

"According to these reports, none," she replied.

Matt felt uncomfortable, not privy to the meaning of their conversation.

He looked around the room, noting its tasteful décor and cleanliness. Pictures of exotic flora and fauna graced the walls, giving it a refined, classy look and feel. The only person who belonged in that room was Ming – the rest of them were interlopers, unworthy of such accommodations. But, noting how they took things in stride, Matt decided to be comfortable, despite the upscale nature of his surroundings.

"I understand that you are already privy to the circumstances surrounding your father's death," Ming began suddenly, looking up at Matt.

Matt glanced over at Bill, then back at Ming.

"Yes," he replied, wondering how she knew this.

"Recently, there's been renewed interest in the possibility that Dr. Uri Kavalov's work may have survived him. Soviet agents pursued this theory early on, but not too vigorously. As far as they were concerned, the matter was closed a long time ago."

She looked at Bill and continued.

"Due to VICORE's interest in this subject matter, the U.S. government has decided to revisit it, calling upon LOC to investigate all details of the original event. Your team will be provided with whatever training and equipment that you require. Offshore facilities will be placed at your disposal. As always, you will operate autonomously, and this action will remain highly classified."

"Understood," Bill replied. "Do you have our cards?"

She reached into her purse and handed them each a driver's license with their photograph and the address of the house they were sitting in displayed just below it. A small, trident-shaped symbol appeared in the upper right-hand corner of the card, with the letters 'NP' engraved on either side of the trident's center fork.

"Anything else?" she asked.

"Yeah," John replied. "Do you have a sister?"

Ming did not react. Instead, she stood up and walked slowly out the front door of the house. She was a shapely woman, both coming and going, but she was all business. By the time she reached the street, a taxi pulled up, and she climbed into the back seat. It drove away slowly, exiting the neighborhood as quietly as it had entered.

"What is this?" Matt said, holding up the card in his right hand.

"It's a driver's license," John said bluntly, offering no further explanation.

"Hold onto it," Bill added. "It may come in handy."

"So, what's this little emblem in the top right corner? And what does 'NP' stand for?"

"It's a trident," Bill replied, "and 'NP' is an abbreviation for a Latin phrase – "*Nolle prosequi.*"

"What does that mean?" Matt asked.

"It means '*Do not pursue.*' " John replied.

Chapter 42

John went into the kitchen and returned with three cold bottles of beer. He placed two of them on the coffee table and sat down with the third.

"Thanks," Bill said, reaching forward and picking up one of them.

Matt looked at Bill, ignoring the remaining bottle.

"Who was that woman, and what was she talking about?"

"She's the Director of VICORE," John explained. "They're based in Reston, Virginia, in a facility adjacent to the U.S. Army's biological research labs. 'Dr. Ming Li' came to America as a child, grew up in California and then moved to the east coast to attend Harvard University. She distinguished herself in a number of branches of biological science, but snagged the attention of the federal government with her work in virology. They offered her the job, and, apparently, they're pretty satisfied with the result. She's managed VICORE's activities for the last five years – the youngest female ever to hold that position. More importantly, she's hot."

"So, what is it?" Matt continued.

"What's what?" Bill asked.

"What's VICORE?" he said.

"It's the Virology Center of Research & Engineering," Bill replied. "It's owned by the federal government, and it employs about thirty of the world's top virologists. Their mission is to design the means to defend against biological weapons. Everything they do is classified, so there's no need getting into it at this point."

"O.K., Matt replied. "So, what's LOC?

"That's us!" John exclaimed. "And, as of now, that includes you."

"Anyone else?" Matt inquired.

"One more," Bill replied. "You'll meet her tomorrow."

"Her?" Matt asked.

"That's right," John replied cheerfully. "We have to have *someone* to look after us."

"I see," Matt said, continuing his questions. "So, what does 'LOC' stand for?"

"Lords of Circumstance," Bill replied, chuckling. "A little handle that I came up with over a couple of beers. What do you think of it? Of all people, you should appreciate that title."

"What do you mean?" Matt asked, puzzled.

"I mean that I personally selected you for this job, Matt, considering your ability to overcome extremely difficult circumstances. In a few days, you'll understand why that's important."

"Amen to that, Brother!" John injected, raising his beer and proposing a toast.

"To those who went before us," he said in a surprisingly serious tone.

Bill tapped the neck of his bottle against John's. Matt picked up his bottle and did the same, thinking of his father.

The beer was cold, and it tingled as it slid down his throat.

Chapter 43

❦

At eight years old, Natasha Ivanov hugged her mother and left Russia with her father. Inquisitive and precocious, she was open to adventure, and this one promised to be singular in nature. For months, her parents had formulated a plan to get her out of the country, in search of a better life. Her mother "fell suddenly and mysteriously ill, unable to care for Natasha alone." The Soviet government saw no threat in allowing the little girl to accompany her father to New York City, where he was assigned the task of studying western engineering techniques used in bridge building.

Upon arrival at New York International, her father immediately requested political asylum for both of them. After an hour of questioning by immigration authorities, they filled out some forms and awaited their decision. It was granted. When the Russians found out about it, KGB agents showed up at her mother's cottage. They questioned and severely beat her, providing her with a legitimate reason to suffer.

The Ivanovs had known to expect this – she and her husband had discussed it late into the night before his departure. Somehow, that made it more tolerable, and her mother was proud to endure it. Her daughter would be safe, and she would have a good life in America. Her own cuts and bruises would heal quickly – a small price to pay, considering how much she loved Natasha.

She spat blood at the feet of the KGB agents as they left, spattering their shoes with the bile of her disdain.

In New York, the FBI kept tabs on Natasha and her father for a while, noting his quiet work in private industry, and her exceptional academic performance in public city schools. At seventeen, she received a full scholarship to Columbia University.

Natasha had a gift for languages and seemed to integrate easily with foreign colleagues. She became fluent in English, German and Italian, adding to her native skills with Russian. When she turned twenty, the FBI offered her a job as an interpreter in Washington, D.C., and she accepted it. She moved into a small apartment off North Quebec Street in Cherrydale and began her new career in the nation's capital. She was well paid, and she converted some of her income into rubles every month and mailed it to her mother. Over the next three years, her work at the Bureau became known. She was recognized as a valued federal employee, with a bright future ahead of her.

In the evenings, she jogged. As a child, she had loved running, and, as an adult, she had maintained her interest in exercise. It provided an outlet for her boundless energy and made her feel strong and fit.

She enjoyed studying the people that she passed along the way, noting their dress and mannerisms. She played a game, guessing where they had come from and where they might be headed.

By six-thirty one evening, she had run three miles from her apartment and was ready to turn back. Recognizing her growing thirst, she side-tracked into a small convenience store, in search of liquids. She smiled at the middle-aged man behind the counter and went directly to the back wall, where a row of glass doors protected refrigerated beverages. Searching for something that would both quench her thirst, and act as good nutrition, she selected a three dollar drink that contained an assortment of fruits and crushed berries.

En route to the counter to pay for the beverage, she unscrewed the lid and took a long drink, quickly reducing its contents by a third. As she reached for the zippered pocket of her jacket, she found that it was missing. Instead, her hand slid into a zipper-less pocket, instantly causing her to freeze.

A sudden, sinking feeling in the pit of her stomach grabbed her as she remembered that she had traded her light blue jogging jacket – the one with a ten dollar bill in its front pocket – for a clean, white one just before leaving her apartment. A newly-discovered stain on the front of her blue jacket had initiated the fatal, last-minute switch.

"Oh, no," Natasha said, looking up sheepishly at the man behind the counter. "I can't believe that I did that."

"Did what?" the man asked.

"I'm afraid I went off from my apartment without any money," she replied.

The man looked down at the open bottle of juice in Nat's hand, already significantly diminished by her thirst. He frowned and put his hands on his hips.

"Do you have a credit card with you?" he asked in a voice that implied consequences if she did not.

"No, I'm afraid I don't," Natasha responded. "But I can run back to my apartment and get the money. I promise that I'll come back and pay you."

The owner wasn't impressed.

"Well, you can't put that container back on the shelf now," he said gruffly. "Either you're going to pay for it, or I'm going to call the cops."

"That won't be necessary," said a firm voice behind her. A strong right arm curled around her side and placed a twenty dollar bill on the counter. The proprietor yanked it up immediately, and Natasha whirled around to discover a man in a Marine uniform, with steel-blue eyes and a brilliant smile. His rugged build conflicted with this sudden act of kindness, and, for a moment, she found herself at a loss for words.

Sensing her discomfort, the Marine focused on completing the transaction with the proprietor. When the man returned seventeen dollars to him, he offered her the change, suggesting that she might need it on her way home.

Natasha studied him a second longer, during which she decided that he had been at war. Something in the timbre of his voice, the color of his skin, the shape of his hands – or perhaps just the experience of looking directly into his eyes – told her that he had recently endured the extremes of human conflict. Whatever it was, it found a home in her soul, and she wanted to know more about him.

"No, no – please," Natasha said. "I'll be fine. It was so kind of you to help me. If you'll tell me where you're based, I'll see to it that you get your money back, with interest."

To Bill, freshly "in-country" from the killing fields of Vietnam, her smile was incredible – stunning – intoxicating. Her green eyes carried on a conversation of their own, and her demeanor was relaxed, yet self-confident. He would be content to say nothing at all, choosing instead just to look at her.

"You don't owe me a thing," he finally replied. "My paycheck comes from Uncle Sam, so just consider this your taxpayer dollars at work."

"Well, thank you," she said, turning toward the door.

"Wait. What's your name?" Bill asked.

She turned around and smiled at him.

"Natasha," she replied. "What's yours?"

"Bill. Bill Hunter," he said.

"Well, it was very nice meeting you, Bill Hunter," she said. She turned around again and exited the store.

"Wait a minute," Bill called after her, following her outside, but maintaining proper physical distance. He didn't want to frighten her.

"Why don't you join me for dinner?" he said.

She paused a minute, then shook her head.

"I really have to go," Nat said. "Maybe some other time."

There was a palpable look of disappointment on his face, and his powerful frame diminished slightly. Nevertheless, he accepted her decision and acquiesced by shoving his hands into his pockets and looking down at his feet. It was exactly the reaction that she was looking for, and it confirmed her opinion of the man who had come to her financial, and, more importantly, personal rescue. Where had he come from? Where had he been? And why did she suddenly feel more alive than she had ever felt before?

She took a couple of steps in his direction and stopped.

"You know what?" she said, a slightly higher tone in her voice. "I think I've changed my mind. I'd like to join you for dinner."

Bill looked up and smiled widely again.

"What kind of food do you like?" he asked her cheerfully.

"Russian," she replied.

"No problem," Bill said brightly, as if it was the cuisine that he ate daily. He pointed toward the parking lot, extending his right arm. "My Jeep's right over here."

Chapter 44

❦

At six A.M. the next morning, Bill stuck his head into Matt's room and informed him that breakfast would be ready soon. It took Matt a second to recall that he was in Alexandria. He detected the smell of bacon and eggs coming from the opposite end of the house, where the kitchen was located. Since Bill was standing in his doorway, he assumed that John was doing the cooking.

Matt got up and went into the bathroom, where he shaved, showered and put on a clean pair of jeans, brown socks and a tan Henley shirt. He slid his feet into a pair of low-top hiking boots that he had purchased back home, the same day that he'd gone into town and run into Bill at the movie theater. His mom had insisted that he replace his worn-out sneakers before returning that evening, and now he was glad that she had. This was the first time he'd worn them, and he was impressed with how strong and comfortable they felt as he walked down the hallway toward the living room.

"Breakfast is ready," called an unfamiliar voice from the kitchen. Matt paused briefly in the hallway, wondering if perhaps John employed a day cook. Her voice had a Slavic accent, with a pleasant tone to it. As he tried to picture what she might look like, Bill came up behind him and nudged him forward.

"Let's eat," he said. "I'll introduce you to Nat."

They turned into the kitchen together, where a well-proportioned young woman was removing warm, homemade cinnamon rolls from the oven. She was slightly taller than the average female, but her body was well toned and slender, with a sinewy, muscular physique. Her movements flowed smoothly from one action to another. To Matt, she appeared to be in complete control of herself, with confidence evident in every move that she made, down to the smallest gesture. Her dark black hair was cropped short, rescued by a cute set of straight, flowing bangs that came to rest just above her emerald green eyes.

She looked up at Matt and smiled.

"Good morning, Matt," she said, smiling. "It's nice to finally meet you."

"Matt Garrett, this is Natasha Ivanov," Bill added.

"Hello," Matt said, a little stunned.

Bill filled the void.

"Nat is the fourth member of our merry little band. She's from St. Petersburg... Russia, that is – not Florida."

"I noticed the accent," Matt said, smiling sheepishly.

"Did you sleep well?" Natasha asked, looking directly at Matt.

"Yes, I did," he replied, nodding his head.

"Would you like some coffee or orange juice with breakfast?" she inquired.

"Sure," Matt said. "Orange juice is fine."

"She turned back to the counter and poured four glasses, setting them on the kitchen table as John entered the room.

"Man, am I glad to see you," John said to her. "I was afraid we were going to have to eat Bill's cooking this morning."

"Bill knows how to cook," Nat replied, defending her colleague.

"And a house painter knows how to paint," John observed. "But an artist like you is an entirely different matter. You, my dear, create beauty, for which we all perpetually hunger."

"Just sit down and eat," Nat said flatly, winking at Matt, who chuckled at the injured look on John's face.

She moved bowls of eggs and bacon from the countertop to the kitchen table. Then, she placed a large platter, filled with fruits and cinnamon rolls, on the Lazy Susan in the middle. The four of them sat down to eat their first meal together as a team.

The food was delicious – the eggs had been flavored with cheese and unusual spices, and the warm, sweet cinnamon rolls were unbelievably light and delicious. Nat enjoyed their extravagant compliments, laughing frequently at their lavish praise. Her delightful company further enhanced the meal, even though the food stood on its own merits.

When they were finished, Matt got up and helped Bill clear the table, while Nat and John went into the living room and sat down to talk.

"Just leave the dishes," John called back to them. "I'll take care of them after you guys leave."

"You mean the housekeeper will do them," Bill challenged.

"Exactly," John confirmed.

Chapter 45

∿

"When will we see you again?" Natasha asked Bill.

"I'll be back tonight," Bill answered. "But we won't have the pleasure of Matt's company for quite a while. He's got some training ahead of him."

"Where?" Natasha inquired.

"Several places," Bill replied. "But he'll start at Quantico. Chances are he'll look a little different the next time you see him."

"What do you mean?" Matt interrupted. "What kind of training? And for how long?"

"As long as it takes," Bill answered. "It's the kind of training that can keep you alive, Matt."

"While making you wish that you were dead," John added.

Bill shot a warning glance at John, who held up both of his hands, surrendering.

"So, what will you guys be doing while I'm gone?" Matt asked.

"John will remain here in Alexandria," Bill explained. "He needs access to Washington. Nat and I have work to do in the Caribbean. I need to get a roof on my place, and Nat will be traveling periodically. She has some important research to do overseas."

Bill continued. "I'm going to drive you over to Quantico this afternoon to introduce you to a couple of friends of mine. They'll get you settled in and will supervise your progress. I'll check in with them now and then to see how things are going. When you've completed your training to their satisfaction, John will pick you up. He'll provide you with a plane ticket and some money so you can join Nat and me in the islands."

"What island is that?" Matt inquired.

"You'll have to earn that answer," Bill replied. He looked down at the floor and spoke in a serious tone. "This training is difficult, Matt – it takes a toll on you. There's always a chance that you might change your mind about us."

"I doubt it," Matt said. "I have a vested interest."

"I realize that, Matt. And that *may* be enough to sustain you. But, until we know that for sure, you don't have a need to know our exact location. It's precautionary – that's all."

"All right," Matt complied. "I understand. I won't ask any more questions."

"Good," Bill said. "Get your things together and we'll put them in the Jeep. Bring your girlfriend with you."

"Did I miss something?" John asked, puzzled.

"He's in love with a Colt that I gave him," Bill explained. "It's time they learned to dance."

Chapter 46

❧

They arrived at Quantico at two P.M. The town was bordered on three sides by a large Marine Corps base, with the Potomac River providing its fourth boundary. Military soldiers and federal agents trained at Quantico, quartered in red brick buildings with asphalt shingle roofs. Bill provided his military ID, along with both of their new "driver's licenses" to the security guard at the front gate.

The Marine guard picked up a phone in the guardhouse, spoke briefly to a superior and then directed them to a small, single-unit apartment that sat near the back of the property. They parked the Jeep beside it and removed Matt's duffle bag from the back. Bill took a small keychain from his pocket with two keys on it. He handed it to Matt as they approached the front door.

"Hold onto this," Bill said. "This is where you'll be staying." When they reached the front door, he said, "Open it."

Matt inserted one of the keys and, guessing correctly, unlocked it. Inside the apartment, he found a single bed, a chair, a small, three-drawer dresser and a tiny bathroom, with a squeaky-clean toilet, sink and shower. A mirrored-door medicine cabinet hung above the lavatory. Bill reached around the back of the cabinet and swung it away from the wall, revealing a hidden storage space.

"Keep your fiancé in here," Bill said. "Hopefully, you won't need her for a while."

"O.K.," Matt replied.

"If you go off-base on your own, take it with you," Bill added.

"All right," Matt said. "When do we meet your friends?"

"They'll be here any minute," Bill replied.

Matt removed the custom Colt .45 from his bag, stowing it in the wall space behind the medicine cabinet, as instructed.

"Sit down for a second," Bill said. "I want to talk to you about something."

Matt went over to the chair and sat down. Bill began to pace about the room, intentionally avoiding eye contact.

"I want you to know that, if this doesn't work out, there are no hard feelings. I'm the one who got you into this, so I'm responsible for the outcome. Very few people would choose this sort of life for themselves. But I want to remind you that your father did, and that the need for this type of commitment may be more important now than ever before. To that end, you're going to be tested here. You may be able to handle it, and you may not. But, if things go as I expect, I'll be seeing you in the tropics in a few months. All you need to remember is not to give up. No matter what happens, *never* give up."

There was a knock at the front door, and two men entered the apartment. One wore a Marine uniform, perfectly fitted to his tightly chiseled physique. The other man was in civilian clothing, with a medium build. Matt stood up and faced them.

"Lieutenant Hunter," said the Marine. "Welcome to Quantico, sir."

"Thank you, Sergeant Hale," Bill replied. "And how are you doing, Reicher?"

"Fine," the civilian responded. "Is this our man?"

"It is indeed," Bill replied. "Matt, this is Sergeant Ben Hale, and this is Special Agent Jack Reicher."

"Pleased to meet you," Matt said, shaking hands with both of them.

"This project is considered priority one, gentlemen, with implications for national security. Is that clearly understood?" Bill said, directing his question to the two men he had just introduced.

"Sir, yes sir," the Marine replied. "General Teague has already advised us, sir."

"Then I'll leave you to your work," Bill said. "If there are any problems, get word to me through the base commander."

"Sir, yes sir," the Marine replied.

Bill turned back to Matt.

"Good luck, Matt" he said. Then, he turned around and walked out the front door without another word.

"Get a good night's sleep," the Marine instructed Matt. "I'll be back at 0500. Wear these."

He handed Matt a paper bag that contained khaki fatigues, a short-sleeved T-shirt, a canvas belt with a brass buckle and a pair of black military boots.

"After tomorrow, you will find a fresh set of clothing on your doorstep every morning," the sergeant informed him. "And you will keep your quarters clean. Is that understood?"

"Yes, sir," Matt replied.

"Call me when he's ready," Agent Reicher said to the sergeant as he turned around to leave.

"Will do, sir" the Marine replied.

Chapter 47

❧

At 0415 the next morning, Matt's portable alarm
clock went off. He crawled out of bed and went
into the small bathroom, where he shaved, showered
and brushed his teeth. Thirty minutes later, he had
made his bed and was completely dressed in the
clothing that had been provided to him by Sergeant
Hale. He unlocked the front door and sat down on
the bed to wait.

At 0455, a Jeep pulled up outside, and he heard
its door shut. Sergeant Hale came through the front
door of the apartment in uniform. Matt stood up and
faced him. The sergeant looked directly at him and
spoke in a loud, forceful voice.

"Mr. Garrett, I have already forgotten your first
name, so from this day forward, I will call you PFC
Garrett or Private Garrett. You, on the other hand,
will address me as 'Sir' and only as 'Sir'. You will speak
only when spoken to, and you will begin all of your
responses with the word 'Sir'. Do you understand me,
Private Garrett?"

"Yes, sir," Matt replied.

Sergeant Hale raised his eyebrows and his voice.

"*What* did you say, Private Garrett?"

"Sir, yes sir!" Matt corrected himself.

"That's better, Private Garrett," the sergeant said. He began to pace briskly from one side of the room to the other, continuing his lecture.

"Private Garrett, you will be placed in a hand-picked group of raw recruits this morning. You will train with them, eat with them, fight with them – do everything except bunk with them. You will return to these quarters nightly, and you will not fraternize with the members of your squad after hours. You will go to sleep every night in pain, with the exception of those nights when you are not permitted to sleep. Most importantly, you will obey every order that I issue without questioning it, or you will be sent packing. Is that clear, Private Garrett?"

"Sir, yes sir!" Matt replied.

"Private Garrett, the squad you will join this morning began their training two days ago. Therefore, we will spend the next half hour getting you caught up on two of the most important skills that a Marine acquires. You will learn how to properly stand at attention, and then you will learn how to correctly salute a superior officer. Is that understood, Private?"

"Sir, yes sir!" Matt responded.

"Pay attention and learn, Private Garrett," he said. He turned to one side and snapped to attention, following this demonstration with a crisp salute to the wall. His eyes remained fixed and steady, focused on an invisible point directly in front of him. Then, he turned to face Matt and repeated the same two actions.

For the next thirty minutes, Matt received intense instruction on the finer points of military posture and the minute details of a proper salute. He practiced each movement, repeating them over and over, while the sergeant physically corrected all deviations.

At 0530, the instruction ended, and he ordered Matt to accompany him to the Jeep. They drove across the complex and entered a small white building with florescent lighting. A single barber awaited them, holding a pair of electric clippers in his right hand. Sergeant Hale instructed Matt to sit in the chair, where his head was completely shaved in a matter of minutes. No words were exchanged as his brown hair fell silently to the floor.

When the barber finished, Matt stood up, and Sergeant Hale placed a set of dog tags around his neck. He followed the sergeant out the front door as instructed. They got back in the Jeep and drove to the center of the compound where a squad of eight men had already assembled. They snapped to attention at the Sergeant's command, their eyes directed forward.

"This man is Private Garrett," the sergeant announced loudly. "Today, this man will join your squad. He will train with you, eat with you and fight with you. However, he will not share quarters with you. *This is a matter of no concern to you!* You are not to fraternize with this man after hours, and you will restrict all communications with him to the training at hand. Is that understood, Marines?"

"Sir, yes sir!" came the familiar response in loud unison.

"Private Garrett, fall in with your squad!"

Matt moved quickly into place at the end of the line, faced forward and snapped to attention.

Chapter 48

❧

Over the next nine weeks, Matt developed an intimate relationship with pain. The physical demands of the training tore his body down and broke his will to resist. He was bruised and battered daily, and his body suffered in the relentless heat and psychological pressure of the Marine Corps regimen. He crawled back to his room every night, collapsing on the small bed, only to be jerked to life again at four A.M. the next morning. He arose, stiff and sore to the bone, treated his cuts and blisters and repeated the same torturous process over and over again.

When his ability to function came into serious question, he reached down deep inside himself and examined his core. He defeated his exhaustion with anger, reacting to the possibility that he might not make it through the training. At the bottom of despair, he formed a mental picture of his father in uniform, and of Bill, waiting for him in the islands. The days droned on as he was reduced to the base of his former self.

The arrival of early fall mitigated daytime temperatures, though the intensity of the training continued. Gradually, his ability to function improved. His muscles hardened, and his body began to reshape itself. He assigned physical pain to the back of his consciousness and increasingly relied on rapid improvements in speed and reflexes to manage new challenges. His mind grew sharper – more alert to details and more responsive to military commands.

Hand-to-hand combat introduced him to the connection between mind and body. He learned to integrate thoughts with motion, compressing the two into a physical flow of energy. He reduced the interval between decisions and action and refined the efficiency of his movements. New techniques modified his approach to dealing with opponents who enjoyed an advantage in size or strength. He displayed a noticeable talent in this area, which quickly gained him the respect of his fellow Marines. Still, Sergeant Hale rode him harder than ever, as if to break his growing self-confidence.

"Too slow, Private Garrett!" he would shout. "Start over, and do it right this time!"

"Sir, yes sir!" Matt would reply, ignoring the injustice and applying himself to the task with renewed intensity. He was accustomed to repetition, and his mind had developed immunity to the pitfalls of reasoning. The combat continued, and he viewed its outcome before it arrived, like a chess player anticipating checkmate half a dozen moves ahead of his opponent.

"That's enough!" the sergeant yelled, after Matt took his latest challenger to the ground and rendered him unconscious. "All of you – get yourselves cleaned up and meet me in front of the armory at 1400 hours."

The physical training was temporarily suspended, and all focus turned to weaponry.

Chapter 49

✎

Each member of the squad was issued a semi-automatic Berretta 9mm handgun and a black, full-auto M16 rifle. The M16s were restricted to three-round bursts for each pull of the trigger to minimize wasted ammunition caused by the natural climb of the barrel during discharge.

Each squad member was taught how to disassemble and clean their weapons, and how to quickly reassemble and ready them for use. Sergeant Hale and two range officers worked closely with the group, developing their overall knowledge of firearms and increasing their individual weapon handling skills. The instructors emphasized firearm safety, proper breathing techniques, body positioning and improved shooting accuracy through hours of practice and repetition. They explained the various techniques and then demonstrated them on live-fire ranges.

Soon, the Marines were on the firing lines themselves, executing the orders of their superiors. From sunrise to sunset they fired their weapons, breaking only for morning and afternoon close-arm drills and brief, but intense reminders of their physical training. Handling firearms became second nature to the Marines, and they found themselves focusing on further refinements in precision shooting. Firearms became an extension of their bodies, and their use became reflexive.

Once again, Matt excelled in his training, due largely to a rare lack of anticipation of recoil. For reasons that were mysterious even to him, he did not suffer the most common deterrent to accuracy experienced by most shooters.

Just prior to discharge, he remained so intently focused on his targets that he failed to dread the weapon's backlash. This left the barrel on point, with no early downward movement, subconsciously intended to counteract recoil. He slowed his breathing just prior to pulling the trigger and achieved an inner stillness that brought to bear the full resources of his mind and body on the target.

His accuracy was natural and uncanny, and his instructors flashed quick glances at each other, but said nothing. They had seen this sort of thing before, but only once or twice among thousands of recruits. It was both strange and exhilarating to witness.

Three weeks into weapons training, Sergeant Hale instructed Matt to bring his Colt .45 to the range. This came as a complete surprise to Matt, since he had no idea that the sergeant was even aware of its existence. Apparently, Bill had mentioned it to him before he left. So, Matt did as instructed, bringing it to the range the next morning. Sergeant Hale disassembled and examined it, then put it back together, shaking his head at its craftsmanship. He opened a case of .45 cartridges resting on the shooting bench and told Matt to get started.

He stood behind Matt and watched, knowing that the Colt .45 was a jackhammer compared to the 9mm that Matt was accustomed to shooting. It had far more recoil, associated with far more knock-down power. He fully expected his first shot to go high, perhaps missing the target altogether. He was partially right.

Matt's first shot climbed to the top edge of the bullseye, straddling the border of the ring that separated it from the one above. Having experienced the shock of its discharge, Sergeant Hale knew that he would over-compensate with his second round, but it landed a half inch lower, piecing the heart of the target.

"Shit!" Sergeant Hale exclaimed. He quickly recovered himself and moved down the firing line to assist the next shooter.

At the end of the day, Matt disassembled and cleaned his custom Colt .45, reassembled it and took it back to his room, storing it behind the medicine cabinet again, as Bill had instructed.

Chapter 50

On a Friday afternoon in the third week of October, Sergeant Hale took Matt aside and informed him that he was not to return to duty until Monday morning. He gave no explanation for his stunning directive. This meant that Matt could "sleep in" for the first time since he had started his training – an unimaginable luxury that he had difficulty grasping.

Matt turned his alarm clock off and went to bed at nine o'clock that night. He slept soundly until four A.M., when he woke up briefly, rolled over and went back to sleep. It was noon before he opened his eyes again and stared at the ceiling. He felt wonderfully refreshed by the extended rest, and he climbed out of bed and went into the bathroom. He took a slow, hot shower and then got dressed and went over to the mess hall, grabbing a couple of quick sandwiches and a can of soda, taking them back to his room to eat. He sat down in his chair and consumed them voraciously while thumbing through a gun magazine that he had picked up earlier in the commissary.

When he finished lunch, he cleaned up his room and walked down to the banks of the Potomac. From the shoreline, he watched sailboats skimming across its surface and anglers casting for rockfish from their boats. Trees along the shoreline were aflame with red and yellow leaves, crisp and gleaming in the midday sun. He stretched out in the grass along the banks of the river and filled his lungs with crisp, fall air. In the distance, he could hear the sharp commands of Marine drill sergeants, driving subordinates to the limits of their endurance.

The afternoon passed quickly, and when he returned to his room, he was surprised to find that it was already five o'clock. He picked up the magazine again and lay down on top of his bed to read.

At five-thirty, he heard a car door shut outside his apartment. There was a knock on the door, and he got up and opened it. An Asian woman stood in front of him in a black, fitted dress, holding out a black suit bag. Matt recognized her immediately. It was Ming.

"It's your birthday," she said. "Get dressed. We're going out to dinner."

She pushed the suit bag into his hands as she brushed past him. A warm, amber smell of perfume filled the small apartment as she sat down on the only chair available.

"What?" Matt said, struggling with the contrast between her refined appearance and the harsh life that he was living.

"But, but – how did you get onto the base?"

"I had a pass," she replied matter-of-factly. "Bill called and asked me to take you into Georgetown and get you a decent meal."

"You're kidding," Matt said. He had completely forgotten that it was his birthday and was a little embarrassed by the fact. He had turned twenty-three and hadn't even noticed.

"Uh, how's Bill doing?" Matt blurted out in a poor attempt to conceal his surprise. "Is he still in the islands?"

"Yes," Ming replied. "He sends his regards."

"What's he been doing?" he asked her.

Ming just looked at him and smiled. He knew immediately that she wasn't going to answer the question.

"Get dressed," she said. "We have reservations."

Matt nodded his head and carried the suit bag into the bathroom, hanging it on the back side of the door as he closed it. He unzipped the front of the bag. Inside was a black suit coat and pants, a black leather belt, a white, long-sleeve shirt and a red tie. A pair of black wingtip shoes with matching socks in them rested in the bottom pocket. He was surprised to find that everything fit, particularly considering his weight loss and altered body shape. Someone was keeping track of him.

In a few minutes, he exited the bathroom, wearing everything except the tie. Ming stood up and looked at him, and he detected a slight rise in the altitude of her eyebrows. She stepped forward and took the tie out of his left hand. Then, she stood on her tiptoes and raised his collar, wrapping the tie around his neckline and tying it expertly into a precise knot. Then, she stepped back, looked at him again and nodded her head.

"Let's go," she said.

She went out the front door of the apartment and walked around to the passenger side of a red Mercedes Sports.

"You drive," she said. "The keys are in it."

Matt was amazed at the smooth power of its engine as they drove across the complex and exited the front gate. The Marine guard waved them through without inspection. In a matter of minutes, they were turning north on I-95, accelerating to interstate speeds and beyond. Forty-five minutes later, they pulled into Georgetown.

Chapter 51

Ming directed Matt to northwest 36th Street, where they parked the car and walked a couple of blocks to their final destination. The *1789 Restaurant* had taken its name from local history, marking the year in which the site was purchased by Archbishop John Carroll, the founding father of Georgetown University – the same year that the Constitution of the United States was adopted and the village of Georgetown was incorporated. The basement of the building housed *The Tombs*, a casual restaurant geared toward university students. But, upstairs, an elegant restaurant waited, revealing stately rooms filled with American antiques and working fireplaces.

The maitre-de seemed to recognize Ming, and he asked them to follow him. He seated them near the fire, placing two large menus in front of them and adding his best wishes for a pleasant evening. Waiters immediately descended upon their table, filling glasses with cold water and placing white linen napkins on their laps. The wine steward brought them a bottle of Alsace Riesling, pouring a small sample of it into a goblet and offering it to Matt.

"Taste it," Ming said.

Matt drank it and indicated his pleasure with a nod.

"That'll be fine," Ming said to the steward. He poured half a glass for both of them, placing the remainder of the bottle in a silver ice bucket, conveniently positioned beside their table.

Matt picked up his menu and studied the first, second and main course offerings. It featured American cuisine that included a variety of steak and seafood offerings. Prices were tastefully printed as double-digit whole numbers to the far right of each item. He lowered his menu slowly and looked at Ming.

"Don't worry," she said, reading his mind. "It's already taken care of."

When the waiter returned to take their order, Matt listened as Ming selected a spiced northern cucumber soup, Maine scallops and Chesapeake Bay rockfish. Matt ordered the same cucumber soup, but settled on linguine with clams and a filet mignon for his main course.

When the waiter withdrew with their orders, Ming raised her wine glass.

"Happy Birthday, Matt," she said with genuine warmth.

He lifted his wine glass, reached across the table and lightly tapped hers.

"Thanks," Matt replied. "You really know how to make a guy feel special."

She looked at him and smiled. Her appearance was classy and elegant, and her beauty was apparent to everyone in the room. Matt understood that she was clearly out of his league, but he could still appreciate her radiance.

"My pleasure," she replied, sipping her wine and studying the changes in his physique since their last brief encounter in Alexandria.

In a few minutes, the first course of their meal arrived, and they began to eat. The food was delicious, introducing an array of unusual flavors – a welcome departure from military fare. It was food of the highest quality, and the service was constant and professional, though not aloof. Matt enjoyed the meal immensely, and he thanked his hostess repeatedly. It had been a long time since he'd tasted food that good, shared with such pleasurable company.

They talked about his training and the other members of his squad. He avoided questioning her about her job, since Bill had said that much of VICORE's work was classified. At one point, though, she volunteered that her role was much like that of a ringmaster in a circus, managing a diverse and talented group of individuals, with quirky talents and inflated egos. But, she also felt that it was important work, and that her involvement served to move their mission forward. It was obvious that she was both intelligent and motivated, but most of the time she kept her thoughts to herself.

Ming decided to dispense with the customary birthday cake celebration, correctly assuming that Matt would prefer to remain low-key. Instead, when the main course was finished, the waiter rolled a three-tiered dessert tray to their table, showcasing a dozen or more temptations. Ming selected a small crème brulee and Matt chose a piece of New York-style cheesecake with strawberry topping. Hot coffee was served with dessert, and, not surprisingly, it was the best that Matt had ever had.

Following dessert, Ming asked if he would like to try some brandy. He declined the offer because he had no idea what it tasted like and was completely content to sip on a second cup of the wonderful coffee. From start to finish, the meal consumed almost two hours.

Matt noticed that no check arrived at their table. Instead, Ming gave a final nod to the waiter, and the two of them stood up, placed their napkins on the table and walked out of the restaurant.

"Have a nice evening," the maitre-de said as they passed by him.

"Thanks. You, too," Matt replied.

"It was a pleasure, as usual," Ming added, looking back at him as Matt opened the door for her. Once outside, they turned in the direction of the car and began walking. Ming pulled a white cashmere wrap around her shoulders to contend with the brisk fall air. Matt slowed his pace to allow for the difference in their strides, and they took their time and enjoyed the stroll.

When they reached the car, they decided to walk farther, bolstered by the idea that a little exercise might compensate for their lavish meal. They turned down Prospect Street, walking parallel to the Potomac River, and continued for several blocks, talking about various aspects of the food they had just shared and the possibility of a return visit to the restaurant once his training was completed.

They passed a few university students, no doubt headed to Georgetown clubs or off-campus parties. Occasionally, adult figures strolled past them, acknowledging their presence with a nod of their head or a brief hello.

Eventually, they turned up Potomac Street, walked one block to "N" Street and turned left to head back in the direction of the car. The evening was drawing to a close, but it had been a fine way to celebrate Matt's birthday, and he had sincerely appreciated it.

"Do me a favor, will you?" he said to Ming. "Tell Bill that I owe him one."

"For what?" Ming inquired.

"For a magnificent meal and the pleasure of your company," Matt replied. "I really enjoyed myself."

"Really?" Ming said, smiling up at him. "I'm sure he'll be happy to hear that. He thinks a lot of you, you know."

"We've known each other since high school," Matt explained. "He's taught me a lot about– "

Matt's voice stopped mid-sentence, as a hard metal object slammed against the base of his neck, and a searing pain shot down his spine. He dropped to his knees and fell to the side, stars igniting in his brain. A large man, with closely-cropped black hair and dark eyes, grabbed Ming's right arm and swung her around to face him. He shoved a 9mm Makarov back into his pocket and took hold of her other arm, drawing her face close to his. Ming's eyes went wide with fear, and her body trembled. She had no experience with violence, and it quickly ravaged her small frame.

"Where is she?" the man shouted angrily, shaking her body for emphasis. He had a thick Russian accent and a dangerous look on his face.

"Wha...? Where's who?" Ming cried.

"Kavalov's daughter!" he shouted at her, shaking her even harder. His crushing grip was hurting her arms, and she screamed back at him.

"I... I don't know!" she cried. "I don't know what you're talking about!"

He slapped her hard, sending her forcefully to the ground. Then, he pulled out the Makarov and pointed it directly at her face, placing his tobacco-stained finger on the trigger.

"You've got one last chance," he said, "before I blow your pretty little head off." He cocked the gun and glared down at her, his eyes gleaming with hatred.

"Please!" she cried. "Please! I don't know anything!"

"That's too bad," he sneered. "I think we could have been very close friends."

He raised his gun and took two steps forward to guarantee accuracy. She held out her hands in an insane attempt to stop the bullet, but it was too late. A terrific blast assaulted the night air – the loudest sound that she had ever heard. The shockwave jolted her body, and in a microsecond, she knew that she was dead. The large Russian man in front of her raised slightly into the air, as a gaping hole opened in the center of his chest and human tissue sprayed across her face.

In the same instant, she realized that she was still an active participant in a world gone mad. Her chest began to heave with emotion, and she screamed at the top of her lungs as the man collapsed forward, impacting the ground beside her with a dull, heavy thud. Immediately, Matt's face came into view. He was positioned on his knees, arms outstretched. Both of his steady hands gripped a large handgun, smoke drifting upwards from the end of its barrel, curling like a snake into the autumn sky.

Matt returned the gun to the back of his waist and crawled forward on his hands and knees. His head was still full of cobwebs, but his motor skills were slowly returning. When he reached her, he sat down and wrapped his arms around her. While she continued to shake violently, he removed a handkerchief from her purse and wiped the blood off her face.

"It's all right," he said. "It's over now."

In the distance, the sound of a police siren sliced through the night, and, soon, a second one joined in. He continued to comfort Ming, until both police cars pulled up, and uniformed officers got out, guns drawn. Seeing no firearms other than the one in the dead man's hand, they quickly focused on Matt, instructing him to get up slowly and put his hands behind his head. He complied, and they immediately approached him, pulling his hands down and cuffing them behind his back.

Ming presented no threat whatsoever, so the second officer helped her to her feet and walked her slowly back to his squad car. There, he did a cursory search of her purse and asked her a couple of questions. He took a warm blanket from the trunk of his car, wrapped it around her, put her in the backseat and closed the door.

Meanwhile, the first policeman checked Matt thoroughly for weapons, removing the custom Colt tucked inside his belt at the middle of his back.

"What have we here?" he said, holding it up to smell the barrel. He could feel its warmth, even with leather gloves on his hands.

When the second officer returned to assist, he bent down to examine the dead man. He rolled the body over slightly and glanced at the large hole in his chest. He looked up at his partner.

"Right through the heart," he said. "Either someone got lucky, or someone knew exactly what he was doing."

"Which is it?" the first officer said to Matt.

He didn't answer.

A third, unmarked police car pulled up and a shift commander got out. He glanced at the woman in the backseat of the squad car and then walked over to his men, who were searching Matt for identification. The shift commander's badge indicated a rank of captain, and he looked both experienced and competent. He addressed the two officers as he approached them.

"What have we got here?" he said to his men.

"A homicide," the first officer replied. "Looks like someone terminated this man with extreme prejudice."

"And who's the perp?" the captain asked.

"Judging from the warmth of this man's Colt, and the size of the hole in that man's chest, I'd say this guy qualifies," the second officer said, nodding toward Matt.

"And who's the woman?" the captain asked.

"Her name is Dr. Ming Li," the second officer replied. "She works at some government facility near Fort Detrick."

"What's your name, son?" the captain said, turning back to Matt.

Matt looked at him, but did not reply.

"Let's see some ID," the commander said to his officers.

"Here's his driver's license," said the first officer, who handed him Matt's card and a flashlight. "The dead guy didn't have any ID."

The captain examined Matt's license carefully, his focus coming to rest on the trident symbol in the upper right hand corner. He glanced up at the two officers and then quickly slid the license back into Matt's wallet and returned it to him.

"Release him," the captain ordered. "The woman, too."

"What?" the first officer exclaimed. "Are you kidding me?"

"No, I'm not," the captain replied firmly. "Get those cuffs off him right now. And give him his gun back. I'll explain this to you later."

The first officer grudgingly complied, assuming that they had stumbled into some undercover drug operation. He removed Matt's cuffs and handed him his firearm. The second officer released Ming from his squad car, and she immediately ran to Matt, wrapping her arms tightly around his waist.

"Do you have transportation?" the captain asked Matt.

"Yes, sir," Matt replied. "That's where we were headed when this guy showed up," he said, looking down at the dead man.

"O.K., then. Get out of here," the captain replied. "I'll take care of the rest."

Matt put his arm around Ming and they walked away from the scene, moving quickly up the street and disappearing into the night. An ambulance passed by them as they reached 36th Street and located their car. Ming was doing much better, but he helped her into the passenger seat anyway. Then, he climbed behind the wheel, cranked the Mercedes Sports and pulled out into the late evening flow of Georgetown traffic.

Chapter 52

❧

They arrived at Quantico at eleven PM. Matt was prepared for a serious confrontation, but the Marine guards passed them through the gate as if nothing unusual had happened. He couldn't be sure if they were oblivious to the events of the evening, or were acting under strict orders not to interfere.

He drove to the back of the complex, expecting Sergeant Hale to be standing in front of his apartment, military police in tow. But no such greeting awaited them, so he shut off the engine, leaned back in his seat and relaxed for a moment. It was a strangely quiet night, and the Potomac River shimmered with streaks of silver moonlight that danced across its watery surface.

"How do you feel?" he said, turning to Ming.

"I feel like you just saved my life," she replied softly, her voice trembling with emotion.

In the pale light, he could see that she was still shivering, so he reached across and wrapped his right arm around her shoulders and placed his left hand gently on her waist. She instinctively leaned into him, and he held her softly while she cried. The events of the night had overwhelmed her, and she willingly surrendered her fears, feeling safe now in Matt's arms.

"It's O.K.," he said to her. "Anyone would feel the same way. It was a terrible thing to witness."

He rocked her gently and waited patiently for her emotions to subside. In a few minutes, she began to calm down, but her face was streaked with tears as she finally let go of Matt and pulled slowly away from him. In the moonlight, he could see tiny specks of dried blood and matted tissue in her beautiful black hair. Her neck, upper chest and the front of her dress also displayed evidence of the violent event. He knew that she would react severely to its presence, so he offered his help.

"Why don't you come in for a few minutes so we can get you washed up?" Matt said to her. "You've still got some stuff in your hair and on your neck."

Ming immediately reached for her hair and felt the dried blood.

"I need to bathe," she said immediately, with a sense of urgency. "I need to wash it off – now." She was agitated, and her voice had a touch of panic in it.

"Sure," Matt replied, trying to console her. "Come inside and you can take a shower. I'll find you something to wear."

He opened his car door, stepped out and walked around to the passenger side. Opening her door, he reached down to assist her.

"Give me your hand," he said.

She placed her small hand in his and stood up, unsure of her stability. At his suggestion, she held onto him as they walked to the front door of the apartment. As soon as he unlocked it and turned on the lights, she removed her spotted cashmere wrap and went directly into the bathroom, closing the door behind her. In a matter of seconds, the shower came on.

Matt hurriedly searched for clothing that might fit her, but nothing was small enough to stay on her petite frame. He selected one of his clean T-shirts and a pair of pajama pants with a drawstring waistband that might manage to stay on her slim figure. He hung them on the bathroom doorknob and waited.

Ming stayed in the shower for a long time. Concerned for her well-being, he eventually called through the door.

"Are you O.K.?" he asked.

"Yes," she replied. "I'll be out in a minute."

"I've hung some clean clothes on the outside of the doorknob. They're not much, but they're all that I could find."

"Would you hang them on the inside?" Ming called. "It's O.K. – I'm still in the shower."

"Sure," Matt consented.

He opened the bathroom door slightly and hung them on the inside handle. He could see her spattered dress lying in a crumpled heap on the bathroom floor in the corner nearest him, so he reached in and removed it. He put the dress in a plastic bag and placed it in the closet, with the intention of having it dry-cleaned for her later. Right now, she didn't need to see it.

Ming came out of the bathroom wearing nothing but his T-shirt over her black bra and panties.

"Sorry I took so long," she said. "I had to get it all off."

"That's O.K.," Matt replied. "I hope you're feeling better."

"The pants didn't fit," she said, smiling demurely at him. "But I think you can handle it."

She was older than Matt, but had taken good care of herself, which made her appear ten years younger. He smiled back at her, surprising himself by wishing that he could see everything that the T-shirt concealed.

Reading his mind, Ming walked slowly up to Matt and embraced him. She turned her face upward, and her eyes searched his. He leaned down and kissed her lightly, then waited for her response.

She smiled up at him warmly, reached forward and began to remove his coat and tie. She kept her eyes on the task at hand, while he studied her shapely body. Her skin appeared incredibly soft and smooth, finer than he had ever seen. She removed his shirt and pressed herself closer against him. The clean, natural smell of her body rose up to meet him, and his hands moved instinctively underneath the cotton T-shirt. He traced the line of her back, and the hourglass shape of her body. His hands brushed up her sides, stopping at the base of her bra. She smiled up at him and stepped slightly back, pulling the T-shirt slowly up and over her head. She let it drop to the floor and then wrapped her arms around him tightly.

He felt her warm, fresh skin, and she responded to his touch. His hands found the back of her bra, unhooking it and freeing her breasts. They rose and pressed against his skin like fire, as she reached up, took his face in her hands and kissed him fully on the lips. There was a warm, flowing feel to her body, as her tongue explored his, and the whole world melted into her movements. He bent down and swung his left arm under her thighs, lifting her easily and placing her gently on the bed.

He turned out the light, removed the rest of his clothing and reached for her in the darkness. She was experienced and knowledgeable, and she took her time with him, instructing gently, placing his hands where they could do the most good.

He removed her panties and explored the softness of her inner thighs. Then, he tasted her breasts and moved up to her neckline, eventually exploring her lips and mouth again. He rolled on top of her, and she opened herself to him, wrapping her legs around his body. They moved slowly at first, and then began to rock together in a strong, passionate rhythm that lasted for several minutes. At the peak of his excitement, she also climaxed, tucking her head into his chest and screaming unashamedly as deep, uncontrollable waves of pleasure swept through her body.

Slowly, their passion subsided, and Matt withdrew from her, rolling his body off to one side. He lay on his back, breathing heavily. Moist with sweat and panting, she climbed on top of him and laid her head on his chest. He wrapped his arms around her small waist, and they drifted together into a light sleep.

Two hours later, he felt her stir. She looked up at his face, moved her fingers through his hair and softly kissed his lips again in the darkness. He ran his hands over her smooth, rising breasts, awakening them once again to his touch. She pressed both of her hands against his chest and sat up, moaning softly as he reentered her. She arched her back and began to undulate, opening her mouth and taking short, rhythmic breaths. Gradually, their pleasure intensified, until, finally, they were both consumed by a second, even more incredible physical and emotional release.

Finally, Ming collapsed upon his chest, gasping for air, her soft hair matted with sweat. He rolled her gently off to one side, fitted his body against her back and fell asleep with his right arm draped over her attentive breasts.

Chapter 53

❦

When he awoke on Sunday morning, Ming was gone. Apparently, she had risen at dawn, dressed in the clothing that he had provided her and slipped quietly out of the apartment.

Matt sat up in bed and looked around the room. His suit hung neatly on the front of the bathroom door, and his custom Colt rested on the chair. He pressed his feet down on the floor, straightened his spine and rubbed the back of his neck, still sore from last night's encounter with the Makarov. He stood up, walked across the room, picked up his handgun and returned it to its normal place of concealment. Then, he shaved, stepped into the shower and turned on the hot water.

When he came out of the bathroom fifteen minutes later, he started to make his bed, but stopped when he spotted an envelope by the lamp. He picked it up and opened it. The scent of amber perfume wafted through the air, as he removed a single piece of tan-colored stationary. Unfolding it, he read Ming's elegant cursive script:

Dear Matt,

When I woke up this morning, I realized that I had you to thank for that. I will, no doubt, feel the same way every morning for the rest of my life.

Please forgive my early departure, but you were sleeping so soundly that I didn't have the heart to wake you. I must return to my work at VICORE, and to the man that I have been married to for more than half of your lifetime. He has treated me well, and does not deserve to be abandoned.

I hope that you will not think badly of me for sharing myself so completely. There is no act more intimate or powerful than saving another's life, and I felt strongly that I needed to repay you in some special way.

It was a terrifying and <u>wonderful</u> night, but I do not want you to pursue me further. You are a young man, with a full and active life ahead of you, while I am older and less accustomed to the challenges of your world.

I leave you to the rigors of your training, knowing that LOC is where you are headed, and where you most certainly belong. They are fortunate to have you.

After you have read this letter, please destroy it, so that I may hold you in my heart as a very personal and private memory.

Always your friend,
Ming

Matt folded the letter and put it back in the envelope. A warm, amber smell drifted through the room again, but quickly faded. He studied the envelope in his hands for a couple of minutes, then carried it into the bathroom and placed it in the sink. Reaching up, he removed a small box of matches from the medicine cabinet and set the envelope on fire, watching as the flames rose and fell, quickly reducing it to ash.

He looked up at himself in the mirror and found a slightly different man staring back at him.

Chapter 54

At the beginning of October, government officials had noted Natasha "Tinski's" arrival in Moscow, but thought little of it, since she had American Embassy credentials. By traveling under an assumed name, they failed to recognize that she also had a mother who lived alone in the foothills near Nelidovo. Natasha's commercial flight had originated in Miami, Florida, which matched the home address on her U.S. passport. They were not privy to the private Learjet flight that had brought her to Miami International from far below in the Leeward Islands.

Upon arrival in Moscow, "Nat" took a taxi to the American Embassy, where they provided her with a middle-aged, gray automobile with Russian plates. That afternoon, she drove to her mother's cottage, bringing her baskets filled with food and wine that she had purchased in the Moscow markets. They shared a warm, pleasant meal together and went to bed before midnight.

The next morning, Natasha drove westward toward Latvia, looking for small border crossings that were less frequently accessed. She spoke discreetly to older men and women who lived in the area, asking them if they remembered anything unusual that had occurred nearby, ten to fifteen years ago. Most of them shook their heads and returned to their labors without comment.

But, near the end of the day, a woman near Sebezh recalled an incident involving a Russian woman and her daughters, all of whom were killed by border guards as they exited Mother Russia on a dirt road ten miles north of town.

According to the authorities, they were carrying illegal contraband. Their van had been stopped by Russian guards, but had suddenly sped away when the officers decided to search it. They had sprayed the back of the vehicle with automatic rifle fire and watched as it veered off the road and burst into flames. It had rolled over and over, as it slid down an embankment on the opposite side of the border and disappeared from view. Latvian guards reported that all occupants had perished in the resulting fire. The woman explained that no one seemed to know who they were, and that, back then, few people dared to ask.

"All of them were killed?" Natasha questioned.

"Da," the Russian woman confirmed.

That evening, Nat crossed the border into Latvia, presumably to visit a sick aunt in the small town of Ludza. She stopped for dinner in a local restaurant and ate borsch and table breads, served with hot, black Russian tea. She inquired about the local schoolmaster and was directed to a cottage near the edge of town. After dinner, she walked to his humble residence and knocked on the front door.

A bearded man in his sixties came to the front door with a wooden cane and an aging wolfhound at his side. He invited her in, and they sat in his modest home and talked. He remembered the accident that the Russian woman had described to Nat, and he shook his head from side to side when he spoke of it.

"It was a terrible thing," he said, lowering his head and voice. "The mother and her oldest child perished, but the youngest was thrown from the vehicle and survived. She walked two miles to a local farmhouse, dragging her little sweater in one hand and a small, wooden jewelry box in the other."

"What happened to her?" Natasha inquired.

"The family took her in," he replied. "They gave her food and shelter for several years."

"What was her name?" Natasha asked.

"Alya," the headmaster replied. "She could not tell us her last name, so her adopted parents gave her their own, which was Stevsky."

"Do you know where she is now?" Nat asked.

He reached down and patted the old wolfhound on the head.

"Somewhere in Switzerland, I guess," he said, with a hint of sadness in his voice. "She went to school here as a child... a very quiet little girl, with straight brown hair and pale blue eyes. She learned to read at a very early age – much earlier than the other children. She had an intense curiosity about the physical world around her.

"Her mind was like a sponge, soaking in knowledge faster than she could find new sources. She loved math and science, and submitted a paper on cellular diseases in insects to the Swiss Academy of Sciences at the age of thirteen. Two weeks later, a Swiss doctor showed up here with an offer of academic scholarship that her adopted parents could not refuse."

He paused and looked up at Nat.

"That was eight years ago," he said. "We haven't heard from her since."

Natasha stood up, thanked him for his time and bid him farewell. The wolfhound rose with her, escorting her to the front door and watching intently as she walked back up the street to the restaurant. She got in her car and returned to her mother's humble cottage in Russia.

The next day, she drove to the American Embassy in Moscow and generated an official inquiry to the Swiss government in Geneva as to the current whereabouts of Alya Stevsky.

Twenty-four hours later, they replied, saying that they had contacted the Swiss Academy of Sciences in Bern, who provided the name of one of her colleagues, since Alya herself had left for a two-week vacation in the U.S. Apparently, her departure had closely coincided with their inquiries.

In fact, Alya, having gotten wind of the fact that government officials were asking about her, had purchased an airline ticket in her own name, but had given it to her roommate, who was very similar in size and general appearance. Her friend had always dreamed of visiting Washington, D.C. – the capital of the free world – so she gifted her with the roundtrip ticket and some money for food and a hotel room.

Alya traded passports with her excited roommate, dropped her off at the airport and then disappeared. Her colleagues at the Academy would not bother to inquire about her for at least two more weeks.

When Natasha arrived in Bern, Switzerland the next morning, she went straight to the Academy of Sciences and spoke to one of Alya's professional colleagues, who described her work in virology at The University of Bern as "cutting-edge science that sets her apart from all the rest." When Nat inquired further as to the exact nature of Alya's current projects, her colleague hesitated, suggesting that Natasha return in two weeks and speak to her in person.

Nat didn't want to raise further suspicion, so she withdrew, thanking him for his time.

As she exited the building, she took note of a large man, with closely-cropped black hair and dark eyes, standing beneath a tree on the opposite side of the street. He was smoking a hand-wrapped cigarette, filled with dark tobacco. When she turned the corner, she glimpsed back at him as he walked across the street and entered the same building that she had exited.

Nat took a taxi to her hotel, where she checked in and went immediately up to her room. She picked up the phone and entered a thirteen-digit number that accessed a switch in Miami, Florida. Soon, a recorded female voice responded mechanically.

"Please enter your four-digit code," it instructed.

Instead, Natasha entered six numbers – the only input to which the switch would respond. There was a brief pause, then a high-pitched tone, indicating that a secure, encrypted channel had been opened. She entered a third series of digits and waited.

"Sailor's Choice!" said a jovial male voice on the other end of the line.

"I'd like to make reservations for four at eight P.M., please," Natasha said. "The name is Locke."

"What's up?" Bill replied.

"We're close," Nat said. "Our suspect's name is Alya Stevsky. But, wait until you hear this; it used to be Alya Kavalov."

"What?" Bill said, stunned. "One of Uri's daughter's is still alive? The word was that the Russians had eliminated his entire family."

"Not quite," Nat said. "Her mother and older sister were killed by Russian border guards when she was a child. They thought that the whole family had perished. But the youngest girl was thrown from the vehicle during a fiery crash on the Latvian side of the border and survived. She was adopted by a rural Latvian couple, who gave her their name. She spent several years living at a farmhouse near Ludza.

"I spoke to the local headmaster in town this afternoon. Apparently, Alya inherited some of her father's intellect. At age thirteen, she was offered a scholarship by the Swiss Academy of Sciences in Bern. She's been there ever since. I don't have specifics on her current projects, but one of her colleagues mentioned that her area of expertise was virology."

"Not surprising," Bill said. "Have you talked to her yet?"

"She's not here right now," Nat replied.

"Where is she?" Bill asked.

"That's why I'm calling you," she said. "According to the Academy, she's on vacation in Washington, D.C., presumably sight-seeing. I think you'll want to contact John in Alexandria and get him looking for her right away."

"Will do," Bill said. "And I'll join him."

"Just a minute," Nat replied. "I think we have another problem that requires attention. I could be wrong, but I believe the Russians have gotten wind of this, too. Right after I left the Swiss Academy, I saw a man who looked Russian enter the same building that I had just left.

"If I'm right about this, it may reopen old wounds. We have to assume that the Soviets somehow got wind of James Garrett's involvement, so, when they find out that one of Uri's daughters survived, and that she is a virologist, everyone even remotely associated with the original Moscow tragedy will become a renewed target of interest to their agents. Matt will be about as safe as anyone could be on a Marine base, but what about his mother?"

"Good thought," Bill said. "I'll get right on it. John can track down Alya on his own."

He was proud of Natasha's ability to grasp the big picture quickly and to anticipate trouble while there was still time to deal with it.

"You may want to have a couple of local FBI agents keep an eye on her place until you get there," Natasha added.

"Will do," Bill said. "I'll leave here tonight. I should be at her place by early tomorrow morning. Good work, Nat."

"Thanks," she replied. "I'm going to hang around here a couple more days to see if I can dig up any more information on Alya's active projects. Let me know as soon as John locates her. I'll be back in the islands by Sunday evening. How's everything going there?"

"Just finishing up," Bill replied. "Everything should be ready by the time you get here."

"Wonderful," Nat said. "I'll see you Sunday."

"Good," Bill replied. "I'll introduce you to Marie Garrett."

"I look forward to meeting her," Nat said. "Love ya."

She hung up the phone and began to unpack her things, spreading them neatly across the foot of the bed. A few minutes later, she went to the closet in search of hangers, and there was a knock on the door. She felt for the Walther PPK in her back pocket and then went to answer it.

Looking through the peephole, she saw a young, blonde-haired woman dressed in hotel uniform, standing beside a pushcart that held a bottle of champagne, a small, silver tray of Swiss chocolates, a white porcelain bowl filled with fresh, plump strawberries and an elegant spray of red roses in a crystal Swarovski vase.

Natasha smiled. Bill was up to his old tricks again.

She opened the door, and the young woman pushed the cart into the center of the room. Natasha followed her, pleased with the thoughtfulness of Bill's gift.

"Oh, my! They're beautiful," Nat said, leaning over to smell the gorgeous roses. As she inhaled deeply, the young hostess withdrew a tiny vial from her apron, covered her own nose with a cloth and sprayed a fine, blue mist directly across the top of the roses.

Caught completely off guard, Natasha reached for her Walther, but collapsed to the floor before she could withdraw it.

Chapter 55

At ten PM, Bill boarded the U.S. government-provided Learjet at the island airport, carrying only a small, black travel bag and his military ID. The Air Force pilot had already filed a flight plan to Miami, which he revised mid-flight to Orlando's McCoy Jetport. A couple of hours later, Bill entered the main terminal of the airport, merging into a sea of tourists and local businessmen arriving on red-eye flights from New York, New Jersey, and L.A.

He went to the rental agencies, where he rented a dark blue Suburban and exited the airport heading east. In a few minutes, he turned south onto Highway 15.

Thirty minutes later, he drove along the shoreline of East Lake Toho and turned up Maryland Avenue toward Matt's home. He passed the quiet house, noting the unmarked FBI car sitting on a side-street nearby. He turned left at the next intersection and circled around to the back of the house, where a second unmarked car was parked. Turning his lights off, he eased up along the driver's side.

The young FBI agent behind the steering wheel was slumped over, blood dripping from his mouth and nostrils. Bill knew immediately that it would be unnecessary to check the other unmarked vehicle.

His senses sharpened, and he slid out of the Suburban, removing a short, double-barreled shotgun from his travel bag. He moved through a neighbor's yard undetected, and approached the side of Matt's house, watching for the slightest signs of movement.

All was quiet, until he reached the front corner of the house and peered around it. In the silver light of a three-quarter moon, he could make out a stocky man standing at the front door, holding a silenced handgun in his left hand, while testing the doorknob with his right.

Bill placed his shotgun on the ground, arced out into the front yard and quickly came up behind him. Suddenly sensing his approach, the Russian whirled around forcefully, just as Bill delivered a crushing blow to the left side of his face. The agent staggered backwards and slammed into the door, face bloodied. Before he could recover, Bill buried his left fist in the man's solar plexus. A great rush of air escaped his lungs, as Bill's third blow destroyed the man's windpipe. He slumped to the ground in a dead-weight heap and lay still.

As the lights came on inside, Bill dragged the man's body around the side of the house, wiped the blood off his hands with the Russian's shirt and then deposited him behind a row of shrubs. By the time Marie put her housecoat on and opened the front door to discover the source of the disturbance, Bill was standing there with a big smile on his face, asking her when breakfast would be ready. She launched herself at him, wrapping her small frame around him and giving him a big hug.

"Oh, my gosh!" she cried. "Where in the world did you come from? Is Matt with you? Is everything O.K.?"

"Of course it is," Bill replied. "I just missed your home cooking."

"Well, come on in!" she said, genuinely happy to see him. "Let me get some clothes on, and I'll fix you something."

"Yes, Ma'am," Bill said, entering the living room and taking a seat on the sofa.

Marie disappeared into her bedroom and returned in a few minutes with slacks and a blouse on. She headed toward the kitchen, but Bill interrupted her, asking her to sit down and talk with him for a few minutes. She looked at him, somewhat puzzled, but gave in to his request.

Ten minutes later, with full assurances that Matt would be just fine, she began to pack two suitcases. Bill had told her that she needed to relocate for a while, but she had no idea where they were going. Perhaps they would end up over at the coast or possibly upstate somewhere. He had spoken in such ardent tones that she decided to trust him. After all, he was like a second son to her.

Since she hadn't been more than fifty miles from home since her husband died, she was a little nervous about leaving. But, Bill had explained that it was necessary, and that Matt would be joining her before long.

That was all she needed to hear.

She gathered her clothing and important keepsakes – family photos, a small necklace that James had given her when Matt was born, Matt's high school ring, her husband's service medals and his first-issued Korean War rifle – an M1 Garand that she wanted Matt to have. Bill protected it in a canvas wrap, saying that he "was certain they could make room for such a fine piece of military history."

Marie remembered being surprised the first time James had shown her the rifle. Engraved on the top, back of the receiver, was the manufacturer's name – International Harvester – the same company that made tractors and agricultural equipment. She had teased her husband about being a farmer in Korea.

"Well, I plowed a lot of foreign soil with that rifle," James had replied, smiling. "I found the manufacturer's name to be strangely appropriate."

While she continued to pack, Bill made a phone call to the Miami switch, which securely routed him to his contact at the FBI. An hour later, as they pulled out of the neighborhood in darkness, two more unmarked cars and a black van passed them on Lakeshore Drive, headed in the opposite direction – the cleanup crew that he had requested.

Chapter 56

Bill drove north on Highway 15 for thirty minutes, then turned into a gated access road that approached the east side of Orlando's McCoy Jetport. Marie did not recognize the road and was surprised to see a military guard posted at the entrance they used. It was well away from the main terminal, so she still wasn't certain where they were headed or what they would be doing once they arrived.

Bill showed the guard his military ID and was immediately admitted. He drove up to the side of a small hangar and parked the vehicle. A sensor-activated light on the roof of the building came on, providing soft illumination to the area Bill had selected. He got out and came around to Marie's side, opening the door and instructing her to step inside the hangar while he gathered her things. She offered to help, but Bill said he would take care of it and for her to go ahead.

Following his instructions, Marie walked around to the front of the terminal, looked inside and froze. The only transport in the hangar was a sleek, white Learjet that was being prepped for flight by a two-man ground crew in plain black jumpsuits. The pilot, dressed in casual clothing, was completing his pre-flight walk-around, running his hands over the control surfaces of the aircraft, looking for anything out of the ordinary. Soon, he noticed Marie standing in the hangar's doorway and walked over to greet her, extending his right hand.

"Mrs. Garrett?" he said, smiling. "Welcome aboard. I'm your pilot. My name is Randy Weston."

"Pleased to meet you, Randy," Marie replied somewhat mechanically. She was stunned, still in shock over what was surely going to be an unusual test of self-control.

Bill came around the corner carrying two suitcases. He walked them over to the ground crew, set them down and then headed back toward the Suburban. As he passed by the two of them, Randy asked if he needed any help.

"No, thanks," Bill replied. "There's just two more items. We're traveling light this trip."

"O.K., then," Randy said in a pleasant voice. "Mrs. Garrett, let's get you settled onboard."

"Uh, but –" she stammered, a worried look on her face.

"Is there something wrong, Ma'am?" Randy asked.

"Oh, no, no," Marie replied. "It's just that I've never…"

Her voice trailed off as she stared at the shiny, custom Learjet, poised like an eagle anxious to take flight. The ground crew opened the small entry door of the aircraft and unfolded a set of carpeted steps that settled on the concrete floor of the hangar.

"You've never what, Mrs. Garrett?" Bill said as he came around the corner carrying his travel bag and the M1 Garand slung over his shoulder in a canvas wrap. He paused and looked at her.

Marie was a little embarrassed.

"Uh– well– I've never been on an airplane before," she finally revealed.

"Oh, you're going to do just fine," Bill assured her. "This little darling is perfect for first-time flyers!"

The pilot looked over at Bill and smiled, knowing that his novice passenger was about to be introduced to flying in the finest possible way. Every seat was first-class on the Learjet, and sunrise over the Leeward Islands was breath-taking to behold, even for seasoned travelers.

"Trust me," Randy said, as he walked her slowly toward the steps. "You're going to love it."

Chapter 57

On the Monday morning that Matt returned to his squad, Sergeant Hale ordered him to the firing range alone. When he got there, no one was around. He waited patiently for further instruction, curious about the sudden change in his daily regimen.

At seven A.M., a man dressed in civilian clothing approached him from the far end of the firing line. Matt recognized him immediately. It was Special Agent Jack Reicher, the second man that Bill had introduced to him when they first arrived at Quantico. He did not fit the rugged image of a soldier, though Matt knew that looks could be deceiving. At first glance, he favored a college professor more than a warrior. The 'Special Agent' preface to his name suggested FBI membership, though it could have signified rank in other government organizations as well.

"Good morning, Matt," he said, smiling. "How have you been? You look a little different than the last time I saw you."

"I feel a little different," Matt replied, agreeing with his observation.

"I'll have to admit – you seem to have weathered those changes better than I expected," Reicher added, nodding his head in approval.

"Thank you, sir," Matt replied. "It's good to see you again. Will you be joining us for today's training?"

Reicher laughed.

"No, I don't think so," he said. "We have some other matters to attend to."

"We, sir?" Matt questioned.

"That's right, Private," came Sergeant Hale's voice from behind him. "You're going to be leaving us today. Special Agent Reicher will be handling your training from this point on. You've finished your training here at Quantico. Pack your bags and go with him. And take this with you."

He held out a brown military envelope, which Matt accepted.

"Open it," the sergeant instructed.

"Sir, yes sir!" Matt replied automatically.

He opened the envelope and pulled out a U.S. Marine Corps military ID. It bore his photograph and a small trident symbol in the upper right-hand corner.

"Semper Fi, Private!" Sergeant Hale said firmly.

"Semper Fi!" Matt replied. "And thank you, sir." He saluted his superior officer.

Sergeant Hale made no reply, turning instead and walking back in the direction of Matt's squad. Matt watched him for a few moments, then turned back to address Reicher.

"Give me twenty minutes, sir," Matt said.

"Take your time, son," Reicher replied. "And you can drop the 'Sir'. From here on, just call me Jack. I'll drive over in a few minutes and pick you up in front of your apartment."

Matt jogged back across the complex to his apartment, where he quickly packed his duffel. He tucked his custom Colt forty-five handgun under the back of his belt and pulled on a gray flannel jacket. He had no idea where they were going, but guessed that it might be to some FBI office in Washington, D.C.

He was wrong.

Fifteen minutes later, when Reicher pulled up outside Matt's apartment in a forest green Land Rover, Matt was already standing in the doorway with his back to him, surveying the interior of his apartment one last time. He left everything clean and orderly, just as he had found it.

"You ready?" Reicher called to him.

Matt turned, closed the apartment door and walked around to the passenger side of the Land Rover.

"Just throw your things in the backseat," Reicher said.

Matt did as instructed, then climbed into the front passenger seat. Reicher cranked the engine and drove slowly through the compound, noting that Matt studied the passing of Quantico's landscape carefully. When they reached the guard gate, they were waved through without inspection.

Soon, the Land Rover was headed north on I-95, in the direction of D.C. Commuter traffic increased as they neared Washington, but they veered slightly west, away from the city, and headed up I-270. In another hour, they arrived at the gates of Fort Detrick, in Frederick, Maryland, home of the U.S. Army's biological research facilities. USAMRIID, the United States Army Medical Research Institute of Infectious Diseases, housed the nation's preeminent research laboratories for cutting-edge military medical research into biological threats.

Matt knew that VICORE was somewhere nearby, but decided not to mention it until he could determine why they were there in the first place.

At the gate, the Army guard asked for their IDs, and both men supplied him with military credentials. He studied their photographs and compared them to their faces. Then, he stepped back into the guard house, closed the door and made a phone call to the base commander. They couldn't hear what was said, but, two minutes later, he opened the door, returned their IDs and passed them through the gate without further discussion.

They passed several brick buildings en route to a large, white concrete structure near the back of the campus, with three ventilation stacks on its roof. The building was unmarked, giving no indication of its purpose. The majority of its floors were below ground level, invisible to those outside. Security guards randomly patrolled the area on foot, maintaining a low-key presence. Those who entered the building used an access card, which they swiped through a reader, just to the right of the only door that Matt could see.

Reicher parked across the street from the building and got out. Matt joined him, and they walked to the front door together. Jack opened his wallet and withdrew an access card, handing it to Matt.

"This is yours," he said. "Don't lose it. Let's make sure it works. Go ahead and give it a try."

Matt slid the magnetic card through the device reader and heard a crisp snap as the lock released, allowing them to enter. Ten feet in front of them was a waist-high kiosk, with a flat, glass plate on top. Both men approached it.

"Quantico sent them your fingerprints some time ago," Jack said to Matt. "Put your right hand on the glass, palm down."

Matt stepped forward and positioned his right hand as instructed. After a brief pause, a pair of thick, sliding glass doors parted in front of the kiosk, and they were granted access into the next security check. An armed guard, seated behind a steel security desk, examined them as they entered.

"How's it going, Jack?" he said to Reicher as they approached the desk.

"Fine, Dan. How are you doing this morning?" Reicher responded. "Dan, I'd like you to meet Matt Garrett. He's just come from Quantico. He'll be with us for the next several weeks, so you'll be seeing him regularly."

"Hello, Matt," Dan said, standing up and offering him his hand. "You've got a top-rate mentor here, you know. Jack's considered the best around here."

Matt stepped forward and shook his hand.

"I'm not surprised," Matt said, smiling. "I seem to be keeping pretty good company these days."

"Good for you, young man," the guard replied. "You'll learn a lot here."

"Looking forward to it," Matt added, though he had no idea what to expect. He had decided to just go with the flow and see where it took him.

The guard had both of them sign in, adding the date and time to their entries. Then, he pressed a button under his desk, and a buzzer sounded as the door to their right unlocked itself. Reicher pushed the door open and held it for Matt.

They entered a short hallway that led to a double-door elevator, where Reicher slid his own card through the adjacent reader. It opened, and they stepped inside and turned around. There was a vertical stack of six lighted buttons on its interior panel. Beside each of them, innocuous labels read 'G', 'P', 'BL1', 'BL2', 'BL3' and 'BL4'. Above them, a ten-digit keypad presented yet another access challenge.

Reicher entered a numeric code and then depressed the 'P' button. Slowly, they began their descent into the darkest chambers of the human heart.

Chapter 58

❦

John Sauter reached into his pocket and removed the small photograph of Alya Stevsky, a.k.a. Alya Kavalov, which Natasha had faxed to him the night before. He had already contacted the FAA and the director of U.S. Customs and had determined that Alya's flight had arrived yesterday at Dulles International Airport. FBI agents tracked credit card records for hotels in the D.C. area, but none existed for an Alya Stevsky, so they assumed that she had registered under a different name and paid cash for her accommodations or was staying with a friend.

When John forwarded a copy of Alya's photograph to the FBI, they renewed their efforts, widening their search grid to include smaller motels and B&B's.

By eight A.M. the next morning, they had spoken to the manager of a small motel on the Beltway perimeter that thought he recognized her as a guest. The manager opened the door to her room, where they found her suitcase and a few small brochures from The Smithsonian Institute in Washington D.C.

They relayed this information to their superiors, and, thirty minutes later, John Sauter was standing on the front steps of the Smithsonian's Museum of Natural History – his best guess at her current location, based upon the pamphlets found in her motel room. He entered the museum and wandered through the exhibits, stopping occasionally to compare the photograph in his hand to women that passed by him.

Just before noon, he spotted a young woman standing in front of the Hope Diamond display that bore similar characteristics to Alya's photograph. He moved around her, studying her face from different angles. Eventually, as she turned to leave, he spoke to her.

"Alya?" he said, smiling.

She ignored him and moved quickly away.

"Alya Stevsky?" he called after her. She quickened her pace, looking worriedly over her shoulder at a man that she did not recognize.

John turned right and cut through a row of gemstone displays, correctly anticipating her escape route. He met her coming at him from around the corner, clearly headed for the exit. He held out his right hand and asked her to stop.

"Please," John said. "I only need to speak to you for a moment."

She paused, six feet away from him and then suddenly bolted for the front door. He caught her by the arm well before she reached it and swung her around, pinning her firmly against the wall.

"Are you Alya Stevsky?" he asked her point blank.

She did not reply.

"Look," he said, "we can do this the easy way, or I can take you down to police headquarters and have them lock you up."

She understood enough of what he was saying to raise the level of fear in her eyes. She struggled briefly, but he maintained his grip on her. She wanted to get away from him, but knew there was no use trying.

"I borrowed her passport!" she blurted out.

"You borrowed whose passport?" John asked.

"Alya's," she replied, straining against his control. "She bought me a plane ticket in her name."

"Let me see your passport," John demanded, releasing her arms, but staying close enough to bar any further attempt at escape.

Reluctantly, she took it out of her coat pocket and handed it to him. He looked it over and told her to calm down. He explained that she would have to come with him for a couple of hours, but that he would return her to the museum shortly after lunch.

"Are you police?" the young Swiss woman asked, still frightened.

"Something like that," John replied, taking her by the arm and exiting the museum. He reassured her that he meant no harm, and drove her to a local restaurant, where he bought her a nice lunch. She calmed down and answered several questions about her roommate while she ate.

He got her real name, and decided to return Alya's passport to her. It was a goodwill gesture that would make it easier for LOC to track her journey home and potentially lead them to the real Alya Stevsky.

He contacted Bill that afternoon to plan their next steps. Using CIA assets in Europe, they probed Alya's apartment, revisited The University of Bern and finally checked back with the Academy of Sciences. No one had seen or heard from Alya since she'd left on vacation. Since they hadn't heard from Natasha lately, it was time to expand their search to wider resources.

Through Interpol, John easily traced the movement of Analiese Greber's passport, apparently in the possession of Alya Stevsky (a.k.a Alya Kavalov), to Paris, but no further travel was documented. She had flown into the city and disappeared without a trace. There were no hotel records, credit card purchases or restaurant receipts. She had dissolved into the fabric of one of the largest cities in the world, and finding her was going to be next to impossible without more help. Agents contacted several of their Parisian resources to no avail. There was no trace of her in the city and no hope of locating her without extensive further investigation.

In fact, Alya Kavalov had caught a ride to Amiens with a middle-aged woman that she'd met on the plane and then hitch-hiked northward to Calais, riding with a group of young college students, then with an elderly fish monger in a rusty brown pickup truck.

The old man was burly and weathered, with a cunning air about him. When she inquired of "quiet methods of transport" to England, he informed her that people routinely made the crossing under the cover of darkness on small fishing boats... for the nominal fee of three thousand francs. He was, in fact, willing to introduce her to his captain – an unsavory man who drank cheap whiskey and belted out immoral nautical ballads all the way across the English Channel.

Late that night, she was unceremoniously deposited in a small cove south of Dover and left to fend for herself. By daybreak, she had made her way to a paved road, where she waved down a local farmer who took her into the nearest coastal town. There, she caught a bus and began the final leg of her journey to London.

Chapter 59

❦

Cruising at thirty thousand feet above the Caribbean Sea, the Learjet felt like it was barely moving. Sunrise had cut a magnificent path across the horizon, splashing an astonishing array of brilliant colors and golden light on the surface of the water below. The pilot began a slow rate of descent over the Virgin Islands, continuing past Anguilla, Saint Martin, St. Barts and Saba.

Marie Garrett looked out her window at the tiny dots of land passing beneath her. They favored a dragon's tail, submerged in the emerald sea. She wondered about the people who lived there – what they looked like, how they lived, what kind of homes they had and work they did. What did they eat? Did they have schools? Attend church? Drive automobiles?

The Leeward Islands curled out in a long, arcing string beneath her. Marie settled back into her beige leather seat, far more comfortable than any in her own home. Bill brought her a glass of ginger ale and sat down across the aisle from her.

"How do you feel?" he asked.

"Like I died and went to heaven," Marie replied, gazing out her window.

"Good," Bill replied. "You deserve it. Are you hungry?"

"Oh, no," she replied. "I'm far too excited to eat. When are you going to tell me where we're going?"

"We'll be there in a few minutes and you can see for yourself, " Bill said, smiling devilishly.

The Leeward Islands were the northern islands of the Lesser Antilles, part of the West Indies. They were positioned where the Caribbean Sea met the western Atlantic, and their sandy beaches ranged from white to tan to pink, contrasted by others with charcoal gray volcanic sand.

As they descended, Marie watched intently as a pair of tropical islands appeared in the distance. One was larger and flatter on the surface, while the smaller, circular one just to the south of it was sharply defined by a single, large, dormant volcano, rising dramatically from its center. It was covered with lush, tropical foliage, and clouds hung lazily about its peak. The volcanic mountain rose from the sea like a vessel, stretching several thousand feet into the air.

In a few more minutes, they landed on its larger, sister island, where one other commercial airliner was parked at the terminal. The pilot set the Learjet down smoothly and taxied it to a private hangar, well away from the main terminal. He shut down the twin turbo-fan engines and unbuckled himself, running through all his post-flight checks.

Still looking out her window, Marie saw a smiling man with light brown skin approach their aircraft. The pilot opened the door and greeted him.

"Hello, Bobbie!" he said.

"Hello, Mr. Randy. How was your flight today?" the brown man said, as he lowered the steps and offered his hand.

"Just fine, Bobbie – smooth sailing all the way," he replied. "Is the hopper ready?"

"Yes, sir," Bobbie said proudly. "She's all fueled up and ready to go."

"Great," Randy replied. "Could you help us with a couple of bags?"

"Of course, Mr. Randy," the brown man, grinning from ear to ear.

"I'll go ahead and open the hangar," Randy said, pressing a button on the upper panel of his cockpit.

The hangar doors parted, revealing a blue and white twin-engine island-hopper airplane.

Bobbie walked over and disconnected the electric cable from a small towing vehicle inside the hangar. He drove it quietly out and backed it up to the front wheel of the island-hopper. He swung a short metal arm down and attached it to the front strut of the plane, pulling it out of the hangar and positioning it to one side of the Learjet.

Then, Bobbie walked around to the baggage compartment of the Learjet and removed Marie's bags, carrying them to the island-hopper and storing them in an external compartment located just back of the interior seats. He transferred the rest of their items and then closed and locked the compartment door.

Randy walked over to him and placed a crisp twenty dollar bill in his hand.

After the passengers disembarked from the Learjet, Bobbie disconnected the tow vehicle from the island-hopper and drove it over to the Learjet. He attached the metal arm just above its front wheel and pulled the jet into the hangar. Once inside, he pressed a button on the inner wall of the hangar and closed the doors.

"We've got ten more minutes of flying," the pilot said to Marie. "Think you can handle that?"

"We've come this far – why not?" she replied, smiling. She was starting to like the idea of flying and actually wanted to see what the twin-engine airplane would feel like, compared to the jet that had just delivered her to paradise.

They boarded the plane and waited as the pilot did his run-up and flight checks. In a few minutes, they lifted off the runway and turned south, toward the small island with the large volcano rising from its center.

As they gained altitude, Marie could see the magnificent profile of the little island against the backdrop of the turquoise Caribbean waters. Tall, royal palms along the shoreline waved in the trade winds, as if to greet them. Small fishing boats and white-canvassed sailboats drifted along the western side of the island, where calmer waters brushed against the sunlit beaches.

"It's too beautiful!" Marie cried. "What is it called, Bill?"

The island-hopper was already descending, aligning itself with a single runway on the northern tip of the island.

"Home," Bill replied. "We call it home."

Chapter 60

∼

"Analiese Greber" stepped off the bus at Holborn Station, exhausted from her arduous travels. She had called ahead two days earlier and rented a one-bedroom flat on Little Russell Street, in the heart of London's West End. The owner was abroad, and the rental company leased the flat to her for six months, with the understanding that she would be doing research at The Imperial College of London, four miles away.

A cursory glance at her Swiss passport and a deposit in British pounds met their requirements, and she settled into the small, upstairs apartment, located immediately above a quaint little photo shop. The furniture was simple, but clean, and she felt safe and comfortable as she looked out the front window at the street below. She unpacked her only suitcase and opened her shoulder bag, taking out her mother's small jewelry box and placing it on the nightstand next to her bed.

She closed the bedroom curtains, undressed and went into the bathroom. The lavatory, toilet and shower were reasonably clean, so she turned on the hot water in the shower and climbed in. Steam rose from the floor of the tub and engulfed her, and she closed her eyes and gave in to its warmth. She thought of her roommate, Analiese Greber, touring the landmarks and museums of Washington, D.C., and, for a moment, she was jealous. It was something that she'd always wanted to do herself, but there were more serious matters to attend to right now.

Her future remained tentative, and her perceived knowledge apparently made her a target of considerable importance to the Russian government. Inquiries had been made as to her whereabouts, which had immediately triggered her flight – a reflex buried deep within her childhood experience. Fleeing Russia, her mother had warned both of her daughters that they must leave the country and never return, and that, if any Russian came looking for them, they were to avoid contact at all cost.

She was aware of the fact that her father had been a scientist, and, as she grew older, she formed her own theories about the sensitive nature of his work. They lacked clarity, but she concluded that his work must have been highly important to the Russian government, based upon their violent reaction to her family's attempt to leave the country. Killing a mother and her children could certainly be perceived as an act of desperation, so Alya had to believe that she would be subjected to the same treatment, if they caught up with her.

In Switzerland, she had buried herself in her studies to escape terrible childhood memories and had earned her Ph.D. in Biological Science by the time she was twenty. Her social life was severely restricted by her dedication to academics, which her colleagues mistakenly viewed as extraordinary self-discipline. In fact, it had been her salvation, redirecting her fierce intellect to matters completely unrelated to the horrors of her mother and sister's death. Since no word of her father had ever surfaced, she assumed that he had met with a similar fate, and that the Russian government was to blame.

She shut off the water and dried herself on the only towel she had brought. Then, she put on a flannel nightshirt and stretched out on the bed. Tomorrow, she would go to the university and visit with an old friend of one of her Swiss colleagues. Perhaps he could share a small corner of his laboratory, so she could continue her research while staying in London. She had all her notes and should be able to continue her work with a few pieces of equipment and his support.

Alya rolled over and looked at her mother's small jewelry box. It contained two small necklaces and an aging black-and-white photograph of her family, taken on the front steps of their apartment building in Moscow many years ago.

She reached over to pick it up, but accidentally dropped it on the floor, sending its contents sprawling across the brown carpet. She rolled onto her stomach and leaned over the side of the bed, picking up the box and gathering its ejected items. One of the small necklaces still clung to the bottom, interior corner of the box, dangling in the air as she picked it up. She turned the box upside down and gave it a tug.

A thin, false floor gave way, popping out of the box and onto the bed beside her. Immediately behind it, a twice-folded cache of papers escaped, fluttering to the carpet and coming to rest against the edge of the nightstand. She looked down at the brown, moisture-stained, back of the note paper and paused. The box had traveled with her since childhood, but she had never known that it concealed anything. Picking up the papers, she carefully unfolded them and began to read.

The first three pages contained her father's coded laboratory notes on the design and development of an engineered virus that he referred to as "Alpha-C." The fourth and final page had suffered water damage, and the writing was completely illegible. The ink had run, damaging the text so badly that no hope remained of discerning its original meaning. She held the page up to the light and was immediately convinced that this portion of her father's work was permanently lost.

Alya drew the pages against her chest and tried to picture him working in his lab, struggling to unravel the mysteries of the microscopic world. Much had changed since that time, but even a cursory examination of his notes made it clear that her father was far ahead of his time. She would have to review this document many times to grasp some of its concepts.

Suddenly, it hit her, and she sat up in bed. This is what the Russian government had wanted. This is what they were looking for!

But, why? Why should it be so valuable to them? And why was it worth the lives of her family members? What power did it possess and for what purpose was it designed? If only she could decipher the last water-damaged page of his notes, perhaps then she could understand. But, there was no hope of recovering its content, not even under the finest microscopes of the day.

All that she could do was to recreate the readable portion of her father's work, with the hope that a logical conclusion would reveal itself. She resolved that it was both her responsibility and her duty to her family to complete the project that he had tried so desperately to preserve.

She laid back down on the bed and fell asleep with the notes in her hand. Sooner than expected, she revisited the disturbing, recurrent dreams of her youth.

Chapter 61

❦

The Swiss doctor who had brought Alya to Bern as an adolescent had left her a reasonable financial endowment in a Zurich bank when he died six years later. It was more than sufficient to live comfortably, since her tastes remained modest. Her need to be noticed by others was virtually non-existent, being contradictory to her survival. She dressed conservatively and seldom spoke to those outside of academic institutions.

This morning, she would have to make an exception, since her stomach was empty, and there was no food in the apartment. She walked to the corner café and ordered a full English breakfast, consisting of two fried eggs, two strips of bacon, a single sausage, fried bread, baked beans, mushrooms and a mug of hot, black coffee.

"When in Rome…" she thought to herself, smiling politely as the waitress placed her meal on the table.

"Thank you," she said. "Do you have strawberry jam?"

"Of course," the waitress replied.

She retrieved a small container from behind the counter and placed it on her table.

"Anything else?" the waitress asked.

"No," Alya said. "This looks fine."

She placed her napkin in her lap and ate ravenously, concerned that others would take note of her gluttonous behavior. But they were consumed by their own interests and took no note of her. Nevertheless, she remained constantly vigilant, alert to any movements nearby. The stakes were higher now, and she wanted to assure that her father's work was resurrected before anyone got to her. Time was of the essence, so she would go directly to the university after breakfast to see about a place to work. She concentrated on finishing her meal.

A few minutes later, in her peripheral vision, she noticed a young man approaching her table. She lowered her fork to her lap, gripping the handle tightly. Every muscle in her body tensed up as she prepared to react to the oncoming threat.

"Good morning, Love!" he said cheerfully with a distinctly British accent. He continued past her nonchalantly and stopped at the counter to pay his bill. The waitress handed him some change, and he exited the restaurant, walking down the sidewalk toward his employer's photo shop.

Alya exhaled softly and wondered what it would be like to have a normal life. Under different circumstances, she would have returned the young man's smile, perhaps even flirting with him briefly, hoping that he might take an interest in her. But that life belonged to someone else.

She finished her meal undisturbed, left the waitress a tip and paid her bill on the way out. She took a taxi to The Imperial College of London and asked the receptionist for directions to the department of Biological Science.

Chapter 62

༄

Dr. Len Watley stood up to greet her. In his early fifties, he was an expert in primate behavior and was known for his extensive studies on aggressive behaviors within monkey and chimpanzee groups. His mahogany desk was covered with stacks of books and papers, and the walls of his office displayed interesting primate photos and framed pictures of indigenous mammals of the jungles that he had visited.

"So, you're Alya Stevsky," he said, smiling. "I'm afraid your reputation precedes you."

"It's very nice to meet you, sir," Alya responded, unsure of whether this meant that she would be welcomed or not.

"What brings you to London?" he asked.

"I've come to stay with a sick friend," she lied. "She's single and is battling cancer."

"I'm sorry to hear that," Dr. Watley replied. "Is there anything that I can do to help?"

"Not really," Alya said. "She's receiving the best medical care available. She just needs someone to comfort and motivate her, so that's why I'm here."

"Did Charles ask you to drop by? How's he doing?" Watley asked.

"Yes, he did, and he's doing just fine. He sends his best regards," Alya responded.

"I'm glad to hear that. He was one of my finest students. We miss him here at the university."

"He's great to work with," Alya agreed. "I have benefitted from his knowledge and friendship."

"Indeed," Watley replied. "He speaks very highly of you as well – and your work. He seems to think that you're the next Pasteur or something."

Alya blushed. It was the first time that a complete stranger had complimented her work.

"Well, thank you," she replied. She hesitated, looking down at the floor and then decided the time was right.

"Dr. Watley," she began. "There *is* one thing that you might help me with."

"Of course," he replied.

"I would like to continue my work here in London. I'll be staying with my friend for six months, but I need a place to continue my research. A small corner of a lab, with a good microscope and a few pieces of standard equipment is all that I would need. Do you know of any such place that I might consider?"

"I most certainly do, my dear," he offered immediately. "You can set up here in my own lab. There's plenty of room, if you don't mind the occasional chatter of primates.

"I'm making another trip to western Africa next week, and I'll be spending at least three months in the field. As a matter of fact, you could be of great service to me, if you would consent to receiving a few lab animals that I will occasionally be shipping back. I'd like you to feed and water them each morning when you arrive. One of my grad students will take care of cleaning their cages at night, so you won't have to worry with that.

"In exchange for your time, I will see to it that you are compensated, and my secretary will be at your disposal to assist with any needs that you might have."

To Alya, it was a windfall of good fortune. Not only would she have access to a lab, but she could have complete privacy as she worked in it. Right now, that perk alone was worth any extra duties that he might ask of her.

"I can't believe it," she said to Watley. "That would be wonderful! It's so kind of you to offer. But, please – no compensation will be necessary. The use of your lab is more than enough payment for my time. And I would be happy to assist you with your project, in any way that you choose."

"Perfect," Watley said. "Then it's settled. I will inform Vivian of our agreement, and you can start on Monday. Since I'll be 'flying the friendly skies' that morning, why don't you come with me right now and I'll show you around the lab. You can ask any questions that you might have."

"Great," Alya replied.

She followed him through the back door of his office, which opened into a lab of considerable size. Her eyes immediately located an expensive, high-end microscope, along with several other pieces of equipment that she needed. A refrigerator, double sink and small freezer unit stretched along the right side of the lab.

Across the back wall, a stack of stainless-steel cages traversed the room. Currently, only three of them were occupied by young, white-collared monkeys. The rest sat empty.

"If you need to order any lab supplies, just tell Vivian," Dr. Watley instructed. "She's a wonder at getting things here quickly. I often accuse her of having connections with organized crime."

Alya laughed appropriately and said, "I won't need much. A few Petri dishes and some microscopic lab samples will do just fine."

"Nothing dangerous, I hope?" Watley said, smiling.

"Oh, no," Alya assured him. "Just the standard fare."

"What are you working on?" he inquired.

"I'm studying the trivalent oral poliovirus vaccine. We're trying to determine why, in eight-to-ten cases per year, people are infected with polio by the vaccine itself. OPV has some paradoxical effects that we need to overcome."

"Sounds like a worthwhile project to me," Dr. Watley replied. "The Imperial College of London will be proud to support your work."

"Thank you," Alya said. "You have been very generous."

"It's no problem at all," Watley replied. "The only thing that I ask is that you remember to lock the place up before you leave each day. Not all of our students can be trusted to take our work as seriously as we do."

"I promise to be careful," Alya replied. "We maintain tight security over our facilities at The University of Bern as well."

"Excellent, then," Watley said. "If there's nothing else, let's go back into my office and I'll get you a key."

"Just one other item," Alya said. "You may want to inform your secretary that I will be working in protective gear. Though the risk of infection is miniscule, I prefer to be extra careful. I wouldn't want to frighten her if she came into your office while I was suiting up."

"Don't worry," Watley replied. "She's seen it before. I wear protective gear on occasion, too, when I'm dealing with an infected animal. Nevertheless, I'll make sure that she gets the message."

"Thank you again," Alya said, as they crossed the lab together.

As they exited the room, Alya noticed a small sign above the door, containing a quote by a German writer, Bertolt Brecht. In bold manuscript, it read:

**Science knows only one commandment –
contribute to science.**

For the most part, it matched her philosophy. She did not concern herself with morality, wealth or prestige – things that were of little interest to her. Her focus remained on research that stretched the boundaries of science, and, like her father, she believed that to be sufficient justification for her actions. It was her birthright, and, through a strange twist of fate, it had reshaped her destiny.

It was time to bridge the gap between her science and that of her father's.

Chapter 63

෩

Matt descended ten feet below ground level with his newest instructor, Jack Reicher. When the elevator door opened, he found himself staring down a long hallway with doors irregularly spaced along the right-hand wall.

Occasionally, one of them would open, and a man or woman would emerge with a stack of papers in their hands or a couple of books tucked under their arms. For the most part, they were in lab coats or clinical attire. Some wore surgical scrubs.

At the far end of the hallway, one door emitted personnel wearing varying degrees of rubberized protective gear.

"Follow me," Jack said, stepping out of the elevator and into the hallway. Matt complied.

"So, what's all this?" Matt inquired.

"This is the Prep floor," Jack explained. "This is where you will live, study and gear up each day for your descent into the lower containment zones. We also have an excellent library here. It's halfway down on your right. You'll spend a lot of time there learning about the organisms that you will meet over the next few weeks.

"The objective is to teach you to identify and understand the potential impacts of the viruses that we work with here. We'll start with some of the less volatile specimens and then work our way down to the more rowdy ones by the end of this month.

"Don't cut any corners on the reading that I ask you to do, Matt. It's important. Your success here is simply a matter of concentration and memorization. You'll need to develop a focused sense of self-control. It's absolutely critical to your survival here, as well as to those around you.

"Slow your mind and your movements whenever you enter a containment zone. You'll need to measure every motion that you initiate in the levels below this floor. I'm sure that you feel that you've already mastered these skills, but I think you'll find that this environment is very different.

"At times, you'll feel like you're staring into the barrel of a loaded gun, but, with the proper mindset, you can handle it. You'll do just fine, if you focus, prepare your mind and never, under any circumstance, panic."

That last reference made Matt a little nervous.

"I'll do my best, sir," he replied.

"That's 'Jack', Matt. Just call me Jack. Otherwise, someone might get the idea that you report to me."

"O.K.," Matt replied. "I'll try to remember that. It's just that I've always had a lot of respect for people who know so much about things that I don't."

"That's why you're here, Matt. We're going to bring you up to speed – fast."

He opened the third door and motioned Matt into the room.

"Leave your stuff in here," Jack said. "This is where you'll be staying. My office is right next door."

The room was larger than his Quantico apartment, and included a number of amenities that might be found in an upscale hotel room. A full bed, a comfortable, brown leather sofa and matching recliner, two Stiffel lamps, a glass-top coffee table and Berber carpeting gave it a relaxed, but professional feel. A decent-sized kitchenette and an ample bathroom, with an enclosed, tile shower convinced Matt that he was going to enjoy his stay – as much as anyone could in a building that contained lethal organisms.

He set his duffel bag on the sofa and exited the room with Jack. Next door, they entered his office. Matt was surprised to find that it was also tastefully done in black walnut, brown carpeting, floor-to-ceiling bookshelves and a large desk that was flooded with papers.

"Sorry about the mess," Jack said. "I've got a couple of projects going right now, and my housekeeping has suffered."

"No problem," Matt replied, smiling. "At least you have everything handy."

Jack went to the shelves behind his desk and slid two books out, handing them to Matt.

"Finish these this week," he said. "As questions occur to you, jot them down on this notepad, and we'll discuss them first thing each morning here in my office. On Friday afternoon, I'll work with you on containment level protection gear and decontamination procedures."

"Will do," Matt replied, looking down at the books in his hands. The first volume dealt with the laboratory identification and classification of viruses. The second featured concise descriptions and associated photographs of human viral infections, along with current methods of treatment. Each volume was two inches thick.

Matt was intimidated, but decided to reserve judgment until he gave himself a chance to study them. Perhaps their contents were beyond his grasp – perhaps not. But he wasn't going to give up without a try. After all, his father had succumbed to a similar engineered, weaponized version of one of these organisms, so he was highly motivated to understand them.

"I have a third volume that I'd like you to skim-read this week as well," Jack added. "I'll bring it in for you tomorrow. It provides a brief history of vaccines in America – their development, application, effectiveness and short-comings. I think you'll find it interesting."

"All right," Matt said. "Anything else?"

"Yeah," Jack continued. "I'd prefer that you remain on the base for the next few weeks. Can you live with that?"

"No problem," Matt replied. "I'm used to it."

"Good," Jack said. "There's a cafeteria in the center of the complex. They serve three meals a day, and the food's not bad. I eat lunch there every day. Just show them your keycard and Uncle Sam will pick up the tab."

"Great," Matt replied, realizing that he was already hungry.

"One other item," Jack said. "Don't discuss your training with anyone outside this building. Everything we do here is highly classified, so keep it to yourself. You'll find that most of the folks that you encounter on the base will behave similarly, so it shouldn't be too difficult for you. Nevertheless, I'll need you to convince me that you understand what I'm saying before we go further. Are we clear on this, Matt?"

"Absolutely, sir – uh, Jack," Matt corrected himself.

"O.K., then. I have a couple hours of work to do before I head home for the night. Why don't you get settled in, get yourself some supper and hit the books."

"Sounds good to me," Matt replied. "Have a nice evening, Jack. And thanks for all your help."

"From what I hear, you're a very bright young man, Matt," Jack said, with a serious look on his face. "It's time to test that assertion."

Chapter 64

❧

Dinner was far better than Matt expected. Military food had been given a leg up at this facility, perhaps to dissuade all the scientists from wandering off the base in search of decent fare. Matt took full advantage of the situation, downing roast beef with horseradish sauce, red-skinned potatoes, yellow corn and a fresh, crisp salad with shredded carrots and plump, ripe tomatoes in it.

He sat by himself at a corner table and studied the uniformed officers around him. They spoke of athletic events, hobbies and family activities and steered away from conversations about their work. Beyond their frequently dangerous military assignments, they seemed to be normal, accessible human beings, with the same interests and challenges as their civilian counterparts.

Matt passed up dessert, thinking that he would do some jogging around the campus before settling in for the night. There was plenty of time, and it would make his brain more alert and receptive to input. He returned to his room, put on a gray military sweat suit and tennis shoes and went back outside.

An hour of light remained, so he made a wide circle around the middle of the complex, picking up speed as he ran. Crisp evening air filled his lungs as he fell into a familiar rhythm that the Marine Corps had taught him. It cleared his head and helped him focus on the task ahead.

By seven P.M., he was back in his room, standing in the shower, with a spray of hot water running down his lean body. He thought of Jack's challenge – particularly his comment about testing the assertion that Matt was a bright young man. He wasn't sure who had made that observation, but he assumed that it was Bill, and he wasn't about to disappoint him based on lack of effort.

He felt that he had mastered most of the physical challenges that had been presented to him. It was just a matter of applying the same discipline to the mental work that lay ahead. He would study like he had never studied before, and he would leave this place with as much knowledge as they could cram into his head in the time allotted.

If the material proved to be difficult, he would get whatever help was necessary. He would read and reread the books that Jack gave him, until the data was branded on his brain. It was likely that he would come face-to-face with most of these organisms in the laboratory, so he would definitely remember them. Having a visual reference was exactly what he needed. Photographic memorization was his forte.

He had been a good student in high school and had taken a particular interest in science, so there was no legitimate reason to back away from this challenge.

He picked up the first book, sat down in the leather recliner and began to read. At two A.M., he reached up, turned off the Stiffel lamp and climbed into bed. A faint rush of excitement stirred in him, as he realized that the material was completely digestible, and that he had a very good chance of retaining what he had learned.

Bolstered by this realization, he added to his excitement by reminding himself again that he would likely get a look at live samples of the viruses that he had just read about. Strangely, it was interesting and exciting subject matter, simultaneously terrible and wonderful in its complexity and design. How such tiny microscopic organisms could bring entire populations to their knees was amazing to him. He felt compelled to understand them, as any good soldier would want to understand his enemy in order to defeat them. A warrior code existed in this miniature world of microscopic slayers. If he could translate their language – if he could learn their strategies and tactics – then perhaps he could be instrumental in the battle to limit their spread and reduce their impacts. In so doing, he would fulfill his father's legacy and put his memory peacefully to rest.

There was a long way to go, but a slight glimmer of light dispelled his initial self-doubt, leading him forward into a deep and dreamless sleep.

Chapter 65

⌒

At four A.M., Matt awoke to the sound of footsteps running down the hallway outside his room. He climbed out of bed and went to his door, opening it slightly to see what was going on. Three men, dressed in medical garb, and a pair of military security guards carrying M16s raced to the end of the hallway.

The Army guards positioned themselves outside the elevator door that led to the containment levels below. One of them inserted a metal key into a panel on the exterior wall and turned it. It appeared that no one would be entering or exiting that elevator without their consent. The three medical staff members rushed through the right-hand door at the end of the hallway and disappeared.

Matt continued to watch as the drama unfolded, deciding to remain inside his room, since he was a newcomer to the site and didn't want to be mistaken as an intruder. Perhaps this was a drill of some sort, but the attitude and behavior of the guards was deadly serious, as if life and death matters were at hand.

In a matter of minutes, the three medical personnel exited the Prep room in full protective suits, with running air supplies. The same guard turned and re-inserted the metal key into the exterior panel, unlocking the elevator's access. Both guards took up defensive positions, with automatic rifles trained on the elevator doors as they opened. Finding it empty, the medical personnel stepped forward and entered the elevator, and the doors closed.

There had been no prior activity that Matt was aware of, so he doubted that a full-scale invasion was underway. Perhaps someone below was in trouble – a heart attack or seizure or something. But why would that require an armed response? Maybe it was standard operating procedure in the event of any emergency. Matt had no way of knowing. If so, it seemed a bit excessive. But, he was a guest here, and it wasn't his place to question how they ran their operation.

For a brief moment, he considered asking the guards what was going on. But, if they conducted their drills like Marine guards, it wasn't likely they'd tell him anything anyway. He decided to leave his door cracked and listen for any other activity.

Forty-five minutes later, he heard the soft ding of an elevator bell. Matt peered out his door again, and the guards leveled their weapons at the elevator and waited. When the metal doors opened, the same three medical personnel, minus their protective gear, pushed a stainless-steel gurney out into the hallway. A black, plastic body bag stretched the length of its surface, revealing the still, unmistakable shape of an adult human being.

An acrid smell of disinfectant pushed down the hallway ahead of them, resembling an offensive blend of bleach and formaldehyde. Matt closed his door quietly, pressing his ear to its inside surface and listening as they passed.

"Get a hold of Jack," one of the voices instructed. "He'll need to contact the family."

"Yes, sir," another voice responded. "Right away. What do you want me to tell him?"

"Tell him it's over," the voice instructed, as their footsteps trailed away.

When Matt opened his door again, they were gone. The hallway was cool, empty and silent, but the distinctive smell of untimely death lingered. He exited his room cautiously and walked to the elevator door, pressing his ear against it. No other sounds ascended from the containment floors below. The entire event had gone strangely silent.

Matt pictured Jack's phone ringing at five A.M. and wondered if he would see him later in the day. The disturbance had ended all thoughts of sleep, so he returned to his room, turned on his lamp and continued where he'd left off, studying the string-like shapes of the Marburg virus that typically killed nine out of ten of its human hosts.

Chapter 66

Jack Reicher didn't show up at all that day. Matt went down to breakfast at seven, but no one seemed to know anything about the disturbance in the middle of the night. If they did, they weren't talking about it. Matt considered asking the security guard he'd met on arrival, but he didn't want to put him in an awkward position. It was unlikely that any of the guards would be free to discuss it anyway. So, he decided to wait until Jack returned. Meanwhile, he would continue his reading.

By noon, he had finished the first book, so he went to lunch, took another walk around the center of the complex and then returned to his room and started reading the second volume. In this book, human exposure to viral agents was explored, along with various attempts at treatment. Images of people infected with smallpox, yellow fever, anthrax, the Marburg virus and Lassa fever leapt from the pages, and Matt found himself riveted by the horrific nature of their suffering. Most anti-viral medications could only alleviate some of their symptoms, but they offered no curative magic.

In the past, this left "ring vaccinations" as the primary defensive mechanism for containing the feeding viral demons. Those individuals already infected were quarantined, confined to their suffering by dedicated doctors and nurses who risked their own lives to alleviate whatever suffering they could. Simultaneously, other medical personnel fanned out beyond the edge of the outbreak and vaccinated still-healthy members of the population.

This approach formed a protective ring – a large, inoculated barrier that surrounded the interior core of infected subjects. Finding no means of exit, the viruses eventually burned themselves out at the center of the ring, going dormant after ravaging the bodies of their unprotected hosts.

Weaponized versions of these viruses were even more capable of rapid distribution, wiping out entire regional populations within days or weeks. The advent of modern air travel had changed the world forever, introducing the very real threat of cross-continent exposure within a matter of hours.

Most disturbing to Matt was the fact that global-scale pandemics could be fueled by laboratory-altered versions of these viruses, intentionally designed to resist traditional methods of treatment. Despite all of the treaties currently in place to discourage biological engineering, there was little doubt that significant steps were being taken in a number of foreign countries to advance the development of these offensive weapons. Since joining LOC, Matt had quickly learned that the Russians were at the forefront of this insane race, with the ultimate, tantalizing goal of world domination in mind. Like his father, he had been selected to interfere with their progress.

Chapter 67

❧

Bill drove Marie Garrett along the Caribbean side of the island in a white Land Rover. Tall palms lined the roadway, and lush tropical forests blanketed the massive slopes of the dormant volcano that rose into the clouds at the center of the island. The land was warm and exotic, vibrant with colorful flora and blessed by gentle breezes that cooled and refreshed. Light brown children in uniforms waved at them as they passed, happy to be headed to their modest, but well-ordered schools.

They passed Cottle Church, Cades Bay and Nelson's Spring. Pinney's Beach on their right gave way to Charlestown on their left.

Nearing the southern end of the island, Bill swung up to the left and began to climb the side of the mountain. Marie looked out across the growing expanse of ocean that stretched beneath them. The turquoise water shimmered and swayed in rhythm with the island itself.

Occasionally, they passed native women bathing in small springs or men harvesting modest crops of bananas or native spices. Small patches of sugar cane and breadfruit grew along the mountainside, and bright red, pear-shaped fruit hung from native trees. The remains of old sugar plantations appeared halfway up the slopes, their history preserved beside beautifully landscaped dwellings.

A mix of Caucasian inhabitants operated small villas that catered to wealthy internationals in search of peaceful repose, unavailable in the large cities and crowded dwellings they had escaped.

This was indeed a place to offset the weight of the modern world, which Marie supposed was why Bill had selected it for his home. She was anxious to see his place – to see how he lived in this tropical Eden. She was curious about what arrangements he had made for her visit.

She was still adjusting to the sudden change in latitude, having been escorted from the familiarity of her own home in the middle of the night and ushered into a completely foreign land just a few hours later. Even so, for reasons that she did not fully understand, she felt safe and comfortable in this place, as if she belonged here – as if it were exactly where she was meant to be.

Looking out across the Caribbean Sea, an occasional ship could be seen in the distance, plowing slowly northward, en route to distant lands. They were heavily laden with supplies, remaining far offshore in the primary shipping lanes. None of them seemed interested in the tiny island that they inhabited, choosing larger destinations that held more promise of commerce and industry.

As Bill and Marie crested the mid-altitude side of the mountain, they saw a small sign indicating the direction of "Hamilton Estate," located on the windward side of the island.

"It might interest you to know that Alexander Hamilton was born on this island around 1755. He spent most of his childhood here," Bill said.

"Really?" Marie replied, surprised that such a tiny place could hold such historical significance. "I had no idea."

"Yep," Bill continued. "He was the illegitimate son of Rachel Lavian and James Hamilton, both from West Indian trading families."

"Huh," Marie mused. "How about that!"

Bill swung the Range Rover down to the right, away from the main road, driving along the lush, southwestern slope. The view of the Caribbean opened up before them as the narrow road wound gracefully along its face. A quarter mile farther, Bill slowed the Land Rover to a crawl and motioned up ahead.

"There it is," he said.

A series of three, beautifully-constructed cottages came into view, perched along the southwestern side of the mountain, with panoramic views of the sun-washed sea below. Hypnotic trade winds drove rhythmic waves across the vast surface of the ocean and played wistfully among the palms that dotted the mountainside below.

Where the sea met the base of the island, a small, private, white-sand beach waited, secluded and empty, unaware of anything but itself. To Marie, the landscape was surreal – like no other place on earth.

"Is this where you're staying?" Marie asked, her voice revealing her child-like sense of wonder. "It's gorgeous!"

"Yes, Ma'am," Bill replied politely. "And so are you. This first cottage is yours."

"Oh, Bill!" Marie exclaimed. "That's got to be expensive! Are you sure that we can afford to stay here?"

"There's nothing to afford," Bill replied. "I built it myself, with a little help from the locals."

"What?" Marie exclaimed. "You – you mean it's yours?"

"That's not what I said," Bill answered coyly.

"But, I don't understand," Marie said softly. "If it's not yours, then whose is it?"

She looked at him and waited. A slow smile spread across his face, and suddenly it hit her.

"Oh, no! No! You can't mean that!" Marie cried.

"That's exactly what I mean," Bill replied calmly.

She brought her hands to her face, touching her cheeks. Her fingers shook lightly.

"But, but – you can't do that!" she exclaimed, completely shocked by his stunning revelation.

"It's already done," Bill replied, matter-of-factly. "You're not going to back out on me now, are you?"

Marie was completely overcome. She looked up at him, took in a deep breath and began to cry. He placed his hand on her shoulder and smiled.

"It's been a long day," he said. "Let's get you settled into your place so you can rest."

"Does Matt know?" she asked, struggling to get the words out.

"Not yet," Bill replied. "I thought I'd wait and tell him about it when he gets here."

Chapter 68

$\backsim$

"So, you heard about it?" Jack Reicher said. "Who told you?"

"No one," Matt replied. "I heard them out in the hallway at four A.M. the night-before-last. Then, I saw them wheeling someone out of the elevator about an hour later. What happened to him, Jack? Was it a heart attack or something?"

"He's been in isolation for the last week," Jack explained. "He was constantly monitored by top-rate Army doctors and nurses who ultimately couldn't do much for him. A momentary lapse of concentration is all that it took, Matt. He dropped a syringe in Level 4 that defeated all odds and landed perfectly vertical on top of his right foot. It penetrated his rubber boot and barely pricked the skin on the top of his foot. He immediately withdrew the needle and reported the incident to his superiors.

"A few hours later, his throat swelled up and his breathing became rapid and irregular. By the next day, small black pustules formed on his arms and legs, then gradually progressed to his genitals, stomach, chest, neck and face. They managed to keep him alive for a few more days, but it was a foregone conclusion. I spent yesterday with his wife and children."

"I'm sorry to hear that," Matt replied. "It must have been very difficult."

"It weren't no picnic," Jack said, conveying his frustration through the intentional use of poor grammar.

"How did they handle it?" Matt asked.

"Poorly," Jack replied. "The funeral's next Friday. I'll have to be there. I'm not looking forward to it, so let's talk about something else. How's your reading coming along?"

"I finished both of the books that you gave me last night," Matt reported.

Jack raised his eyebrows. "Any questions?" he asked, somewhat surprised at Matt's progress.

"Just a few," Matt replied. "But they can wait until later, if you've got other things to do."

"There's always other stuff to do, Matt," Jack said. "But my orders are to move you along as quickly as possible. Frankly, I'm not too comfortable with this plan. As you've already seen, haste makes *more* than waste in this business. But, my orders are clear, so I'll do my best to teach you what I can as quickly as I can. It's up to you to stay alive while I'm doing it."

"O.K.," Matt agreed. "I'll do my best."

"Let's get your questions answered first," Jack said. "Then, we'll introduce you to some lightweight protective gear. After lunch, we'll visit the first two containment levels below."

"Sounds good," Matt responded.

Things were getting real much faster than Matt had anticipated. What had just been 'ink on text' a few hours earlier was about to become virulent, living subject matter, with the potential to kill without compunction. He thought of Jack's plea for concentration, and, subconsciously, he began to practice slowing his movements. It was clear that, in this world, the smallest mistake could have dire, irreversible consequences.

Mind and body would have to work together to succeed here, and the delicate bridge between courage and panic would have to be carefully negotiated. Matt already knew that the ancient, primal fear of certain death could have devastating effects on the mind, turning relatively simple physical tasks into nightmarish challenges. So, he began to concentrate on his breathing and raising his level of awareness of everything around him. His best chance for survival was to follow Jack's instructions to the letter.

Once the question and answer session was completed, Matt followed Jack to the end of the hallway and entered the Prep room, where personnel prepared for descent into the lower levels of the building. A variety of protective over-garments hung on the walls, most with stenciled names on them. Their construction ranged from lightweight, polyurethane materials to heavier, rubberized gear with umbilical cords that attached to life support systems. Some were simple in design, while others were more advanced – completely self-contained, allowing for maximum unrestrained movement within the laboratory.

Jack opened a locker labeled "LOC" and withdrew a brand new set of light green pants, shirt, gloves and boots made of rip-stop nylon. He handed them to Matt and told him to strip down and put them on. Meanwhile, he opened his own locker and withdrew matching gear.

"There's not much to be worried about in the first two levels that we'll visit today," Jack said. "Still, you'll want to be careful that you don't underestimate our less potent residents. They won't necessarily kill you, but they can make you sick enough that you'll wish you were dead.

"When I ask you to handle virus samples, please use both hands to lower the risk of dropping them. Examine them in the same order that I give them to you. When you're finished looking at them under the microscope, I'd like you to put them back where they came from, one at a time. As we work, I'll give you a bit of information about each virus, and I'll expect you to remember what I tell you. Is that clear?"

"Yes," Matt replied.

"You'll be wearing a simple surgical mask," Jack said, "so we'll be able to talk to each other throughout today's session."

"O.K.," Matt acknowledged.

Jack reached into the top shelf of his locker, pulled down his own mask and put it on. Matt followed suit. When both of them were ready, they exited the Prep room and entered the elevator. Jack punched in a code on the numeric keypad and then selected the button labeled "BL1." The elevator began its slow descent, and, thirty seconds later, the doors opened into another world.

Chapter 69

❧

"**B**io-Safety Level 1 is pretty low-key," Jack explained to Matt.

Rows of black-surfaced lab tables, covered with beakers poised on metal stands, glass tubing, microscopes and small stainless-steel containers supported a flurry of research activity. Scientists and technicians moved quickly around the room, dressed in relaxed lab attire.

"These folks only work with clearly-defined strains of viable microorganisms that are *not* known to cause disease in healthy human beings. Standard microbiological practices are sufficient to protect them here. So, the first thing you'll notice is that no primary or secondary barriers are necessary to work with the samples in this lab. Personnel are required to make use of their sinks for thorough hand washings, but, beyond that, there's little else to worry about."

Jack guided Matt through the room, asking him to observe samples of *infectious canine hepatitis, bacillus subtilis niger* (used to model anthrax), and *naegleria gruberi.* Matt had seen pictures of *naegleria* and recognized it immediately, which did not escape Jack's notice.

"What can you tell me about it?" Jack challenged.

"Well, I remember that some strains of *naegleria* are deadly, but *naegleria gruberi* isn't."

"That's right – it's harmless," Jack said. "Can you give me an example of a *naegleria* strain that isn't?"

"*Naegleria fowleri* is the only one that I remember," Matt replied. "It can contaminate fresh water and infect human beings while they swim or bathe. I believe it enters through the nose and gets into the brain as a parasitic invader, causing amoebic meningoencephalitis. If I remember correctly, it's almost always fatal. Right?"

Jack was impressed. It was already looking like this young man was going to live up to all the hype that had preceded him.

"That's correct," he replied. "You've been paying attention."

"It's interesting material," Matt replied modestly.

"That's exactly the right response," Jack thought to *himself.*

"O.K., then," Reicher continued. "Now that you've seen some of the organisms that they work with here, let's wash our hands good and have a look at BL2."

Matt followed him to a sink near the exit. After Jack finished washing, Matt scrubbed his own hands and forearms thoroughly. He took one last look at the personnel in the room and then followed Jack out to the elevator. A minute later, they had descended to the next containment level. From the moment the elevator doors opened, Matt began to take note of significant differences in the landscape.

In BL2, disposable scrubs were worn by everyone, including masks, gloves and booties. All personnel worked with biological samples positioned under clear, Plexiglas hoods that provided a splash barrier between their infectious sample and its human handler. Jack offered further explanation.

"As you can see, more precautions are taken in BL2, where we work with a broad spectrum of moderate-risk agents. All of these specimens are associated with human diseases, with varying degrees of severity. To work with these agents, we must do what we can to reduce the possibility of splashing fluids or spreading aerosols. We want to minimize the risk of percutaneous exposure, which includes needle sticks, sharp instrument injuries and the related exposure of skin or mucous membranes to blood or other infectious biological material. Using effective microbiological techniques, we are able to avoid these types of hazards."

Matt noticed that the movements of the scientists and technicians working in BL2 were somewhat slower – more deliberate and calculated. Physical separation was emphasized, with generous spacing between each work station. The atmosphere was a bit more serious here, and conversation was held to a minimum as workers focused on their tasks.

"This gentleman is working with the *hepatitis B* virus – also known as 'the silent killer'," Jack said, as he moved among the work stations. "This one is doing research on *salmonella*, and the woman on the end of this row is comparing the neurological impacts of *toxoplasma gondii* on the brains of cats, mice and humans."

"There's a theory that it can alter behavior and emotions. Right?" Matt said.

Jack was surprised at his comment.

"It hasn't been proven," Jack said, "but some folks believe that the Soviets are doing mind control experiments with it. Frankly, I think they're barking up the wrong tree."

"Let's hope so," Matt quipped.

As a change of pace, Jack handed Matt slides to examine on his own under an impressive microscope positioned at the back of the lab. He provided Matt with brief explanations of what he was looking at and asked him questions about each of them. Time and again, Matt demonstrated his grasp of the written materials that Jack had given him. He was a quick study – a natural when it came to this type of material, and Jack made a mental note to request more in-depth, formal training for this young man once his current assignment was completed.

Then, they moved carefully through the lab, observing and discussing other specimens with various scientists who slid back from their stations and provided insights into the nature and goals of their unique research. Matt did not hesitate to ask them for more details, figuring that Reicher would override his curiosity if he went too far. But Jack gave him free rein, and the information flowed.

Matt had always been fascinated by people who chose to serve others anonymously, who needed no recognition or rewards to motivate them. They seemed content solely with the knowledge that they were helping others. It was an aspect of human behavior that intrigued him, and, in his opinion, it set those who adhered to this philosophy widely apart from all others. They gave completely of themselves, expecting absolutely nothing in return. He looked across the room full of dedicated professionals and wondered if he could do the same.

"You have to have something greater than yourself in mind," Jack said. He had been watching Matt, apparently reading his thoughts.

"I guess so," Matt replied. "You must be very proud of them."

"I am, indeed," Jack replied. He motioned toward a side room near the front of the lab. "Let's go through the basic DECON room, wash up and lose these clothes. We can exit through there and head back up to my office in a pair of clean scrubs. I have another book that I want you to read."

"Great," Matt said.

"See if you can get through it tonight," Jack added. "We've got a busy day ahead of us tomorrow."

"Will do," Matt said, as they headed through a door labeled "DECON."

By the time Matt went to dinner that evening, his head was spinning with all the information the scientists had provided. They were a dedicated and talented brain trust, serving their country silently, completely invisible to the public that they strove to protect.

Chapter 70

❧

M att was ready for Jack's questions as soon as he
arrived the next morning. The reading that
Jack had assigned him provided historical perspective
on the development of biological agents, used for
centuries with varying degrees of success. The U.S.
had not developed an offensive bio-warfare program
until 1941, in response to the growing threat of such
weapons being developed and tested by Japan.

Much of the U.S. program that spanned the next
twenty-eight years was cloaked in secrecy and was
controversial from day one. Highly effective research
had been implemented by the military, with the
majority of the work being done here at Fort Detrick,
Maryland. Production and testing of these offensive
biological weapons had taken place at Pine Bluff,
Arkansas and the Dugway Proving Ground in Utah.

During that time, very little effort was devoted
to the development of bio-defensive measures,
until the president decided to halt the design and
development of offensive biological weapons in 1972.
The International Biological Weapons Convention
sought to stop all development and retention of

such weapons, though no successful means of global verification was forthcoming.

Within the ranks of the intelligence community, it was generally felt that the Soviets were secretly continuing their efforts to develop offensive biological weapons, though no one knew the extent to which it was true. Massive stockpiles of smallpox virus had been produced and stored at various locations inside Mother Russia, in direct opposition to the Biological Weapons agreement they had signed. Their goal was to improve both its killing power and resistance to treatment through genetic engineering.

In addition to this, they continued their research on even more effective weaponized viruses, intent on reaching their elusive goal of world domination.

Meanwhile, the work at Fort Detrick, Maryland turned to the physical and medical countermeasures necessary to protect both the military and the general public from the threat of biological attacks, both naturally-occurring and man-made.

Jack had also provided Matt with a small manual on the procedures and equipment used in BL3 and BL4's containment levels. He studied it carefully and realized that several of the shots he had received weeks before coming to Fort Detrick had, in fact, been vaccines meant to protect him from several BL3 agents. Tuberculosis, encephalitis and hepatitis were one thing. But immunizations alone would not help him in the lowest containment level, where the Marburg virus, hemorrhagic fever, and a handful of unidentified monsters awaited him.

Air locks, negative-pressure air-handling systems and extreme filtration of all outflow air were also insufficient. Only filtered, positive-pressure total-body suits could protect them from the hellish demons in BL4, assuming that they adhered strictly to all decontamination procedures and didn't lose focus or panic.

Matt felt certain that he could handle it.

But Jack knew that it was like going into combat for the first time. You never really knew how a person was going to react until he came into direct contact with whomever, or whatever wanted to kill him. Then, and only then, would Jack know if Matt was cut out for this type of work.

PART III

That fate forgives the tortured soul
Belies the progress of the mole.

Chapter 71

෧

When Peter went back into Dr. Kavalov's Moscow lab, he descended into its lower chambers and immediately began to switch out the decontaminate container at the back of the locker room with the metal canister of accelerant that would incinerate the entire facility. Once the new connection was made, he returned to the monitor, reached behind it and located the switchbox used to activate the accelerant's dispersal through the overhead sprinkler system after a five-minute delay.

Ten minutes later, the phosphorus igniter in the lab would initiate the intense conflagration that would destroy all organisms within it. No evidence of their existence would remain.

He took a deep breath, placed his finger on the switch and allowed himself one last look at the monitor's screen.

The occupants lay contorted and still, but a small, sudden twitch of the forefinger on the American's right hand caught Peter's eye. He drew in a quick breath and removed his finger from the switchbox, unsure of what he had just witnessed. Had he imagined it?

He pressed his face closer to the monitor's screen and waited.

If the American had actually moved, was it merely a post-mortem reflex, or was he still alive? He strained to see if the man was breathing, but no movement of his chest or ribcage was discernable. Surely, it was not possible. No one could have survived the biological weapon that had done such horrible damage to his Russian adversary. Still, the American had no apparent open wounds on him, which could have made a difference. Peter struggled with the possibilities.

A second later, the American's forefinger twitched again. This time, Peter was sure that he saw it, and he stood upright, trying to assess the situation. He began to pace nervously around the locker room, struggling to decide what to do. If there was any chance that the man was still alive, he would have to do something. He could not allow himself to burn a man alive. No God could forgive such a sin.

He rushed to the shower wall, removing one of the two bio-safety suits still drying from earlier use. He put it on and returned to Uri's locker, opened the door and pulled out the emergency first-aid kit where he hoped to find smelling salts.

Instead, he was surprised to discover two small vials of clear fluid, alongside two sterile syringes tightly sealed in plastic wrap. In Uri's Cyrillic handwriting, the vials were marked "Anti-viral C / beta," with the warning "Untested" immediately beneath their labels. Peter removed the items, along with a small, palm-sized mirror and put them in a plastic bag.

He couldn't find smelling salts.

He switched on the power unit of the positive pressure suit and felt the air flowing around him. Then, he went to the hatch that led down into the lab and entered the combination that Uri had taught him. The hatch opened, and he descended into the hot zone, where both friends and enemies had found their final resting place... except, perhaps, for one of them.

When he reached the floor of the lab, it was eerily quiet. The only sound was the air flowing inside his bio-suit. Peter crossed the room carefully, bent down and placed the small handheld mirror at the base of James Garrett's nose. A tiny fog of oxygen formed on its surface, immediately spurring Peter to further action.

He withdrew the items from his plastic bag and unwrapped one of the syringes. He sunk the needle into the vial of clear fluid, slowly withdrew its liquid contents and injected it into James' thigh. Completely unconscious, the American did not react. His breathing was barely detectable – faint and erratic. Peter knew that he would have to move quickly, if there was to be any chance of their mutual survival.

He rolled the American onto his back, grabbed both of his hands and pulled him up to a sitting position. Then, Peter straddled his body, put his hands under his arms and lifted him to his feet, pulling him in close to support his weight. Slowly bending his knees to lower himself, Peter allowed the American to collapse over the top of his left shoulder. He lifted him up and carried him to the base of the metal stairs. Looking up at the steps in front of him, they seemed impossible to conquer. The unconscious man was limp and heavy, and it would be an epic struggle to get him up the metal stairs and out of the laboratory. Still, Peter knew that he would have to try.

One difficult step at a time, he made the arduous ascent with the American. At the top, he pinned the man against the metal stairs with his left hand and opened the hatch with his right. Ten minutes later, he had managed to push the American through the hatch above him, where he slumped lifelessly onto the locker room floor.

Peter crawled out and fell down beside him for a few minutes, his chest heaving with exhaustion. He took deep breaths and willed his body to rise again to close the hatch. Then, he dragged the American into the shower stall and poured decontaminate fluid all over him, soaking him to the bone. Next, he drenched his own bio-suit with the same fluid, covering it multiple times, using far more decontaminate than normal. After letting it soak for a few minutes, it was time to expose his own body to the invisible risks that waited outside his protective gear.

Peter shut off his bio-suit's power supply and removed his protective gear. He picked up the plastic bag, took out the second vial and syringe and injected himself with Uri's untested anti-viral fluid. Then, he removed the American's clothing and placed him in an upright, seated position, with his face away from the shower head. He reached up and turned on the water.

The American's skin was flushed and red, but his breathing had improved somewhat. Peter washed him thoroughly with soap and warm water. Then, he pulled him carefully out of the shower, dried him off and wrapped him in a warm blanket.

While the American slept, Peter gave himself the same shower treatment, dried off and then put on his street clothes. As he pulled on his shoes and overcoat, he looked down at the man on the floor, rolled up in the thick blanket like a chrysalis.

"Who are you, my friend?" he said aloud, looking down at him in disbelief. "And what has kept you alive?"

Receiving no response, Peter shook his head and walked over to the monitor. He reached behind it and flipped on the switch to activate the timer for the accelerant's distribution and ignition. He would have fifteen minutes to get the American upstairs and out the back of the building, where his rusty van was waiting to facilitate their escape. There was no time to waste. They needed to distance themselves from the area as quickly as possible.

Chapter 72

❦

The conflagration lasted well past noon, burning the entire facility to ground level and below and consuming both buildings on either side of it. The initial fire fighters arriving on scene were forced to fall back from the extreme heat and let it burn until reinforcements arrived, armed with special, military-grade flame retardants.

In the end, nothing remained of the laboratory or its deadly contents. Authorities theorized that illegally-stored chemicals had started the inferno, possibly ignited by spontaneous combustion. They contacted the aged property owner, who denied any knowledge of illegal substances stored onsite. He expressed little interest in the outcome of the fire, since he was in very poor health and had recently resolved himself to the close proximity of his own death.

Earlier that morning, before dawn, Peter and his unconscious passenger arrived at the front gate of a large, Russian Orthodox monastery in Sergiev Posad, forty-five miles northeast of Moscow. He looked up at the white archway, where he could barely make out a painting of Christ standing over the bed of a man who appeared to be dead.

It was time to separate himself from the unfortunate American, who remained unconscious, his breathing still shallow and labored. Peter knew there was nothing more that he could do for him, and that, at this point, the man would live or die by the grace of God's hand.

Peter would escape into the Urals, where he would live alone in the forest, far away from those who would soon hunt for him. There was certainly no hope of the American surviving in the cold, mountainous terrain of the Urals in his current state. It was best to leave him here, where the monks would discover him when they set about their chores after morning prayers.

Hopefully, they would take the stranger in and provide him with care and shelter in his final hours, safe from the angry world outside their walls. By daybreak, the KGB would be looking for their missing agents, and they would relentlessly pursue the blood trail of the man who had shot Poloff in the stairwell of the Kavalov's apartment building. Ultimately, the trail would lead to Peter, and, when it did, the American would have a far better chance of survival on his own, here at the monastery.

Peter laid him gently at the front gate and covered him with a second blanket. He looked down at the man with compassion.

"Sbohem a hodně štěstí," he said in his native tongue.

Having bid him farewell and good luck, he climbed back into his van and drove slowly away.

Peter traveled due east for a couple of hours. On the far horizon, he could just make out the western slope of the Ural Mountains.

In the middle of nowhere, a sudden thirst assailed him, and he searched for a place to stop for water. He raised his right arm to wipe his brow and noticed a pattern of web-like lines that originated from a small cut just below his bicep. It had already spread across the top of his forearm and hand and had moved upward, disappearing underneath his shirt sleeve. He realized that he was sweating in the cool morning air, and when he felt his forehead, it was uncharacteristically warm.

He pulled the van over and got out, looking for water to quench his growing thirst. There was none to be found, so he climbed back into his vehicle and continued a few more kilometers until he began to feel severely dizzy. The van swerved off the road and plunged into a thick stand of trees that engulfed the vehicle as it came to a final stop.

Peter was suddenly aware of a sharp, debilitating pain in his lower back that quickly spread higher, following the path of his spine. He slid the van's gear into neutral and waited. An intense headache set in, and soon he began to vomit and convulse. His legs shot out, straight and stiff, and his right foot slammed down on the accelerator permanently. The engine raced wildly, protesting the limits of its aging mechanical components.

In another minute, Peter heard himself screaming loudly as a sharp crack bent him forward, slamming his forehead against the steering wheel and tearing his skin open. Blood quickly blocked his vision, and panic set in. In the biological fury of his demise, he remembered the Russian man, curled up like an animal on the floor of Uri's lab, disfigured by the agony of his scientifically-engineered death.

Peter's hands tore at his throat as it swelled tightly shut, cutting off his airway. Starving for oxygen, his brain began to shut down. Within seconds, he was unconscious, and the blessing of death followed close behind. The overheated engine of the van burst into flames, quickly incinerating everything within a hundred feet.

Chapter 73

❧

Jack Reicher attended his former employee's funeral on Friday morning. Matt stayed behind and focused on his reading, anticipating their planned visit to BL3 and BL4 later that afternoon. He hadn't known the man who died and would have felt uncomfortable around his family. It was best to spend his time preparing for their upcoming descent into the same chambers that had claimed the dedicated scientist's life.

He had just finished the latest book that Jack had given him and was covering the equipment and procedures manual when the phone rang.

"Matt," said the voice on the other end, "this is Dan down at the security desk. There's someone here to see you – says he's from the Veteran's Administration."

"From the what?" Matt replied, confused.

"From the V.A." Dan repeated.

"Who is it?" Matt asked.

"Says his name is John Sauter," Dan replied. "Do you know him?"

Matt was embarrassed. It had been months since his trip to Alexandria, and John's sudden visit had taken him by surprise. He gathered himself and spoke calmly to the guard.

"Does he have a Hawaiian shirt on?" Matt inquired.

"As a matter of fact, he does," Dan responded, somewhat surprised by Matt's clairvoyance.

"Keep him away from your female employees," Matt said half-seriously. "I'll be down in a minute."

"O.K.," Dan replied, smiling into his handset. "I'll keep an eye on him." He turned to the man standing in front of him.

"Nice shirt," Dan commented.

"I'm retired," John replied casually.

"He's on his way down," Dan informed the visitor. "You can have a seat over there, if you'd like."

A female lab technician carded into the front door of the building. John turned around to look at her and smiled.

"I think I'll stand," he replied, keeping his eyes on her until she disappeared into the elevator.

A minute later, the same elevator door opened, and Matt walked briskly down the hallway toward John, extending his right hand and smiling.

"I'm sorry," John said with a look of amazement on his face. "I was looking for Matt Garrett. Who the hell are you?"

"I'm afraid I'll have to do, Mr. Sauter," Matt replied, grinning from ear to ear. "How have you been doing, John?"

"Apparently, not as well as you have," John said, shaking his hand vigorously. "Quite a metamorphosis!"

"We all have to grow up sometime," Matt replied modestly.

"I'm sorry to hear that," John quipped, enjoying the exchange. "But, it looks like you've made the most of it."

"Sir, yes sir!" Matt responded in the familiar tone of a Marine.

"Enough of that," John said, putting his hand on Matt's shoulder and directing him aside, just outside the range of Dan's hearing.

"We've got a serious problem, my friend," he said in a low voice. "You need to get your bag and your fiancé and come with me right now."

"What?" Matt asked, confused. "What's up? Where are we going?"

"You're headed to Miami to meet Bill. I'll drop you off at Andrews Air Force Base. There's a military flight waiting for you. Now, go get your stuff and come with me. I'll explain on the way," John promised.

"But, what about Jack Reicher?" Matt inquired. "He's expecting me to be here this afternoon."

"He's already been informed," John replied. "Just get your things and meet me in the parking lot in five minutes."

"All right," Matt replied.

He turned and moved quickly down the hallway to the elevator. His mind was racing.

Something had to be seriously wrong for LOC to pull him out of training. They had not made contact with him since he'd left Alexandria several months ago. What was happening that required such a sudden and dramatic change of plans? A sense of dread arose in him, countered only by the primitive thrill of the unknown.

Chapter 74

⚭

John stopped at the gate, showed his military ID to the guard and had Matt do the same. They were immediately cleared to enter, and John drove to a large hangar on the south side of Andrews Air Force Base. An Air Force F4 Phantom sat on the tarmac, fueled up and ready to go.

The pilot sat in the jet's forward cockpit, already geared up and running system checks. The ground crew directed them into a small mobile van, where Matt was unceremoniously installed in a pressure suit and fitted with a flight helmet. As they dressed him, they provided rapid-fire instructions and tried to give him some idea of what to expect.

"Have you ever flown before?" the crew chief asked.

"I'm afraid not," Matt replied, looking a little embarrassed by his lack of experience.

"Well, this is a helluva way to introduce you to it," the crew chief said. "Just relax and leave the driving to us."

John knew that Matt would not show his fear, even if he felt it, so he did what he could to make him feel comfortable.

"Don't worry, Matt," John said reassuringly. "This flight won't last long. You'll be in Miami in less than an hour. Tell Bill I'll be on post by the time you get there. Anything that you guys need, just call me."

"O.K.," Matt replied. "I'll tell him. Oh – and thanks for getting me here, John… I think."

"Just find her," John said bluntly as he turned to leave.

It was more like a command than a request, but Matt understood what he meant. On the way, John had explained that Natasha was missing. It was time to get down to business.

The crew members helped Matt up the ladder into the rear cockpit and buckled him in. After a few last words on ejection procedures, they withdrew. The canopies closed, and the F4 pilot taxied onto the runway. Matt's heart rate increased as the pilot spoke to the control tower. He had no idea what to expect.

"We've been cleared for take-off," the pilot said calmly to Matt through his radio headset. "Just relax."

"Why does everyone keep telling me that?" Matt thought to himself.

In the next thirty seconds, he understood. The aircraft roared to life and screamed down the runway, leaping purposefully, with strangely agile force, into the air. It claimed a wildly vertical angle, climbing into the heavens like a scalded eagle.

Its rate of ascent pressed Matt firmly back into his seat, where his stomach awaited him. For a moment, he felt certain that he would be sick, but he willed himself to control it. He closed his eyes and thought of Natasha, imagining her desperately in need of their help.

Matt felt the aircraft roll to one side as it turned southward and continued its climb. He opened his eyes and looked down at the earth as it grew smaller beneath them. White puffs of sunlit clouds slid by the canopy, passing like cotton daydreams. The blue intensity of the sky crystallized their outlines and, thankfully, began to reduce his unfounded apprehension.

Matt reasoned his way forward, taming his fear with logic. The pilot in front of him had flown thousands of man hours, and it wasn't likely that he'd be up here if he felt there was undue risk involved. He was safe, and he might as well take it all in and enjoy the ride.

The thought of seeing Bill again added focus to Matt's thoughts. He had not realized that Bill and Natasha had developed a relationship outside of their profession. No one had told him until John explained the situation on the drive to Andrews. But, now that he thought of it, they seemed well suited to each other. Apparently, Nat had made some sort of critical discovery in Russia that had led her to Switzerland, where she had disappeared without a trace shortly after a phone conversation with Bill. John said that Bill would provide all the details in Miami.

The F4 Phantom leveled off in the thin atmosphere of forty thousand feet, and Matt relaxed even more. The aircraft streaked effortlessly across the sky, with remarkably little noise or vibration inside the cockpit. At this altitude, the air outside was thin, crisp, clear and cold, but they remained comfortable inside their metal cocoon.

The color of the sky above them had deepened to a regal, azure blue, resembling the jewels of royalty. Matt looked up and scanned the spherical dome of heaven, briefly wondering what lie beyond the reach of his vision.

"How fast are we going?" he asked the pilot over his voice-activated microphone.

"Just passing Mach 1," the pilot responded coolly. "We're at cruising altitude."

For a couple of minutes, the F4 continued to increase speed. Then, while maintaining course, speed and altitude, the pilot communicated with Miami International's air traffic controllers. Fifteen minutes later, they began a slow descent to the earth below.

So much had happened to Matt in the past few months that it was difficult for him to put it all in perspective. Perhaps he would have time to do that later. Right now, his friend was waiting, and he needed his help.

Chapter 75

When they landed in Miami, Bill was waiting for him at the gate. His skin was well-tanned, making his broad smile even brighter. Matt thought that he looked stronger than ever, possibly due to the work that he was doing on his island home.

"Good to see you," Matt said, smiling and extending his hand as he approached him.

Bill pushed it aside and gave him a powerful hug.

"Good to see you, too, buddy" he said. "How was the flight?"

"Amazing," Matt replied. "What a way to travel! It took us less than an hour to get here."

"That was the idea," Bill said, stepping back. "It's been a while – let me have a look at you."

He spun Matt around and slapped him on both arms simultaneously.

"You're looking pretty fit, young man," Bill said. "It's remarkable what a few months on a Marine base can do for you."

"They treated me like an animal from day one," Matt stated proudly.

"And yet you survived," Bill observed. "As a matter of fact, it looks like you've flourished."

"There were some ups and downs," Matt conceded. "By the way, thanks for sending Ming on my birthday. We had a great time in Georgetown, until some crazy mugger tried to kill her."

"Whoa!" Bill said, looking surprised. "First of all, I didn't send Ming anywhere. The fact that she looked you up on your birthday had nothing to do with me. You must have made quite an impression on her in Alexandria."

"What?" Matt replied, confused. "But she said…"

"Hey – don't look a gift horse in the mouth," Bill advised. "She's a classy lady, with a mind of her own."

"Yeah – well, we ran into a little trouble after dinner that night," Matt said. "It's a good thing you told me to take my fiancé with me anytime I went off base. Some nutcase tried to do her in."

"I heard about that," Bill acknowledged. "The FBI in Washington got a call from a Georgetown police captain who described what happened to you, including the ID that you produced. He also sent them the assailant's prints, which didn't match anything they had at the Bureau. They contacted our boy, John, who forwarded the prints to Interpol. They immediately identified your attacker as Yakov Vasiliev, a Russian 'tourist' who had just arrived the night before. He was also KGB, until you punched his ticket."

"KGB!" Matt exclaimed. "Why on earth would the KGB want to *kill* Ming?"

"I'm sure they wouldn't have stopped with her," Bill said, indicating that Matt would have received the same treatment. "I understand that your marksmanship convinced him otherwise."

"A lucky shot," Matt replied. "I was a little groggy at the time."

"Too much sherry?" Bill mused.

"Too much Makarov," Matt replied, rubbing the back of his neck.

Bill smiled and indicated the direction that they should go.

"You have a lot of information to catch up on," Bill said. "We'll discuss it on the plane."

"Wait a minute," Matt protested. "What about Nat? Has she shown up yet?"

"Not yet," Bill replied. "We'll talk about it on the plane."

"What plane?" Matt said. "Where are we going?"

"Just come with me," Bill replied, ignoring his questions.

"Wait," Matt said, hesitating. "Do I have time to call Mom? I sent her a few letters from Quantico, but I haven't had a chance to talk to her in quite a while. I'd just like to know how she's doing."

"Trust me," Bill said, looking back at him with a Cheshire cat grin on his face. "She's doing *just fine*. We'll visit with her as soon as we get back. Right now, we need to catch a flight and find out what's going on with Nat."

Matt could see that Bill was restraining himself, hoping to convey only a professional concern for

Natasha's safety and well-being. But, Matt had known him since high school, and he knew exactly what was going on inside Bill's head. He decided to forego the phone call to his mom for now – Bill's problem was more important.

They descended to the lower level and exited through a private door, manned by plain-clothes airport security. An impressive Learjet waited just outside, the pilot already strapped into the cockpit. The white surface of the aircraft beamed in the bright Miami sunlight, as waves of heat rose from the tarmac. Bill took Matt's only bag and handed it to a member of the ground crew, who quickly stowed it in the baggage compartment.

"After you," Bill said, indicating that Matt should board first.

"Do we need a ticket?" Matt asked.

"Not on this flight," Bill replied.

Matt climbed the aircraft's stairs and entered the cabin.

"This is definitely not a military flight," he thought to himself as he looked around.

"Sit anywhere you want," Bill instructed.

There were only six passenger seats, each covered with tan, supple leather, designed for first-class comfort.

"Is this a corporate jet?" Matt asked.

"Yep," Bill replied. "It's on long-term loan to 'LOC, Incorporated' by the U.S. government. I'll introduce you to the pilot once we reach cruising altitude."

Chapter 76

❧

They landed in Zurich, Switzerland at ten P.M. Bill wanted to approach Bern using common transportation, so they took the train – yet another first for Matt. An hour later, they were standing at the front desk of the Bern hotel where Nat had stayed.

The hotel manager emerged from a side office and asked how he might help. Bill identified himself and questioned the manager about Nat's stay. According to him, she had checked in early the previous Friday morning and had gone out for most of the day, returning a couple of hours before dark.

"About nine o'clock that evening, we found one of our female staff members in a downstairs storeroom, bound and gagged. She was unconscious, and her uniform was gone. An ambulance rushed her to the hospital, where she recovered, but she had no idea what had happened. Someone had approached her from behind and placed a cloth over her mouth and nose. The next thing she knew, she woke up in the hospital.

"Later that evening, one of our security personnel noticed that the door to Ms. Ivanov's room was ajar.

He knocked, but got no response, so he entered the room to check on her. She wasn't there. There were no signs of foul play, but her absence seemed strange, particularly with the door open and her clothing, luggage and purse lying out in plain view on the bed. We alerted the local police, and an hour later someone from the American Embassy showed up. That's about all that I can tell you."

"Could we see her room?" Bill inquired.

"Of course," the manager replied, removing a key from the wall behind the front desk. "Please, come with me."

The manager took them up to the room where Nat had stayed. At the request of Interpol, the room had remained exactly as she had left it, her clothes still spread across the bottom of the bed and her suitcase still open just above them. Her purse rested on its side near the head of the bed. Bill found three hundred U.S. dollars in it, along with the rough equivalent in Swiss francs. Whatever had happened to her, burglary was not the motive.

Bill had a quick look around the room. If anything was to be found here, Interpol would have advised him. Satisfied that there was nothing more to discover, he turned to the manager and explained that he would be removing Natasha's belongings for safe keeping, and that the hotel could return the room to normal use again.

"Thank you," the manager said. "When you find Ms. Ivanov, please tell her that we would be happy to have her as a guest again. She was a pleasure to meet.

I spoke to her the morning that she arrived and gave her directions to The Swiss Academy of Science."

"Sure," Bill replied. He shot a quick glance at Matt, as if something wasn't quite right.

The manager departed as Bill and Matt began placing her clothing and purse inside the suitcase.

"What's the matter?" Matt asked as soon as the manager left the room. "Is something wrong?"

"He's lying," Bill replied.

"Who? The manager?" Matt asked.

"That's right," Bill said coldly. "Nat went directly from the airport to The Swiss Academy of Science. She checked into the hotel afterwards."

"Sounds like we need to have a little chat with him," Matt said.

"Yes," Bill replied. "But not here. The embassy dropped off a car for us in the hotel parking lot. Perhaps he would enjoy a ride."

"He'd make a wonderful tour guide," Matt agreed. "He seems to know the area quite well."

"Let's check the car and make sure there's room for him in the trunk," Bill said.

They stopped by the front desk and asked for any messages left in Bill's name. The desk clerk handed him a brown envelope that contained a set of keys and a brief note, with a license tag number and the address of a Bern residence. Outside, they found a black Mercedes with matching tags. Bill opened the trunk and removed a small bag, placing it in the back seat of the vehicle.

"What's that?" Matt inquired.

"The keys to the city," Bill replied.

He turned toward the hotel's side-entrance and began to walk. Matt followed him.

"I don't have time to negotiate with this guy," Bill said, stopping briefly on the sidewalk. "You may want to wait out here."

"I understand," Matt replied. "I'm going with you."

They moved quickly through the side entrance and into the manager's office, surprising him as he withdrew a small packet from a wall safe behind his desk. He spun around to greet them just as Matt closed the office door.

"Why, Mr. Hunter!" the manager said, startled at their sudden appearance. "What else can I do for you?"

Remembering the packet in his hands, the manager turned around and placed it back in the safe. Before he could close the door, Bill moved quickly around the desk and pressed a small handheld device, with short metal prongs, firmly against the side of his neck. The stunned manager immediately went catatonic, and his eyes rolled back in his head.

Bill withdrew the weapon, and Matt caught the man's slumping body, tossing him over his shoulder like a sack of potatoes. Bill picked up a small envelope on the manager's desk and went quickly to the door, opening it slightly and peering out into the lobby. While he timed their escape, Matt withdrew the small packet from the manager's wall safe, stuffed it in his pocket, closed its door and spun the lock. Bill turned and spoke to Matt.

"Give me a minute," he said. "As soon as I distract him, get out."

Bill slipped out the office door and walked calmly across the lobby to the front desk. The clerk looked up and asked how he might be of help.

"Would you give this message to Ms. Ivanov if she returns?" Bill requested, pushing the small envelope across the desk.

"Of course, Mr. Hunter," the clerk replied.

As he turned around to place the envelope on the message board behind him, Matt slipped silently out of the manager's office and carried him out of the lobby, exiting the building through the same side entrance they had entered. In the parking lot, he deposited the man rudely in the trunk of their Mercedes and closed the lid. Bill arrived just as he was cranking the engine, and they made their exit unnoticed.

Pulling a city map from the glove compartment, Bill searched for the street name mentioned on their note.

"Make a left on Viktoriastrasse, then right on Wyttenbachstrasse," he instructed. "At Breitenrainstrasse, you'll make another right. The safe house should be the third one on your right."

"At your service," Matt replied. "By the way, I got you a little present."

He pulled the small packet out of his pocket and handed it to Bill.

"Our trunk buddy seemed pretty fond of this," Matt said. "I thought you might want to have a look at it."

"Nice work," Bill replied, taking the packet.

He opened it and found twenty thousand dollars in Swiss francs, along with a receipt from a foreign currency exchange, revealing that the money had been converted from Russian rubles.

"Looks like our hotelier may have some knowledge of what happened to Nat," Bill said. "Perhaps we can convince him to part with it."

"No doubt," Matt concurred. "Something tells me that he'll be quick to reveal his sources. Can't imagine he'd want to withhold information. He seems intelligent enough to value his own life."

"We can't waste any time convincing him," Bill added coldly. "As soon as he comes to, he'll have to talk, or suffer the consequences."

Matt hoped that the hotelier talked fast. He'd seen that look in Bill's eyes before. Desperate to find Natasha, the thin veil of civilization had eroded in him to a wisp of porous restraint.

Chapter 77

∽

D
r. Watley's secretary, Vivian, offered to locate a protective lab suit for Alya to prevent her from having to purchase one during her brief visit at The Imperial College of London. Alya Stevsky, a.k.a. Alya Kavalov, accepted her offer graciously and thanked her twice. By nine o'clock the next morning, she was wearing full protective gear, borrowed from the university's equipment lab, and had begun work on her father's notes in Dr. Watley's exceptional laboratory.

Already, her excitement mounted as she thought of fulfilling her father's legacy and possibly bringing his work to its full potential. The world would soon recognize his genius, and the treatment of his family would become public, severely damaging the reputation of those responsible for their demise. They would be made to suffer, as she had, and their identities would be exposed on the world stage of science and national politics. She would destroy them or destroy herself trying.

Alya worked long days and nights, eating infrequently and resting only when her eyes could no longer stay open.

By the end of the second week, she began to receive a few crated laboratory monkeys from Western Africa. Unexpectedly, they were green monkeys, with golden-green fur, pale hands and feet and pale blue scrotums.

It was clear that Dr. Watley was shifting his focus from the three white-collared monkeys still in his lab to this new breed in his study of aggressive primate behaviors. Alya made a mental note of this.

She fed and watered the new residents each morning, as she had promised. Their cages were cleaned after midnight, apparently by the grad student who Dr. Watley had mentioned, although Alya never saw him. Vivian had described him as "a loner named Chad" who never slept, which made him perfectly suited to the task.

By the beginning of the third week in Dr. Watley's lab, Alya had experimented successfully with the remaining portion of her father's notes that were still legible. His concepts were complex, but she was developing an improved grasp of his work.

She had tested several viral adaptations from his notes, studying their growth in Petri dishes that remained carefully housed in a six-foot bio-safety cabinet. Her work showed promise, and her attention slowly turned to live subjects.

Since the good doctor no longer seemed interested in the three white-collared monkeys that remained in the lab, they would be perfect for her experiments. If they became ill, she would dispose of them in the basement incinerator and would tell Dr. Watley that they had died of natural causes.

She selected what appeared to be the most viable of the viral adaptations that she had created in the Petri dishes. Then, she trapped each of the three white-collared monkeys against the back of their cages with a flat-ended board, mounted at the end of a metal rod. With her other hand, she used a pole syringe to inject each of the white-collared monkeys with the most promising viral strain that she had cultivated.

Over the next three days, Alya observed their behavior, occasionally tranquilizing them to draw blood samples for study under the lab's powerful microscope. One of the monkeys, who had appeared sickly even before the injection, slowly became ill and died after hemorrhaging from his mouth and anus. Later that evening, wearing her protective suit, Alya removed the dead primate from its cage and quietly disposed of him downstairs in the basement incinerator.

The other two white-collared monkeys remained uneffected, continuing their normal diets and behaviors. The next morning, she drew fresh blood samples from them, returning to the microscope in search of an explanation. They were clearly infected with the designer virus that she had injected in them, and it was slowly spreading through their bodies. Yet, no outward symptoms of disease were evident. The death of the first primate had likely been coincidence, unrelated to the injection.

The written portion of her father's work that was still legible had only produced a lentivirus – a very slow, steady-growth virus. This one was unique only in the fact that it morphed into a variety of shapes and sizes as it spread. However, it seemed to have little impact beyond that.

How could this portion of her father's work have been significant? Why was it so important? And why was it worth her family's destruction? Obviously, the missing portion of her father's notes was critical, since she had already exhausted the parts that were readable, yielding unimpressive results.

Alya realized that, unless she could extrapolate the final components of her father's viral design, she was doomed to defeat. In the sparse, fitful hours of her sleep, she would have to come up with a solution.

Chapter 78

❧

Natasha Ivanov awoke in a cold, dark room, with concrete walls and a single wooden table, on which her bruised and battered body rested. She was positioned on her stomach, with her hands tied behind her back. A second piece of rope drew her bound ankles backward and was tied to the rope around her wrists. A soiled piece of rag was stuffed into her mouth, and the smell of petroleum and blood flooded her nasal passages.

She turned her head painfully from side to side, struggling to see who else might still be in the room, but darkness denied her any reference point. As far as she could tell, they had taken a break from their work, but she knew that they would return.

She had not given them the information they wanted, and they were growing increasingly frustrated. Physical beatings were one thing, but when they brought out the tools, life could get very interesting, very fast.

"It's a funny thing," she thought to herself, "to know that your life is coming to an end. There's so much more that I

wanted to do. But, I suppose that's what everyone thinks when they realize they're going to die."

She gathered her courage and waited for the coup de grâce.

An overhead door opened in front of her, and a shaft of light streamed down a wooden staircase against the far wall. Squinting, she could just make out the figure of a heavy-set man carrying a leather bag as he descended into the basement. He was smoking a dark cigarette. She instantly recognized its smell as Russian tobacco. She had not seen this man before – he was not among her initial persecutors. Apparently, he had been called in to extend the boundaries of her "debriefing."

He walked over to the table, grabbed a handful of her hair and raised her head just enough to see her eyes.

"Ah, I see you're awake, Ms. Ivanov," he said, addressing her in Russian. "Perhaps now you are ready to tell us who you work for and where Alya Kavalov is?"

Realizing that she could not respond with the rag in her mouth, he reached down and removed it.

"Eat shit and die," she said dryly to him in perfect English.

"You first," he replied in Russian, slapping her cruelly across the face and stuffing the filthy rag back into her mouth to soak up the fresh blood.

"I had a feeling you weren't going to cooperate," he replied coldly, "so I brought a few things to motivate you."

He opened his leather bag and withdrew a selection of sharp instruments, a couple of liquid-filled syringes and a small, hand-cranked electric generator with wire leads that terminated in shiny, metal gator clips.

"You know, Ms. Ivanov, I'm a man who truly enjoys his work," the Russian said, sneering. "You won't mind if I take my time, will you?"

Natasha knew that he was telling her the truth. She felt her body begin to shake involuntarily. She had survived three long nights of relentless questioning, light deprivation, cold, thirst and hunger. Her resistance was ebbing, and her physical and mental reserves were exhausted. There was nothing left to do but die. She would tell them nothing about LOC, and she had no idea where Alya Kavalov was at this point. Of course, the man who was about to administer her painful death had no way of knowing that. And, even if he did, it wouldn't have mattered. Telling him or not telling him would produce the same result. She had been a fool to allow herself to be taken in the first place, and now she would have to pay the price.

"Why don't we start here?" he said.

Her Russian tormentor picked up the small generator and turned the hand-crank several times. Then, he grasped the insulated handles of the gator clips, lowered them in front of her face and drew the metal ends close to each other. A ragged stream of electricity arced across the gap between them, hissing and snapping loudly. Then, he touched the metal ends together, and a spray of white-hot sparks shot into the air. Natasha instinctively closed her eyes tightly and drew her face back from the dangerous current.

"Don't worry," the sadistic Russian said cruelly. "We're not going to clip them to your eyelids. At least, not yet."

He set the clips down carefully, took Natasha by the shoulders and rolled her onto her side. Then, he tore the front of her shirt open, exposing her bra.

"A woman's body offers the perfect set of terminals," he said smiling.

He removed a scalpel from his leather bag and sliced the front of her bra in two. Then, he picked up the generator and turned the hand-crank vigorously, preparing it for maximum electrical output. Satisfied that it was fully charged, he set the generator on the table, picked up the gator clips and turned to Natasha.

"Anything you'd like to say before we proceed?" he asked, feigning interest. He had no intention of stopping now.

Natasha's eyes, wide with fear, began to shed the last of her tears. In the terror of her last moments, she thought of her mother and father and of Bill sitting on the front porch of his tropical island bungalow. And, oddly, through the fog of her tears, she imagined the face of the young man of Alexandria – Bill's best friend who was destined for Quantico – except that, in her vision, his face had matured now, morphing into that of a warrior – an angel of vengeance, approaching her failing body without the slightest indication of fear or remorse. In the confusion, she imagined that she saw the face of God.

Chapter 79

∾

The snap of electricity that assaulted Natasha's ears had actually been the crack of the Russian's spine and neck, snapping like a stubborn branch as he crumbled to the basement floor. His arms and legs shot straight outward in a decerebrate posture, indicating that severe brain damage had also occurred. He began to seize violently, his body slapping coldly against the concrete floor.

Incredibly, Matt's face came suddenly into view. He had slipped in quietly through a small ground-level window and had quickly dispatched her tormentor. He immediately removed the filthy rag from her mouth and drew her blouse closed with his left hand. With his right hand, he pulled a fighting knife from his back pocket, instantly snapping it open and severing the ropes that bound her. He rolled her onto her back and gently gathered her sobbing frame into his powerful body.

"It's O.K., Nat," he said. "It's all right. You're safe now. They won't hurt you anymore. Bill's coming. He's right behind me. He'll be here any second."

She buried her face in his chest and cried out loud.

Simultaneous to Matt's arrival, Bill had sliced three Russian men into hideous stacks of shredded flesh above them. The rapid fire of his silenced, Heckler & Koch MP5 had ripped through Natasha's persecutors like a hailstorm, while the weapon's flash suppressor kept the late-night evidence of his work to a minimum. Having eliminated multiple threats upstairs, he closed the front door behind him and raced down into the basement.

"Natasha!" he called. "Natasha! Is she all right, Matt? Is she all right?"

"She's fine, Bill. She's going to be just fine. Just some cuts and bruises," Matt said, trying to assure both of them.

In fact, she looked bad, but Matt wanted to calm her as much as possible by understating the severity of her wounds. He lifted her fragile body off the table and turned around. When Bill saw her, he dropped to his knees.

"Oh, my God," Bill said, covering his mouth. For the first time in his life, Matt saw fear in Bill's eyes.

"Let's get her to a hospital," Matt said, indicating that time was of the essence.

Bill immediately got to his feet and transferred Natasha into his arms.

"It's all right, Nat," he said, trying to convince himself of the same. "It's all right, Baby. Everything's going to be O.K. I'm here now."

She looked up at him through swollen eyes.

"What took you so long?" she said, smiling weakly.

In that brief moment, Matt glimpsed the true nature of their relationship. It had the markings of a lifetime commitment.

"I assume you've completed your business upstairs?" Matt asked, refocusing Bill on the task at hand.

"With extreme prejudice," Bill said coldly. "Lead the way."

Matt pulled out his custom Colt, in case any loose ends popped up. He went up the staircase first, with Bill carrying Natasha close behind him. Finding no further obstacles, they exited the front door and rushed Nat into the backseat of the warm Mercedes. Bill climbed into the backseat with her, wrapping her in a soft blanket. Matt pulled a small kit from the glove compartment and removed a syringe, handing it to Bill. He injected Natasha with the pain killer and tried to get her to drink some water from a plastic bottle.

As he drove, Matt dialed the car phone. Through LOC's Miami phone switch, he quickly made contact with John Sauter in D.C.

"John," Matt said, with a sense of urgency in his voice. "It's Matt. We've found Natasha. I'm driving west on Breitenrainstrasse street in Bern, Switzerland. We need to get to the nearest hospital quickly. Can you help us?"

"No problem," John said immediately, recognizing that this was a serious request. "Standby..."

In the background, Matt heard John giving sharp voice commands.

"Switzerland. Bern. Hospitals."

There was a slight delay, and then his voice came back on the line.

"You're in luck," he said. "Take a right at the next intersection. Follow that street for five blocks and then look to your left. You'll see The University of Bern's hospital rising up on that side. The emergency room entrance is on the east side of the complex."

"Thanks, John. I've got it," Matt said, accelerating the powerful Mercedes engine.

"Good luck, buddy," John replied. "I'll call the hospital to let them know you're coming. Is she breathing?"

"Yes," Matt replied. "But tell them she's been badly beaten. Lots of cuts and bruises and possible internal injuries – we're not sure yet. Tell them we've administered five milligrams of morphine."

"Got it," John said. "I'll contact the embassy as well. They'll get extra security over there."

"Let's leave the embassy folks out of it this time," Matt replied. "We need to figure out how the Russians knew she was here in the first place."

"O.K.," John said. "I'll arrange for alternative security."

"Thanks," Matt said. "We'll get back to you."

He hung up the phone and raced toward the university's medical center.

Chapter 80

❦

Two days into her hospital stay, Nat had made great progress. Most of her swelling had subsided, and her bruises and cuts looked much better.

Bill had not left her side the entire time, overdoing his protectiveness to the extent that he irritated the nurses. In private, Natasha asked for their patience, explaining that this was his way of trying to help. They yielded, but insisted that he leave the room occasionally for treatment and improved periods of rest for their patient. Gradually, the nurses convinced him that Nat was safe, and he left them to their work.

Matt dealt with the hospital's administration and communicated with two plain-clothes Special Forces squads, dispatched from a U.S. military base in Germany by order of the president. John Sauter had requested their assistance to act as security and to clean up the results of LOC's encounter with the Russians.

Once Bill was available, Matt asked him what he wanted to do next.

"According to Natasha," Bill said, "Alya's trail went cold for her, too. Let's get Nat back home, make sure that she's comfortable and spend a few days planning our next moves. Then, the two of us will return to Paris and try to pick up Alya's scent. We've already delayed the Russian's efforts to find her. It'll take them a week or two to regroup, following the loss of six of their assets."

"Six?" Matt inquired. "I only know of five."

"I'll tell you about the other one later," Bill replied.

"O.K.," Matt said, somewhat confused. "I'll talk to John and have him make the arrangements."

Bill had not mentioned the attempt on Marie Garrett's life to Matt, since any distraction could have been dangerous at the time.

"Tell him the Lear will do fine," Bill instructed. "We'll want to leave here about ten o'clock tomorrow morning. The doctors are planning to release Nat early."

"Does this mean that I'm finally going to see your place in the Caribbean?" Matt asked.

"It's not much," Bill lied, looking away. "You'll probably be disappointed."

"I'm sure it'll be great," Matt argued. "as long as you have a roof over it now."

"Be it ever so humble," Bill replied, keeping his poker hand close to his chest.

By now, the locals should have completed the tiered landscaping of his property, and a small tropical garden of fruits and vegetables should have been planted under the watchful supervision of Marie Garrett. What Matt didn't know could fill a book, and Bill had hastened Natasha's recovery by secretly plotting "the reveal" with her as she improved. They both looked forward to surprising him.

"When we get there, I'll give Mom a call and see how she's doing," Matt added.

"Sure," Bill replied casually.

By nine A.M. the next morning, they wheeled Natasha out of the hospital and into the same Mercedes that had brought her there. Two additional security cars escorted them to the airport where the shiny white Learjet was waiting. They thanked their Special Forces escort and helped Nat slowly into the aircraft, settling her into a reclining leather seat with warm blankets.

She begged them to stop fussing over her, as they kept a constant stream of delicate foods and hot or cold liquids in front of her. Eventually, she gave in to their over-zealous service and consumed some of both.

By eleven A.M., they were well on their way, and she had drifted into a deep, calm sleep – the best that she'd had in several days.

Matt and Bill selected meals of their own and settled into their seats opposite each other. When they finished eating, they checked on Natasha again and found her sound asleep. Satisfied that she would rest easy for a while, they reclined their seats and got some well-deserved rest of their own.

Seven hours later, Matt awoke to the smell of coffee. Bill was standing over him with a cup in his hand, talking softly with Natasha, who was sitting up drinking the same brew.

"So, how are you feeling, Nat?" Matt asked, looking back at her and stretching as he sat up in his chair.

"Much better, thank you," she replied, smiling. She looked fantastic compared to her previous state, and Matt couldn't help but notice that her green eyes glowed with anticipation, as if she knew something that he did not.

"What have you two been talking about?" Matt asked, sensing that he had missed something important.

"Oh, nothing," she replied. "We're just excited about getting back home for a while."

"So what's the name of this little island of yours?" Matt asked, addressing Bill.

"Nevis," Bill replied. "Ever heard of it?"

"Nope," Matt answered honestly. "What made you pick it?"

"See for yourself," Bill said, pointing out Matt's window.

They were just beginning their long descent toward the island of St. Kitts, where the Learjet was normally hangared. Below them, the long arc of the Leeward Islands stretched out, waves of amber, gold and green lights dancing across the turquoise surface of the Caribbean Sea. The horizon was still drenched in good light, but the promise of a splendid sunset waited patiently at the razor edge of the earth's rim.

Just beyond St. Kitts, the tip of Nevis Peak peered through a brilliant white halo of clouds, taking on the appearance of a French pastry from above.

As they descended toward the airport on St. Kitts, Nevis' thirty-two hundred foot mountain loomed just to the south of them, a stereotypical sentinel of tropical paradise. It was a tiny refuge of lush greenery, rising above a vast stretch of blue-green ocean.

"Incredible," Matt said, stunned by the natural beauty of Nevis. "It's like something out of a travel magazine."

"It is," Natasha agreed.

"How did you *find* this place?" Matt asked Bill.

"Got lost," Bill replied, "and decided to stay."

Matt studied the landscape and understood why.

"You're a lucky man," he said to Bill.

"So are you," Bill replied, an odd inflection in his voice.

Chapter 81

❦

At the age of forty-five, Don Hanson had been a highly-paid Soviet mole at the American Embassy in Moscow for more than eighteen years. As a communications specialist, he had unique access to information passing between the U.S. and their American Embassy employees in Moscow.

He had been a young informant at the time of the arrival of the tape from Uri Kavalov's lab, which had explained the bizarre nature of his comrades' deaths at the hand of a fellow agent, an American spy and a deadly virus. He shared that information with his Soviet contacts.

It was thought that the secrets of Dr. Kavalov's incredible biological weapon had perished with him, until they got wind of the possibility of Alya Kavalov's amazing survival. This information had rekindled their interest in the details of her father's work, since no equally formidable weapon had been forthcoming from their remaining stable of Soviet scientists.

Agents were immediately dispatched to find Alya, extracting information along the way from anyone who might know of her whereabouts. It was a long shot that she would possess such sophisticated knowledge, but, once they discovered that she was a virologist by profession, their interest peaked sharply. The use of deadly force was authorized to achieve their goals, and six of their best agents were dispatched to complete the mission.

Don Hanson remained at the American Embassy, tracking any similar efforts by Washington to locate Uri's daughter. Initially, there had been little interest on the part of the Americans, but Natasha Ivanov's visit drew Don's attention. She had shown up under a false name with embassy credentials and had been issued an automobile.

Don immediately alerted the KGB, recommending that they keep close tabs on all of her movements. He emphasized the need to maintain a safe distance, in hopes that she might ultimately lead them to important information. Their agents spent a sleepless night in the woods outside her mother's cottage and shadowed Natasha as she probed along the Russian border.

Eventually, they followed her into Latvia, where she met with an elderly schoolmaster, previously unknown to the KGB.

After her departure, they, too, had visited with the old man and his dog. He had been reluctant to let them in, suspicious about why two men would come asking about his conversation with the gentle woman who had just left. They did what they could to convince him of the harmless nature of their visit, but he grew increasingly agitated and uncooperative. Finally, he asked them bluntly to leave.

One of the agents, whose patience had worn thin, forced his way into the cottage, grabbed the schoolmaster by the throat and pushed him savagely back into his chair. With terror in his eyes, the old man turned to his dog and shouted.

"Nahpahst' nah neekh!" he commanded in a loud, angry voice.

The Russian wolfhound leapt to its feet with surprising agility and lunged at his master's attacker, burying his sharp teeth deep into the agent's thigh. The KGB thug cried out in agony, but before his scream was completed, his partner pulled out a silenced nine-millimeter handgun and shot the animal twice through the chest.

"No!" the schoolmaster cried out.

As the great hound collapsed to the floor, he placed another round through the dog's head for good measure.

The two agents jerked the old man out of his chair and slammed him onto the kitchen table on his back, binding him to it with bailing wire. When he refused to answer their questions, they injected him with a powerful truth serum, at which point he could no longer resist their questions.

Once they had extracted all of the same information that Natasha had acquired, they lifted the heavy carcass of the wolfhound and placed it across his face, perpendicular to the old man's body, forming the shape of a letter "T". The schoolmaster struggled for a minute or two and then went limp, having suffocated under the weight of his best friend.

The man's housekeeper found them the next morning, and the people of the small village buried them side-by-side in the cold soil of their ancient cemetery.

Things were looking up for the KGB, until a series of debacles on U.S. and Swiss soil cut off their efforts at the knees. Within a matter of two short weeks, all six of their highly-trained agents had disappeared and were presumed dead. To make matters worse, the Soviets had absolutely no idea who had terminated them.

CIA agents in Eastern Europe and Russia were carefully tracked by the Soviet government, but none of them appeared to be involved. Natasha Ivanov was an interpreter for the FBI, but seemed to have few skills beyond that which qualified her for this type of work. To them, she was just another pretty face, with no remaining associates inside the Soviet Union, aside from a few embassy employees and her own aging mother.

Perhaps another country had gotten wind of the prize – someone in search of power – someone interested in bringing the world to its knees. Who else would seek such knowledge? Virtually any government with a grudge stood to benefit from acquiring a biological weapon of this magnitude. Even private interests could have taken up the hunt, using mercenaries to execute their plans.

It was time the Russian government found out who had killed their agents. More importantly, they needed to renew their efforts to find Alya before anyone else did.

Only then could they determine if she sheltered the information that could boost their ascent to the coveted peak of world domination.

Chapter 82

୶

One hundred and fifty miles north of Nevis, on the western edge of Anegada, a rusty, tin-roofed shack stood at the end of a stagnant salt pond, its faded yellow clapboard sides baking in the tropical sun. Its sole inhabitant, Damas Kingston rose slowly from the torpor of his midday nap and went outside to check his previous night's work. He had buried his father at the warm, muddy edge of the salt pond after slicing his throat with a bolo knife and relieving him of the few coins that remained in his pockets.

Satisfied that his labors left no tell-tale signs, he gathered up a few sweet potatoes and bananas, placing them in a cloth sack. Then, he went out back to the unpainted shed that he had lived in for the last five years, amidst the stench and squalor of chicken droppings and the sparse remains of small pigs that he managed to steal and eat.

Damas had been large enough to claim his impoverished mother's life during childbirth, and his father had abused him every day thereafter. He had barely survived his childhood, scorned by others due to his large size and strangely misshapen head, the top of which contained an unseemly depression. This gave unusual rise to the sides of his cranium, so that he appeared to wear a bowl on his head, out of which grew a thick, shock of black, unruly hair.

Denied all knowledge of the basic tenets of hygiene, his body developed a permanent stench in the island's sub-tropical heat, and, as he grew older and larger, he was completely shunned by his peers. He had no schooling, and his life served no purpose beyond that of a nuisance. His father moved him into the backyard shed, declaring that he looked and smelled like the animals that found shelter there.

Now almost twenty years old, he had grown much larger than expected, filling his stomach with fish and dark turtle meat to supplement his diet of small mammals that he took from the properties of local inhabitants. Domestic animals frequently went missing, including cats and dogs.

The year before, a young girl had disappeared from the small island during a fierce tropical storm that had flooded its low-lying land. The family had assumed that she was swept away, drowned in the fury of an angry sea. In truth, Damas had claimed her, first toying with her through the night and then turning her into a gluttonous meal at daybreak to prevent her from revealing his unspeakable sins. He tossed her bones into the salt pond, where they were picked clean by voracious red crabs and quickly dissolved into the concentrated saline solution.

The time had come to leave the island, before his father's disappearance raised new questions that would soon draw the police to his property. He would take his father's boat, sailing southeastward in the wooden skiff, using its outboard motor only when necessary to conserve the remaining fuel in its tank. He would gather food from the sea and would refresh his other supplies at each island that he encountered.

Damas was certain that he was stronger than any man alive and that he could crush anyone who got in his way. Confident that the world would yield to him, he gathered his cloth sack, his casting net, several jugs of water and his freshly-sharpened bolo knife and loaded them into the skiff. He set sail at dawn, never once looking back at the small island so profoundly blessed by his departure.

By noon the next day, he anchored his small boat off the eastern shore of Moskito Island and went ashore in search of red meat and water. Finding little, he returned to his boat and sailed across a narrow strip of water to the northern tip of Virgin Gorda. He skirted along the northeastern shoreline looking for a place to anchor his boat and swim ashore. He chose a spot near a deserted strip of beach and went ashore, his bolo knife tucked under the side of his belt. Under a line of low palms, he found a small fishing boat, with nets drying across its bow. Beneath them lay a small, rusting tank of gas, half full. He would collect this on his way back to the boat and float it out to the skiff.

Farther inland, he came across a dirt road that led away from a small village of native residents. He followed it for a while and came to an aging wooden house, barely big enough to live in. An old woman sat on the front porch, chewing sugar cane and talking to a healthy mixed-breed dog that barked at Damas as he approached. Realizing that the odd-looking man was a stranger, the old woman stood up and turned around to enter the house.

"You have water?" Damas called to her from the edge of the road.

She turned momentarily and looked at him, then continued into the house, ignoring his inquiry. Damas drew his bolo and approached the front porch. When the angry dog attacked, he sliced its head cleanly off and forced his way through the front door. The old woman backed away, a look of terror rising in her eyes.

"You are de devil!" the terrified old woman cried out.

Her voice fell on deaf ears as Damas stepped forward and opened her stomach wide with the bolo knife, spilling her entrails onto the floor. A stunned look on her face, she collapsed in a heap of blood and bile.

Moving quickly, Damas stuffed what little food he could find in the house into his shirt and exited. On the way out, he bent down and picked up the dog's torso, slinging it over his shoulder like a bag of potatoes. He returned to the beach, entered the water and swam out to the skiff, pushing the gas tank in front of him, with the dog's bloody body trailing behind him. Before any sharks could arrive, he was out of the water and setting sail. Soon, he was out of sight, continuing southward, following the shoreline of Virgin Gorda from a safe distance.

That night, he put ashore on a deserted stretch of sand below Spanish Town and cooked the dog over a stack of burning driftwood. The meat was delicious, and he felt his strength returning after two long days at sea. He went to sleep under a hammock of palm trees and awoke at daybreak to the sound of people approaching. He quickly gathered his things and returned to the skiff, weighing anchor and moving away before anyone took note of him. He set a course for Saba, where he would take on more supplies.

By the next day, he was running dangerously low on water. The last of his plastic jugs was near empty, and the midday sun was already starting to dehydrate his large body. Sensing this, Damas cranked the outboard motor and pushed the small boat through the water, hoping to make landfall that evening.

By six P.M., the island came into view, and, by seven, he put ashore at Torrens Bay. He tied the handles of his plastic bottles together and hiked up into a lush mountain forest, where he found a small waterfall, with two local children playing at its base. When they saw him, they ran away, squealing like frightened little monkeys. He claimed the space they had deserted and gathered huge gulps of cool, clear water. When he finished drinking, he filled his plastic jugs and secured their lids. Then, he paused briefly to rest before beginning his descent.

A soft breeze blew across the forest floor, picking up small leaves that flipped over and settled a few feet away from where they had started. In the brief lull that followed, the sound of heavy footsteps could be heard as a man's shape appeared out of nowhere.

The children had alerted their father to the presence of a stranger, and as he approached, Damas rose to his feet and glared at him.

"Hullo," the Saba man said, lifting his hand. He was broad-shouldered and stocky, with a look of power and self-confidence. His obvious lack of fear told Damas that he needed to act quickly to gain the advantage. He must not allow this man to prepare for battle.

In a flash, Damas drew his bolo knife menacingly. This sudden, unanticipated response to his arrival took the man by surprise, and he instinctively crouched down and began to swing his body from side to side, sizing up his ugly opponent. The long blade of the trespasser's knife left no doubt in his mind that he was facing a dangerous man. The stranger's incredible size and filthy appearance had also frightened the unarmed father of two.

Recognizing this, Damas relaxed somewhat and managed a sadistic smile. Then, he suddenly lunged at the man, bringing his sharp bolo knife down hard, burying its blade deep into the Saba man's right shoulder. The broad-shouldered father issued a blood-curdling scream and stumbled back against the roots of an ancient forest tree. Damas bent down and withdrew the blade from his shoulder. After a brief pause, he raised it above his head again.

The cowering father held up his opposite arm, desperately trying to shield himself, but the trespasser completely severed it with a swift, downward stroke. It separated from his body, settling into the lush green grass beside him, staining it crimson red.

For a few moments, the poor man screamed even louder, until he finally passed out.

Damas left him there to bleed to death while he raced down the mountain carrying his plastic bottles full of critical, life-sustaining water. He loaded them into the boat and put to sea quickly, heading southeastward toward St. Eustatius.

He had already decided to bypass that island, due to its proximity to Saba and the events that had just occurred there. He needed desperately to put more miles between his deeds and his person.

Just beyond St. Eustatius lay the sister islands of St. Kitts and Nevis.

Chapter 83

On Thursday morning, Alya Kavalov awoke to the familiar symptoms of her annual sinus infection, accompanied by its usual intense, dry sinus headache. She went into the bathroom and draped a hot wash cloth across the bridge of her nose, hoping to relieve some of the pain caused by clogged sinus passages. She looked at her face in the mirror and groaned. Her hair was askew and her eyes were red, irritated by the shortage of moisture associated with the affliction.

Her misery was compounded by knowledge of the fact that she had been at an impasse with her lab work at the University for several days, making little progress toward her goal of completing her father's work. The two white-collared monkeys that she had injected continued to show no ill effects from the lentivirus that she had designed, going about their daily business of eating, playing and non-stop chattering.

Alya was weary from lack of rest, and now she was sick. To make matters worse, it was raining and cold outside, and the thought of trudging into the university through foul weather was more than she could bear. She picked up the phone and called Dr. Watley's secretary.

"Dr. Watley's office," said the healthy voice on the other end of the line.

"Vivian, this is Alya Stevsky," she said, using her surname known to those in the academic world. "I'm afraid that I won't be in today. I'm a little under the weather."

"Oh, dear. Sorry to hear that, Love," Vivian replied. "You don't sound too good. Do you have a cold?"

"A sinus infection, I think," Alya responded. "I seem to get them at least once a year."

"That's too bad," Vivian sympathized. "Can I do anything to help?"

"No, no," Alya replied. "I stopped by the infirmary after work last night and a kind doctor wrote me a prescription for some medicine. I dropped it off at a pharmacy down the street last night. They should deliver it this morning. I just wanted you to know that, based on how this usually goes, I probably won't see you until Monday."

"Put some tea on the hob," Vivian said, "and don't worry about your work, Love. Just concentrate on getting better."

"Thanks," Alya replied. "Hopefully, I'll see you soon."

She hung up the phone, went back into the bathroom and found a bottle of aspirin. She took two of them, went into the kitchen and made herself a cup of hot tea with honey.

Within an hour, a young man delivered her medicine to the flat. She went to the door in her bath robe, paid him and downed the prescribed dosages immediately. Then, she returned to her bedroom and snuggled back into the comforting warmth of her bed.

She stared at the ceiling for a while and finally fell asleep as the medications began to take effect.

Two hours later, she awoke feeling a little better, went into the kitchen and fixed herself a bowl of hot lentil soup. She sat down and ate it with crackers, regaining some of her strength. Then, she moved into the living room and looked over some of her notes.

Within an hour, her sinus headache had returned. She retrieved two aspirin and downed them with a second cup of hot tea.

Rain continued throughout the night and halfway into the next day. As expected, her condition deteriorated somewhat. She continued to take the prescribed medications and slept more than usual.

Friday and Saturday were the worst days, but by Saturday night, her body had begun to recover with the help of the antibiotics and decongestants that the doctor had provided. Her head stopped hurting, and her nasal passages finally opened.

By Sunday morning, her eyes were clear and bright again, and, later that day, she ventured down to the little restaurant on her block and had a pleasant lunch.

She got a good night's sleep on Sunday and returned to the Imperial College of London on Monday morning, feeling refreshed and healthy.

"Well, hello there, stranger!" Vivian said cheerfully, greeting her as she came through the office door. "Welcome back. How do you feel?"

"Much better," Alya replied. "How are you today?"

"Well, I'm fine," Vivian declared. "And I'm really glad to see you looking so well."

"Thanks," Alya responded. "I think I slept through the whole weekend."

"Well, it looks like it did you a world of good," Vivian observed. "Maybe you should get sick more often."

"Ha!" Alya chuckled. "That might not be a bad idea. Right now, though, I've got a lot of work waiting on me."

"Well, just don't overdo it, dear," Vivian instructed. "And let me know if you need anything."

"Thanks," Alya replied, smiling. "I certainly will."

She walked through Dr. Watley's office and into the lab. The busy chatter of the growing population of green monkeys met her ears immediately.

She walked across the room and placed her coat and bag on top of a table positioned along the far wall. Then, she pulled up a chair and sat down.

As she unpacked her lab notes and organized her equipment, she began to sense that something had changed. It gnawed at her subconscious as she continued her preparations, until, eventually, it surfaced. Something was not right. Something was missing.

She slid her chair back and stood up, listening to the normal sounds of the lab.

Suddenly, it hit her. The familiar chorus of primate chatter did not include that of the white-collared monkeys that she had injected. They produced a distinctly different sound, which was noticeably absent from the lab. She whirled around and looked at the cages positioned along the back wall of the room.

Two of them were missing. Her test animals were gone.

At once, the thought that the white-collared monkeys had died flew through her head. Perhaps the grad student had removed them to the basement incinerator to dispose of their bodies. She stood up and exited the lab immediately, racing downstairs to prove her theory.

Sure enough, when she opened the basement door, the two cages sat empty, stacked on top of each other near the back wall.

She made a mental note to speak to Chad later that night and have him bring the cages back up to the lab to house more green monkeys as they arrived from West Africa.

Growing excitement arose in her as she realized that the death of the white-collared monkeys probably indicated that she was closer to realizing her father's dream than originally thought. Perhaps more intense testing could yield the results that would finally reveal his genius to the world.

She was beginning to understand the poetry of her father's scientific designs, and she felt fiercely proud to be his daughter. All that was left was to expand his work to its logical conclusion.

Alya returned to her testing with renewed zeal, working well into the night. As soon as she could develop the next carefully-altered, viable strain of the virus, she would select two of the green monkeys to serve as replacement subjects. Since they belonged to an entirely different species, the test results could vary considerably. But, based upon the fairly rapid deaths of the white-collared monkeys, she was cautiously optimistic that the green monkeys would be similarly affected, demonstrating a broader range of impact on different species.

Just before midnight, she fell hard asleep at the table, her head resting on top of two well-worn lab books.

Chad, the loner, arrived at one A.M., cleaned all the cages and departed without disturbing her.

Chapter 84

∾

A warm, tropical breeze met his skin as Matt stepped out of the Learjet's air-conditioned interior onto the tarmac at St. Kitts.

"Could you give me a hand, sailor?" Nat said as she slowly exited the door of the Learjet behind him.

"Oh – sorry – sure," Matt replied, turning around and taking her hand to steady her descent down the small set of steps.

Bill exited the aircraft last, carrying her blanket and medical supplies.

"I doubt you'll need this, but we'll take it with us anyway," he said to Natasha, referring to the blanket draped over his left arm. He waved at a brown-skinned ground crew member, who returned his greeting and began to unload their bags.

"Wait here with Nat and I'll get us some transportation," Bill said to Matt.

He disappeared briefly into the terminal, leaving them to survey their surroundings. Once inside, he placed a quick phone call to Marie to let her know that they had arrived on St. Kitts and would be home in about thirty minutes.

"I'm so excited!" Marie said. "I get to hug my son again and meet your girlfriend for the first time, all on the same day. I have a little surprise for you, too."

"What's that?" Bill asked.

"Come see for yourself," Marie replied. "I think you'll like it."

Two minutes after Bill went into the terminal, the Learjet pilot pressed a button inside the Learjet's cockpit and the doors of the hangar in front of them opened. The blue and white island hopper was rolled out by the ground crew, and the Learjet took its place inside the hangar.

Randy, their pilot, helped the two of them get seated in the twin-engine island hopper as Bill returned to join them. In a few minutes, the pilot had completed his run-up and was taxiing down the runway. As soon as they took off, Nevis rose up to greet them across a short expanse of blue-green Caribbean water. Ten minutes later, they set down on the small runway at the northern end of the breath-taking island that was their final destination.

When Matt stepped out of the airplane, the exotic smells of Nevis' bountiful landscape drifted across the short runway. He looked up at the magnificent slopes of Nevis Peak.

"It's even more impressive from the ground," he thought *to himself.*

"Home, sweet home!" Natasha said, as Bill helped her out of the plane. "What do you think, Matt?"

"I think I died and went to heaven," Matt replied, scanning the gorgeous terrain and smiling.

"I know exactly what you mean," Nat said. "The first time I saw this place, I cried. It's just so beautiful!"

"It certainly got more than its fair share," Matt agreed.

A white Land Rover pulled up beside them and a light-brown-skinned man walked over to Bill and gave him the keys.

"Nice to have you back, Mr. Hunter," the man said. "How was your trip?"

"It was fine, Bobbie. How's everything here?"

"Warm and wonderful," Bobbie replied. "Let me help you with your bags."

Natasha insisted that Bill let her ride in the backseat of the Land Rover to provide Matt with an unobstructed view during his introduction to the island. Bill helped her get settled, and they departed the small runway in the Land Rover, heading due south.

Riding along the western shoreline, insanely gorgeous beaches stretched along their right-hand side, with the heavily-foliaged mountain slope rising majestically on their left.

Native Nevisians walked along the main road, balancing open baskets of fruits and vegetables on their heads with one hand, while throwing up the other to wave as the Land Rover passed. Their pace was in sync with the island itself, slow and graceful – a smooth, artful motion that ignored the passing of time. Matt marveled at their effortless strength, feeling that there was something to be learned from these people that he could not yet grasp.

A couple miles farther, Bill swung the Land Rover to the left and began to climb the side of the mountain. Small patches of crops clung to the slopes, bathed in brilliant tropical light. Occasionally, they passed simple dwellings of wood or stone, with small children playing in the yard, monitored by older siblings or grandparents. Higher up, a few small villas appeared, intermixed with the aging stone ruins of sugar cane mills or the remains of long-abandoned Colonial estates.

As they crested the mountainside, Bill turned back and away from the main road, guiding the vehicle upward along the southwestern slope. The narrow road, perched above a fantastic view of the Caribbean Sea, curved gracefully along the mountain's side. A quarter mile farther, the road leveled off, and Bill slowed the vehicle to a stop.

Up ahead, a line of three recently-constructed wooden cottages, with inviting front porches and galvanized tin roofs, came into view, separated by a hundred feet or so of lush native growth. From their front porches, the vast wealth of the Caribbean Sea could be seen. Stretching far to the south, the view offered endless solace to the soul of weary travelers.

Even Bill was surprised at the progress of the three new tiers of land that had been recently shaped and cultivated just below the cottages. An impressive array of fruit trees and vegetables had been freshly planted, and half a dozen native workers busied themselves watering the new crops.

"This is it," Nat said excitedly. "Bill, let's walk from here."

Matt was unsure of her meaning and turned to Bill for an explanation.

"We're staying in one of these?" he asked.

"Not exactly," Bill replied, smiling.

He stepped out of the driver's side and walked around to help Natasha. Matt opened his door and stood up, looking all around for any other dwellings that might be hidden among the tropical foliage.

"So... if we're not staying in one of these, then where are we staying?" he asked Bill.

Before Bill could answer, a woman appeared on the road, wearing a broad-brimmed straw hat, blue Capri pants and a white blouse. Her skin was well-tanned, but Matt could tell that she was Caucasian. As the woman approached, she quickened her pace, until, fifty feet away, she began to run. At first, Matt had not recognized her, but, as she drew closer, he realized that he knew her face. Her cheeks were wet with tears, and her arms stretched wide apart as she neared him.

"Mom?" he said, incredulously.

Before he could get anything else out, she was upon him, wrapping herself around him in a full hug, crying.

"Where in the world did you come from?" Matt said, choking back his own emotion. He could tell that she was strong and healthy and that she seemed, miraculously, to have retrieved some of her youth.

"How in the world did you get here?" he said to her.

"In a jet!" she cried. "Can you believe it?"

"I brought her down a few weeks ago," Bill explained. "I didn't think you'd mind."

Natasha wrapped her arms around Bill's waist and hugged him.

Finally, Marie Garrett drew back from her embrace and turned to Nat.

"Oh, my," she said. "I've been so rude. You must be Natasha."

Nat stepped forward and offered her hand.

"It's so nice to meet you at last, Mrs. Garrett," Natasha replied.

Marie could see that she had been injured. She noted the cuts and bruises on her face and arms, as well as the protective nature of Bill's care for her. As a mother, she instinctively ignored Nat's outstretched hand, stepped forward and gave her a gentle hug instead. Then, she turned back to Matt.

"Well, now, young man," she said, wiping the tears away from her cheeks. "Let's have a look at you."

She took him by his forearms and spun him around, studying him from top to bottom. To Marie, Matt had changed in almost every way possible.

He was handsome and had developed an impressive physique, not unlike his father's at the time they had met. It was obvious that Matt's military training had served him well, forging him into a man to be reckoned with.

Marie knew that his strength was backed by purpose, and she could not help but be proud of the vocation that he had chosen. Dangerous as it was, it seemed to be exactly what he was meant to do, and, for that reason alone, she accepted it.

"You look great, Matt," she said softly. "You should be very proud of yourself." She hugged him again for emphasis.

"Well, I'm not so sure you'd say that if you knew some of the things that I've done," Matt replied.

"Do you mean like saving my life?" Natasha submitted in a serious tone.

"Bill did most of the work," Matt replied, deflecting her praise.

"Yeah, I guess we can give him a little credit, too," Natasha teased, looking up at Bill and smiling.

"You don't need to explain anything to me about your work, Matt," his mom said. "Just do what's right – that's all I need to know."

Bill interrupted.

"It looks like you've been a little busy while I was gone," he said to Marie, pointing down at the terraces of freshly-planted crops.

"I've managed to make some new friends," Marie replied. "I've been entertaining their children after school until they get home from work. In exchange, they've been teaching me how to plant tropical foods. If it's O.K. with you, I'd like them all to share in the harvest."

"Sure," Bill said. "Looks like there's going to be plenty to go around. Natasha's going to be here for a while, so, once she heals up, you might even get her to help you."

"Oh, I'd love to!" Nat agreed. "Would you teach me, Marie?"

"Why, of course I will," Marie replied enthusiastically. "But, first, let's get you well. You'll stay at my place. I've got plenty of room."

Nat looked up at Bill as if to get his permission.

"That's fine with me," Bill said, grinning at her. "Maybe now I can get a little rest."

Natasha jabbed him playfully in the ribs.

"Good, then" Marie said. "That's settled."

She took Natasha by the arm and started up the road toward the first cottage.

"Come on, Matt," Bill said. "I'll show you where you're staying."

Marie put her arm around Nat's waist to support her as they climbed the front porch steps and disappeared inside her cottage. Bill and Matt continued to the next cottage – the middle of the three structures.

"Here we go," Bill said. "You'll find everything you need inside, including cold beer. Come on over to my place when you've changed, and we'll have one together."

"I don't get it," Matt said, a little confused. "How can we afford to rent all three of these places? They look pretty expensive. Is Uncle Sam paying for this? How long are we staying here?"

"That's up to you," Bill replied, casually continuing down the road alone in the direction of the last cottage.

Matt shook his head, turned to his left and looked out across the vast, blue-green ocean. It was a timeless seascape that had the ability to quickly put things into perspective. He took a deep breath and surveyed the beautiful expanse.

On the neatly terraced land just below him, a brown-skinned man in a flop-brimmed hat looked up from his labors and waved.

Chapter 85

❦

At daybreak, the stranger sat quietly, listening to the morning prayers of his fellow monks. Afterwards, they shared a simple breakfast. When he was finished eating, the man stood up and went outside to tend the garden, planted within the sacred walls of the Trinity St. Sergius Monastery. The stranger dropped to his knees and began to weed the narrow rows of beans and potatoes.

"Will you speak to us today, Lazarus?" an older monk inquired of him.

Captain James Garrett looked up at him with a blank expression. His body had thinned, and his bearded face wore the perpetual look of someone lost in a deep forest. Internally, he struggled daily to recall his past, but nothing came to him. His brothers in the monastery had long ago accepted this and had assigned him the biblical name of 'Lazarus' to facilitate their communications regarding his care.

In some sense, the stranger had, indeed, "risen from the dead," though Peter's anti-viral injection, coupled with the monks' constant care and feeding over a period of several months had been the actual cause of his miraculous recovery. Of course, the monks attributed this miracle to God's grace, which served to make Lazarus even more welcome in their midst.

The stranger rarely spoke, but occasionally managed a simple "yes" or "no" in response to questions concerning present matters. He seemed to find solace outdoors and was assigned permanent duty in the garden and adjacent grounds. After years of questioning local citizens, they had given up on determining his true identity. The monks' resources were limited, and their focus was on the routines of daily worship. A man in such condition could not survive on his own, so they viewed it as their solemn duty to provide him with food and shelter on an indefinite basis. Would not Christ have done the same?

Fearing that he might get lost, the monks had decided to keep him within the boundaries of the monastery walls. On the surface, the stranger seemed to prefer this, but, internally, he struggled to cope with his mental and physical confinement. Some days, they found him huddled against the monastery wall, his eyes tightly shut and his hands reaching out as if to grasp something. At such times, they waited patiently nearby, until he was released from his trauma and they could return him to his room and let him rest. Usually, they would not see him again until the next day, when he rejoined them at morning prayers.

Endless days of routine had passed, his mind wandering through an opaque abyss. But, recently, strange, fragmented images had begun to appear in his head, jarring him awake in the middle of the night. He did not recognize them or understand their meaning. Sometimes, they involved tiny shapes that shifted kaleidoscopically. Other times, bits and pieces of random numbers appeared out of nowhere, dancing across the roof of his mind. He reached out for them in the darkness, but they dissipated into a fine, gray mist. The next morning, he tried to remember the images, but they were just beyond retrieval.

Frustrated by this experience, he resolved to write them down as soon as they appeared. The next day, he found a shred of paper and a small, discarded pencil in a waste basket and placed them on the nightstand next to his bed, alongside his candle and matches. When the images appeared again, he would be ready.

Over the course of several nights, he managed to piece together the oddly-shaped parts of seven random numbers, which he wrote down in the same order as they had appeared. The digits – 4529667 – meant nothing to him, but he clung to them anyway, hoping that, one day, they might give meaning to his otherwise meaningless existence. He went about his daily routines and ignored the mild headaches that often followed his dreams.

Three days later, he sat among his brothers at morning prayers, listening to the lyrical tones of their recitations. Even though they spoke in Russian, he recognized the structure of their phrases and understood the approaching conclusion of their prayer. As they traced the sign of the cross on their bodies, the words softly slipped from the stranger's tongue.

"In the name of the Father, the Son and the Holy Spirit."

The monks immediately looked up at Lazarus, who, for the first time, had uttered a phrase in English. It lacked a British accent, leaving only one other possibility. They looked at each other and whispered.

"The abbot must be told," they said to each other.

The monks kept an eye on Lazarus and wondered what was going on inside his head.

"I feel sorry for his family," the abbot said when they reported the incident. "If only we knew who they were."

Formerly, the good abbot had privately doubted that they would ever know. They had all resigned themselves to the fact that the stranger would live out his life among them, wrapped in the protective arms of the Trinity St. Sergius Monastery. It was, after all, a good life for those who served the Lord.

But, this new revelation changed everything.

Chapter 86

∾

Matt turned around and climbed the front steps of the center cottage. The porch contained a few pieces of white wicker furniture and a small table made of native woods. He entered the front door of the cottage and stood for a moment, admiring its unique design and quality construction.

Rich, warm woods greeted him – tongue and groove walls, made of knotty white pine, with exposed-beam ceilings that coordinated with beautiful hardwood floors. Well lit by a number of skillfully framed windows, the room had an open, spacious feel.

To his right, against the wall, a staircase made of the same wood led upstairs to a loft area, which contained a bedroom, bath and a small study with dormer windows.

The downstairs kitchen and dining area consumed most of the first-floor space. The kitchen cabinetry was made of the same clear-sealed, knotty white pine found throughout the cottage.

Black, metal door handles and hinges added necessary contrast to the interior woodworking.

A white, recessed refrigerator and stove, along with a stainless-steel sink set in black, slate counter tops, gave the room a clean, efficient appearance. The surface of the kitchen's island, also covered with black slate, matched the color of the wooden chairs positioned around the hardwood dining table.

Behind the back wall of the kitchen, a full bath had been built, with a shower, sink and toilet.

To his left was the living room, with a comfortable couch, a dark-patterned oriental rug, a wicker end table and lamp and a native-hardwood coffee table.

Mounted on the living room wall was a heavy mantel, made from the ancient plank of a wooden ship. Clay vases rested on both ends of it, boasting fresh sprays of native wild flowers – no doubt his mom's doing.

Just above the mantel, an impressive rifle was cradled in padded wall mounts. Matt recognized it immediately. It was his father's M1 Garand that he had used in Korea.

Worn, but sturdy, the ambiance of its history had been improved by the proper application of protective oils. The wooden stock and metal components were carefully restored, preserving its character without altering its functionality.

The work had been performed by someone who knew what they were doing – probably someone with a military background.

Matt stared at it, wondering how it came to be there. Most likely, Bill had something to do with it.

The back, left side of the floor contained the master bedroom, constructed of the same floor-to-ceiling, tongue and groove white pine. Inside, a comfortable double bed with two pillows was covered by a simple, blue cotton spread. A modest wooden dresser, a nightstand with a lamp and a cane-backed chair completed the room's furnishings.

Matt went into the bathroom and washed his hands and face. Then, he took his bag into the bedroom and placed it on the bed. He unzipped the top and pulled out a pair of shorts, a T-shirt and sandals. He changed into them and then went into the kitchen.

When he opened the refrigerator door, he found lunch meats, lettuce, tomato, Cokes and a half dozen bottles of Carib beer, imported from Trinidad.

He selected a bottle of Carib and removed its cap. After a couple of short swigs, he exited the dwelling, walking down the narrow road toward the last cottage.

Bill had already settled himself on the front porch and was preparing for the conversation they would soon have.

As Matt covered the hundred feet of distance between them, he glanced down the mountainside and noticed the small, white-sand beach that rested at its base.

"Are we allowed to use that?" Matt asked as he reached Bill's front porch and climbed the steps.

Bill was sitting in a green, wooden rocking chair, nursing his own bottle of Carib.

"I don't see why not," he replied calmly. "It's ours."

"What? Do you mean that's part of your property?" Matt exclaimed, amazed.

"All the way to the water's edge," Bill replied. "Beyond that, you're on your own."

"How could you afford all of that?" Matt asked incredulously.

"See for yourself," Bill replied.

He pulled a small, green bank book out of his shirt pocket and handed it to Matt.

When Matt opened it, he was surprised to find his own name printed inside. It detailed a number of financial transactions, resting in a "robust" international bank account.

A series of monthly deposits had been recorded, ranging back to the time that he had signed the confidentiality agreement that Governor Rice had presented to him. At the bottom of the list of deposits, the resulting total contained six digits to the left of the decimal.

"Sorry I didn't tell you about that earlier," Bill said, referring to the small, green bank book in Matt's hand. "I just didn't want you to blow it all on expensive booze and loose women before you had a chance to visit us down here."

"What?" Matt said incredulously. "Do you mean to tell me that this is *my* money?"

"Don't worry," Bill said. "I've got a little green book just like yours, and they haven't asked for any of mine back yet."

Matt stared at the account book. He didn't know what to say.

"Look," Bill continued. "They're not going to ask us to do this kind of work for nothing. You've already seen how dangerous it can be. As a matter of fact, I'd say that poor Nat deserves a bonus."

"But – it's too much!" Matt said, unfamiliar with such salaries.

"So, spend the extra money on your mom," Bill suggested. "She certainly deserves it. Let's face it, buddy – anyone who'd put up with you all these years deserves a medal."

"Ha, ha," Matt replied flatly. As an afterthought, he added, "She really does look great, doesn't she?"

"I'm telling you, that woman belongs here," Bill replied. "Wait until you see how she does with the locals."

"I can just imagine. She's pretty remarkable, I'll admit," Matt concurred. "I really appreciate you bringing her down here, Bill. It's obviously been a great break for her."

"Actually, there's a little more to it than that," Bill replied. "In the middle of the night, I had to remove a piece of Russian trash from her front doorstep in Florida. It was right after you took out the Russian who threatened Ming in Georgetown."

"What?" Matt exclaimed. "Why didn't you tell me?"

"What for?" Bill replied. "I took care of it."

"Well, of course, I'm grateful for what you did, but you should have told me sooner," Matt complained. "What happens when she goes back? Will she continue to have protection?"

"I'm hoping that she doesn't *go* back, Matt," Bill explained calmly. "She has a home here now... and so do you."

Matt's mouth hung open briefly. Then, he took a long draft of his Carib and set it down sharply on the table.

"What are you talking about?" he said. "Have you lost your mind?"

"Well – uh – yeah," Bill replied, smiling, "but that was a long time ago. By the way, if you happen to run across it, let me know. I could really use the extra gray matter."

Matt threw up his hands in exasperation. None of this made any sense to him.

"Listen," Bill said, altering his voice to a more serious tone. "I built all three of these places, with a little help from the natives. I had all the materials shipped in from Miami eight months ago, and we finished the construction just before you and I went to Zurich.

"I've been thinking about this little project ever since I was in Nam. I promised myself that, if I ever got out of that hell-hole, I was going to do it.

"Now that it's finished, I'm giving two of these places to you – one for your mother – God forbid that she should have to live with the likes of you – and one for you.

"The way I look at it, you're the only family that I've got left. If you think you can be happy here, I'd like you to stay. If you can't, then you're free to do whatever you want. I'll rent the cottages out to tourists or something."

Matt turned around and looked at the magnificent view of the Caribbean Sea that spread before them. He was trying hard to digest what Bill had said.

"What sane person would turn down such an offer?" he *thought to himself.*

Matt turned back to Bill and addressed him in a business-like tone.

"You'd have to let me pay you back, Bill," he declared. "I can't just take something like this and say 'thanks.' That's not enough."

"Fine," Bill replied. "I'll take a dollar apiece for them."

Matt frowned at him and then paused, feeling like he had overlooked something.

"Wait a minute," Matt said. "What about Nat? She deserves a place to live, too."

"I've already worked that out," Bill replied, enjoying his advantage. "She can stay with your mom until we get back from Paris. Then, if I have my way, she'll be moving in with me."

Matt picked up his beer, took another drink and then set it down.

"You know, that doesn't surprise me at all," he said. "You two look like the perfect fit."

"Let's hope she agrees," Bill replied. "She may change her mind when she sees me in a bathing suit."

"Somehow, I doubt that," Matt said, rolling his eyes. Bill was in as good, or better shape than he was.

"O.K., then," Bill continued, "Now that our living arrangements are somewhat settled, let's get down to business.

"We'll plan to leave for Paris on Sunday. That'll give you some time with your mom, and the two of you can discuss my offer.

"Meanwhile, we'll keep an eye on Natasha and make sure that she's healing normally. If she needs any other medical attention, we'll fly someone in from D.C.

"I'm going to make a few contacts that can assist us in Paris. I also need to check with John Sauter and see if any new intel has surfaced on the whereabouts of Alya Kavalov."

"Sounds good to me," Matt replied. "Let me know if you need any help."

"I'll be fine," Bill said. "Just relax and enjoy your stay. Oh, and you're welcome to use the Land Rover, if you want to explore the island. It won't take long – there's not that much of it. If you like what you see, maybe you'll decide to stay."

"Well," Matt replied, "I can tell you right now that, if it were up to me, you'd never be renting these cottages to strangers. This is an amazing place, Bill, and you've done an incredible job with the construction of these homes."

"Thanks," Bill replied, "but I can't take all the credit. The locals did a fair amount of the work, too."

"I'll be sure to thank them as well," Matt added. "You know that I'd love to stay here, Bill – nothing would make me happier. But, first, I need to check with Mom and see what she wants."

Bill chuckled.

"What is it?" Matt said. "What's so funny?"

"I'd like to see you try to take her off this rock," he replied. "I have a feeling you'd have to drag her, kicking and screaming. Just wait – you'll see what I mean."

They finished their beers together, and then Matt returned to his cottage to finish unpacking his things.

Later that afternoon, a small group of five island children, dressed in blue school uniforms, showed up at the front doorstep of Marie's cottage. She met them with a tray of warm, freshly-baked cookies.

Natasha came out on the front porch and sat down to watch them.

"Thank you, Miss Marie," they said in unison, excited by the special treat that she had made for them. They sat on the front steps and consumed the cookies voraciously.

Marie went back into the cottage and returned with glasses of cold milk. After each child had taken one, she sat down on the top step to listen to them share the events of their school day.

Standing just inside his own front porch, Matt observed their warm interaction and knew that Nevis would be their home.

Chapter 87

At midnight, John Sauter put in another call to The Swiss Academy of Sciences in Bern, where it was eight o'clock in the morning. He asked to speak to the man whose name Natasha had provided. He had called twice before, but Alya's illusive colleague had been out of the office most of the week.

This time, when his secretary answered, she transferred him immediately to his desk.

"Dr. Perin, my name is John Sauter. I'm a friend of Alya Stevsky. I've been trying to reach her for a few weeks now, but haven't been able to get a hold of her. Would you happen to know where she is?"

The man cleared his throat.

"Interesting that you should ask," Dr. Perin replied. "Until about ten minutes ago, I had no idea. She hasn't been into the office for quite a while now. A month or so back, she went on vacation for a couple of weeks, but never returned. We figured she'd run off with some rich American, until we got a letter this morning."

"What did she have to say?" John asked.

"The letter wasn't from her," the doctor revealed. "It was from an English colleague of mine who's studying primates in West Africa. He mentioned that he was sharing his laboratory at the Imperial College of London with Alya while he was away. Apparently, she's doing some sort of research on the trivalent oral poliovirus vaccine. Frankly, we were stunned to hear this. It seemed strange that she wouldn't even call to let us know where she was."

"I know what you mean," John replied, trying to establish rapport with him. "I've been worried about her, too."

"It just doesn't make any sense to me," Dr. Perin added. "I know that she was happy here. I just can't imagine what would cause her to leave like this."

"Women," John said flatly. "Who can figure them out?"

"Well, I hope that she's happy, whatever she's doing," Dr. Perin added. "She has a brilliant scientific mind."

"I'm sure she'll get in touch with us when she's ready," John said reassuringly. "Meanwhile, could you do me a favor and not share this information with anyone else? As a friend, I'd like her to decide on her own when she's ready to explain her actions."

"I agree," Dr. Perin replied. "Let's just respect her privacy and see what happens."

"Thank you, Dr. Perin," John said. "It was a pleasure talking to you."

He hung up the phone and dialed the Miami switch, which securely routed his call to Bill Hunter's cottage on Nevis.

They had caught an unexpected break that could swing the odds in their favor. If they got to Alya

Kavalov before the Russians did, perhaps they could persuade her to transfer her work to America. If she was willing to share her knowledge, they could offer her a job at VICORE, where Ming Li would closely monitor her research.

All indications were that Alya Kavalov was capable of a major biological breakthrough. Whatever it was, the Russians were willing to kill to get their hands on it. In all likelihood, it was related to her father's work.

John Sauter had seen the tape of Dr. Uri Kavalov's death and the subsequent mayhem that had followed. Occasionally, he still awoke at night with images in his head of the incredibly rapid viral attack that had occurred after the lab monkeys were shot, their blood sprayed across the white tile walls.

Something about the ravenous assault of a tiny, invisible creature made his skin crawl. And, from what he had seen on tape, the strain of virus that Dr. Kavalov had created was fast, virulent and most likely impossible to contain, if intentionally released.

Finding Alya Kavalov was a race that they could not afford to lose.

Chapter 88

❦

After dinner, Matt decided to explore some of the windward side of the island on foot. He walked back to the main road and traveled eastward, crossing the southern half of the island. Gradually, the road swung to the north, moving up the Atlantic side of Nevis.

Following the main road, he made good time, slowing only to acknowledge others or to get his bearings. Before long, he came to one of the more populated areas on the island.

Named after the valuable ginger crop once grown there, the parish of Gingerland rose up before him. The bright red roof of St George's Anglican Church, near Market Shop, welcomed him first. He studied its architecture briefly and then pressed on.

Fascinated by their differences, he traveled through several of the parish villages – Chicken Stone, Zetlands and Zion, where people waved casually as he passed by.

Situated on the windward side of the island, these small villages faced the steady breezes of the trade winds. Many of them rested at altitudes of a thousand feet or more, with fertile soil and ample rainfall. As a result, they enjoyed cooler temperatures than the coastal villages situated below them.

Matt enjoyed the refreshing temperatures and spoke to several Nevisians as he walked past their small farms and villages. These people supplied most of Nevis with its fruits and vegetables, and their goats and sheep ranged freely along the mountainside. Cows, horses and pigs were fenced or tied.

Finally, he dropped down toward Coconut Walk Estate, situated near the Atlantic shoreline. Its tall windmill tower could be seen well before arriving at the site, giving silent testimony to the strength and skill of the early slave and free craftsmen of Nevis. The aging, stone-walled building, with its wooden roof and rusting iron cogwheels strewn about the unkempt yard represented the last sugar cane factory to operate on the island.

Matt glanced at his watch. This would be his last stop – it was time to turn back.

As he approached the ruins of the sugar mill, the shrill sound of a woman's voice rang out.

"Annika!"

Suddenly, the brown body of a middle-aged woman, dressed in island clothing, flew out from behind the stone building, hurled by a powerful, invisible force. Her cry went silent as she hit the ground.

Her scream was followed by a second, higher-pitched cry. It sounded more refined and helpless, though no less traumatized. The pure terror in the second female's voice stirred something deep inside Matt that he had felt only once before in his life.

A galvanic skin response raced up his arms, and, before he realized it, he was running toward the ruins. As he approached the structure, his senses peaked, and his mind shifted mechanically into a different mode, functioning purely on instinct.

When he reached the front of the building, the raw, booming voice of an angry man assaulted the air. His deep, guttural curses drowned out the desperate cries of his second victim.

As Matt edged quickly along the side of the building, the woman's terrified voice was cut off abruptly, stopping as suddenly as it had started. He rounded the corner to the back of the building, pausing for a split second to assess the situation.

Twenty feet away from him was a six-and-a-half-foot tall, three hundred pound giant of a black man, standing directly in front of a white woman. With his massive left hand gripping her throat, he had lifted and pinned her body against the back wall of the stone building. His blonde-haired victim thrashed wildly as she struggled to breathe, her arms flailing helplessly in the air. Her eyes had opened widely, and her face was turning blue.

The huge man roared with laughter and then slapped her fiercely across the face with his right hand, rendering her completely unconscious. Using the same filthy hand, he immediately began to tear at her clothing.

The first woman, who had been tossed through the air like a ragdoll, was coming to, twenty feet away. She sat up and screamed.

"Annika! Annika!"

Matt was already bearing down on her attacker. As he swept deftly forward along the side of the building, he scooped up a wooden post lying on the ground, three inches in diameter.

Ten feet away, Damas became aware of Matt's rapid approach, and he released the woman. As she dropped to the ground, he swung his left arm upward, just in time to meet the arc of the aging wooden post as Matt slammed it down toward his misshapen head.

The top third of the post shattered across the giant man's forearm, sending a shower of splinters through the air. Damas brought his right arm around quickly, delivering a heavy blow to the side of Matt's head that sent him tumbling across the ground.

Matt came up on his feet and instinctively reached for his Colt .45, which wasn't there. He had left it back at the cottage, certain that there was no need for it in paradise. Simultaneously, Damas slid a long, sharp bolo knife from the side of his belt and grinned at him with jagged, yellow teeth.

For a brief moment, Matt tasted the bitter onset of fear. His advantage had disappeared, and hand-to-hand combat with an armed opponent of this size and strength wasn't likely to go well. The long, sharp edge of the bolo knife glistened, threatening serious, permanent injury.

As Damas started toward him, Matt pushed aside his fear and focused on survival. He bent down and picked up a fistful of sand.

When Damas drew close, he swung the bolo savagely at Matt's head, barely missing him as he ducked beneath the blow. When Matt came up, he strafed his attacker's eyes with sand, causing momentary blindness. Then, he slammed his right fist into the man's lower abdomen and punched him viciously in the throat with his other. The giant man stumbled backward, coughing and spewing, but regained his balance quickly.

Enraged by his first real experience with pain since reaching adulthood, Damas roared at the top of his lungs and raised his bolo high above his head. He attacked like a wild animal, cursing the man who had dared to strike him.

Matt picked up the longest remaining piece of the splintered fence post, turned around and retreated, running at half speed toward the beach, away from the battered women.

Damas, in immediate pursuit, could taste the growing certainty of victory as he gained on his opponent.

"I kill you! I kill you!" he bellowed at the top of his lungs, excited by the carnage that would soon follow.

Matt looked back over his shoulder fearfully, selling his terror at being pursued by his executioner. He increased his speed slightly, as did his attacker.

Soon just three feet behind him, Damas raised his bolo knife high above his head with both hands and began the downward swing that would slice his opponent in half.

Suddenly, with lightning speed, Matt went to the ground in a single motion, crouching in a forward-bent position, head lowered as if in prayer. He braced the blunt end of the fence post deep in the fine, white sand and slid the opposite, jagged end of the weapon, angled forty-five degrees upward, back underneath his right arm, gripping it tightly with both hands.

Damas met the sharply-splintered end of the pole with the full force of his body weight, amplified by the rage of his downward swing of the bolo. The wood pierced his diaphragm at the base of the sternum and continued completely through his body, exiting just beneath his shoulder blades. A torrential gush of bright red blood issued from his mouth, drenching the back of Matt's head in its angry heat.

In slow motion, Damas' giant body collapsed to the side, hitting the sand with a resounding thud. His reign of terror had ended.

Matt stood up and turned around. The brown, island woman had struggled to her feet and was making her way unsteadily toward the young white woman, who remained unconscious at the base of the sugar mill wall. He looked down at his hands and feet, which were covered with blood that didn't belong to him. He could feel it running down his face and neck as well.

Knowing that this would frighten the women, he turned back around, went to the water's edge and washed himself off. Then, he quickly returned to check on them.

Fearing that she was dead, the island woman was bent over the young woman's crumpled body, embracing her and crying softly. Matt took her gently by the shoulders and sat her up so he could determine the younger woman's condition.

When he looked down at the young woman's face, partially concealed by her long, blonde hair, Matt felt an unfamiliar surge of electricity in his body, inexplicable under these circumstances. He brushed it aside, knelt down and placed two fingers on the front side of her bruised throat to check for a pulse. She was still unconscious, but alive. Her breathing was shallow and labored, and he knew that she needed medical attention.

Matt turned to the island woman.

"Are you O.K.?" he asked. "What is your name?"

At first she was too frightened to answer. Shaking slightly from mild shock, her lips trembled and tears welled up in her eyes.

"It's all right now," Matt assured her. "It's over with. Please, tell me your name."

"I am Sharine," the brown woman replied.

"And who is this?" Matt asked, referring to the unconscious woman.

"That's Annika," Sharine replied. "She's my friend and she's hurt! Can you help her?"

"We need to get her to a doctor," Matt said. "Is there one nearby?"

"Yes," Sharine answered. "In my village."

"Good," Matt said. "Let's go."

He picked up the unconscious woman and looked at Sharine.

"This way," she said, pointing back toward the main road that encircled the island.

Fifteen minutes later, they reached the doctor's office. Matt carried the woman into the examination room and instructed Sharine to stay with her. Then, he went back to the waiting room and asked the receptionist to contact local law enforcement.

Soon, a white ambulance showed up outside the doctor's office, and the injured white woman was transported to the island's only hospital in Charlestown. Sharine rode with her, thanking Matt profusely as they left the doctor's office.

Ten minutes later, two men from The Royal St. Kitts and Nevis Police Force showed up. Matt explained what had happened and took them back to Coconut Walk Estate, where Damas' skewered body was already being examined by sand crabs. They called the island's only coroner and helped him collect the massive body for transport to the morgue.

Law enforcement officials quickly identified Damas as the man from Anegada who had left a trail of dead bodies all across the Leeward Islands. By midnight, they released Matt on his own recognizance, feeling that he had done both them and everyone else on the island a great service.

Matt took a taxi to the hospital, where he inquired of the injured woman's status. A friendly night-shift nurse explained that she had sustained a serious concussion and had been heavily sedated to help her rest. Sharine had checked out O.K. and had been sent home to her family, with the promise that she could return to visit her close friend, Annika, first thing in the morning.

"Could you do me a personal favor?" Matt asked the nurse, pulling the same one hundred dollar bill from his wallet that Governor Rice had given him almost a year ago.

"I'd like her to have some nice flowers when she wakes up," Matt said smiling. "Could you manage that? Whatever's left, please apply it to her bill."

"Of course," the nurse replied, smiling at him. "I'll take care of it."

At one A.M., the same taxi dropped Matt off in front of his cottage. He went inside, took a hot shower and collapsed on the double bed in the master bedroom. He closed his eyes and retraced the evening's events.

Who was the young woman, sleeping now in the island's only hospital? Where had she come from? What was she doing there?

Through the bedroom window, the vibrant sounds of the tropical landscape mingled with the distant rustling of an impatient sea. He fell asleep, with every intention of answering those questions the next day.

Chapter 89

෴

At eight A.M., Marie knocked on Matt's front door. Hearing no response, she called out to him.

"Matt, come to breakfast!" she yelled. "Bill will be joining us, too. Eggs, bacon, sausage and biscuits."

Matt sat up in the bed and swung his feet out onto the floor. He went into the bathroom, washed up, got dressed and combed his hair. Then, he shoved his Colt .45 into the back of his belt, determined not to leave the house again without it.

"Even in paradise, chance favors the prepared mind," he thought to himself.

As he exited his cottage ten minutes later, Bill was coming down the road.

"Good morning," Matt said, rubbing the back of his neck.

"Long night?" Bill asked, noticing his grogginess.

"I'll tell you all about it later," Matt replied.

"They'll be plenty of time on the plane," Bill said. "John Sauter just called. We're headed to London this morning."

"London? What's going on?" Matt asked.

"He's located Alya Kavalov," Bill replied. "She's working on viruses at The Imperial College of London, using the name Alya Stevsky."

"What kind of viruses?" Matt asked.

"The kind that kill people," Bill replied. "If Natasha's doing all right this morning, we're leaving right after breakfast. The Learjet is being prepped on St. Kitts. It should be ready shortly after we get there."

"How did John find her?" Matt inquired.

"Pure luck," Bill replied. "We need to get to her before the Russians do."

"I'm right behind you," Matt assured him. "Let's check on the ladies and grab some breakfast."

Natasha looked much better. Marie had catered to her every need, including the wonderful breakfast that the four of them shared together. She raved about "Miss Marie's hospitality" and fully convinced Bill that she would be fine in her care.

"Just leave us to ourselves," Marie said to Bill. "And don't worry about Natasha. We've got lots to talk about. You know – girl talk."

"That's what I'm worried about," Bill replied. "By the time we get back, she'll know way too much about me. That could be hazardous to my health."

Marie winked at him.

"I'll put a nice spin on it," she said.

When breakfast was finished, Bill and Matt got up to leave. Natasha stood up and hugged them both.

"Be safe," she said, knowing that it was unlikely.

"I hate to have to leave here so soon," Bill replied, "but, hopefully, we'll be back in a few days. Take good care of yourself."

"You, too," Nat replied, kissing him quickly on the lips.

They thanked Marie for breakfast and left, returning to their respective cottages to ready their travel packs. Matt finished quickly and stood in his living room, watching for Bill's Land Rover to pull up outside.

While he waited, he took his father's M1 Garand off the wall and examined it closely. He had memorized every detail of this rifle years ago, but it was particularly gratifying to see it in its present condition. Bill had done a great job of restoring it to its former glory. As he studied it, he reflected on what had brought him to this point in his life.

Right after Matt signed Governor Rice's confidentiality agreement, he had been shown the lab tape of his father's death. Governor Rice had felt that Matt deserved to know the whole truth, as painful as it was to witness. It had sealed Matt's decision to move forward and had forged his will to withstand any pain or difficulties encountered during training.

Over the past several months, those images had never failed to motivate him. Not only had he survived his training – he had excelled at it.

Looking back now, it seemed strange to think that, by this time tomorrow, he would be talking with the woman whose father had sought the help of his own, and who, unintentionally, had been the cause of both of their deaths.

Two minutes later, Bill pulled up outside and tapped on his horn. Matt returned the Garand to its place above the mantel and joined him in the Land Rover. As they drove by Marie's cottage, she waved at them from the front steps.

"Stay out of trouble!" she called. "I don't want to have to come get you."

When they reached the main road, they turned left and headed up the Caribbean side of the island. Bill could tell that Matt had something on his mind.

"Could we stop by the hospital in Charlestown on the way?" Matt asked suddenly. "I'd like to check on a friend. I promise it won't take more than ten minutes."

Bill could tell that it was a serious request.

"Who would you know in Alexandra Hospital?" Bill inquired.

"Someone I came across last night," Matt explained. "I'd like to know how she's doing before we leave."

"She?" Bill probed.

"Yeah, she," Matt replied, and then went silent, staring out the passenger-side window.

"Far be it from me to come between you and your lady friends," Bill said, smiling and raising both of his hands as if to surrender.

Figuring that it was best to wait for further explanation until they got on the plane, Bill drove to Alexandra Hospital without saying another word. When they arrived, Matt opened his door and got out.

"Be right back," he said to Bill through the window.

"Take your time," Bill replied. "They're still prepping the plane."

Matt nodded at him and then turned around and hurried into the building. Visiting hours didn't start until two P.M., so he checked with the woman at the front desk.

"Are you family?" she asked him.

"Yes," Matt lied. "I'm her brother."

"Well, you can check with the hall nurse," she replied. "She might let you see her for a few minutes. She's in room twenty-one. Take a right as soon as you go through those doors."

"Thanks," Matt replied. "We're very concerned about her."

Matt went through the doorway, turned right and followed the numbers until he came to room twenty-one. As he entered the doorway, Sharine looked up from her bedside chair and smiled.

"Mr. Garrett!" she said, completely surprised by his appearance. "How did you get in here?"

"I might ask you the same thing," Matt replied, teasing her.

"My sister works here," Sharine said. "She's a nurse."

"Well, lacking your advantage, I told them that I was Annika's brother."

"Ha!" she laughed. "Annika doesn't have a brother."

"She does now," Matt quipped. "How are you two doing?"

"Oh, I'm fine – just fine," Sharine said. "But, I'm afraid Annika's not awake yet. Come and sit with us anyway. I'm sure she'd like to meet you."

Matt entered the room slowly. A large spray of beautiful flowers sat on the nightstand beside her bed.

"I'm afraid I can't stay long," Matt replied. "I'm headed to London with my partner. He's waiting for me outside."

"London?" Sharine asked, somewhat confused. "You don't sound British."

"A business trip," Matt replied, "for some very fussy clients."

"I see," Sharine said. "I suppose you're the one who sent those flowers. They're wonderful. Annika will love them."

Matt drew closer to her bedside, getting his first good look at her under semi-normal circumstances. Her hair had been combed, and her face and arms had been washed. She wore no makeup and had a slender build, with delicately-arched eyebrows and dark eyelashes. Her skin was a pearlescent tan, and her long blonde hair curved gracefully around her face, flowing down the front of her hospital gown.

"She's beautiful, isn't she?" Sharine said, looking up at him. She paused briefly and then added, "Inside and out."

"Has the doctor been in yet this morning?" Matt asked, deflecting her comment.

"Yes," Sharine replied. "He said that he spoke to her parents last night and told them they would be keeping Annika here a few days for observation. Her parents should arrive here later today."

"Does she live on the island?" Matt asked.

"She's from Sweden," Sharine explained. "Her parents have a villa in Golden Rock where they spend their summers. I took care of Annika when she was growing up. She still comes to visit me whenever she can."

Matt reached down and lightly touched the back of Annika's hand.

"She's lucky to have a friend like you," Matt said to Sharine.

"And a brother," Sharine replied, winking at him.

Matt smiled and looked down at his watch. Fifteen minutes had already flown past.

"Well," he said apologetically, "I'd better get going."

As he withdrew his hand to leave, Annika stirred, a soft moan issuing from her lips. For a tortuously brief moment, she opened her eyes and looked peacefully up at the man who had saved her life. Deep wells of Caribbean blue flashed around her dark pupils, framed by the blessing of long, black eyelashes. Her head tilted a millimeter, and her lush lips parted slightly, as if to speak, but nothing came out.

Matt had never seen or felt anything like it before. The same unfamiliar surge of electricity that he had experienced at the ruins of Coconut Walk raced unabatedly through his core, cauterizing deep, long-standing wounds.

As quickly as they had opened, Annika's eyes closed, and she drifted back into sedation.

Matt stood still for a moment, fixated.

Finally, Sharine broke the silence.

"Don't worry," she said. "I'll be here."

"Everything O.K.?" Bill inquired as Matt slid back into the passenger seat of the Land Rover.

"Fine," Matt replied, somewhat distracted. "Just fine."

"All right, then." Bill said. "Let's dance."

He cranked the engine and headed for the airstrip at the northern end of Nevis, where Randy was waiting for them with the island hopper. When they arrived, they parked the Land Rover out front and collected their packs.

As they walked through the terminal, a middle-aged Swedish couple was speaking anxiously to a taxi driver. The woman glanced up at Matt as he passed by them.

He recognized her eyes immediately.

Chapter 90

‿

When Dr. Perin arrived at The Swiss Academy of Sciences the next morning, he found his office torn to shreds. Chaotically scattered about the room were the contents of all of his file cabinets, bookshelves and desk. His university papers and personal correspondence were randomly strewn across the floor, as if an angry child had thrown a tantrum.

He immediately called security.

Soon, it was determined that an exterior window at the back of the building had been forcibly entered, following a knowledgeable disarming of the security device attached to it. Only Dr. Perin's office had been disturbed.

Questioned by security personnel about possible motives for the break-in, Dr. Perin could supply little information to assist them. At the time, his research held no real commercial value and would have been of little interest to foreign governments.

Ultimately, they attributed the incident to random mischief, and Dr. Perin and his secretary set about the business of restoring order to his office. Two hours later, he sat down at his desk and began to work.

Something repeatedly disturbed his concentration, though initially he could not grasp it. He pushed the annoyance aside, preferring to address the heavy workload in front of him, exacerbated by the absurd invasion of privacy that had started his day.

Nevertheless, the feeling persisted, until, finally, he identified it.

Dr. Len Whatley's letter was missing.

Chapter 91

❧

The Learjet streaked high above the mid-Atlantic, en route to London Heathrow. Lunch included shrimp cocktails, followed by tuna salad served on warm bakery rolls. An assortment of fresh fruits and vegetables complemented the meal.

Matt selected a ginger ale from the galley's cooler and pulled out a Coke for Bill. They returned to their seats to enjoy the meal.

"Swedish, huh?" Bill announced suddenly.

Matt looked over at him, astonished by his comment.

"How did you know that?" he asked incredulously.

"I'm psychic," Bill declared, taunting him.

"Seriously, though – how did you know that?" Matt demanded.

"I got a call from the Royals this morning," Bill explained, referring to the Royal St. Kitts and Nevis Police Force. "Seems you made quite an impression on them."

"So you heard all about that, huh?" Matt acknowledged. "I hope I didn't put you in an awkward position."

"On the contrary, *hero*," Bill replied. "They just wanted to thank us for taking out their garbage."

"Well, the truth is, he took himself out," Matt replied. "He got all excited about chasing a fence post."

"That's what I heard," Bill said. "I suppose you didn't have anything to do with helping him catch it, did you?"

"It was the least that I could do," Matt responded.

Bill smiled at him and then took another bite of his sandwich, chewing it with a degree of satisfaction. He knew that such encounters further sharpened Matt's survival skills.

"Did you show the Royals your trident ID?" Bill inquired.

"No," Matt said. "It wasn't necessary."

"That's good," Bill replied. "I'd rather keep our island profile separate from our work."

"We're in good shape so far," Matt said. "And I'll try to tone down my presence a bit."

"Are you sure about that?" Bill teased. "That Swedish girl might have something to say about that."

"Look," Matt said. "Don't jump to any conclusions. All I did was help her out of a jam. She doesn't even know my name."

"Is she good looking?" Bill probed further.

"I don't know," Matt answered. "I was too busy trying to stay alive."

"But, what about at the hospital?" Bill asked. "They let you in to see her, didn't they?"

"Just for a couple of minutes," Matt replied. "She was sedated."

"And?" Bill said, waiting for him to finish.

"And, what?" Matt replied.

"And, how did she look to you?" Bill asked with growing impatience.

"Sleepy," Matt responded flatly.

Bill threw his hands up in the air, exasperated.

"Look," Matt said. "She only opened her eyes for about one second."

"So?" Bill said slowly. "How did the *rest* of her look?"

"I didn't notice," Matt replied honestly. "I couldn't take my eyes off hers. They were very unusual."

"Ah-ha!" Bill shouted. "Now we're getting somewhere!"

Randy, the pilot, leaned over and looked back through the open cockpit door.

"Is everything all right back there?" he asked.

"Right as rain!" Bill replied, smiling broadly and taking another enormous bite out of his sandwich.

Matt frowned at him, embarrassed by the small amount of information that he had unwillingly divulged.

"Don't worry, ole buddy," Bill added. "Your secret's safe with me. You'll have plenty of time to investigate when we get back. It shouldn't take long to locate Alya Kavalov and convince her to share her secrets."

"What makes you think she'll be willing?" Matt asked.

"When she realizes that we've found her, she'll know that the Russians can do the same," Bill replied. "Based on the history of how they treated her family, I'm sure that she'll prefer our company. Protective custody in the U.S., with the promise of continuing her work under close supervision, beats the heck out of the alternative."

"What if she's unwilling to cooperate with *either* side?" Matt asked.

"Then the Russians will kill her," Bill replied. "But not before they extract every ounce of information they can from her. It won't be pleasant."

"So, where does that leave us?" Matt inquired.

"In a very difficult position," Bill replied. "We can only do so much to convince her to come home with us. Beyond that, we have a job to do. We can't allow the Russians to get to her."

Something in Bill's voice disturbed Matt. The "leopard of his youth" seemed ready to pounce again, but this time, it was different. The prey was small and defenseless – an unseemly target for such a ferocious predator. Would he actually execute such an order?

This was the job that Matt had signed up for, and he understood the incredible danger of leaving her to the Russians. Perhaps it would not come to that, and she would willingly return to America with them.

If not, what was necessary would not come easily. He shuddered to think of having to live with it for the rest of his life.

Chapter 92

Immediately after Natasha's rescue, John Sauter had ordered around-the-clock monitoring of all pay phones within a three-block radius of the American Embassy in Moscow. It was a long-shot, but John thought they might get lucky if an employee was communicating classified information to the Soviets, using publically available and, therefore, innocent looking telecommunications. CIA agents in Moscow installed tiny bugs in the mouthpieces of all pay phones in question.

The possibility of an embassy breach of security had been raised by Matt's hesitancy to use their security personnel for additional protection while Natasha was recovering at the University Hospital in Bern. The Russians had initially gotten to Dr. Perin at virtually the same time that LOC had, and a female agent had followed Natasha back to her hotel and overcome her.

Matt felt that this could only mean that someone in the embassy had alerted them to the fact that Natasha had been quietly issued a vehicle upon arrival at the embassy, had secretly left for her mother's cottage on her own and was worthy of pursuit.

John Sauter followed up on Matt's theory by checking up on the aged Latvian professor that Natasha had mentioned to them. Discovering that he had been recently murdered by Soviet agents, John was even more convinced that Matt was right.

For two days, no pay phone communications of interest were captured by the CIA. But, on the third day, the gamble had paid off.

CIA agents recorded a conversation between an English-speaking subject and an innocuous government office worker describing an event that had taken place earlier that day. The initiator of the call had witnessed a letter hand-delivered to the American Embassy by an unidentified, robed monk that was addressed to the ambassador. He had no idea of its contents, but thought it was worth mentioning, since such things rarely took place.

It was unlikely that the monk was soliciting financial support from the Americans, since the Soviet government frowned on all such activities. This left serious questions about the nature of this communication and the monk's reason for taking such a risk. The informant was instructed to find out what was in the letter and report back immediately.

Voice analysis confirmed that the informant was an embassy employee – a communications specialist by the name of Don Hanson.

Within the hour, John Sauter was standing in the office of the Secretary of State, talking with a small handful of top government officials. After brief discussions, he picked up a secure line and called the American ambassador's home in Moscow, where it was eleven o'clock at night. His wife answered the telephone.

"This is John Sauter calling from the State Department in Washington. Is he in?"

"Yes," she responded. "Hold on a minute."

When the ambassador came to the phone, John introduced himself and asked if he might put the call on speaker phone so the Secretary of State could participate in the conversation.

"Of course," the ambassador replied. "What's up?"

"Ambassador, the LOC team has determined that there's a mole in your shop," the Secretary said. "We need your help to divert all sensitive information away from this man, without alerting him to the fact that we are on to him. We'll be sending a member of the LOC team to take him into custody and return him to the U.S. quietly."

"All right," the ambassador replied. "Who is it?"

"Your communications specialist, Don Hanson," John Sauter said. "Evidently, he's been at it for quite a while."

"Don Hanson?" the ambassador said, completely taken aback by the idea. "Are you sure?"

"We've got him on tape talking to his Soviet contact about a letter that was delivered to the embassy by a monk, addressed to you," John replied. "Does that ring any bells?"

"Why, yes," the ambassador confirmed. "I received it this morning, but I haven't opened it yet. There were several more pressing issues to deal with, so

I never got around to it. I have it in my briefcase, though. Would you like me to get it?"

"Yes, please," the Secretary of State responded. "We're curious to know what's in it."

"Give me a minute," the ambassador replied. "I'm going to lay the phone down while I get my briefcase."

A minute or so later, they heard the locks on his briefcase snap open and the rustling of papers as he located the letter. The ambassador returned to the phone and continued the conversation.

"I have it," he said. "The envelope is very simple and has no postage on it, which confirms that it was hand-delivered. One of my attachés brought it to me this morning. He must have spoken to Don Hanson on the way up to my office. Just to confirm, you'd like me to open this now? Is that correct?"

"That's right," the Secretary replied.

On the other end of the line, they could hear the ambassador tearing the letter open and removing its contents. There was a brief pause as he examined its contents.

"Hmmm," the ambassador said quietly. "That's very strange."

"What is it?" John Sauter inquired anxiously.

"There's a note in the envelope, written in some sort of ancient Cyrillic. I'm afraid I can't be of any help to you with this, gentlemen."

"Can anyone at the embassy translate it?" John asked.

"Not that I know of," the ambassador replied. "There's also a small slip of paper tucked inside, with a seven-digit number penciled on it. I can tell you this; whoever wrote the number wouldn't win any contests for penmanship."

"Give us the number," John instructed.

The ambassador recited it, but it held no significance to anyone on the call.

Chances were that the whole letter was the product of some religious zealot, warning of the world's eminent demise. It was probably a waste of Don Hanson's time to pursue it and theirs as well. But, they preferred to error on the side of caution.

"Ambassador, do you have any means of securing that letter in your home?" the Secretary asked. "We'd prefer that it does not return to the embassy."

"Yes," the ambassador replied. "I have a small wall safe that I can store it in."

"Excellent," the Secretary said. "We'll have someone there by tomorrow evening to pick it up. He'll have embassy credentials and will carry trident identification. Please allow him to transport the letter back to the U.S. for analysis."

"Certainly," the ambassador replied. "Anything else?"

"He'll need someone to pick him up at the airport," John Sauter added.

"I can arrange that," the ambassador said. "As long as he has embassy credentials, there shouldn't be a problem."

"One more time, Ambassador," the Secretary added. "Make sure that no sensitive information is exposed to Mr. Hanson before we collect him. Is that understood?"

"Absolutely," the ambassador replied. "I'll see to it."

They said their goodbyes and hung up. The ambassador immediately contacted embassy security and instructed them to enter his office, open his desk and files and relocate all sensitive materials to the basement vault. Additionally, he requested an immediate call-back upon completion of this task.

Chapter 93

❧

Air traffic controllers at London Heathrow cleared the Learjet for landing just before midnight. Randy taxied the aircraft to a private hangar on the south side of the airport and powered down the engines.

Matt and Bill gathered their packs, deplaned and entered the hangar where an automobile was waiting for them. Randy stayed with the aircraft as it was serviced, expecting a quick turn-around flight back to the U.S. before daybreak. He reclined in one of the passenger seats to grab a few hours of sleep.

Bill drove the black Mercedes, with its right-side steering wheel, exiting the airport gates. Matt was amazed at how quickly he adapted to its steering as they turned east on the M5 motorway, en route to the heart of London.

Matt studied his map and directed Bill toward The Imperial College of London, which would be closed that time of the night. This would allow them to carefully examine the office and laboratory of Dr. Len Whatley, currently being used by Alya Kavalov.

When they arrived, all was quiet, save a few inebriated students wandering across the campus in search of companions. They drove around to the building marked "Biological Sciences" and parked the car behind it. Bill removed a small set of lock picks from his backpack and exited the vehicle. Matt joined him, approaching the poorly-lit back door.

Three minutes later, they had bypassed the alarm and entered the building undetected. Using a small flashlight, they studied the directory posted on a nearby wall. Soon, they were moving quietly up a flight of stairs and entering a long corridor that provided access to several classrooms.

Dr. Len Whatley's office sat along the west side of the building, halfway down the hall. The upper half of the outer door was glass, and they could just make out his secretary's desk, as well as Dr. Watley's office just beyond it. Both were dark.

Through the upper half of the door at the back of Dr. Watley's office, they could see a small table lamp burning on the far side of the lab. Its soft white light silhouetted a seated woman in a white lab coat, pouring over a series of notes that rested on the table's surface. As she studied their contents, she paused occasionally to record additional details.

"Looks like she's burning the midnight oil," Matt said to Bill. "Whatever she's working on must be pretty important."

"Maybe she's just a night owl," Bill replied. "Fewer interruptions."

"Until now," Matt added.

They entered the outer office and checked the surface of Vivian's desk. Finding nothing of interest, they proceeded into Dr. Whatley's office, checking his desk as well. Then, they moved to the back door of his office, which led into the well-equipped lab.

Alya continued her work, unaware of their presence. Slowly, Bill turned the door handle and swung it partially open. He stopped suddenly and crouched down, signaling Matt to join him.

A young man, with dark, disheveled hair, entered the same lab through a back door. Ignoring Alya, he went to the monkey cages at the back of the room and began to clean them.

Alya stood up and faced him.

"Ah! You must be Chad," she said to the young man. "I've been meaning to talk to you."

"Right-o," he replied. "What can I do for you?"

Matt and Bill listened intently to their conversation.

"I wanted to ask you to bring those two cages back up from the basement," Alya explained to him.

"And what cages are those, Mum?" Chad asked, a little confused.

"You know," Alya replied. "The ones that belonged to the two dead white-collared monkeys that you incinerated in the basement last week."

"Oh, *those* cages!" he exclaimed. "I'd almost forgotten about them."

"We'll need them for the next round of green monkeys that come in," Alya explained.

"Of course, Miss," Chad replied. "I'll bring them right up this evening."

"Thank you, Chad," Alya said, sitting back down. "I appreciate your help."

"You're welcome," he replied. "But, there's just one thing..."

"What's that?" Alya asked.

"Those two white-collar monkeys didn't die," he said calmly. "Miss Vivian asked me to crate them up in the same boxes that the last shipment of green monkeys arrived in."

"Why would she have you do that?" Alya asked, confused by the information.

"So she could ship them back to West Africa, Miss," Chad replied. "Dr. Whatley didn't need them, so he asked her to ship them back to him."

"Why didn't anyone tell me?" Alya exclaimed.

"You were out sick, Ma'am," Chad replied. "They didn't want to disturb you with the task."

Slowly, reality set in on her.

"Oh, no!" Alya cried. "What did Dr. Whatley do with them?"

Seeing that she was upset, Chad lowered his head and spoke softly.

"As far as I know, Miss, he released them back into the wild. He's a good man, you know – Dr. Whatley. He wouldn't kill an animal needlessly."

Chapter 94

∽

Alya was crushed. She looked down at her father's notes, and a feeling of despair swept over her. The white-collared monkeys were alive and well, released back into their native African habitat. All of her hard work had ultimately produced nothing remarkable at all.

She had failed her father and her family miserably, unable to extrapolate the intended design of Dr. Uri Kavalov's work. She would have to start all over again, testing her latest strain of viruses on an entirely different species of monkeys.

She sat back down, and her shoulders slumped.

Her next test results might be different, but she was running out of time. Dr. Watley would be back in a couple of weeks, and she would have to suspend her efforts and set up shop elsewhere. The delay would be costly, and she was increasingly concerned about foreign governments catching up with her.

If they found her with her father's notes, she would likely be arrested and imprisoned – perhaps even tortured and killed. She had grown so paranoid over the possibility that she now carried a small cigarette lighter in her pocket, in case she was threatened. She would incinerate her father's notes before she would relinquish them to anyone else.

From across the lab, Chad could see that Alya was unhappy, so he returned to the business of cleaning the cages at the back of the room.

Bill stood up in the darkness of Dr. Whatley's office and motioned for Matt to follow him into the lab. As he reached for the doorknob, a sharp, hissing snap sounded at the back of the lab.

The young, male lab-worker's body drew upright, and his hands grabbed at the hole in his chest. He fell backwards, causing the nervous monkeys to erupt into a chorus of loud screams.

Alya stood up and shouted.

"Chad!"

Simultaneously, a large man and a small, blonde-haired woman entered through the same back door of the lab, both of them wielding handguns of Russian design. They turned and looked at Alya.

Instinctively, Alya turned back to the table and grabbed her father's notes. She ran five steps in the opposite direction before the Russian woman shot her in the back.

Bill was already through the front door of the lab, swinging his firearm across the room. The female KGB agent took a bullet in the stomach and doubled over. Bill finished her off with a second round that angled down through the top of her chest. At the same instant, a nine millimeter bullet tore through his left shoulder, sending him to the floor.

Matt hurled himself out in front of Bill, releasing a hail of .45 caliber bullets at the large man who was firing in their direction. Matt split the side of the Russian's head open with his first shot, planting another round in his center body mass as he went to the floor. In seconds, the battle was over.

Matt turned immediately toward Bill. He was grimacing, but definitely alive. Pulling his pack off, Matt removed two sulfa packs and a roll of tape. He applied both to Bill's wound, reassuring him that he would be all right.

"Shit!" Bill cursed. "Go check on Alya."

Across the room, they could hear her crawling slowly across the hardwood floor. Suddenly, the sound stopped, replaced by two short clicking noises.

Matt stood up and scanned the room with his firearm. As he worked his way cautiously through the lab tables, alert to the possibility of other intruders, a small stream of smoke arose from the vicinity of where Alya lay.

By the time he reached her, her father's delicate papers were aflame. A small lighter rested on the floor beside her, as she stared up at him with terror in her eyes. Blood drained from the corner of her mouth, and she struggled to breathe.

Matt stomped on the burning lab notes, trying to extinguish the flames. It was too late. For the most part, they were already ruined.

He bent down and raised Alya's head.

"What were you working on?" Matt implored. "Were you successful?"

Alya did not answer him. Instead, her eyes rolled back in her head, and her body slumped.

"That's it. She's gone," Matt said to himself.

He turned and walked over to the Russian woman, rolling her onto her back to get a look at her. Her face matched the description of Natasha's kidnapper, possibly aided by the large Russian man who lay bleeding ten feet away from her. In her waistcoat pocket, Matt found a letter from Dr. Watley to his colleague, Dr. Perin, at The Swiss Academy of Sciences. He placed it under the lamplight that Alya had used and read it.

"Well, that explains how they found her," he thought to *himself.*

He picked up Alya's lab journal lying open under the lamp. Then, he gathered the charred remnants of her father's notes, placed them inside the journal and stuffed it into his shirt.

He returned to Bill and explained that Alya was dead.

"Too bad," Bill said. "She might have given us some remarkable science."

"Question is, are we better off without it?" Matt replied.

In the distance, a police siren could be heard winding its way through the center of London.

"Come on," Matt said, helping Bill to his feet. "We need to get you to a hospital. I saw one on the way in."

"Call John Sauter and give him an update," Bill said, grimacing from the pain.

"Will do," Matt replied.

They made their way out of the building and into the Mercedes, departing the campus just before the police arrived.

Chapter 95

❧

When Bill woke up the next morning, his left arm was taped to his chest. Matt was sitting beside his hospital bed, going over a map of Moscow. Three British men in plain clothes were positioned around the room, with two more visible officers just outside his door.

When Bill stirred, Matt looked up at him and smiled.

"Glad to have you back, *William*," Matt said, knowing that Bill hated that name.

"Don't call me that, *Matthew*," Bill replied. "How long have I been out?"

"Let's see…" Matt replied. "They took you into surgery about two A.M. this morning, and it's almost noon now, so I'd say you've had about eight hours rest so far."

"Who are these guys?" Bill inquired, motioning toward the British security agents.

"Just a few of James Bond's friends that the Prime Minister sent over," Matt replied. "He sends his regards."

Bill chuckled.

"Did you get a hold of John yet?" he asked.

"Yep, I talked to him last night," Matt replied. "Right after they took you into surgery. He got in contact with Natasha. I'm supposed to let John know as soon as you're awake."

"Tell him I'm fine," Bill said.

"You can tell him yourself," Matt replied. "They should be here in a couple of hours."

"They?" Bill repeated, confused.

"John and Natasha," Matt clarified.

"What?" Bill complained. "Why in hell are they doing that?"

"Couldn't stop them," Matt replied. "Apparently they're both just as stubborn as you are."

"But, that doesn't make sense," Bill complained.

"Apparently, they're going to escort you home on a commercial flight," Matt explained. "First class, of course."

"And what about you?" Bill asked, confused.

"Me?" Matt replied. "Oh, well, I'm headed on to Moscow to collect some garbage."

"What garbage?" Bill asked.

"John identified the embassy's mole," Matt explained. "I'm being sent to collect him. They want him back in the States for some 'communications training.' I'll deliver him to federal agents in Miami. They'll take him on to Washington. I should make it back home shortly after you do."

"Do you think you can handle all of that without me?" Bill asked facetiously.

"I'll do my best," Matt replied. "Meanwhile, I want you to give this to John when he arrives."

Matt pulled Alya's lab journal out of his pack and handed it to Bill.

"Have John get this to Ming," Matt said. "I picked it up in the lab as we were leaving. She might be able to decipher it."

"You got it," Bill replied, tucking it under the bed covers.

"Leave the nurses alone and get some more rest before the troops arrive," Matt advised him. "These guys will keep an eye on you while you're here."

Bill looked around the room.

"If only they spoke English," he said sarcastically to Matt, pressing the button to raise the back of his bed.

"What's a guy gotta do to get some food around here?" he shouted.

Matt looked up sheepishly at the security detail and then turned back to Bill.

"I'll speak to the nurses on my way out," Matt assured him.

"Keep your head down, Matt," Bill warned. "Things are probably a little dicey in Moscow right now."

"I'll see you back in paradise," Matt replied, standing up and walking out the door.

He exited the hospital and made his way back onto the M5, heading west toward Heathrow Airport, where the Learjet was already fueled and waiting.

Chapter 96

❧

At ten A.M. that morning, the CIA recorded a second conversation from a different pay phone located only a block away from the American Embassy in Moscow. The call lasted three minutes.

Don Hanson had volunteered to go for pastries at a local bakery. As soon as he left the building, embassy security called the State Department, who immediately got word to the CIA.

"Something's wrong," Don Hanson told his Soviet contact. "When I got to the embassy this morning, they informed me that they were sending me back to the U.S. for training on some new communications equipment."

"What's so strange about that?" his Soviet contact inquired.

"What's strange is that they're sending some guy with me that I've never heard of," Don replied. "They've never done that before."

"Perhaps he is in need of training, too," his contact suggested.

"There's more," Don added. "I went through the ambassador's office this morning while he was in a meeting."

"And?" his contact asked, waiting to hear the outcome.

"There wasn't a single piece of information even remotely sensitive on his desk or in his briefcase. And the monk's letter was nowhere to be found."

"And why should you worry about this?" his contact inquired, knowing full well that something wasn't right.

"Because nothing was locked," Don explained. "Not his desk, his briefcase or his file cabinets. It's not normal, unless, of course, you have removed everything worth protecting."

"And why would they do that?" his contact inquired, probing for more information.

"I don't know," Don replied. "Maybe they're on to me."

There was a brief pause in the conversation. Then, his contact spoke up again.

"You can't assume this," he said, reasoning with Don. "They could be doing an inventory of their sensitive materials."

Don thought it over for a minute. It seemed unlikely to him.

"Well, they've never done it before," he commented.

"I wouldn't worry about it," his contact said, reassuring him. "If they knew something, they would have arrested you by now. Right?"

"Maybe," Don said nervously. "I don't know. It just doesn't feel right."

"Stay calm," his contact advised him. "Everything will be all right."

"I have to go now," Don said. "I've got to pick up some pastries on the way back to the embassy."

"Call me tomorrow," his contact instructed. Then, the line went dead.

Don Hanson hung up the pay phone and walked down the street to the corner bakery. He went inside and selected warm apple babkas, along with a half dozen plum and almond tarts. The Russian woman wrapped them in brown paper and placed them in a white paper bag for him. He paid her in rubles and turned around to leave.

As he opened the front door of the bakery, a green, four-door Russian VAZ, similar in design to the Fiat, turned the corner and paused. A Soviet marksman in the backseat put one round from an AK-47 through Don Hanson's forehead and then sped away.

He was dead before he hit the ground.

Three hours later, the head of the Moscow Police called the American ambassador to inform him of Don Hanson's murder and to express his deepest regrets. He offered to return the body for burial as soon as the investigation was complete.

"That won't be necessary," the ambassador replied calmly. "Feel free to cremate the body and spread his ashes in Mother Russia, where they belong."

The ambassador hung up the phone before the Soviet officer could reply.

Chapter 97

༄

The flight from London to Moscow took a little
over three hours. Matt slept most of the way, until
he felt the Learjet begin its descent. Twenty minutes
later, they landed at Domodedovo Airport, fifteen
miles south of the city. Randy taxied the aircraft to
a tie-down location near a hangar on the west side
of the airport and shut down the engines. Then, he
unbuckled himself and walked back to Matt.

"You go ahead," Randy said. "I'm going to stay
with the plane and have it refueled. I'll be staying at
The Aerotel."

He handed Matt a note with the hotel's phone
number on it.

"It's within walking distance of the airport," Randy
explained. "Let me know if you need anything.
Otherwise, just call me when you want to leave, and
I'll have the Lear fired up and ready to go."

"Thanks," Matt replied sincerely. "I'll probably see
you around noon tomorrow."

Matt gathered his pack and exited the Learjet at
eight P.M. Moscow time. It was still light out, and

he caught a ride to the main terminal on a small passenger transport.

Once inside, he submitted his passport and American Embassy credentials to the head of security, and they passed him quickly through customs without further inspection. An embassy driver was waiting for him just beyond the customs area.

"Mr. Garrett?" he asked, recognizing Matt from the small copy of his passport photo that the ambassador had been given.

"Yes," Matt replied.

"May I see your identification, sir?" the driver asked.

"Certainly," Matt replied.

Matt pulled out his credentials again and waited as the driver examined them. Five minutes later, they had exited the airport and were underway, headed north on the M4 toward the American Embassy in Moscow.

"Have you been to Russia before?" the driver asked him, making light conversation.

"First time," Matt replied.

"It's a little different," the driver commented.

They passed a number of unfamiliar vehicles – cars and trucks shaped by typical Soviet styling; squarer and more box-like than most American automobiles. Single-tone gray, green, black or dingy white colors dominated the roadway, with exhausts that were not shy about emissions.

"The ambassador has asked me to deliver you to his private residence," the driver informed Matt. "His wife is serving roast duck with orange sauce for dinner. They've invited you to stay the night as well."

"That's fine," Matt replied. "How close are they to the embassy itself?"

"Less than a mile away," the driver replied. "We should be there in about ten minutes."

"Great," Matt said. "By the way, there'll be two of us in need of a lift to the airport tomorrow."

"That's what we understood," the driver replied, "but, unfortunately, there's been a change of plans."

"What do you mean?" Matt asked, surprised by the news.

"The ambassador will explain it to you this evening," the driver said. "We just got wind of it while you were en route from London."

"Why didn't they contact us?" Matt inquired.

"Because they still need your help on another matter," the driver replied. "If you don't mind, I'd rather let the ambassador explain it to you this evening."

"O.K.," Matt replied. "That's fine."

He wasn't panicked by the news, but the sudden change in game plan put Matt on alert. He slipped the custom Colt out of his pack and placed it under the back of his belt, concealed by the lightweight jacket that he was wearing.

They entered the city and made their way to the ambassador's residence – a rugged stone and mortar house near the banks of the Moscow River. When the driver pulled up outside, Matt gathered his pack and thanked him.

"I'll see you again tomorrow," Matt said as he opened the door and got out.

"Enjoy your dinner, Mr. Garrett," the driver replied. "Take care."

The embassy car pulled away as Matt turned and walked up to the house. As he approached the front door, a delicious aroma floated through the evening air.

"If nothing else," he thought to himself, *"at least this meal will make the trip worthwhile."*

He rang the doorbell, and a pleasant-looking man with silver-tipped hair approached the front door from a spacious living room area. Through thick glass panels, Matt could see that he was in his early-to-mid fifties. He moved with the confidence of a successful negotiator.

As he opened the door, the exotic aroma of roast duck with orange sauce enveloped Matt.

"Ah, Mr. Garrett," the ambassador said, "Welcome to Moscow. Please, come in."

He stepped back, inviting Matt into the living room. As Matt walked through the house, he noticed a well-stocked library to his left, with a rich, mahogany-wood-paneled study opposite it. The kitchen and dining room were located at the rear of the house, with living quarters on either side of the living room.

"You've arrived just in time for dinner," the ambassador said. "My wife will be thrilled."

"That's very kind of you," Matt replied. "Thanks for having me."

"Before we sit down, a formality... " the ambassador said.

Matt already had his passport and embassy credentials in the front pocket of his jacket, figuring that he should be prepared to prove his identity. He pulled them out before the ambassador could finish his sentence.

"I'm sorry to put you through this," the ambassador said apologetically. "But consistent procedures are a necessary evil here in Mother Russia."

"I understand, sir," Matt replied.

"We were told that you are a member of the LOC team," the ambassador said. "Is that correct?"

Matt recognized this cue as well and pulled his wallet out, handing his U.S. driver's license to the ambassador.

"That's right," Matt replied. "Two of our other members are healing up from workplace injuries, and I believe you've spoken to John Sauter before."

"Yes," the ambassador replied. "As a matter of fact, we've gotten to know each other quite well over the last two days."

The ambassador examined Matt's driver's license and then returned it to him, having verified the unusual trident symbol in its upper right-hand corner.

"I understand that there's been a change of plans," Matt said as they stood in the center of the living room.

"I'm afraid so," the ambassador replied. "Looks like you won't be escorting Don Hanson back to the states tomorrow."

"Really?" Matt replied. "Why not?

"Just a few hours ago, we were informed that he had been murdered. He left the embassy about ten o'clock this morning to purchase some pastries for his colleagues. Someone shot him once in the head, killing him instantly."

"Any idea who did it?" Matt replied.

"According to eye witnesses," the ambassador continued, "the bullet was fired from an AK-47 out of the backseat of a dark green VAZ – a Russian automobile, which immediately sped away from the scene.

"An hour later, we were told that the real reason Don had left the embassy was to make a phone call to his Soviet handler. The CIA recorded it. Unfortunately, he expressed serious concern to his Russian contact that we were on to him.

"Apparently, the Russians didn't want him questioned, since revealing their relationship would have caused an international incident. So, they took the safe approach. They terminated him."

"Interesting," Matt said. "So, why am I here?"

"To have roast duck, of course," the ambassador replied, smiling at him. "Let's go into the dining room and eat while it's still hot. We'll adjourn to my study afterwards, and I'll give you something that needs to go back to the States with you."

"Great," Matt said, following him to the dinner table.

The ambassador's wife wasn't exactly what Matt had expected. She was vivacious and funny, with a lively sense of humor. When Matt was introduced to her, she stepped back to examine him, and her eyes lit up.

"Wow!" she squealed, as if pleasantly surprised. "Now I remember why I miss the United States so much!"

Matt understood what she meant, but wasn't sure how to react.

"All these Soviet men look like the butt end of a boar," she complained. "It's so refreshing to have a nice, young American guy in our home again."

Matt chuckled.

"Well, uh – thanks... I guess," he said, slightly embarrassed.

"Don't mind Hilary," the ambassador replied, smiling. "She has a mind of her own. But she's a wonderful cook, as you're about to discover."

"Thanks for having me, Ma'am," Matt said looking down at the lavishly-arrayed dinner table. "It smells wonderful."

"My Chanel or the duck?" she quipped.

"Both," Matt replied, opting for the safe out.

Chapter 98

☙

After an entertaining dinner that included his first introduction to roast duck, Matt complimented the chef profusely, thanking her for the wonderful meal and enjoyable company.

"Breakfast is at eight," she replied. "Don't be late, or I'll feed it to the dog."

"I'll fight him for it," Matt responded quickly.

The ambassador stood up and thanked his wife as well.

"Great job, honey," he said. "What would I do without you?"

"I hesitate to think," she replied, winking at him.

Matt followed the ambassador into his study, where he removed a beautifully-framed print of Monet's *San Giorgio Maggioriore-Soleil Couchant* from the wall behind his mahogany desk. A small, recessed safe was revealed, with a black spinner lock on it. As he opened it, he explained his actions.

"Yesterday, I brought an unopened letter home in my briefcase that I had received at the American Embassy earlier that day. Frankly, I just hadn't had time to look at it yet. It was handed to one of our employees on the front steps of the embassy early yesterday morning, but it was addressed to me.

"From what I was told, the monk who delivered it just turned and walked away without saying a word, heading to the north. Our staff member reported that the man was wearing a simple, black cassock, indistinguishable from most other Russian Orthodox monks.

"When he called after him, the monk just held up his staff and waved it from side to side, without looking back at him. My man mentioned that it had a blue triquetra on top of it."

"Sorry?" Matt said, interrupting the ambassador. "What's that?"

"You know," he replied. "the three-part, interlocking fish design that symbolizes the Trinity... the Father, the Son and the Holy Spirit."

"Got it," Matt replied. "Please, continue."

"At the time, I didn't think much of the letter, figuring that it was probably a request for a donation to some religious order. In retrospect, though, that seems unlikely, since the Soviet government would not approve of such activities on embassy grounds.

"Anyway, John Sauter called me at home last night from the Secretary of State's office and said they had identified a mole in our shop. Through recordings done by the CIA, we discovered that Don Hanson also had an interest in the monk's letter, being suspicious of its contents. When he reported this to his Soviet contacts, they directed him to pursue it.

"Of course, when Don searched my office this morning, it was nowhere to be found. I left it here for safe keeping.

"All other sensitive materials had been removed from my office as well, which is probably what spooked him. If he would have kept his concerns to himself, he'd probably be flying home with you tomorrow, only to be arrested and tried for treason in Washington.

"I don't mind telling you that, to me, justice was better served by what happened."

The ambassador paused a moment and then continued.

"Last night, The Secretary of State directed me to open the monk's letter and read it to them over the secure line. When I described its contents, they asked me to turn it over to you for safe transport back to the U.S."

"What does it say?" Matt asked.

"I have no idea," the ambassador replied, "and neither will you. It's written in some sort of ancient Cyrillic language. No one on my staff can interpret it, so you'll have to get it back to the States and have some academic experts examine it there. Chances are, it's just some religious psycho-babble, but, just in case it isn't, the State Department would like to have a look at it."

"Of course," Matt said. "Would you mind if I have a look at it?"

"Not at all," the ambassador consented. "It's all yours now."

He pulled the letter out of the wall safe and handed it to Matt.

Matt opened the parchment envelope and pulled out a light brown note, folded in half. When he unfolded it, a small slip of paper fell out and floated gracefully to the floor, dancing about like a butterfly.

He looked at the letter still in his hand, which was completely unreadable, with a mix of words and symbols that meant absolutely nothing to him. Then, he bent down and picked up the small piece of paper, glancing at the seven, barely-legible numbers on it, penciled by an unsteady hand.

He quickly returned both items to the envelope and looked up at the ambassador.

"I'll see that it gets home safely," Matt said. "Anything else?"

"Not that I know of," the ambassador replied. "Let's have a nightcap, and then I'll show you to your room."

"Wonderful," Matt replied. "You and your wife have treated me like family. I hope that you'll come visit us when you finish your work here."

"Be careful," the ambassador warned. "We might just take you up on that."

"I certainly hope so, sir," Matt replied.

An hour later, Matt was shown to the guest bedroom, where he secured the monk's envelope in his pack. He undressed, took a hot shower and crawled into bed, pulling the warm duvet over his body. For a few minutes, he lay there wondering how Bill was doing in London, with the rest of the LOC team fussing over him.

Matt looked forward to getting back. By this time tomorrow, he would be in Miami, where he would turn the monk's letter over to federal agents. Then, he could head back home to check on the status of the people that he cared about, including a young woman whose eyes still haunted him.

Soon, he drifted into a deep sleep.

Chapter 99

In his dream, Matt was sitting in the living room of his remarkable new home on Nevis. A warm, tropical breeze wandered through his cottage, and the ever-present sounds of the Caribbean Sea could be heard in the distance.

He stood up from his chair and went to the wooden mantel. Once again, he reached up and removed his father's M1 Garand from the wall. Holding it with both hands at waist level, he admired its rich, warm finish and solid stature.

Suddenly, a rustling sound overhead caught his attention, and he looked up. A clear strip of film detached itself from the ceiling and floated downward. He tried desperately to reach up and grab it, but the ten-pound weight of the Garand suddenly felt like a hundred.

He stood there, watching helplessly as the strip floated downward toward him, dancing about like a butterfly in the warm tropical air. It passed his face and continued its descent.

As it neared his waistline, a small, seven-digit number on its surface came into focus. In slow motion, the clear strip of film landed softly on the top, back of the M1 Garand's receiver, precisely overlaying the rifle's serial number… an exact match.

Matt bolted upright in the middle of the night, his chest heaving and his mind racing wildly, like an engine thrown suddenly into neutral during a high-speed chase. He threw the warm duvet completely off the bed and leapt to his feet. Flailing about in the darkness, he finally located the nightstand's lamp and turned it on.

Immediately, he checked his wrist watch. It was one A.M. The only sound in the house was the steady ticking of the grandfather clock in the hallway, clearly out-paced by his pounding heart. He called on his military training, forcing himself to calm down.

A minute later, he was under control.

There was no mistake – he was certain of it. Nevertheless, he went to the dresser and opened his pack. Removing the monk's letter, he took out the small slip of penciled paper inside and studied the numbers.

His body began to tremble.

How could a monk, half a world away from his father's rifle, have knowledge of its serial number?

A coincidence? The statistical odds against it were astronomical. As far as he was concerned, there was only one explanation.

Soldiers were forced to memorize the serial numbers of their rifles, required to repeat it frequently in front of drill sergeants and other officers. It was a fundamental tenet of their early military training regimen.

Matt had never met an older Marine veteran who could not recite the serial number of the weapon issued to him, even decades after active duty.

He gathered his clothing and dressed quickly, struggling to control his emotions. As he busied himself collecting the tools that he would need, he began to reason. He would not wake the ambassador or his wife. If he were caught, it would be best if they could honestly deny any knowledge of his actions.

Matt tucked his custom Colt into the back of his belt and pulled a small set of lock picks, a brass-encased compass about the size of a quarter and a tiny penlight from his pack. Then, he located his map of Moscow and the surrounding area, sat down on the edge of the bed and opened it under the lamp light.

As he studied the map, he tried to recall what the ambassador had said about the monk's strange behavior when he delivered the letter.

Two things had stuck in Matt's head; the monk had departed in a northerly direction, and he had waved a staff that revealed a symbol of The Trinity on its head.

Remembering the ambassador's library, he made his way quietly through the living room with his pen light and entered the multi-shelved collection of books. A section of the library was devoted to Russian art, literature and religion. He selected a volume on the history of Russian monastic life and returned to his room.

Rushing through its pages, he came across a list of Russia's Orthodox Christian monasteries. There were many, but he quickly eliminated those that lay to the south, concentrating on those that were north of Moscow.

As he studied the list, his eyes froze on one name – The Trinity-Sergius Lavra, Russia.

Located in the town of Sergiev Posad, it was a large, white-walled monastery, housing an array of medieval buildings with blue and gold-domed tops. The text described it as the spiritual center of the Russian Orthodox Church, founded in 1345.

Suddenly, Matt realized that the monk had indeed spoken as he departed the embassy – he just hadn't used words. The triquetra symbol was a guidepost, intended to identify his monastery. The symbol of The Trinity was, in fact, Matt's inconceivable destination.

Chapter 100

❧

A t five P.M., Governor Owen B. Rice was packing his briefcase at the end of a busy day of legislation, preparing to return to his Tallahassee home, located five miles from the state capital. His wife had called ten minutes earlier to remind him that she was planning dinner at six, hoping that he would be on time.

As he started for the door, his secretary stepped into his office and informed him that he had a phone call.

"Is it my wife?" the governor asked. "Tell her I'm on the way."

"No, sir," his secretary began, "but…"

"Well, whoever it is, tell them I've left for the day," Owen instructed. "I need to hit the road."

"Uh… I think you better take this one, sir," his secretary replied. "It sounds important."

"Who is it?" the governor inquired, concealing his mild irritation.

"He says his name is Matt Garrett," the secretary replied. "He's calling on a secure line from Moscow."

"Moscow?" the governor asked. "Moscow, Russia?"

"That's right," his secretary replied. "He says it's critical that he speak to you."

"Put him through immediately," the governor instructed, setting his briefcase down and returning to his desk. "And close the door to my office as you leave."

"Of course," his secretary replied as she exited the room.

When the call was transferred to his desk, Governor Rice picked it up instantly.

"Matt?" he said. "Is that you? What the hell are you doing in Moscow?"

"Making new friends and winning hearts," Matt replied. "I'm on a secure line in the American ambassador's home in Moscow right now. I hope you're doing well, sir."

Owen detected the controlled excitement in Matt's voice and knew that something unusual was going on.

"Well, I'm fine," the governor replied, still a bit dazed by Matt's call. "Just a little surprised to have you call from Russia. What's up?"

"Well, sir," Matt began slowly, "you're not going to believe this one. Are you sitting down?"

"As a matter of fact, I am," the governor replied. "But something tells me that I won't be for long."

"I need your help, sir," Matt explained. "I think you'll agree that it's a matter of considerable importance."

"Just name it, Matt," he replied. "You know that I'll do whatever I can."

"Great," Matt said. "Before I explain what's happening, I need you to write down a couple of numbers. Do you have a pen, sir?"

"I'm ready," the governor replied, picking up a pen and notepad. "Go ahead."

Matt recited an eleven-digit number, followed by a seven-digit number, both of which the governor carefully recorded.

"The first number is the Aerotel Hotel, adjacent to the Domodedovo Airport in Moscow," Matt said. "I need you to contact my pilot there, Randy Weston, and pass on some operational orders from me. He'll be asleep when you call, but it has to be done. He's very professional – he won't mind, particularly when you explain to him what's going on."

"And what might that be?" Owen inquired, anxious to get to the root cause of Matt's unexpected call.

"That brings us to the second number," Matt replied. Initially, there was emotion in Matt's voice that concerned the governor a bit, but it quickly shifted to professional precision – the kind that Owen recognized as the influence of disciplined training.

"The seven-digit number that I gave you belongs to an old friend of yours," Matt said.

"A friend of *mine*?" the governor said, puzzled by Matt's claim. "I can't think of anyone that I know who's still serving in that part of the world."

"That number is the serial number of Captain James R. Garrett's service rifle – his M1 Garand," Matt said, already anticipating the governor's next response.

There was a brief pause as Owen contemplated the meaning of this.

"O.K.," the governor said slowly. "I believe your mother still has that rifle. Right?"

"Actually, she gave it to me last week," Matt replied. "It's hanging on my living room wall in Nevis."

"I heard about the cottages that Bill built for you," the governor remarked. "How does Marie like it down there?"

"We all love it," Matt replied, "which is one of the reasons that I want you to come visit."

"Well, thanks for the invitation," the governor replied. "I might be able to fit it in sometime next month."

"I think you'll want to move that up a bit on your schedule when you hear about the other reason," Matt replied.

"Oh, yeah?" the governor said. "What's that?"

"Are you still sitting down, sir?" Matt inquired.

"I am," Owen replied.

"It's one-thirty in the morning here, and I'm about to borrow a car and drive up to the Trinity St. Sergius Monastery in Sergiev Posad. It's about forty-five miles northeast of the city."

"Now, why would you risk that in the middle of the night?" the governor asked, concerned for Matt's safety.

"Because one of their members dropped off a slip of paper with that rifle's serial number scribbled on it at the American Embassy in Moscow yesterday. The monk that delivered it departed immediately, without saying a word."

There was a long pause on the other end of the line as the details of Matt's words sunk in.

"How did *they* get it?" the governor asked, completely confused.

"You tell me," Matt replied.

A second, longer pause ensued. Owen Rice was having a hard time wrapping his head around the whole idea.

"It doesn't make any sense," the governor finally declared. "We all saw the tape."

"The tape ran out," Matt reminded him.

"But, it's not possible," the governor said, struggling to grasp the concept.

"That's what I intend to find out," Matt responded.

"What did the ambassador say about this?" Owen asked.

"He doesn't know yet," Matt replied. "It was a private revelation that just hit me. The ambassador and his wife are still asleep. I'm going to look into this on my own. I don't want them involved, in case I run into any trouble."

"I see," the governor said, still confused. "All right, what can I do to help?"

"I need you to call Randy Weston," Matt repeated. "Have him file a flight plan to depart Moscow for London at six A.M. and have him meet me at the fence line immediately in back of where our Learjet is parked just before dawn. Tell him to bring a pair of wire cutters and a small roll of aluminum wire."

"Got it," the governor replied. "What else?"

"I also need you to contact John Sauter. He and Bill and Natasha are probably on a commercial flight back to the states by now, en route to San Juan and then on to St. Kitts and Nevis. Bill's recuperating from a shoulder injury that he sustained in London, so they crossed the pond to escort him back home."

"I heard," the governor replied. "How's he doing?"

"Mean as a junkyard dog," Matt replied. "Even worse since he was shot. Have John tell Bill what I've just told you. They'll know what to do. I really need to get underway here as soon as possible."

"I understand," the governor replied.

"Just one more thing, sir," Matt said. "I'd really like you to be down there to help with my mom if this thing turns out to be for real. It's hard to predict what impact it might have on her."

"I can certainly relate to that," Governor Rice replied. "God, I hope you're right!"

"I can't think of any other explanation, sir," Matt said. "Anyway, I've got to get going."

"Don't worry, Matt," the governor assured him. "I'll take care of everything immediately. As soon as I finish making the contacts you've requested, I'll call the Secretary of State and update him as well. Chances are he'll want to communicate with the Director of Customs in Miami. Then, I'll head for the airport and catch a flight down to St. Kitts and Nevis. If this turns out to be a false alarm, we'll just have a nice little visit together."

"Thank you, sir," Matt said. "I remain in your debt."

"Not if you pull this off," the governor replied. "Listen, Matt. Be careful. The Russians aren't fond of Americans going sight-seeing on their turf in the middle of the night."

"If I have it my way, they'll never know about it, sir," Matt replied, confident that his plan would work.

"Good luck," the governor added.

"Thank you, sir," Matt replied.

He hung up the phone and wrote a quick note to the ambassador and his wife, apologizing for his sudden call to duty and thanking them again for their hospitality. He added his mailing address and left the note on the dining room table.

At one-forty A.M., he slipped out the back door of the ambassador's residence and made his way quietly up the street on foot. Three blocks away, he selected a black Russian automobile, picked its door lock and hot-wired the engine.

He pulled away quickly, heading northward through the streets of Moscow, his compass and pen light resting on top of the open map beside him.

In ten minutes, he was clear of the city, turning northeast onto a road that was lightly traveled. An occasional truck passed by, headed into the city to deliver produce or other goods, but traffic thinned to almost nothing as he got farther and farther away from Moscow.

Somewhere out there in the darkness was a monastery that knew something about the father that he hadn't seen or heard from in almost fourteen years.

Was there another explanation for the numbers? Was this some sort of cruel, practical joke that God was playing on him?

He pushed the thought out of his head and concentrated on the task at hand.

Chapter 101

❦

Marie was sitting on her front porch, waiting to hear from Natasha, when a white, four-door Mercedes pulled up in front of her cottage. A middle-aged couple, neatly dressed in European clothing, got out of the front seat.

A much younger, blonde-haired woman opened the back door, and the man came around and helped his daughter to her feet. Once upright, she steadied herself, as if dealing with an injury. Marie noticed bruises on her neck, but the girl proved sturdy enough to walk on her own.

They looked up at Marie and smiled, greeting her with an accent that was obviously not American. Marie stood up and responded in kind, opening the front porch door and inviting them in.

"You are Matt's mother, perhaps?" the wife asked, guessing from her age and appearance.

"I am, indeed," Marie replied. "Won't you come in?"

The three of them made their way slowly up the steps, keeping an eye on their daughter's progress.

"We are Rodger and Marta Eriksson," the husband said with a distinctly Swedish accent, "and this is our daughter, Annika."

"It's so nice to meet you," Marie replied. "Please, sit down and join me. My name is Marie... Marie Garrett."

"And you have a son named 'Matt'?" Rodger inquired as he settled his daughter into a cushioned wicker chair.

"Yes, I do," Marie replied. "I'm very proud of him."

"You have every right to be," Marta said.

Marie turned and looked at her, wondering what experience her judgment was based on.

"Is your son home right now?" Rodger asked politely. "We'd really like to meet him."

So far, the daughter had not spoken. Marie glanced over at her and got a close look at the young woman's eyes. They were an unusual color of blue, reflecting the island's light in a way that made her appear both regal and compassionate.

"I'm afraid he's not back yet," Marie replied, turning back to her father. "Would you mind if I asked what this is all about?"

"You mean you don't know?" Marta asked, looking at her curiously with eyes that favored her daughter's.

"Know what?" Marie responded.

"He didn't tell you?" Rodger asked.

"I guess he didn't," Marie replied, completely at a loss. "Is something wrong?"

Finally, the young woman broke her silence.

"He saved my life," the daughter said softly, with velvety, smooth warmth in her voice. "I wanted to thank him."

"Matt did?" Marie exclaimed. "My Matt?"

"Yes," Rodger confirmed. "He took on a much larger man who attacked Annika. And he didn't even know who she was. We are deeply indebted to your son, Mrs. Garrett. If he had not intervened, Annika would not be sitting here today."

Marie was stunned. Matt had said nothing to her about it. Why would he keep such a thing to himself? *You just wait until I get my hands on you, young man!"* *she thought to herself.*

"Well, I don't know what to say," Marie replied at last, breaking an uncomfortable silence. "He's always been protective of women, perhaps because of his concern for me. Matt became the head of our household at an early age. His father died in the military when he was only ten years old."

"I'm very sorry to hear that, Mrs. Garrett," Marta said with genuine sympathy. "You've certainly managed to raise a fine young man, though. He even visited Annika in the hospital the morning after the attack. She was sedated, but he left flowers for her anyway."

"He also paid part of her hospital bill," Rodger added. "We just can't believe that he did all of that for a complete stranger."

His voice trailed off as he contemplated his own words. Marta filled the gap.

"He's a remarkable young man, Mrs. Garrett. We look forward to meeting him."

Marie liked them both immediately. Anyone who thought that much of her son certainly deserved her friendship and support.

"Would you like something to drink?" Marie asked, smiling at them. "I'd love for you to stay and visit a while. I have coffee and tea already made."

Her guests looked at each other, agreeing to accept her invitation.

Marie went inside and soon returned with a tray of tea, coffee, cream and sugar.

"I'll be right back," she said, returning to her kitchen.

Ten minutes later, she was serving them hot, crab meltaways on triangular slices of English muffin, fresh from her oven broiler. She sat down with them, poured herself a cup of coffee and looked over at Annika.

"Now, dear" Marie said in an upbeat tone. "Tell me all about what happened."

By the time they left at six P.M., it felt like they were old friends. Marie promised to let them know as soon as she heard from Matt, and they insisted that she and Matt come to dinner at their villa in Golden Rock as soon as he returned.

All three of them hugged Marie as they left. Annika's embrace left an inexplicable impression on her.

Chapter 102

෨

A half hour after the Eriksson's left, Bill's Land Rover pulled up in front of Marie's cottage. She walked out on the front porch to greet them.

Looking much improved, Natasha got out of the back seat and opened the passenger-side door for Bill. When he stood up, she could see that his left arm and shoulder were wrapped in a blue, white and red sling, bearing the design of the British "Union Jack" flag.

"Bill Hunter!" she exclaimed. "What have you done to yourself now?"

"Don't worry, Mrs. G," Bill said. "I just took a little tumble and injured my shoulder. Got anything to eat? I'm famished. Airline food sucks."

When the driver got out, he was wearing a tacky Hawaiian shirt, blue jeans and leather sandals. He looked up at Marie and waved.

"And you must be John Sauter," Marie called to him, smiling. "Bill's told me all about you."

"And you're still willing to let me come inside?" John quipped.

"Only if you'll stay for dinner," Marie responded.

John smiled and headed toward the steps behind Bill and Natasha.

"Where's Matt?" Marie asked, directing her question to Bill.

"He's on the way," Bill replied matter-of-factly. "I had to take a different flight to accommodate all of my entourage. He'll arrive on the Lear about eleven o'clock tomorrow morning."

"Why so late?" Marie inquired.

"He insisted on seeing Big Ben before he left," Bill lied. "You'd think that he'd be more concerned about my welfare than some old clock, wouldn't you?"

"That boy!" Marie chuckled, both amused and mildly frustrated. "Did you know that he actually saved the lives of two women on this island right before he left here?"

"What?" Natasha exclaimed, having no knowledge of the event whatsoever. "When did he have time to work that in?"

"I don't know, but it's true," Marie insisted. "The younger of the two women showed up here with her parents this evening wanting to express their gratitude. You can imagine how I felt, being totally in the dark like that."

"Hmmf," Bill added, tongue in cheek. "Whatever are we going to do with that boy?"

"Oh, shut up," Natasha said, chastising him softly.

"Anyway, dinner's almost ready," Marie said. "All of you come inside and make yourselves comfortable."

John Sauter looked back over his shoulder at the magnificent view of the Caribbean Sea.

"Hey, how come you didn't build me a place down here, too?" he complained to Bill.

"Isn't it obvious?" Bill replied flatly and kept on walking.

The exotic smell of pork ribs, sweet potatoes and stir-fried island vegetables met them as they went, single file, through the front door. Just as Marie was about to close the door behind them, an island taxi pulled up and stopped behind the Land Rover.

A tall man in a crisp, black suit, carrying a matching leather travel bag stepped out of the backseat and paid his Nevisian driver. When he turned around, Marie realized that it was Governor Owen B. Rice.

"Wow!" he remarked as she came out on the porch. "This is quite a place you've got here, Marie. I hope you don't mind the intrusion."

"Are you kidding me?" Marie exclaimed, hurrying down the front steps to greet him.

"Matt called and invited me down," the governor explained. "He said I could bunk at his place."

"What a wonderful surprise!" Marie replied, giving him a big hug. "And you've arrived just in time for dinner. Come on in. Everyone's here except Matt. He should arrive in the morning."

"Great!" the governor said. "I'm anxious to see everyone again."

"Isn't it wonderful what Bill did for us?" Marie commented as they went up the front steps. "He's such a special young man."

"You've got a couple of those, don't you?" the governor commented.

"I've been very fortunate, indeed," Marie acknowledged.

"Lady, you have no idea," the governor thought to himself as they entered the cottage together.

After a wonderful dinner, Marie slipped away into the bedroom and made a phone call, fulfilling her promise to the Eriksson's.

While she was gone, Governor Rice went over the plan with the LOC team.

Chapter 103

❧

At three-thirty A.M. Moscow time, Matt turned his headlights off as he pulled up alongside the white-walled fortress of the Trinity St. Sergius Monastery in Sergiev Posad. There was light snow on the ground, but the sky was crystal clear. With the help of a tightly-bound length of rope that he kept at the bottom of his pack, he scaled the ancient stone wall and dropped into the courtyard undetected.

A series of magnificent stone buildings were scattered about the area, bathed in the still light of a waning moon. He could just make out the beautiful architecture of their domes, decorated with stars and symbols of Orthodox Christianity. A five-tiered bell tower soared above the complex.

He made his way silently across the courtyard and entered the shadows of a large building that served as the refectory. The monks took their meals here in silence, but no lights came through the windows yet.

Matt continued past the refectory and located the monks' dormitory, with ground-level access directly into the gold-domed Trinity Cathedral. A tiny ray of light escaped from a small office at the back of the structure.

Matt entered the main cathedral door and moved quickly in the direction of the light, passing the austere chambers where the monks slept.

At the end of the hallway, he peered into the office of the abbot, who was placing his prayer book in the pocket of his black cassock in preparation for morning prayers. His long, black hair reached down to the sides of his matching full beard. When he sensed Matt's presence, he turned around without alarm.

The abbot studied Matt for a few seconds.

There was no mistaking the resemblance.

"You have come for him?" the abbot said calmly, as if expecting him.

Matt held out the parchment letter.

"Wait here," the abbot instructed, ignoring the letter. He walked around him and disappeared silently down the hallway.

Matt's heart pounded in his chest as he waited.

In another minute, the abbot was standing over the stranger's bed. He bent down and shook him gently.

"You must rise, Lazarus," he said. "You have a visitor."

James Garrett stirred and then slowly opened his eyes. Looking up at the abbot, he whispered quietly.

"Is it time for prayers, Father?" he said, somewhat disoriented.

"No, my son," the abbot explained. "You must come with me. There's someone here to see you."

"Who?" Lazarus inquired.

Since entering the monastery, James had never had a visitor. The very idea seemed absurd to him.

"Perhaps you'll recognize him, Lazarus," the abbot replied. "Put on your cassock and come with me."

Matt heard the footsteps of two men approaching from down the hallway. He faced the doorway and held his breath. In another minute, the abbot entered the room and stepped to the side.

When the second man entered the room, Matt drew in a deep breath and exhaled sharply. He felt the warmth of tears slipping down his cheeks, and he brushed them away in an attempt to control himself.

Standing before him in a simple black cassock was a man who was clearly related to him. He seemed smaller and somehow more distant, but he appeared to be relatively healthy, despite his experience. The monks had taken good care of him.

In spite of his father's illness and years of separation from his family, Matt found himself looking at an image of himself.

"Lazarus," the abbot said to him, "Do you know this man?"

The quiet monk did not reply, but continued to stare at the young man before him, who looked vaguely familiar. He struggled to lift the veil from his memory, but could not remove it.

"Lazarus," the abbot repeated. "Do you recognize this young man?"

He tilted his head slightly and furrowed his brow, trying with all his strength to identify him.

"Dad," Matt said gently. "It's me – Matt. I am your son. Don't you remember me, Dad?"

The sound of his voice renewed his father's struggle. Fragments of information swirled about in his mind, but he had trouble organizing them. Nothing he tried could bring them together in meaningful relationship to each other.

Matt reached into his pack and pulled out a small object, handing it to his father. Lazarus accepted it and looked down at the small metal soldier in his hand, curious about the gift of a child's toy.

The well-worn soldier held a tiny M1 Garand in its miniature hands. Lazarus locked onto it, and, in a few seconds, a string of seven numbers danced inside his head.

Suddenly, he looked up at the young man in front of him, eyes bright with realization.

"Matt?" he cried. "Matt!"

He reached out for him, and Matt stepped forward, embracing him tightly. Together at last, they wept.

The abbot left the room quietly, giving them some time to themselves. When he returned, he carried a staff, with a blue Trinity symbol on top of it.

"Lazarus," the abbot said. "Take this with you to remember us. We will keep you in our prayers."

Captain James Garrett withdrew from his son's embrace to receive the abbot's gift.

"Father, I am so grateful to you."

"Go now, Lazarus," the abbot instructed. "You must return to your family. We will pray that no harm comes to you or your son."

Matt reached into his pack and pulled out an envelope that he had prepared at the ambassador's residence. Inside, he had placed two thousand dollars, in the unlikely case that he actually located his father. Now that he had, he knew exactly what to do with it.

"Father, I want you to have this money," Matt said, placing the envelope on the abbot's desk. "Use it to feed and clothe the monks who have cared for my father so well."

The words were no sooner out of his mouth than he realized how foolish they were. The monks had no such needs. They raised their own food, and they had no need for clothing beyond their simple cassocks, which they wove themselves.

The abbot sensed Matt's realization and reassured him.

"We will use your gift to feed and clothe the poor," the abbot said. "It is our duty to help them."

"Thank you, Father," Matt replied. "I know that you will put it to good use. I cannot tell you how grateful my family is for what you have done. It was truly an extraordinary act of kindness. How can I possibly thank you?"

"By restoring your family," the abbot replied. "Clearly, it is God's will."

He turned to Lazarus for the last time.

"Go now, my son," the abbot instructed. "From the accent in your son's voice, I believe that you have a long journey ahead of you. May God protect you both."

"Thank you, Father," James replied. "I will never forget you."

They embraced each other, and then Matt and James Garrett turned and exited the abbot's office together. As they made their way down the hall, they could hear the monks beginning to rise for early morning prayers.

Out in the courtyard, the moon progressed across the night sky, reminding Matt that time was short. They would need to reach the airport by five A.M., while darkness was still on their side.

Matt selected one of the archways nearest his vehicle and unlatched its door, opening it into a world that his father had not seen for many years. He guided him to the parked car and settled him into the passenger seat. Then, he slipped behind the wheel and cranked it, pulling away slowly through the quiet streets of Sergiev Posad.

Chapter 104

∽

In five minutes, they were clear of the town, turning southward onto the same road that Matt had traveled before. Once again, traffic was sparse, and, for the next half hour, they made good time. A light snow began to fall, covering both sides of the roadway with a fresh, thin layer of white.

Thirty minutes later, traveling through the woods outside of Moscow, a low, dense fog set in, and Matt was forced to slow their speed. The speedometer fell to sixty kilometers per hour – not fast enough to soothe Matt's apprehension. Time was critical, and the fog was a setback.

He looked across at his father, who was holding onto the Trinity staff that the abbot had given him. Matt realized how difficult this must be for him. He had been rushed out of a slow-moving, secure environment into a world that moved quickly and contained real dangers.

Matt looked over and started to speak to him, when a flash of motion caught his eye. He turned back just in time to see a stag horn deer, frozen in his headlights, directly in front of their car. Instinctively, he slammed on the brakes and swerved to the left.

As he struggled to correct the automobile, the right rear panel of the automobile struck the animal as it slid underneath the car. They felt a hard bump, and then the vehicle swung back across the right-hand side of the road and came to a stop.

Matt shut the engine off and reached across to check on his father. He was shaken, but all right.

Matt instructed him to remain in the car as he got out and walked around to the back of it. The right rear tire had blown out, a four-inch piece of stag horn protruding from its side. The trunk had popped open from the impact, and blood was sprayed across its lid.

The twisted carcass of the deer lay still along the side of the road, thirty feet behind the vehicle.

Matt reached into the trunk and removed the spare tire, which was low on air and balding, but still usable. A rusting jack lay beneath it, so he retrieved his pen light and used it to illuminate the elevation of the rear quarter of the vehicle.

Meanwhile, his father sat quietly in the car, staring out the passenger-side window. James Garrett's eyes came to rest upon the bright red splashes of deer blood, spread across the contrasting surface of the freshly fallen snow. *Deep inside his mind, the veil lifted once again, and images of Chinese soldiers in white battle dress rushed into his consciousness, their uniforms spattered with a matching red substance. Astonishingly, a man that he recognized came into focus, fighting for his life behind a large boulder as Chinese soldiers closed in on him. It was*

Owen – Sergeant Owen Rice – his best friend, lost to him for so many years.

Halfway through the removal of the damaged tire, Matt stood up as an approaching vehicle slowed down, pulled off the road behind them and came to a stop in back of their car.

The driver left his lights on when he got out and walked toward Matt. When he got closer, Matt could see that the man was a young, Russian police officer. For a split second, Matt considered reaching for his custom Colt, but decided against it.

"Hello," the young officer said in Russian.

Matt didn't speak Russian, but he replied in kind, figuring that it was a greeting of some sort.

"Need any help?" the officer inquired in Russian.

Matt deduced from the slight rise in inflection at the end of his sentence that he was asking a question. Odds were that he was offering assistance.

"Nyet," Matt replied, smiling and continuing his work.

"Where are you headed?" the Russian officer asked in Russian.

Matt stood up slowly and faced him. The officer was similar in size, though slightly thinner.

"Nyet," Matt replied, taking his chances.

The officer immediately went on the defensive, placing his hand on his sidearm and addressing him firmly.

"Your identification, please," he said in Russian, extending his left hand to retrieve it.

Matt realized that he wanted identification, so he reached into his pocket and pulled out his passport.

As he stepped forward to hand it to the officer, he stumbled slightly and intentionally released it from his hand.

Instinctively, the young Russian officer reached downward to catch it, momentarily taking his eyes off of Matt. A hard blow struck the back of his neck, and he went to the ground unconscious.

Matt retrieved his passport and removed a pair of hand cuffs from the officer's belt, temporarily placing them in his own pocket. Then, he bent down and lifted the young officer over his shoulder.

He quickly carried him fifty feet into the woods and set him down against a small, sturdy tree trunk. He pulled the Russian's arms behind his body and cuffed them around the tree. Then, he removed a handkerchief from his pocket, balled it up and stuffed it into his mouth.

Matt returned to his vehicle and quickly completed the tire swap, grateful for the additional light that the officer's headlights provided. He rolled the damaged tire away from the vehicle, threw the jack back in the trunk and closed it. Then, he pulled his pack out of the backseat, walked to the officer's car and climbed into the driver seat.

He drove the police vehicle into the woods, turned off its lights and engine and left the keys in the ignition. Then, he took a small bottle of rubbing alcohol and a rag from his pack and wiped down all of the surfaces that he had touched. The snowfall would cover the vehicle's tracks.

He removed a blanket from the backseat of the officer's car and wrapped it around the Russian's shoulders as he left.

When he returned to their "borrowed" vehicle and sat down, his father looked over at him.

"He'll be O.K., Dad," Matt reassured him, glancing down at his watch.

Twenty minutes had been lost. They would have to hurry.

He hot-wired the vehicle's engine again. It struggled for a moment and then cranked. Matt pulled back onto the road and accelerated quickly, praying for the fog to lift.

As they neared Moscow, he checked his watch and the map. They were late, but they were close to their destination. He turned down an access road that led to the airport, racing against the approach of dawn.

Chapter 105

When Matt pulled up along the western fence line of the airport, he shut off his headlights. Slowly, he made his way to the tie-down area, where he hoped Randy was still waiting for them. They were twenty-three minutes late, but when he spotted a small penlight flashing on and off, he knew that they had made it. He pulled his own pen light out and signaled their identity.

Matt parked the car near his pilot's location. Randy had already cut a four-foot vertical slice in the fence. He pushed the wedge open as two men got out of the car and hurried over to the fence.

"Dad, this is Randy," Matt said quickly to his father. "I want you to go with him. He's going to put you on that plane over there. I have to go through customs, but I'll join you in a few minutes."

"It's great to meet you, sir," Randy replied, ignoring his strange monastic attire. "Come with me. I'll take care of you."

"What about the guys in the hangar?" Matt asked.

"Don't worry about them," Randy replied. "There were only two of them, and I served them a cup of my famous Brazilian coffee this morning as soon as they removed the tie-downs and chalks from my plane. They're sound asleep in the hangar. They'll be out for another thirty minutes or so."

Matt shoved the Trinity staff through the fence first, and then both of them helped Matt's father through the opening. Randy placed three short pieces of wire in Matt's hand. Then, he picked up the staff and led Matt's father quickly to the plane.

Matt closed the gap in the fence line, wrapping the aluminum wires around the slice at three points, making the damage more difficult to spot. Then, he climbed back in the vehicle and drove around to the front of the airport.

He parked the car in the midst of several others, using the last of his rubbing alcohol to wipe down all of the surfaces that they had touched on both sides of the vehicle.

Matt straightened his clothing, organized his pack and placed his embassy credentials and passport in his front pocket as he walked through the terminal. He passed through customs quickly and caught a ride on the same, small passenger transport that he had used on arrival.

When they dropped him off in front of the Learjet, the sun was just beginning to crest over the horizon. The twin turbo-fan engines were already running. As the passenger transport pulled away, Matt looked down at his watch.

It was five-fifty-three A.M.

He climbed onboard and closed the hatch. When he turned around, he saw that his father had already been strapped into one of the plush leather seats. His staff was resting beside him.

Matt sat down across from him and buckled his seat belt. Through the open cockpit door, he could hear Randy talking with ground control. The Learjet's engines revved up as they pulled away from the hangar and onto the taxiway. Five minutes later, they were airborne.

Chapter 106

As soon as they cleared Soviet airspace, Matt got up and went into the galley. His father was sleeping, lulled by the smooth progress of the Learjet, following the frantic start to his day. He was unaccustomed to such activities, and his body demanded rest. As much as he wanted to talk to him, Matt decided to let him sleep.

In the galley, Matt made a pot of coffee and heated a breakfast tray for Randy.

By the time Matt reached the cockpit door, Randy had the plane on auto-pilot, en route to London Heathrow for refueling before the trans-Atlantic leg of their flight. He handed him a cup of coffee and a plate of eggs, bacon and buttered toast.

"Thanks, partner," Randy said.

"Thank *you*," Matt replied sincerely. "I owe you, big-time."

"No problem," Randy responded. "Life's not worth much without a little excitement. Wouldn't you agree?"

"Yeah," Matt replied, "But this ride's going to be hard to top."

"You're right, my friend," Randy agreed. "Can you imagine what it's going to be like when your mom sees him?"

"I just hope she survives it," Matt said, with a look of genuine concern on his face.

"Don't worry, Matt," Randy replied. "From what I hear, she's a remarkable woman. She'll get through it."

"I hope Governor Rice made it down there to help her," Matt added. "It's going to be a traumatic moment when she lays eyes on him again."

"Don't kid yourself, Matt," Randy insisted. "It'll be the happiest day of her life. I wouldn't miss it for all the gold in Fort Knox!"

"Me neither," Matt replied. "I just hope it's not too hard on her."

"Hey, by the way," Randy added. "I've got some extra clothes in my bag that I always bring along on trips. Do you think they might fit your father? We're pretty close in size."

"I hadn't thought about that," Matt replied. "I guess it would be less of a shock if we could get him out of that cassock and into some normal clothing."

"Feel free to try mine," Randy offered. "I've got plenty more at the house."

"Thanks, Randy," Matt said. "We might just take you up on that."

Matt returned to the galley and got himself a cup of coffee. He stood there drinking it, watching his father sleep. Eventually, he poured a second cup and returned to his seat, reclining in a futile attempt to relax.

Two hours later, they landed at London Heathrow Airport. James Garrett sat up and stretched, watching out the window as ground crews refueled the jet. Randy filed a new flight plan and, by seven A.M. London time, they were climbing out over the Atlantic Ocean, headed west-southwest to Miami International Airport.

Matt prepared breakfast for his father and himself. The meal was served hot, and his father seemed to enjoy it. Occasionally, James Garrett glanced over at his son and wondered where his new home would be.

He had only a vague remembrance of his former life… scattered images of Korea, of his son playing baseball in a backyard that he didn't recognize and of a woman whose name he could not remember.

He thought of his brothers back at the monastery, rising to find that he was gone, saddened by the fact that they would not see him again.

Matt got up and went into the galley to pour another cup of coffee for Randy. When he handed it to him, Randy looked up and smiled.

"Thanks," he said. "I can use the caffeine."

"If you can get us home safely, I guarantee you a week of surf and sun on Pinney's Beach," Matt replied.

"No problem," Randy joked. "I can do this in my sleep."

"Why does that make me a little nervous?" Matt countered.

After their conversation, Matt returned to his seat and settled in, keeping close watch over his father.

Soon, James Garrett drifted back to sleep again. Satisfied that he was O.K., Matt gave in to his own fatigue and joined him.

Chapter 107

❦

Eight hours later, the plane landed at MIA. Two federal agents were standing on the tarmac when Randy lowered the Learjet's steps. Matt came out first and displayed his passport and LOC credentials. His father stepped off the plane right after him, came down the steps and stood beside him.

"And you are Captain James Garrett? Is that correct, sir?" the first agent asked, turning to Matt's father.

"I am," his father replied.

"Then I think this belongs to you, sir," the man said, holding out a small, blue booklet, with a gold-embossed seal of the United States of America on its cover. "Welcome home, sir."

He handed James Garrett his passport, which had been updated to reflect current validity. In his photograph, James looked younger, but, under the circumstances, he had held together fairly well.

"The Secretary of State asked us to give this to you as well," the second agent said, holding out a small, black box with a formal letter underneath it. It was issued by the President of the United States.

"The Secretary wanted to be here himself, sir, but he didn't want to cause a stir with the press," the other agent explained. "He figured your privacy was more important right now."

Captain James Garrett, wearing Randy's khaki pants and blue cotton shirt, accepted the gift and thanked the agents.

"You won't need to go through Customs, sir," the first agent informed him. "That's already been taken care of. The Secretary felt that you'd be anxious to get home."

"Thank you, gentlemen," Matt interjected as his father studied the objects in his hand. "We'll be underway as soon as the plane is refueled. Please give the Secretary our warmest regards and thank him for all of his help."

"We certainly will," the agent replied. "And, once again, Captain Garrett, thank you for your extraordinary service to our country."

They shook hands, and the two agents turned around and disappeared back into the terminal.

Randy came over and stood beside Matt's father.

"Why don't you open it, sir?" he encouraged him.

James Garrett handed the letter to Matt and opened the black box in his hand. Inside was a Meritorious Service Medal, awarded for outstanding service to The United States of America. The letter that accompanied it was signed by the President.

"We'll hold onto it, Dad," Matt said. "You can put it with your other medals when we get home."

"What other medals?" James inquired.

Matt chuckled.

"I'll show you when we get there, Dad," Matt assured him.

He handed the objects to Randy for safe keeping and put his hand on his father's shoulder.

"You know what?" Matt said cheerfully, "You could use a haircut. Let's step inside the main terminal and see if we can find a barber. I have some things that I need to talk to you about, anyway. We'll be back in thirty minutes, Randy."

"No problem," Randy replied. "We should be ready to go by then."

Chapter 108

❧

By ten-thirty A.M., the Learjet began its decent to the island of St. Kitts. James Garrett, freshly groomed and well rested, peered out of his window at the turquoise water below. To him, it felt like a dream, from which no man would wish to awaken.

Five miles south of their landing site, at the center of an even smaller island, the majestic summit of Nevis Peak waited patiently, encircled by a crown of pure white, sunlit clouds.

The Learjet taxied to a stop in front of the hangar that housed LOC's blue and white island hopper, the twin-engine plane that would complete their long journey from Russia. Light brown men rolled it out of the hangar and onto the tarmac beside them.

Fifteen minutes later, they had exchanged their means of transportation, departing St. Kitts for Nevis.

Chapter 109

❦

"Matt's going to be so surprised!" Marie said excitedly.

The whole LOC team had decided to come, wanting to see Matt's reaction to Governor Rice and the Eriksson family showing up to greet him. In fact, Governor Rice and the LOC team were far more anxious than Marie was, hoping for a miracle of unspeakable possibility.

At eleven o'clock, the blue and white island hopper landed. It turned around at the end of the runway, taxied up to the terminal and shutdown its engines.

Inside the terminal, Marie stood waiting between Governor Rice and Bill, with Natasha and John on either side of them. The Eriksson's stayed back a bit, not wanting to interfere with their initial greeting. They had no idea what was about to happen.

When Matt came through the door, he was carrying a strange staff in his left hand. He paused briefly, spotting the LOC team, Governor Rice and his mother. Then, he turned back and wrapped his right arm around the shoulder of a second man, who entered the door behind him. Together, they walked slowly toward the group.

Marie felt the governor's hand slip around her waist just before her knees gave way. Her hands covered her mouth and her eyes opened widely, as if she had seen a ghost.

"Oh! Oh! Oh!" she cried repeatedly, her breathing instantly becoming rapid and heavy. For a moment, Matt thought that she would pass out, but Owen Rice supported her, while a couple of tears ran down his own face.

"Marie?" the apparition said. "Is that you?"

James separated himself from his son and walked toward her alone. Five feet away from her, he stopped and held out his arms.

"Is that you, darling?" he said softly.

Her whole body began to tremble and she began to cry.

"How can this be?" Marie thought to herself, her mind struggling to grasp what her eyes were seeing. "He's dead! He's dead! How can this be?"

In the next second, she was pushing herself free of Owen's support and running to her husband. She wrapped herself tightly around him and held on for dear life. Her tears soaked the front of his clean blue shirt as he brushed his fingers repeatedly through her hair, speaking to her in soothing tones.

"It's alright, Marie. It's O.K., honey. I'm home now," he said. "I'm home now, and I'm never going to leave you again."

"You'd better not!" she wailed, looking up at him and grabbing his face. "I'm never taking my eyes off you again!"

Matt came up behind them and wrapped his arms around both of them.

John Sauter looked over at Bill, whose broad smile was beaming.

"This may take a while," John quipped.

Natasha clung to Bill's good side, crying like a little girl. Governor Rice stepped forward and spoke to James.

"Captain Garrett," he said. "Welcome home, sir."

"Owen!" James replied. "Owen Rice. It's so good to see you."

"Likewise, my friend," the governor replied. "We've all missed you."

James Garrett reached out his hand and grasped him behind the neck, pulling him into the fold.

The other members of the LOC team looked at each other with anticipation.

"Oh, what the heck!" Bill said.

They moved forward as a team, surrounding the Garrett's and the governor in a group hug.

Randy Weston stood in the doorway, taking it all in and smiling.

Suddenly realizing that their Swedish guests had no idea what was happening, Natasha separated herself briefly from the pack, walked back to where they were standing and explained it all to them. As soon as they understood, Natasha returned to Bill's side.

A few minutes later, Matt looked up to catch his breath. Across the room, he spotted the same Swedish couple that he had passed here in the same airport as he had departed Nevis for London. They were smiling warmly at him, as if they knew who he was.

He released his parents, slipped through his team members and began to walk toward them. Annika stepped out from behind her father in a white sun dress, with delicate flowers embroidered across the top of it. Her long, blonde hair cascaded over the front of her left shoulder, and her eyes grew moist as he approached her.

She was slender, and her movements were fluid as she walked up to him and stopped, two feet away.

"Annika," Matt heard himself say. "I'm so glad to see you looking well."

He held out his right hand to shake hers.

She stood perfectly still, looking up at him with the same unnerving Caribbean blue eyes that had formerly captured his soul.

Her gaze had already penetrated the barrier of self that all men present to the world and was examining the core of his being. For a moment, he felt naked – unable to conceal his innermost thoughts.

Sensing his discomfort, she reached out and grasped both of his hands by the back of the wrists, pulling them forward and wrapping them slowly around the back of her waist, where they instinctively held their ground. As she released them, she reached up and pulled his face down to her own.

She carefully placed her first, slow kiss high on his cheekbone, just beneath his left eye. Her second landed gently at the corner of his mouth.

Her third and final kiss met his lips squarely, adding to the certainty that no other day in his life would ever be as wonderful.

Chapter 110

❦

"**D**inner's ready," Marta Erikkson called to her daughter from the veranda of their Golden Rock villa.

Grilled mahi-mahi and conch fritters graced the table, served with skewers of red and green peppers, tomatoes, onions and zucchini.

"Hold on a minute," Annika whispered into the receiver of her bedroom telephone.

"Be right there!" she called obediently to her mother.

Turning back to her Russian contact, she completed the communication quickly.

"He's hooked," she said. "I'll keep you informed."

Epilogue

～

Two months later, in the thick, tropical forests of Western Africa, Saa Tumba tore through the underbrush, in pursuit of a pair of white-collared monkeys. Occasionally, the sting of whistling thorns tore at his flesh as he drew ever closer to his frightened prey. Ignoring the pain, he raced ahead, knowing that just one of the monkeys could feed his family for a week.

As he ran, he raised his sharpened spear and flung it into the tree overhead, piercing the body of his supper. The screaming simian careened to the warm forest floor, landing at his feet with a dull thud.

Saa Tumba immediately drew his knife and slit the animal's throat. Its blood sprayed across his arms and legs, mingling with his own as the white-collared monkey's unusual life ended.

On the rise of the next full moon, Saa Tumba took note of a small, web-like growth beneath the surface of his skin, just above his right ankle. His wife, who had prepared last month's bush-meat delicacy, shared traces of the same intruder on the back of her busy hands.

About the Author

᭡

A graduate of Guilford College and The University of North Carolina at Greensboro, Mike Leach began his career in secondary education as a guidance counselor and A. P. English teacher. After seven years in this field, he transitioned to the high-tech world of large computer system support at AT&T. A quarter century later, Mike retired from AT&T as a Senior Systems Manager. While pursuing his love of writing, he divides his time between Central Florida and The Blue Ridge Mountains of North Carolina. He is a member of ASU's *Institute for Senior Scholars* and the *High Country Writers* group in Boone, NC.

"I grew up in St. Cloud, Florida – the 'Veterans of Foreign Wars' town referenced in <u>Lords of Circumstance</u>. As a child, I was strongly influenced by contact with veterans of World War II and the Korean War. They taught me about service and sacrifice, imparting a deep respect for those who protect our country. Most importantly, they instilled the timeless reminder that 'freedom is not free' and that perpetual vigilance is the price of maintaining it. Even back then, I understood that these were lessons that I would take to the grave.

"I married a girl that I grew up with from elementary school age. She is my best friend, my first-read copyeditor and the deeply-ingrained love of my life. We have two beautiful daughters, Wendy and Paige, who, along with their husbands, have given us three wonderful grandchildren: Aidan, Benjamin and Addison."

Mike Leach – m1garands@gmail.com

Made in the USA
Middletown, DE
22 February 2019